Praise for Rivers Wilde

"From the cover, to the characters, to the intricate plot and interesting secondary characters, it just worked and I loved everything about it. Highly recommended!"

~ Book Twins Reviews

"You can tell Allen poured herself into this story completely because it exudes everything that is her. Brilliance, awe inspiring, riveting, captivating, emotional, inspirational, unexpected and spectacular!"

~ 4_the_love_of_books

"Epic Love...they had it in spades!!! Remi's story was a roller coaster of emotions...a ride I never wanted to end!"

~ Keri Loves Books

"...I love Dylan Allen's writing so freaking much! Just Get this book as soon as it comes out and do yourself a favour."

~ The E-Book Addict

"The drama, the mystery, the intrigue and the love...all the love. It's like the tv show Dynasty and The Notebook had a love child...and it's beautiful!!"

~ Bibliophile Chloe

"It's an angst fueled roller coaster. Buckle up, and enjoy the ride."

~ The Romance Rebel

"The Legend by Dylan Allen gripped my heart from the beginning and stole my breath away completely. This story was simply mind blowing and captivating. This beautifully written epic saga of timeless love is full of angst, drama, heartbreak, passion and every delicious feeling."

~ PP's Bookshelf

The JEZEBEL

The JEZEBEL

A RIVERS WILDE NOVEL

DYLAN ALLEN

The Jezebel
A Rivers Wilde Novel

ISBN: 978-1-968707-97-2

Published by Blue Box Press, an imprint of Evil Eye Concepts, Incorporated

v.72620-DA

Dedication

To my niece, Laila.
I can't wait to watch you set the world alight with your magnificent mind.
I love you.

Until the lion learns to write,
history will always glorify the hunter.

~ Proverb of unknown origin
that my father shared with me.

WELCOME TO RIVERS WILDE

The Jezebel is the third stand-alone in the Rivers Wilde Series.

The fictional enclave of Rivers Wilde, carved into a parcel of some of the most valuable and coveted land in all of Houston, TX, is home to the two families that it's named after.

The Rivers are old, Texas money. Sugar, oil, and natural gas are how they made their fortune. And with that bounty, they helped found the city of Houston.

The Wildes are the new money. They built their wealth in restaurants, grocery stores and real estate. And they have made a fortune that casts the old money into the shade.

In the 1980s, the oil markets were crashing and the Rivers found themselves hard up for cash. With no other viable options, they sold part of their precious land to the usurpers they'd previously refused to even acknowledge.

Seeds of resentment burrowed deep into the fertile soil of their dislike and grew tenacious roots. Thirty years later, the rivalry continues. Even though, now, no one remembers what started it and just *why* the blood between the families is so bad.

Today in Rivers Wilde, a new generation is coming to the helm of power in both families. Will they put the past behind them and usher in a new era of cooperation between the two ruling families in Houston? Or will the sins of their fathers continue to cast a shadow over them?

I hope you enjoy finding out!

Welcome to Rivers Wilde.

Present Day

HOUSTON, TX

The Jezebel's Undoing

REGAN

"I need to speak with you."

The unexpected sound of my husband's voice nearly stops my heart. My reflexive gasp draws soap and water into my nose and throat, and I cough violently to clear it. I turn the water off and meet his unreadable gaze in the mirror.

The burn of mint scented face wash invading my nostrils and stinging my eyes barely registers against the shock of seeing him standing in my bathroom when he should be on the other side of the Atlantic Ocean.

I grab a towel from the small pile on my counter and wipe the soap off haphazardly and turn to face him. "Why are you here?" I demand.

He raises one gray flecked eyebrow as if surprised by my question. "This is my house. You are still my wife." He curls his lip and drags a possessive gaze over my towel clad, shower damp body.

I resist the urge to cross my arms over my chest and glower at him. "Please leave, now."

He shakes his head slowly; one side of his thin mouth curls upward in a sneer. "I'll wait for you in the bedroom." He informs me, and then he turns and walks out of the bathroom.

I release the breath I was holding, and rush into my closet, slide the door closed behind me and start to pace. Mounting dread compounds my shock, but I can't afford to indulge either.

Since our confrontation after he received the divorce petition, he's been radio silent. I've been praying, unceasingly, he'd stay that way. Marcel being here today is a very, very bad sign and even worse timing.

The State of Texas gives a respondent twenty days to respond before granting a divorce by default. This morning, I woke up and drew the nineteenth red "X" on the small calendar I keep on my bedside table. It was like hearing a key slide into the lock of a door that had been sealed shut for years.

Just one day left. I could *taste* my freedom. And, for the first time ever, I dared to imagine welcoming Stone to Houston as a single woman.

It was stupid to think Marcel would make this easy.

I glower at my reflection, this time, the sting in my eyes from tears I won't allow to fall. There's no reason to cry. Marcel will drag it out and make it as painful as possible, but he can't do anything to stop the divorce. This is just one battle in a war that, ultimately, I know I'll win.

I take my time getting dressed, pulling on my softest pair of leggings and a t-shirt Stone bought me in Todos Santos. I stride into my bedroom, walking past him toward my bed without stopping or looking at him, my voice projecting irritation and impatience. "Whatever this is about, I wish you'd called first. I have a very busy—"

"Who is he?" Marcel speaks in a quiet, insouciant voice, but his question lands with the potential lethality of a grenade before it detonates. I have no idea if it's a dud or if my whole life is about to go up in flames.

I quell that flare of panic. There's only one *he* that matters, and Marcel can't know about him. *No one* does. Stone is my heart's most closely guarded secret. With that certainty as my shield, I ignore the explosive question, turn my back to him, and start making my bed.

"Regan, I am speaking to you." The easy confidence in his voice is splintered by indignation that provides another balm to my rattled nerves. He's much easier to manage when he's angry.

"Oh, I'm sorry," I drawl and glance over my shoulder in his general direction, one eyebrow raised in apathetic curiosity. "I didn't hear you." I resume my task without meeting his eye or waiting for an answer.

A second later, a black smartphone lands face down on the bed. "My mother was right about you. You are the devil in disguise." he snarls behind me.

I sigh loudly at his dramatics before I pick up the phone and turn to face him. "What is this about?" I snap.

He nods at the phone in my hand. "See for yourself, *Jezebel.*"

Those tendrils of trepidation hiss like agitated snakes in my gut and drawn my grudging gaze to the phone and the shield I'd been so sure of crumbles as the grenade I'd dismissed for a dud, detonates.

The headline written in bold red all caps reads, "La femme de Landel montre au monde qui elle est: La Jézabel" *(The wife of Landel shows the world who she is: Jezebel.)*

It's splashed over a picture I looked at just this morning with sweet longing and tentative hope. Me and Stone kissing, his hand grasping my bikini clad bottom, my tattoo glaring the small of my bare back. My arms are twined around his neck, obscuring the sliver of his profile that the brim of his hat didn't hide. I scan the article and see the words "unknown companion".

Amidst the discordant bells of devastation, disbelief, horror, and humiliation tolling inside my head, is a note of relief. But my knees still buckle under the weight of this disaster and I sit on the bed, dazed.

"I want you out of my house, faithless woman." Marcel issues his order like a tyrant who expects complete obedience and my head snaps up. His eyes glitter with the anticipatory menace of a spider preparing to devour the unfortunate prey trapped in its web and I've never been so afraid in my life.

But, after years of living with his flagrant infidelity, Marcel's righteousness spawns rage so ardent, it momentarily overwhelms my fear.

I raise my head and meet his raptor like glare with one of my own. "This is *my* home. The kids and I aren't going anywhere."

His thin-lipped sneer spreads into a malevolent smile that chills me to the bone. "The *children* aren't going anywhere. But *you* most certainly are."

Heart-stopping fear steals my breath. "No, they wouldn't...you couldn't. They need me..." My throat throbs with unshed tears of helplessness and fury. The phone slips from my hand and lands at my feet with a clatter that's muted by the panic thundering through my veins like a band of unbroken stallions.

The polished tips of his bespoke *Aubercy* loafers come into view. And he presses a finger to the underside of my chin and lifts my face to his. I'm too shell-shocked to resist.

Disdain draws furrows between his brows, scorn etches grooves around the edges of his lips and he leans forward until I can smell the cognac on his breath. "After you have so thoroughly disgraced yourself, me *and* them, do you think they will want to be with you?"

Oh God. My children. The thought of them seeing that picture fills my gut with an unbearable ache.

At my silence, his sneering lips curl into a satisfied smile. He drops his hand from my chin and takes a step back. "*You* will leave. *They* will stay here. And if you tell me who the man is, I will call this newspaper and have them take this article out of circulation. This was published at midnight in France." He checks the time on his wristwatch and purses his lips, his eyes narrowing thoughtfully. "It's only 2am there, now. One phone call, and I can make it go away. I will spare you the humiliation of your children knowing what kind of woman you are. Just tell me who he is. Then, it will only be *his* life I burn to the ground."

Disgust cuts through my apprehension and I find my voice. "You would use our *children* as pawns?"

His eyes narrow in condescending pity, "But, that is exactly what they are, Regan. The prenuptial agreement we signed saw to that."

"I will fight you, Marcel" I vow. That document is more than ten years old and if I've learned anything from my brother, is that there is no such thing as an unbreakable contact.

He shrugs. "And I'll win. That picture, whether the publication removes it or not, means I hold all the cards. Tell me his name and all you will lose is what you have already forfeited—custody of the children."

"My face isn't showing, you can't prove it's me." I grasp at straws.

"Will your brother perjure himself and risk his law license to help you prove that in court? Because that's where this is headed if you fight me."

I can see the picture in my mind as clearly as if I was still looking at it. Our faces aren't showing. Yet, the glint of my gold body chain, the riot of dark curly hair that cascades down my back are distinctive but combined with the tattoo that adorns my lower back, it might as well be DNA evidence.

But, there's no way to prove that's Stone's hand cupping my bottom. My chest aches at the thought of him. And what being embroiled in this could mean for the career he's worked so hard for. I won't let that happen.

I just don't understand how this picture that was on my personal cell phone got into the hands of a newspaper in France. One Marcel claims he has the power to command.

I grasp at that thread of suspicion like it's a lifeline and use it to pull my head above the surface of guilt and terror I'm drowning in. "How did they get that picture? I don't understand," I make my voice sorrowful, keep my head bowed, but keep a surreptitious eye on him through the veil of my lashes.

His smug smile falters, and his eyes dart over my shoulder. But he regains his composure so quickly I'm not sure it wasn't just wishful thinking. "Maybe your lover handed it over to make a pretty penny," he sneers.

My head snaps up, and I scoff loudly; dismissing his statement for the conjecture it is. "He doesn't—"

"*He* what?" Marcel's keen eyes narrow and I curse my near slip up.

"Nothing. He is no one." My heart thuds in protest at my necessary lie.

"And that's *exactly* what I will tell your children. That you threw their family away for *no one*."

I blanche at the malicious glee in his voice. That he would relish hurting our children fills me with a crushing despair, so heavy that I can't bear it and my own weight. I sit on the small dark leather trunk at the foot of my bed, drop my face into my hands and I search my disordered mind for a way to stop this. To keep them safe, with me and ignorant of their parents' failings.

"Time is ticking, Regan," Marcel taunts.

I lift my head to glare at him. "We haven't lived together for five years. A quiet, straight forward divorce would have barely made a ripple. Their lives wouldn't have changed at all. But this…you are taking them to Paris in the middle of the school year?"

He snorts a derisive laugh. "Their lives will not be disrupted. I will continue residing in Paris and will make more frequent trips to see them. And when school is over, they will come to me."

Incredulity slackens my jaw and widens my eyes. I gaze over at him. "Don't be ridiculous, the children can't stay here alone."

"They're not. Hanna is moving in."

I shoot to my feet, my fear and despair burned away by a surge of primordial rage.

"You *wouldn't*." I growl.

He swallows thickly, his eyes dart away from my brimstone gaze. He tugs the cuffs of his shirt, collects himself and looks back at me, the challenge back in his beady eyes. "The children know her and like her. You are the only one who had a problem with her."

"Because she was our *nanny* and you got her *pregnant*." I scream, incandescent anger propelling me toward him.

He takes a step away from me. "Lower your voice," he hisses.

"I will *not*. I've never cared where you have dallied. I still don't. But if you do this—I will see you in hell." His eyes dart past my shoulder again, this time, his tongue darts nervously over his thin lips.

I swivel in the direction of his gaze. There's nothing there but the huge gold leaf framed mirror that hangs over my fireplace.

"What the hell are you looking at?" I demand, searching the wall for whatever keeps drawing his attention.

"Anything but you." He means the words to sting, but his cadence is stilted. His unease, in a moment where he holds all the cards, plucks at my suspicion.

I erase any trace of it from my voice and my expression and turn back to him with a narrow-eyed glare and scornful scowl on my face. "Why? Because I'm not eighteen and under your employ?"

His haughty, self-righteous stance is back. But I don't miss the flash of worry in his eyes. Or the way his throat bobs behind his starched collar.

"You must stop this delusion about Hanna."

"Is the baby she popped out with *your* fucking eyes *a delusion*?" I ask incredulous that he's still denying it.

"You have no proof. Whereas, I have this picture." He waves his phone in my face, and his sneer turns taunting. "You're nothing but a common slut and soon, the whole world will know."

I bristle. "Well, they already know that *you* are the king of sluts, so they'll just think you finally rubbed off on me."

He flinches as if I slapped him and then his face flushes scarlet and he bares his teeth in a feral snarl before he rushes toward me. With more speed and strength than I thought him capable of, he shoves me. I land flat on my back. The rug cushions the impact of my fall, but I lay there, dazed and disoriented. He drops to his knees beside me and grips my cheeks, squeezing so tightly that I can't move my lips.

"Is he the reason you asked me for a divorce?" Spittle sprays my face and shock at the violence of his touch stuns me silent and still.

"Fucking answer me." He tightens his hold on me and my teeth cut into the inside of my cheek. The salty metallic taste of my own blood is an elixir—neutralizing my fear and feeding my fury.

I gaze into the wrathful face of the man I wasted too much of my life on. The last ember of goodwill I feel for him, dies. Whatever he sees in my expression startles him—his eyes widen and his grip on my face slackens. I yank his hand away, press my palms to his chest and shove him off me. He lands in a sprawl beside me.

I pull myself up with as much dignity as I can muster and wait for him to do the same. And then I step to him and stand close enough that I can see sweat beading on his cowardly upper lip.

My hands curl into tight fists at my side, the bite of my fingernails in my palm keep me grounded and in control of the tempest that wants to fly free and beat his ass the way my brothers taught me to. But I am not going to jail for this asshole. "You will never, *ever* touch me again, Marcel. Not ever."

His jaw trembles, but his voice is as sharp and smooth as the edge of an assassin's blade. "I don't have to lay a hand on you to hurt you, Regan. You smug, faithless woman. I am going to ruin you. And when I find out who dared to cuckold me, I'll do the same to him."

"Mom?" At the sound of my daughter's trembling, tear clogged voice, we both freeze. I brush my cheeks, clear my expression, and with my heart in my throat, turn to face her.

"You should be sleeping, Angel, are you okay?" It's an asinine question. It's clear from the way her stricken gaze darts frantically between her father and me that "okay" is the last thing she is. My gut clenches at the sight of tears trailing down on cheeks and the trembling hand pressed to her mouth.

She rushes to me, her arms circle my waist, and she presses her wet cheek to my chest. My heart burns with something that scares me. I hug her tight, press kisses to the top of her head, and will my voice to steady. "It's okay, baby. I promise. Let me take you back to bed. Daddy and I will finish talking and then, I'll come see you." I try to pry her loose. I am desperate to get her away from us and our disaster.

She shakes her head violently and tightens her hold on me. "The man downstairs said you're leaving. I want to come with you. Please, Mommy."

My eyes boomerang back to Marcel, and a shiver of dread runs down my spine at the triumph in his eyes. "What man?" I demand.

"The one who is going to throw you out if you refuse to leave on your own," he informs me in an even casual tone.

I push my daughter behind me and bare my teeth. "I *dare* you to try."

He claps twice and just like *that;* the battle of my life begins.

Eighteen Years Ago

RIVERS WILDE
HOUSTON, TX

Chapter 1

NO RIGHT OR WRONG

REGAN

"Have you learned *anything* from me?" My mother's exasperated question isn't rhetorical. As always, she's more interested in obedience than truth.

This is one of the rare times that I can give her both. "I've learned *everything* from you, Mom." Even the things she didn't mean to teach me. She's the reason I floss like it's my side hustle, exercise like it's my religion, and will *never* get married or have children.

"Then *why* did you go to your grandfather when I already said no?" She snaps.

I roll my eyes, something I only dare when she can't see me. "You *told* me to ask him." I remind her, fighting to keep my own exasperation out of my voice.

She scoffs. "He was supposed to say no, too. I swear sometimes I think that man forgets that you're *my* daughter," she seethes.

"How could he? When you remind him so often?" I quip.

"Don't get smart with me, Regan. You may have that man wrapped around your finger, but if I say no, not even he can save you." Her warning douses ice cold water on the giddiness that's made me reckless tonight. I know how far to push my mother and I just danced a little too close to the line. "I was just joking. I'm sorry," I say, filling my voice with contrition.

"Apology accepted," she says with the condescension of a queen granting a pardon. Her ruffled feathers smoothed; she returns to the original conversation. "Now, tell me what agreement you two made about your schedule and how you'll keep up with everything else at the same time"

I've been prepared for it, but my heart skips a beat at her question. My answer will either be the key to her approval. "I'll be home by midnight, I'll go straight to bed. I don't have to leave for school until 7:45. All my homework is done, I took a nap, worked out, ate dinner and still had time to beat Pops at a round of checkers." I rattle off my itinerary without pausing to take a breath. When I'm done she's

"That's a good plan. I'll withhold my kudos until I see how well you execute it."

I grit my teeth to stop myself from scoffing. "I think you'll be impressed. My grades are just as important to me as they are to you."

She sighs. "Don't let that wild heart of yours lead you astray. I know it's loud, but never forget that your greatest asset is your brain. We have great expectations of you."

She hangs up before I reply and I'm not even annoyed that she had the last word.

I won.

I put my cell phone, also known as my electronic leash, into my purse. The only reason I didn't "forget it" at home tonight is so I can text Weston and let him know the coast is clear before he heads over to meet me.

I grin in anticipation.

He's got hair the color of flame and eyes the color of the sky—a palette of heaven and hell that draws sighs from nearly every girl in school.

Except me.

I turned him down every time he asked me out. I didn't return his sly, slow smiles or giggle at his jokes.

He thought it was because he wasn't the all-American boy next door or the tall, dark and handsome scholarly type my mother would approve of and I let him.

It was easier than explaining that I had my eyes on a different prize.

My brothers, Remington and Tyson, have been raised with the expectation that one day, they will take over the business that, in just one generation, has become a multibillion dollar empire.

My grandfather and mother have made it clear that my role in furthering the family's interests would look very different.

They expect me to marry someone who comes with the one thing their money hasn't been able to buy—access to spaces and opportunities that require having at least one ancestor who could vote when the constitution was ratified.

I was thirteen and saw an interview of Desiree Rogers right after she was named as the CEO of Johnson Publishing. She was everything I wanted to be—beautiful, successful, impactful, and single

She credited her time at Wellesley College—an all women's college in Massachusetts—for giving her the confidence to pursue career opportunities in fields that, traditionally, had been the domain of men.

I wasn't sure what I wanted to do with my life—the only thing I'd ever loved was writing and cooking. But right away, I knew if I was going to be more than a trophy wife, I wanted to go to Wellesley, too.

Aside from my family's anticipated opposition, the odds of getting in were heavily stacked against me.

Only 5% of applicants are accepted and I was already a grade behind my age group. So I put my head down and focused on honing myself into the ideal candidate. By the beginning of my senior year, I had a perfect GPA and near perfect SAT score to show for it.

I kept my plans for school to myself and let my mother think I was on board with her plan for me to attend Southern Methodist in Dallas.

The day she hosted a lunch at the Junior League for a group of SMU alumni, I stopped by the post office to mail my application to Wellesley before driving over to join them.

When my admission letter arrived, I took it to my mother beaming with pride and disbelief and expected her to at last begrudgingly proud of me.

Instead, she scowled tossed it on to her desk without a word. Then, she handed me an envelope with my name scrawled on the back in her strident, slashing handwriting and said. "Absolutely not." Before she left me sitting in her office alone and dejected.

I opened the envelope to find an offer of admission and a full ride from Southern Methodist University.

A small yellow sticky note clung to the first page.

On it, she'd written, "I know better."

My grandfather, who usually took my side, wouldn't intervene.

The year before he exhausted any credit he had with my mother when he helped my twin brother, Remington, in his bid to attend a college she didn't approve of.

They'd had the element of surprise on their side, then too. But after losing *that* showdown, she'd been ready for me.

The roots of her opposition ran deep and were fed by a constant supply of pride and resentment. She wouldn't budge.

But I wasn't ready to concede.

I applied for a scholarship.

But a school like Wellesley, that only takes the best and brightest, didn't offer incoming freshman academic scholarships. All awards were based on financial need. With a family fortune in the billions behind me, there was no chance of that. My dream was crushed under the heel of my mother's will.

I wouldn't make the same mistake twice. I vowed to never ask anyone, but *myself*, for permission again.

If they wouldn't give me my due, I'd just take it.

I mailed in my acceptance form to SMU that very day.

Then, I pulled out my old yearbook and found the phone number Weston scribbled over his senior picture and called him.

The son of a local drug dealer, he isn't the all-American boy next door or the tall, dark and handsome scholarly type my mother kept trying to set me up with and that, I'd entertained in an attempt to stay on her good side in hopes that she's say yes to Wellesley.

I drove out to his house the next day after school and let him take my virginity.

Brief and not as painful as my mother swore it would be, the thrill of knowing that I was breaking one of my mother's cardinal rules made it feel delicious.

I'm aware of what a cliché I am—the poor little rich girl dating the bad boy to stick it to her mother. But after a lifetime of glass towers and short leashes, the afternoons with him left me high on the rush of rebellion.

When my mother became suspicious about my disappearances after school, she started inventing errands for me to run that ate into all of my free time during the day.

After two weeks of that, I saw a sign in our bakery window for a kitchen prep position that went from 8pm to midnight.

I went to my grandfather and offered to take this position and let him sample the ginger lemon scones I wanted to bake exclusively for our bakery.

He was ecstatic and made a call to the division that oversaw our stores and in a matter of minutes the job was mine. I love to bake, am a night owl by nature, and this gave me the perfect cover to see Weston. He's set to come at ten which will give me plenty of time to do my work.

I unlock the bakery and catch the glow of a light on in the back. Curious, more than worried, I head for the kitchen.

"Hello? Is someone here?" I call and push open the double doors that lead to the back rooms. There's no response, but the snick of a door closing, is all the answer I need.

My heart skips a beat. Marlene, the bakery manager, told me that the lock on the back door was broken but no one was worried about break-ins in Rivers Wilde.

Nevertheless, I pull out my keys and fumble for the small bottle of mace on it. I hold it in front of me and hold my breath as I yank the door open and step into the cavernous room where we store our dry supplies.

The room is completely empty. I scan the space and notice one of the huge cabinets that line the walls is slightly ajar. The sound of sharp, shallow breathing as I get closer confirms my fear.

Whoever is in there can't be a big person. But danger comes in all shapes and sizes. At this time of night, nothing good could be lurking here.

"I know you're there, so you might as well come out." I nudge the door with my foot again and hold my breath.

Nothing happens.

"I'm gonna count to three and then I'm opening this door... I've got a gun." I add that lie in hopes that they'll come out slowly enough to give me a chance to bolt if I need to.

"One…two…" The cabinet door swings open and a small, pale hand reaches out from the dark recess of the industrial sized cabinet. I stop counting. The hand is joined by a skinny, freckled arm. A head, topped by a thick, unruly, wavy mop of sandy brown hair appears next and I come face to face with my trespasser.

He's just a boy, doesn't appear to be any older than seven or eight, dressed in a school uniform I recognize.

A few months ago, when I was still keeping up appearances, I dated a boy who attends the prestigious all boys boarding school, Blackwell Academy. I remember him mentioning a ten-year boy enrolling in ninth grade at the start of this school year. This kid looks younger than that, but this *has* to be him.

His face is pointed at the floor, his shoulders hunched in on himself. His little body is rigid, the hands he shoves into the pockets of his navy-blue uniform pants, ball into fists.

"What are you doing here?" I make my voice as calm as possible.

"Hiding," comes his disgruntled, sarcastic reply.

"I got that part," I return with the same snark.

"Then, why'd you ask?" The defiance in his voice belies his posture.

But I recognize little boy bravado when I see it. He's hiding from someone, or something, or both.

Unfortunately, he can't do it here. Not with Weston coming and not when putting a foot wrong could jeopardize this last vestige of freedom I've managed to carve out for myself.

"Okay, how about I don't ask you anything else? How about I just call the police and let them ask you all the questions they want?" I ask, bluffing in hopes that he'll scurry away.

"Wait," he cries. His head snaps up, revealing a tear streaked, freckled face, red-rimmed dark eyes magnified behind thick, black plastic framed glasses. They magnify the dark smudges under his eye. I scan the rest of his face and gasp at the fresh split in his lower lip and a smear of blood on the tip of his nose.

His eyes narrow as he takes me in, too. "You don't have a *gun*."

I raise my eyebrows at his indignant, accusing glare. "And *you* have no business being here."

His swollen mouth tightens, and he winces, his tongue prods his raw lower lip and my annoyance transfers from him to whoever hurt and scared him.

"What happened to your face?" I ask him

"I got punched, Captain Obvious," he says with a roll of his big eyes.

I smother the urge to chuckle at his precociousness and frown instead. "I can't imagine why. You're *so* polite."

"I thought you were calling the police."

"Thanks for the reminder." I pull out my phone and dial the number Remi set up as a prank and pray it's still in service.

He smirks and leans against the cabinet and crosses his legs at the ankle. He watches me with an ennui that's so convincing I almost believe that he doesn't care.

"It's ringing." I lift my eyebrows in exaggerated excitement and give my brothers a mental high five.

"Yeah right, you're probably calling your bestie or something," he says with a churlish little laugh.

I hit the speaker button just as the call connects, "911, do you need police, medical or fire?"

His eyes nearly bug out of his head at the recorded voice. "Stop," he bellows and then springs off the cabinet and races to me, hands straining ahead of him, his eyes trained on my phone.

I hightail it out of the storage room and out into the kitchen, racing to put the huge marble top prep surface between us.

I hold the phone up over my head. "Don't come any closer, and I'll hang up."

He screeches to a stop across from me. His dark, tear damp eyes are blazing, his flushed nostrils flare. Thank goodness he isn't the same size as his anger—he'd fill this entire room.

"Why couldn't you just pretend you didn't see me?" he seethes through clenched teeth. His eyes shimmer with unshed tears.

Guilt and compassion replace my annoyance.

He's just a kid.

And he's scared. The last think I want to do is add to that already overflowing bucket. "I didn't really call, okay?" I put the phone down and lift my empty hands so he can see I'm as defenseless as he is. "Now, tell me who you're hiding from."

His eyes widen just enough for me to know I hit that nail on its head before he narrows them angrily. "No one," he insists.

"You can trust me," I coax softly. Instead of the reassurance I hoped to inspire, his bottom lip trembles and his throat moves convulsively. I reach across the counter, my palm open in invitation.

He stares at my hand with wide, wary eyes before he lifts his gaze to my face. The bleak, haunted look in his eyes makes my breath hitch.

"I won't let them hurt you again."

"You can't do anything," he snarls then turns to make a run for the door.

I sprint to get ahead of him, stop short, and pivot with my arms open to catch him. He may be small, but he packs the punch of a freight train and his momentum sends us crashing to the floor.

I roll over and wrap him in a bear hug. The press of his too-prominent rib cage against my arms and the thud of his sprinting heart and against my torso firms my resolve to find out what happened to him.

"Let me *go*," he screeches and bucks against me. His head flails between my breasts and I crane my neck to move my face out of harm's way. My wildly beating heart is lodged in my throat and my arms ache. But compassion firms my conviction to hold him until he understands I'm not trying to hurt him.

"You're safe with me." I whisper The touch seems to startle him and instantly, but for his heaving chest, he goes completely still.

"Please, please let me *go.*" His voice is still colored by anger, but it breaks at the end of his sentence.

His hot tears dampen the front of my shirt.

I rest my cheek atop his head. After a few seconds of this, I risk loosening my hold and move my hand to caress circles in the center of his back. He stiffens and then our embrace changes.

His fisted hands were trapped between us. Now, they slide around my ribcage, his small hands press into my back. He holds me so tightly it's uncomfortable and cries like his entire heart is broken.

I recognize the weight of the grief radiating from him. There aren't many things that can make a child cry like this—they laugh in the face of almost anything.

My father died before I was old enough to have a single memory of him. But I've felt his absence so deeply at times that it felt like a piece of my soul had been hacked away. I cried so much I felt like I was drowning in tears.

What always saved me from those emotional hurricanes was having a safe place—usually my grandfather's arms—to see the storm through. He didn't insult me with platitudes and promises he couldn't keep. He'd let me get it out, chuck me under the chin, and send me on my way.

"Whatever you've lost, is gone. But you're still here, and you deserve to be happy." I repeat one of my favorite meditations in a soothing cadence. I was even younger than him the first time I heard it.

His sobs soften but he doesn't let go of me.

Pity squeezes my heart. My family isn't perfect, but I've never not had a place to go when I was low. Whoever and whatever he lost has left him so alone that he's managed to find his way here on a school night without triggering an Amber Alert.

We lay there silent, the buzz and hum of the appliances and overhead lights mingling with our breaths and heartbeats.

After a few minutes, his arms slacken and a half sigh, half snore confirms that he's fallen asleep.

I press a kiss to the top of his head and close my eyes as the familiar scent of Johnson's baby shampoo assails me. Oh God, he's *so* young.

My phone buzzes in my pocket.

Shit. Weston.

I stifle a groan and chew the inside of my lip while I consider the child asleep in my arms. I need to figure out who he is and how to get him back to school.

The time I'd set aside to get some of my work done ahead of his arrival is gone. I may be brazen enough to sneak him in here, but I'm not crazy. This work has to get done and on time, too.

I reach for my phone, moving gingerly to not wake him and read Weston's text.

"OMW"

I make a snap decision and type back a response.

"Not alone. Can't meet. Sorry! Call you 2morrow."

His reply comes right away, "Cool. L8r".

It stings my pride that he didn't even pretend to care. The scowl forming on my face softens when I look down at the sleeping, bruised face pressed to my chest. Weston can wait a few days, but I'm not sure that he can.

I manage to lift and carry him into the bakery's restaurant. I lay him on one of the plush sofas, rush back to the workroom, and grab the pashmina in my bag to drape over him. It covers him completely and makes him look impossibly vulnerable. I *need* to know who hurt him. When he wakes up, I'll coax it out of him with some milk and scones.

Then, I'm going to make sure the person who did this *and* the adults who let it happen make things right for him.

I engage the deadbolt so he can't leave through the front door. Then, I get back to work.

The butter I'd taken out has softened too much to be used in my scone recipe, so I pop it into the freezer. I set a timer for twenty minutes, pop in my Love Jones soundtrack CD and get to work zesting lemons and ginger. I'm only on the second lemon when the sound of shattering glass from the restaurant splinters my focus.

I drop everything, grab the chef's knife off the wall, and run. Images of him bleeding, or in the clutches of whatever villain broke that glass make me dizzy with fear.

With my arm raised to strike, I take a fortifying breath and burst through the swinging doors with a primal scream that nearly chokes me when I take in the scene.

He's gone. An entire pane of glass is missing from the store front window. And one of the small silver footstools my mother handpicked lays sprawled on the sidewalk in a sea of fractured glass.

What an *idiot* I am. I bet he wasn't even really asleep.

I run to the window, stick my head out of the gaping hole he made and look each way down the deserted street. He could have gone anywhere, and I don't have time to go looking for him now.

I need a *really* good story that explains how that window got broken. Otherwise, my whole plan is shot to hell and I can forget this sliver of freedom I carved out. I glower at the yawning hole in the glass and curse the little delinquent and my irrational instinct to protect him. As angry as I am with him, it's clear that the kid has enough problems without adding Owen Wilde to them.

That little shit may have escaped my grandfather's wrath, but he won't escape mine.

Chapter 2

I WANT TO FIGHT

REGAN

"Come on, gimme a kiss, Regan. You used to like it, remember?" Billy, aka Mr. Boring Enough to Make my Mother Happy, leans across the center console of my car with his eyes closed.

I roll my eyes skyward and lean as far away as the small interior of my Ford Mustang will allow. I don't remember if I liked kissing him or not, and I have no intention of refreshing my memory.

In the distance, a bell rings and I put a hand on Billy's chest and imbue my voice with regret. His eyes pop open and confusion creases his brow.

"I don't want to make you late." I glance at my watch meaningfully.

"That was just the warning bell, we've got time. If you want that schedule, it'll cost you." His smile is smarmy, his voice heavy with entitlement as he grabs my wrist and tugs me forward to close the space between us.

His eyes drift closed, and I let him draw me closer while I keep *my* eyes on the piece of paper he's holding as ransom. He *should* have been holding it out of my reach.

I snatch the paper from his distracted, slack grasp and yank my wrist free.

"What the fuck?" he snaps, shoving away from me with a huff of disgruntled annoyance.

"I'll just take this and skip the kiss," I say with a tight smile.

"Aren't you even going to say thank you?" he asks, peevish resignation in his voice.

Even though I didn't engage them when he got in, I hit the switch on the door locks for the sound effect. "Thank you," I deadpan, and eye him impatiently.

His expression crumbles and he pouts. That little kid has more backbone than him. "Aww, come on, Regan. At least let me see your titties."

I level him with a disgusted glare. "Get out of my car before you piss me off and force me to tell Tyson about this."

He pales and draws away. "For fuck's sake, I was just kidding."

With a churlish flash of his middle finger, he climbs out of my car.

Tyson's pain in the ass obsession with scaring my dates has finally paid off. Even though he's four years younger than me, he's bigger than most of the boys my age and the last boy who tried to coax a kiss out of me on our doorstep got a black eye for his trouble.

My grandfather bought my story about throwing the stool in fright because I thought I saw a mouse. But he was still docking my pay to cover the cost of repairing it. Tracking this kid down and holding him accountable for the trouble he caused was an all-consuming compulsion when I woke up this morning.

So, I called Billy under the guise of returning a book that a kid wearing their school uniform left in the bakery.

As soon as I said kid, he laughed and said "What the *fuck* is Stone Rivers doing in Rivers Wilde? Isn't your family like... his family's enemy or some shit?"

I'd been stunned silent. That little boy is *Stone Rivers*? But...how could the son of one of the richest and most powerful families in the entire state of Texas be beaten up, bloody nosed and have no one to turn to?

Gripped by a burning curiosity, I threw caution into the wind and told Billy I'd meet him if he could get me his schedule. In his eagerness to agree, he didn't even ask why I needed it.

My gut knots as I recall that his father, Jason Rivers died recently and that Hayes, his older brother, was sent to Europe to live with an aunt. That explains his tears. But it doesn't explain the busted lip.

I scan his schedule. He has study hall in the library next. I hurry from my car, find the library on the campus map and walk over to wait. I perch on a bench outside of a building with the words *Rivers Hall* etched into the marble. I take in the perfectly manicured grassy quadrangle that is flanked by four brick buildings with a gothic façade. Their piss-poor security aside, Blackwell is one of the most elite boarding schools in the country. Only the brightest students gain admission.

The school boasts two former presidents, a Vice President and a slew of ambassadors, CEOs, United States Senators, and visionary inventors as alumni.

That Stone is here at the tender age of ten means he's something more than bright. Another bell rings, and the doors of the classrooms that line the corridor arc open in near perfect unison and liberate streams of teenagers. They fill the quiet with a cacophony of shouts, laughs, and curses.

The library is set apart from the rest of the campus and I have a good view of the students as they make their way into the big grass covered quadrangle. Nerves assail me as I start searching the crowd for my quarry. The throng clears without any sign of the tiny human who should stick out like a sore thumb.

And then, I hear it. That raucous, collective laugher that, when made by a group of unsupervised teenage boys, is a universal signal that they're up to no good.

I head toward the sound, filled with an inexplicable certainty that those laughs are the reason Stone hasn't made it here yet.

I round the corner of a building and find myself in a service alley that's lined with garbage dumpsters. All the way at the end of it, four boys stand in a huddle with their backs to me.

One of them is holding Stone up against a wall, his spindly legs dangling, while the other three seem to be trying to undress him.

He doesn't make a sound or move. His eyes are closed, his expression devoid of emotion. Like he's playing dead.

"What the hell do you think you're doing?" I call out and the outrage burning in my chest turns my voice into a menacing growl. Stone's eyes pop open and he blinks a couple of times before he seems to believe his eyes. He stares in stupefied amazement as I prowl toward the group of boys who have all turned around. The one still holding Stone watches me over his shoulder, wide-eyed with surprise and suspicion.

"Get your fucking hands off him," I snarl.

He relinquishes his quarry with a sadistic smile that I want to wipe off with my fist. Stone lands on his feet, stumbles slightly and steps away from his tormentors He straightens his uniform and keeps his eyes trained on me.

"Are you okay, Stone?"

Instead of returning my attempt at a friendly smile, he glowers at me like I'm the one who was holding him against the wall. "What are you doing here? And, ho-how do you know my name?"

The boy who was holding him against the wall shakes off his fear, puts on a cocky smile and crosses his arms over his chest as he steps into my path and blocks Stone from my view.

He's an inch taller than me and tries to look down his nose at me. But I'm not scared of him. Bullies are the lowest hanging fruit. So pathetic and easy to take down once you recognize them for the cowards they are.

"Who the hell are you?"

"*You* don't get to ask me questions, motherfucker," I growl.

One of his friends snickers and he shoots him a quelling glare before he returns his smug gaze to my face. "This is a private campus. Stone doesn't know you, and so you better leave before we call security."

I laugh, but my eyes harden, and I enjoy watching his self-satisfied smirk disappear when I pull my phone out and hand it to him. "Go ahead. I can't wait to hear you explain why you were trying to undress a boy half your size."

He scoffs. "Our word against his and his...nanny or are you his maid?" The boys share a round of chuckles that stop abruptly when I join in.

"What's fucking funny?" the ringleader barks.

"Your joke," I say, wide-eyed with feigned bemusement.

"*What* joke?" he demands.

"The one where the school takes *your* side over the one of the boy whose family's name is on that building." I point back to the library.

For all the academic smarts these boys have, they're remarkably lacking in common sense.

He tries to stare me down, and only lasts two seconds. "Whatever. This is lame, We're outta here. We'll see *you* later, Rivers," he tosses the thinly veiled threat over his shoulders and shoves past me.

I grab him by the collar and drag his face to mine. "No, you *fucking* won't see him later. If you look at him again, much less touch him, I'll be back, and I won't be alone. And what my friends will do to you, will make you *wish* you'd been expelled," I warn through gritted teeth.

His face pales he yanks his collar out of my grasp and scowls at me while he smooths it back into place. "We were just fucking with him. This is high school. If he can't handle it, he should go back to the baby school." He shoves past me and his friends, who I've named Pathetic and Predictable, follow him.

I turn to Stone, who is standing there looking like he wants to kill someone, and I sigh.

"Did I just make things worse for you?" I ask

"Hello, Captain Obvious, good to see you haven't changed." He quips, no hint of gratitude or camaraderie on his face.

I bark out an incredulous laugh, "Wow, is that the thanks I get for saving you?"

"Thank you. Now, why are you here?" He adjusts his rucksack on his shoulders and taps his foot like I'm keeping him from an important appointment.

"You broke the window last night; did you think I was going to let that go?" I cross my arms.

He rolls his eyes. "You shouldn't have tried to lock me in."

My neck snaps when I lurch backwards in surprise. This kid... "Huh? Have you forgotten that you *broke* into my bakery and then fell asleep after you cried all over me?"

His cheeks flush red with embarrassment, but he doesn't let it show anywhere else. His eyes are calm, his thumbs hooked into the pockets of his jeans, his smile the picture of devil may care. "I didn't break in. The door was unlocked. And I only cried because I wanted to leave, and you wouldn't let me."

Now it's my turn to roll my eyes. "The door wasn't *unlocked.*" But I allow him his pride, and don't push back on the rest. "However, you got in, you shouldn't have been there at all. Are you going to tell me why or are you going to force me to turn you in?"

"You can't prove I was there," he pushes.

"We have video surveillance," I lie.

He crosses his arms over his bird-like chest and gives me a long assessing look, like he's trying to decide if he can trust me and then sighs in resignation, his shoulders slumping like the weight of the world just landed on them. "I study there. I don't touch anything, and I don't make any trouble. I won't be back. If you tell how much the window costs, my family accountant will send you whatever you need."I shake my head in grudging respect. He's a little shit, but he's braver than that group of boys combined.

"Oh, you're going to pay me back alright. But it's not going to be as easy as calling *Jeeves*. You're going to keep coming to the bakery. And when I'm done with my work, you're going to clean up. You're going to work until you've done enough hours to pay the insurance deductible on that window," I inform him and wait for the outrage.

It doesn't come.

Instead, his shrewd little eyes glitter with interest. "You mean, like baking?"

"No. I mean like cleaning up, sweeping, wiping stuff down. You can study while I bake and when I'm done, you can clean up."

"Oh." He frowns and his eyes narrow and I can practically hear his brain rerouting itself.

"What time do you want me to come by?" he asks, and I smile, impressed with how quickly he made up his mind. I expected he'd do like my brothers whenever they have to help in the kitchens—kick up a fuss and whine.

"I'll be here to get you at 8pm."

His smile disappears. "You're gonna *come* get me?"

I fold my arms over my chest, assuming a stance of authority. "I don't know how you got to the bakery yesterday, but you're too young to be going anywhere that time of night alone."

He balks. "I rode my bike like I always do. It's fine." His somber expression reminds me of all of the things he's recently lost. I relent.

"Fine, but when we're done, I'll throw your bike in the back of my car to bring you back. That's the deal." I add when he opens his mouth to argue. "You get to study while I work, and *then* you help me clean up. When you've worked enough hours to earn the $500, you're free to go."

"Okay," he croaks out. He looks sharply at the ground, but not quickly enough to hide the tears that well in his eyes.

My heart squeezes in empathy.

I hate for people to see my tears, too.

I walk over to him. I bend so we're eye level and grab his chin and turn his face up to mine.

"I'm sorry about your stepfather."

He blinks up at me in surprise. "Sure, thank you." His eyes mist and he blinks to clear them and gives me a heartbreakingly brave smile. I run a hand over his hair and it's not my imagination when he nuzzles against my palm before stepping back.

"I know it feels like the entire world is too small to hold your hurt, and there's no shame in crying. if you need to talk, I won't mind listening."

His tongue darts out and he licks his lips and then bites the lower one. They're very swollen still. My fists curl in on themselves itching for a chance to punch those boys square in their stupid, smug faces.

"Have you lost someone?" he asks.

"Huh?"

"Last night, you said something that made me think maybe you lost someone, too," he elaborates. "Why are you looking like that?" he asks when I just gape at him.

"Just that, I thought you'd a been too busy scheming to have heard anything I said."

He rolls his eyes again, but an embarrassed blush colors his cheeks and a shy smile dances on the corners of his cherub's mouth. I chuckle, utterly charmed by him. He's guileless and brave, but he needs someone looking out for him. "I did lose someone, a long time ago, yes."

His gaze sharpens. "Who?"

"My dad."

He nods absently as if he's processing my answer. "And…you're okay now?" His voice is innocent, but his expression intent, like my answer, is the most important thing in the world to him.

So, I answer with a candor I only share with a few people. "Most of the time…yes. Life goes on. But the first thing you have to decide is whether you're going to let grief rule you or if you're going to fight for every morsel of joy you can squeeze out of life."

"I want to fight," he says with a fierce light in his big eyes. "It's better than being a chicken," he challenges with an up tilt of his stubborn, surprisingly strong little chin.

I raise an eyebrow in response. "Not every battle is worth fighting. It takes courage to walk away from those, too." I hold a finger up to stop whatever rebuttal he's prepared.

"Just trust me on this one, okay?"I know you're smarter than everyone else in this place, but there are some things only time can teach you." I cringe inwardly at how much I sound like my mother.

He casts me a dubious glance and nibbles the corner of his lip, but his eyes don't lose the gleam of determination. "Can I start tonight?"

Relief courses through me, relaxing the muscles I didn't realize I was tensing. I don't know why this matters so much. The smart and safe thing would be to let this all go. But it's more than him paying for what he did. This child needs someone. And I'm compelled to be that person.

"Yup. At fifteen bucks an hour it's gonna take you a while to earn it—"

"It'll take approximately thirty-three hours. If I work 2 hours a night, we'll be square in as few as 17 days."

I blink in surprise. "How did you do that so fast?"

He quirks an eyebrow. "In my head, Captain Obvious." He taps his temple.

"Very funny. The answer only seems obvious because you're answering the wrong question."

He shakes his head. "You asked me *how* I did it. That's a very specific question. You should have asked how I did it so quickly. But seeing how I'm 10 years old and in high school, that's got a pretty obvious answer, too."

I open my mouth to retort and shut it again when I realize that he's right.

His cheeky smile widens to a grin at my deepening scowl.

Outwitted, I scowl. "No one likes a know-it-all."

I regret my quip when his eyes fall to his shoes and mutters a barely audible, "I know."

What is it about this kid and the way he tugs heartstrings I didn't know I had?

"No one, but me, that is," I add in a voice devoid of sympathy. The unexpectedly joyous smile he beams up at me feels like a trophy. I smile back and ruffle his mop of dark brown hair. I catch a glimpse of the time on my wristwatch and start backing away.

"I'll see you tonight. Come in by the *front* door. I got that back door fixed," I inform him with a meaningful look before I turn to hurry back to my car.

"Uh, Regan?" he calls. I turn to find him running toward me.

"I didn't tell you my name." I raise an eyebrow in suspicion. He stops a few inches shy of bringing us toe to toe and gazes up at me with hopeful eyes.

"You didn't have to. You're exactly like everyone describes you." He shoves his glasses up the bridge of his nose and clears his throat. His cheeks flush flame red and he drops his gaze to the ground.

"And how's that?" I ask, not sure if I should be flattered or concerned that "everyone" is talking about me.

He shrugs, and looks up at me through his lashes, but his gaze is direct and intense light in them.

"That you don't look like anyone they've ever seen... and really pretty." He drops his gaze again and I'm grateful.

Heat rushes up my neck and floods my cheeks and I curse my sun starved skin as my embarrassment makes itself plain as day. I've heard myself described that way before and I don't understand it. I have a twin. We're not identical. But there is no doubt that we're siblings. And, I look just like my mother. I clear my throat and "I have to go and you're late for study hall, I'll see you tonight."

"Wait." He grabs my arm to stop me from turning away. His head remains bowed and his grip on my hand tightens as if for moral support.

"Yes, what is it?" I ask when he doesn't say anything.

"About the window. I was…" he rushes the words out and then comes to a sudden, stuttering stop. He lets out a long, heavy sigh, his hair sways with the baleful shake of his head that follows. "There's no good reason for it. I'm just sorry." Hope shines out of his remarkably clear hazel eyes. I put a hand on his shoulder and smile at him as wide as I can. "I forgive you. Thank you for apologizing."

His frown is skeptical. "Your smile looks like you don't mean it."

"I know. It's just how my face is. I promise that all is forgiven. We've got a clean slate."

I hold my hand out for him to shake.

He ignores it, takes a step forward and wraps his arms around my waist. His head comes just to the top of my torso. He rests it there and squeezes me tight.

It's so sweet and sincere, and the unexpected warmth so welcome, that my embarrassment falls away and I return his embrace automatically, "You know that I came here to punish you, right?" I ask when he doesn't let go.

"You could have, I would have deserved it. But you're helping me instead. Thank you, so much," he says with his mouth pressed to my belly. I let him hold on for a minute more before I lean back, so I can look him in the eye.

"Maybe Stone, *just maybe*, you deserve this, too." I give him a wink and walk away.

Chapter 3

ALCHEMY

STONE

"Hey, come in here for a few minutes," Regan sticks her head through the door of the office she set up for me to work in. I glance at the clock in surprise. I've only been working for thirty minutes. But I put my pen down and close my notebook. "Oh, okay…Are you ready for me to start cleaning already?"

She shakes her head and smiles. "Nope. I have a treat for you. Can you take a break?" Surprised, I look up at her and instantly forget what she asked me.

She's so pretty. I know I shouldn't even be thinking it, but I can't help myself. She has the darkest eyes I've ever seen. Her lips may not be made to smile wide, but the way her eyes twinkle when she's happy more than makes up for that.

"Well, can you?" she asks, when I don't answer. I've still got at least an hour's worth of work to do, but after this afternoon, I would do anything she asked me to.

"Yeah, I can. I just need to finish this equation. I just need a few more minutes?"

"Okay, see ya," she calls as she disappears down the hall.

I glance at the now repaired back door and smile when I remember the first time I came to this bakery. Thankfully, for me anyway, a faulty lock wasn't a high priority on anybody's to-do list in places like Rivers Wilde.

This is a community that behaves the way a family *should*. And that includes trusting their neighbors to walk past a broken lock and not see it as an invitation.

But since my stepfather died, and my brother Hayes left to live with his aunt in Italy, I've been repeatedly reminded that in the eyes of most of the people I've called friends since I was three years old, I'm nothing *close* to family.

My mother is seen as the person who drove the much beloved and respected head of the Rivers Family, to an early grave. The Rivers family is without an official leader even though my Uncle Thomas is acting in his place. He can barely manage his own life, much less an entire empire.

It threw Houston's philanthropic community into a tailspin and created enough uncertainty to send the Rivers family's business, Kingdom, stock value into free-fall.

Fortunes have been lost or greatly reduced in the last few weeks, and *my* mother is viewed as the person who knocked over the first domino.

I came back to campus after the funeral and learned the hard way that being her son, too small, a*nd* way too smart for my age, was a triple curse.

Life at Blackwell turned into a game of survival. During the day, I had to be on constant alert for pranks and traps my bullies set. I couldn't focus enough to study. I got a C on the first exam I took after the funeral and it scared the hell out of me.

The school had been hesitant to admit a student as young as me. Despite my test scores and performance on the assessments they gave me, it took funding the library's endowment and my stepfather's clout to convince them. With him gone, I'm afraid they'll kick me out of here so fast, my head will spin.

I can't afford to let that happen. Not just for my sake. But for my two younger brothers as well. I'm the only responsible person in their lives now. My mother will ruin them, just like she ruins everything else she touches. The sooner I graduate, the sooner I can take care of them. When I walk into the kitchen, she's sitting at the counter with a plate full of biscuits and two glasses of milk in front of her.

"Come on, sit down. I want you to try these. I created the recipe myself."

"Okay..." I wasn't expecting her to feed me, but I'm glad. I'm too busy watching my back to actually eat anything at mealtime.

Most of the kids come back to school with care packages or get them regularly from home. I don't have anything like that, and I usually go to bed hungry. I sit down and pick up one of the tender, golden biscuit looking things and examine it.

"Looks weird. What is it?"

"It's a scone." She says scone like she's saying diamond.

I frown at her. "Looks like a biscuit."

She presses a finger to my lips, her eyes wide with alarm "Hush, before you hurt its feelings. Taste what it's made of, then you'll know why it's special."

I cast her a skeptical look but bite the biscuit thing before she starts talking about it like it's a human being again. It's as light as air, and practically melts on my tongue. I groan, my eyes roll heavenward. The butter, ginger, lemon and sugar are like biting into sunshine.

"I know," she croons.

I nearly choke on my biscuit. She's smiling wide, even though she'd said she couldn't. But yesterday when I said it, she looked like she wanted the ground to swallow her whole. So, I keep the thought to myself and take another bite of scone, intending to play it cool this time.

But I can't.

It's just too delicious.

"These flavors together -*this* is alchemy," I exclaim and then bite my tongue. I know how my vocabulary annoys people.

Her eyebrows raise up and she smiles down at me, something like pride shining in her eyes.

"Alchemy? That's a great word. How does it feel to be so incredibly smart?"

My stomach knots and I don't want to talk about *this*, not with her. I shrug. "I'm only kinda smart, but mainly I read a whole lot."

She smiles "I know you don't think it's great now but when you're older, you'll be so glad--"

"Yeah, obviously." I hate how people seem to like telling how much I'll love being me when I'm an adult. But that doesn't make it feel better right now. I want to be normal.

Embarrassed by the attention and not wanting to say anything else, I grab the glass of milk and wash down the rest of the scone.

She hops off the stool she's perched on and walks over to the huge cabinet and starts taking out bowls and baking sheets. "It's not so bad to be misunderstood and ahead of your time... Jesus, Jane Austen, Malcolm X, Winnie Mandela—they were all revolutionaries who were ahead of their time. People thought they were weird, chased them, teased them, rejected them. But they didn't stop. And neither will you."

"I won't?" I ask absently. I'm mesmerized by the economy and precision of her movements as she lays out her tools.

She gathers up her long, straight dark hair and ties it up on top of her head in a huge bun.

"Nope. Because we can't stop being ourselves. Just because you're not like everyone else, doesn't mean there's a single thing wrong with you. You're perfectly made."

I can't speak around the tears clogging my throat, my heart feels too big for my chest. No one has ever spoken to me like this.

"Okay, you go to do your homework while I get to work. I'll have tons of clean up for you by the time you're done." She points me in the direction of a dark corridor but doesn't even spare me a glance as she dons her crisp white apron and gets to work.

"Are you sure you don't mind me being here?"

She shakes her head, her bun bobs as she ties the strings around her waist. "After living with my two brothers, hanging with boys is my forte. You couldn't possibly annoy me half as much as they do."

She cocks her head to look at me, that half smile on her pretty mouth, and my stomach feels weird, like I'm on the Texas Cyclone at Six Flags. I'm afraid that I'm gonna fall off the stool, so I stand up and grab the counter. "Give it a couple of days. My mother says I could try a saint," I warn her.

"Well...I'm made of sterner stuff than some old saint. Besides, you're like me...a giver. And I've heard it said somewhere, that when two givers get together, it's like...alchemy." Her eyes twinkle and this body that's always felt too small for the soul inside it, relaxes and I draw in a deep lungful of air. And then she says the words that, later on, I'll recall as the ones that made my heart hers forever. "I water you, you water me. Together, we're going to grow."

"You did good. Cleaning up my colossal messes just might be your calling." It's a few minutes past midnight and Regan just locked up the store.

"As if it takes any talent to wash dishes," I grumble, glad the dark is hiding the blush that blooms at her praise.

She nudges my shoulder as we make our way down the main street of Rivers Wilde. "I don't know if it takes talent, but it certainly takes determination to scrub every last burned-on crumb off those cookie sheets. I used to think spotless baking pans were the sign of a dispassionate baker. Now, I'll think of them as fruits of a committed dishwasher's labor."

We walk in silence the rest of the way to her blue Mustang and she pops the trunk for me to drop my BMX inside the surprisingly roomy compartment. When she starts the car, music blares from the speakers so loud that it rattles the windows. She winces and turns the volume down to just above audible.

"Sorry, I listen to it like that when I'm alone."

"It's cool," I shrug and stare out into the night, still lost in my thoughts as we make our way toward the exit of Rivers Wilde.

She didn't go easy on me tonight. She gave me *all* the work she would have done if I wasn't there. And I loved every minute of it.

I'd never washed a dish in my life before—I've been missing out. It felt good to see that sparkling, empty sink clear of the dirty whisks, mixing bowls and measuring spoons that she'd dropped into it. In fact, the whole night was nice.

"I failed second grade." Her unexpected statement draws my eyes to her. She's got her eyes on the road, but her jaw flexes in sync with her hands' grip on the steering wheel.

"Why?" I ask when she doesn't elaborate.

She shrugs. "I failed math, social studies, and science." Her voice is light, and when she glances at me, there's an embarrassed half smile on her face. But her jaw is still tight when she turns back to the road.

"Yeah but, *why*?" I press.

"According to my report card, I didn't grasp the material."

"Okay. But that can't be why." I can't believe she's *ever* failed to grasp *anything*.

She glances at me again; her expression has gone from embarrassed to assessing. "You're the first person to ever say that. So, I'll tell you why, but you have to swear that you're not some sort of spy for your family."

Family. How I wish. Longing twists like a hook in my heart. "Hayes and my little brothers are my only family and they can't afford to hire me, at least not yet. So, don't worry. Your secrets are safe with me."

She exhales the way my mother does when she's trying to calm her nerves. "I didn't want to be in the same class with my twin brother for the rest of my life."

That's the last thing I expected her to say. "Didn't you have to live together, too?"

"I didn't hate *him*. It was everyone else. He's great at everything. He's charming, and funny, and smart. They couldn't help but compare us, and I was never anyone's favorite." She says it like it doesn't matter, and maybe it doesn't, anymore. But, if she failed a grade and added an entire year to school to get away from him, it must have mattered a whole lot. "I'm sorry," I say and hate how dumb it sounds.

"Don't be. It was one year, and I've recovered nicely. I know it must make you twitchy seeing how you're in a rush and all."

That hook twists tighter "Not by choice. I have to take care of my brothers. I'll peak early and then, I'll do an Aaliyah or a Biggie, and that'll be it.".

"What?" she chuckles.

"They all peaked early and died early. I'm ten, and five years ahead in school. Figure I'll finish college by the time I'm 18, and then I'll get a job, kick butt and then kick the bucket by 30, max. So, I'm not gonna get married or have kids. Better not to have people left behind who need me."

"But...that's ridiculous," she sputters.

"Tell that to Selena, Ricky Valens, Tupac, Kurt Cobain, River Phoenix, James Dean." I counter.

"Are you s*erious?*"

"You look like I just told you I was from Mars."

She groans. "So, what about Oprah Winfrey, Margaret Thatcher, Vera Wang, Betty White, Viola Davis?"

"Violin *who?*"

She darts an unimpressed glare in my direction and shakes her head in disappointment.

"I'm going to teach you some *women's* history while you're cleaning. They're all legends who have lived long after their moment of glory. My dad died young; I know my time could come any day. But that just makes me want to do something worth being remembered for. Your life will have more than one peak, and more than one valley. You might die young and it's good to live like this might be your last day, because hell. who knows? But you better *plan* like you're gonna be here until you're a hundred and three."

"And, we're here," she announces breezily, oblivious to the seismic shift her words have caused inside me. She pops the trunk before turning to face me. "See you tomorrow?"

"Yup." I croak and grab the door handle.

"Oooh, I almost forgot. One sec…" She reaches into the back seat, pulls out a white wax lined bakery bag and holds it out to me.

"Scones. In case you get hungry between classes tomorrow."

I take the bag and hope that she can see the gratitude in my eyes. I'm afraid that if I try to speak, I'll cry.

I hold the bag with as much delicacy as I can while I walk my bike up to the side entrance. I turn to look back at where she dropped me off, she's still there watching until she's sure I'm going to get inside safely, something my own mother has never done. I lift a hand to return her wave goodbye and slip past the gate.

That night, for the first time since my stepfather died, I don't cry myself to sleep.

Chapter 4

JUST MY IMAGINATION

STONE

The last four months have been the best of my whole life. Regan gave me more than a place to study; she transformed my whole life. When I walked into class the morning after my first night with her, the ever-present ball of dread in my gut wasn't so heavy.

I'd been afraid to fight back because I didn't want to get kicked out. But I saw their faces when she reminded them that I'm a Rivers and I know they don't want trouble either. They only pick on me because I let them.

The next time they cornered me, I swung my backpack at the one whose face was closest and broke his nose.

He bled all over the hallway.

We were both hauled to the principal's office, and before I could say anything, he announced that I'd hit him accidentally.

They never bothered me again.

It only took me one month to work enough hours to earn the $500 I owed her. When she told me my tab was settled, I kept coming anyway. With my bullies vanquished I didn't need the space to study anymore. So, I started spending the entire evening with her in the kitchen.

She's a universe of knowledge and she shares it all with me. From baking to history, politics to Pokémon evolution, she knows everything. And when she's talking to me, I get the feeling that she's been waiting to tell someone all the things she's sharing with me.

Some nights, we just listen to music and work on our own. She plays music I've never heard before. Her favorite is "Just My Imagination" by The Temptations. When that comes on, she sings along. Her voice is nice enough. But it's the smile she wears when she's singing it that makes it my favorite.

Other times, she brings her laptop and gives me an education on movies shot in Houston. We watched *Terms of Endearment*, *Jason's Lyric*, *Armageddon*, and *Selena*. All of them were sad, but *Selena* is the only one that made her cry.

And on the nights when we get every scone off the cookie sheets without any of them sticking, she plays this song called "Southside" and makes me dance with her. She smells like those scones she makes: lemon and ginger and vanilla… I could smell it all day, every day, and still never get tired of it.

The loud, long screech of a car horn shakes me awake just in time for me to stop myself from walking into the crosswalk. I jump back onto the sidewalk and clutch my backpack to my chest.

My heart thuds against the hardbound book inside. This signed special edition copy of Cosmos by Carl Sagan is my most prized possession. I'm giving it to her as a graduation gift. Last week she found out she's going to be her class Valedictorian.

I wish I could go watch her graduate. But I'd have to ask my mother to drive me all the way to Hofheinz Pavilion. If she knew I'd even *met* a Wilde, much less spent time with one, she'd raise hell and this small peace I've found would be taken from me.

So, I'm taking her my present now. I've read it at least a hundred times in the two years since my stepfather brought it home for me. I can recite entire chapters with my eyes closed. But there's one in particular, about the planet Venus, that made me decide to give this book to Regan.

The transits of Venus—the point in its orbit when it moves between the earth and the sun—only happens once a century. It is the rarest of predictable astronomical phenomena—and one of the most important. Before we had high powered telescopes and the ability to launch satellites into space, scientists used its occurrence to map our entire solar system.

The book has taught me more than planetary order. It helped me understand that even in chaos, there's order.

When my stepfather died, I read it obsessively to remind myself that there is no such thing as bad timing, or coincidence, or luck. As intelligent as we are, we're no more important than a speck of stardust compared to the age and size of the universe.

Just like those planets up there - we're on a collision course with our destiny and everything we do, everyone we meet, shapes that journey and becomes part of it.

Regan has become part of mine.

I wrote an inscription on the inside of the book that says, "You're my Venus and I'm your Mars."

It's simple, but when she reads the book, she'll understand. She'll see I'm not some ordinary kid. When I finish school, I'm going to marry her. I used to think I'd never get married, because I didn't want to leave people behind the way I was. But I'd do it with her.

I gulp down the cool night air to calm my racing heart. The sidewalks here are pristine strips of large red pavers that line the glass fronted stores on the street. The leaves and petals of the hanging plants that give it a small town feel during the day, cast eerie shadows now.

The telltale glow of light from the back of the store makes my heart skip a beat. I'm early, but I wanted to have time to give her my present before we got to work.

I've just opened the door and am about to call out for her when a shrill, short scream rips through the quiet of the bakery.

I freeze, my heart beating like a jackhammer. Another scream, this one followed by a man's rumbling voice scares me into motion. I press the white button on the wall to trigger the silent alarm and tip toe toward the kitchen.

The rush of blood in my ears is so loud, my ears throb. If anything happens to her…I move faster, but soundlessly through the hallway that leads into the kitchen and stop to grab a knife from the wall where they're mounted.

"Get over here and show me what a slut you are," the man's voice isn't angry. But I've heard the boys at school call girls that and I know it's not something you say to be nice.

"You wish," she responds in that taunting voice of hers. She doesn't sound afraid, but her scream when I first walked in is practically ringing in my ear.

I creep to the door and pause to listen for sounds of him coming this way. I don't hear anything, so I flatten my back to the wall of the dark hallway and move as fast as I can and creep unnoticed into the service area of the restaurant where they're standing.

His back is to me, Regan is on her knees in front of him and his hand is in her hair, tugging it back and forth. Regan is gagging. He's saying all sorts of filthy words to her that even Hayes wouldn't say to anyone. I see red and tighten my grip on the knife handle.

Seeing him hurt her, *my* girl, makes something in me go solid. All of the crap of this year bubbles up to the surface. I don't think about what comes next. I just heed my instinct that's screaming at me to protect her. I rush toward them with the knife poised to strike. I'm fully prepared to take this man's life to save hers.

Regan's thick, dark lashes flutter and then her eyes pop open just as I lift the knife. I shake my head, mouth "I'll stop him," and watch them go from dazed to terrified as I plunge it into his back.

And then all hell breaks loose.

Chapter 5

DO YOU LOVE HIM?

REGAN

Weston's howls are interspersed with grunts of pain. He claws desperately at his back to try and grasp the handle of the knife, twisting and turning wildly. In stark contrast. Stone is completely still and silent as he stares in rapt, morbid fascination.

If this nightmare wasn't happening to me, I would laugh.

The horrifying, manic scream Weston unleashes when he manages to grip the hilt and yank it out, shakes me out of my stupor. I take a cautious step in his direction, "Weston, let me have that," I nod at the blood tipped chef's knife in his hand.

He jerks away from my extended arm. He eyes Stone with wild, enraged eyes. "Who the *fuck* is this kid?" he roars lurches toward him.

I'm afraid he's going to turn the knife on Stone, but he drops it and reaches around to probe his back. He lifts a trembling bloody stained hand in front of his face and pales.

"Are you okay?" I ask him and reach for him again.

As soon as I touch him, he wrenches away, protecting his injured flank and turning his ire on me. "What the fuck do you think? I got stabbed in the fucking back and I'm bleeding," he cries.

"We should call 9-1-1," Stone's voice is toneless and so cold, it sends a shiver up my spine. I glance at him and gasp at the undisguised malice in his eyes.

"Don't you fucking call *anyone*," Weston hisses through clenched teeth.

"You need a doctor," I argue, incredulous as he starts to gather the small pile of keys, phone and wallet he'd dumped on the white marble serving counter that runs along the entire front of the bakery.

"*And* the police," Stone chimes in.

"*Fuck* the police," Weston pushes a lock of blonde hair off his sweat damp forehead.

"Why not? I stabbed you, don't you want me to pay for it?" Stone asks in a taunting voice. His expression is keen and knowing. His voice is grave and there is not a hint of regret in his expression. If anything, he looks like he's sorry Weston *isn't* dead. There's no hint of the compassionate kid I've gotten to know.

"You're fucking lucky I don't like cops. I know some bruisers in juvie hall that would turn your little ass inside out," Weston growls.

"Weston!" I shoot him a quelling glance over my shoulder.

He looks at me like I grew another head. "Are you seriously yelling at me? The little *shit* fucking stabbed me."

"He was scared," I snap at him and step into his line of sight so he can't see Stone anymore.

"He doesn't scare *me*." Stone's voice trembles.

I turn around, cup his face in my hands, and tilt it up until I can look into his eyes. They're luminous with unshed tears. "Why?" I whisper.

He opens his mouth, but he doesn't say anything before he presses his lips together like he's holding back a scream. He swallows hard and he looks into my eyes like his life depends on it.

"I'm fucking bleeding, can you have your little moment later?" Weston groans from behind me.

"He's just a kid, let me get him sorted," I say in annoyance over my shoulder, and tense when Weston struggles to his feet.

His face is pale and waxy. Pain etched in lines that crease his forehead and bracket his mouth. He takes a few steps and then slumps into one of the chairs.

He needs medical attention. But first I need to get Stone out of here. "Are you ready to go back to school? I'll take you."

"I'm not a kid." Stone stands, arms crossed, glaring at me.

I sigh in frustration. His lack of remorse rankles. I know he's got the courage of his convictions, but he's gone too far.

"*Yes*, you are. And you stabbed someone tonight when you shouldn't even have been here. You should at least apologize."

He steps back like I slapped him.

"I thought he was hurting you," he says, his little hands balled into fists.

"No, not at all. What we were doing is what boys do with girls they like."

"Is he your boyfriend?" Stone asks and I frown, my brow furrows so deeply that it gives me an instant headache.

"No, honey, I..." I have no idea how to explain this thing between me and Weston.

Weston hefts himself up with a grunt of pain. "We're fucking and that makes me much more than her titty sucking *boyfrien*d."

I wish he'd act like people on tv when they got stabbed and pass out, or *something*. "Shut *up*," I snap.

"*You* shut the fuck up, you bitch," he grits out, his finger pointing menacingly at me. His face is contorted by outrage as he staggers toward me. I'm not scared of him, but I take an instinctive step back.

"Stop saying bad words to her," Stone yells.

"What are you, five years old?" Weston taunts, raising the pitch of his voice in a mocking mimic of Stone's.

"I'm ten and a half," he levels a contemptuous gaze on Weston. "I'm glad I stabbed you, you dirty mouthed jerk," And then, he lunges at him with so much force that he manages to drag me forward a few steps before I can stop him.

Weston's howl of pain before he falls to his knees makes me jump back in surprise. He drops to his side on the floor clutching his balls and moaning in agony.

Stone's little face is grim, his eyes wide and on glued to Weston's now prostrate, writhing body. "I kicked him," he says like he can't believe it himself.

I reach out to him. He eyes my hand warily, but when I cup his shoulders and pull him into a hug, he comes willingly. He wraps his arms around my waist and hugs me tight.

Even in the midst of this disaster, affection and love overwhelm everything else, and I hug him back. "You don't have to be afraid," I murmur into the top of his sweat-dampened hair.

"Like hell. If he's still here when I get up, I'm gonna skin that fucker alive," Weston grits out, spittle foams in the corners of his grotesquely contorted mouth.

"I thought he was hurting you," Stone roars suddenly and pulls away from me with a violent jerk of his little body.

We all jump at the same time when the sound of the emergency vehicle siren rips through the quiet air. They're closer now.

"You called the cops?" Weston groans and starts to stand, but he slumps back in his chair, pale and sweaty.

"No, I didn't call anyone."

I rush to the window and peer out at the long stretch of Wilde Way. In the distance, I see the unmistakable flash of lights. Like the proverbial deer, I'm momentarily frozen by fear even as my mind races to think of how to salvage this.

Stone can't be caught here. He'll be expelled. And my grandfather will kill me if he knows I've been giving aid and comfort to a Rivers.

"You have to leave." With my heart in my throat, I grab Stone by the shoulders and turn us toward the back exit. When he digs his heels in and won't move, I lean down and bring us face to face. "If they find you here, you'll be in a lot of trouble," I plead.

The anger and hurt in his eyes so raw and naked, that it steals my breath.

"You lied to me, Regan." He wrenches out of my hold.

"About what?" I ask, bewildered and anxious at the same time.

His chest is heaving, and his lip is trembling. He blinks and squeezes his eyes closed sending tears spilling out of the corners of them.

The sight of this sweet, thoughtful, sensitive soul who I've grown to care about over the last few months, crying because of something I did, intentionally or not, hurt him brings tears to my eyes.

"Everything was perfect until you ruined it. I love you, but you like h*im*. Even *I* can tell he's a bad man. I wish I'd never met you."

The force of his outburst hits me square in the solar plexus and I have no clue how to respond to what he just said.

Stone, on the other hand, has no problem saying what he thinks. He glances at Weston, and his lip curls in disgust.

"I should have let him choke you to death with his penis," he growls and then turns and sprints for the backdoor.

Dismayed, I start after him, but the flashing lights and screeching sirens outside the bakery, stop me mid-stride. So, I let him go.

But as I turn back to deal with Weston and disaster that's bubbling over in the bakery, I have a terrible feeling that I'll never see that little boy again.

At that thought, my heart breaks, too.

One Year Later

PALESTINE, EAST TEXAS

Chapter 6

PALESTINE

REGAN

"Reggie, are you sure you know where you're going? We're in the middle of nowhere." My friend Matty peers futilely out of her window at the fathomless dark while we zip down the winding back roads that were cut through the dark forest.

"We're in Jerusalem, Texas and the people who live here would be pretty offended to hear you call this little pearl, *nowhere*," I drawl in an exaggerated twang.

"A pearl? Wow, the dark must hide *all* its charm," Matty, quips dryly.

"And the machete wielding madmen," Jack chimes in from the back seat.

"You two are such city girls, you'd think you'd never been out in the country before." I chide, tongue in cheek. I haven't even been camping before. I think these woods are creepy as hell.

"So are *you*, your $1000 cowboy boots don't make you an expert, okay?" I can hear Matty's eye roll without looking at her.

"No, but they'll sure make me feel like one if we run out gas and have to walk. Good luck running from coyotes in those four-inch Manolo's—hey," I yelp and arch away when her fingers dance over my ribs to tickle me.

"Are there really coyotes out here? Do they eat people?" Jack asks, nervously.

I groan with exaggerated impatience "Calm your tits, tricks, we've got plenty of gas and I know where I'm going. I promised you an adventure and I'm delivering. Just sit back and enjoy the ride."

Matilda and Jacqueline, aka Matty and Jack are my best friends from freshman year. We all had internships at Wilde World this summer. They've been staying with me at my family's house this week. And we've been having the time of our lives. My mother seemed to have mellowed and except for her horror over the way I wore my hair, she barely had a word to say about anything.

Growing up, Houston's humid summers made my hair impossibly frizzy and my mother would drag me to the African hair braider on West Alabama to get my hair braided every week. In the fall and winter when the air was dryer and cool, we spent Saturdays getting our hair rolled, blown out and then pressed with a flat iron.

It was an ordeal. But in Tina Wilde's eyes, an unruly coiffure was a sign of internal disorder. One of the things I looked forward to most about leaving home was autonomy over my own hair.

In the weeks before I left for SMU, I spent hours reading Black hair blogs. I learned my hair was considered a 3C texture and figured out which products were best for it and went down to Solid Gold on W. Bellfort to buy them.

Before I left, we spent half the day at the beauty salon getting it pin straight, the way she liked it.

The first thing I did after she dropped me off on campus was wash my hair. I walked out of my room and headed to orientation with it loose and free for the first time in as long as I could remember.

I stopped to ask someone for directions. She gave them to me and when I said, "Thank you" the girl responded with, "What are you?"

I laughed and answered, "An Aquarius," tongue in cheek because it was such a vague question.

She gave me an impatient sigh and spoke in a slow, deliberate tone. "Are you, like…Dominican, or something?"

"Nope, I'm from Texas." My ignorance was feigned, but only because I wasn't sure how to answer.

If she'd asked *who* I was, the answer would have rolled off my tongue. I'm Regan Naomi Wilde—daughter, sister, dreamer, womanist, ally, writer, reader, rebel.

But *what* I was? I'd never given much thought to. In Houston, my family's history is practically local lore and even though my grandfather is Irish, we were raised by our mother and have always thought of ourselves as Biracial Black people.

Over the course of my first week on campus, I found myself being asked that question, "What are you?" repeatedly. The response to my ambiguous and vague answers was, almost universally, disappointment. And it only made me feel more alone than ever.

One night, I stared at myself in the mirror and tried to see what stood out the most. But all I saw was a near perfect blending of both parts of my heritage.

My eyes are the same deep dark brown as the famously rich soil in the Blue Mountains of Jamaica where my mother spent her childhood.

The spray of freckles on my left cheek are a gift from my maternal grandmother who was born in the town of Letterkenny, Ireland.

In the summer my skin drinks in the sun and turns deep brown. By the end of winter, I'm so pale Tyson calls me Casper.

I joined the Caribbean Student Union and the Irish American Student Coalition to try to figure out where I might fit. I found things and people I loved in both organizations, but I realized that no matter what I called myself, my resting bitch face was a universal language that made friendships hard to cultivate, no matter where I was.

It was in the bowels of the library, researching a piece to submit for a spot on the school paper's staff that I felt most at home. I guess it should have come as no surprise that it's also where I met my best friends.

The submission prompt asked us to pick a historical figure that was notorious, scandalous, or is widely despised. We were to cite reliable sources and tell a different story. One that was just as true, but perhaps, more inconvenient.

I knew right away who I was writing about—Jezebel. The biblical Phoenician princess whose name has become synonymous with ruin and deceit is, in my opinion, one of the most misunderstood women in all of history.

I've been obsessed with her since my grandfather told me that she was actually a ruler whose name was dragged through the mud because she was so ahead of her time. For a little girl, who often, felt misunderstood and underestimated, hearing her story made me angry. The budding storyteller was itching for a way to set the record straight, and this was my chance.

My very first conversation with Matty was an argument in the stacks over a book we were both intent on checking out. When our heated exchange revealed that we'd picked the same subject for our newspaper pieces, we quickly settled our quarrel. She invited me to join her and her roommate, Jack, for dinner.

We spent the evening talking about our shared outrage over the way, both history and myth alike, make men heroes and describe women as treacherous sirens, child-eating monsters, or husband murdering gold diggers. Our food grew cold, and our friendship caught fire.

The rest is history.

"So, how do you know this guy?" Matty asks, breaking into my wandering thoughts.

"Weston is my walk on the wild side from high school," I say with a mischievous and lascivious laugh. But, if I'm completely honest, I have no idea what to expect tonight.

The last time I saw him, he called me a "disloyal cunt." He was carrying an unlicensed weapon and had bags of weed in his backpack that night at the bakery. He was handcuffed to the gurney that took him to the hospital for treatment of his stab wound.

My grandfather was furious when I called him to try and do damage control, and my late-night shifts came to a swift end.

"Oh my God, is this the guy who pierced your hymen?" Jack asks excitedly.

"Can't you just say I lost my virginity?" I groan.

"Why? You knew what I meant, right?"

"Fine." I cede the point and roll my eyes at the satisfied smile on her face. "And yes, that's him. I don't know what to expect, because the last time I saw him, it wasn't exactly hearts and roses."

"So, what was high school Regan like? Were you the girl everyone wanted to be, and every boy wanted to fuck but who no one could touch?"

I laugh at the irony of how completely opposite my experience was. Besides my brothers, Stone had been my only other real friends.

"Hardly. There's nothing in the world that could compensate for what is, according to my mother, my greatest flaw—I don't smile enough."

Matty doesn't say anything, but after sharing a dorm room with her all year, I understand her silences as well as I do her spoken words. If she's quiet, she's thinking. I glance at Jack in the rearview mirror, and her sad smile makes me self-conscious.

"Don't feel sorry for me. I take initiative when it matters. I'm not crazy about people in general. I don't really mind that they leave me alone." Silence falls and when I look in my rearview mirror at Jack, I notice a pair of headlights far behind us. It's the first car I've seen since pulled off the 45.

Matty breaks the silence. "I'd seen you before that day we met in the stacks. I'd heard your family was rich. And I thought…a girl who looks like you, with money, who doesn't smile and eats alone… I thought you were a snob. I was surprised when you suggested I use the book first. I should have known better; I know what it is to be judged for things I can't help. I'm so sorry." She leans over to hug me and I give her an awkward pat but keep my eyes on the road. "You're going to make me drive off the road." I grumble, but with a smile on my face.

"I thought your magical cowboy boots could save us from any-thing," Matty wiggles her fingers at my ribs again, and I shriek with laughter.

A glance in my rearview mirror smothers my good humor.

The car is closer now. So close, I can tell that he's going faster than me. This is a two-lane road; I could let him pass me. But I'd rather stay ahead because the shoulder is nonexistent, and I don't want to risk being side swiped.

I punch the gas and speed up to keep a good distance between us and try to relax for the rest of the drive. I need tonight and all the debauchery it promises.

I've spent the summer with my hair tamed, my clothes tailored, my legs stockinged and my smile plastered on. I'm itching for a little bit of Weston's dark.

I turn off at the exit when the GPS instructs me to. The car that had been so far behind us is only a few car lengths away now and pulls off the exit behind us.

This close I can tell it's a big truck and I speed up as soon as I come out of the curved bend of the exit. But no matter how fast I go, it keeps pace.

When we turn down the road that leads to the cabin where Weston is having his party, it does too. I know this area well enough to know that these lanes usually have a single house on them. They must be going to the party. I don't know why my stomach knots like a ninny.

When it doesn't follow us as I turn into the drive, I almost sag in relief.

Until I see the house.

There are only two cars parked in front. And no lights on in the cabin. It looks abandoned. Hardly the makings of the house party he claimed he was throwing.

"Is this it?" Matty asks just as bright lights cut slices into the car and land on my rearview. The truck is stopped a few feet behind my car and the lights blaze into my car and make it so we can see each other properly for the first time.

I look at my friends and see that neither of them look worried.

"We must be the first people here," I say and turn the car off.

"Come on, let's go in. I promise this is going to be a night like you've never had."

Over the next seventy-two hours, I'll wish for a return to my normal everyday boring life, more times than I draw breath.

The two women who I called sister will suffer for my poor judgment and our relationships will be forever altered.

The man who I called a walk on the wild side, will become my mortal enemy.

And the man I will love above all others, though he wasn't present when my world shifted off center, set it all in motion the night he thought he was saving my life.

Six Years Later

HOUSTON, TX

Chapter 7

SOS

REGAN

"Call me back."

I read Matty's text with eyes still blurry from sleep. My boyfriend, Charlie mutters in his sleep and pulls the comforter up over his shoulder and turns his back to me.

I slide out of bed and hurry into the bathroom of the hotel room we booked for tonight and close the door behind me.

My phone says Matty called me four times before she sent that text.

Alarm sends my stomach into a free fall, and I can't get my normally pragmatic brain to pull the brakes on my fear. We've barely spoken in the last month.

I take a deep breath and with still trembling fingers unlock my phone to call her back.

But it rings before I can. The caller id flashes Jack's name this time I answer it before the second ring. I hear Matty's deep voice shouting a steady stream of curses in French and a man shouting too.

"She's still not answering," Jack sounds distressed and desperate.

"Jack?" I shout to make sure she hears over the pandemonium in the background.

"Oh my God Reggie, thank *God,*" Jack's breathy, frantic voice is barely audible over the shouting behind her.

"What's wrong?" I cover the mouthpiece to try and muffle my voice.

"No, no, no, no, no, no," she cries and then I hear the unmistakable sound of a gun being fired. My blood turns cold and terror sinks claws into my chest and holds me in its grip.

"Jack! What's happening? I'm going to call the police."

"No *no*, Regan you can't call the police. Please don't," she shouts but part of it is muffled as if she's covering the phone. All I can make out is the general sound of chaos and irritation mingles with my fear.

"Jack, if you don't tell me what the hell is going on, I don't care what you say I'm hanging up and calling the police."

"No, no—please wait" She sucks in a breath and when she speaks again her voice is much steadier. "We're not hurt, but we do need your help. We're at Dan Harrison's house. We need you to go to his office and get his laptop and bring it over, please?" she asks

At the mention of my grandfather's personal secretary, dread joins my fear. "Why? And who fired a gun at who?"

"We'll tell you when you get here," she says impatiently.

"No, you'll tell me now or I'm not coming," I snap, even though I'm already on the move.

"I told you," she says in a voice made rough with annoyance.

"Told me what?" I ask confused

"Not you, Reggie. Hold on." She covers the phone to muffle her voice. I'm about to hang up when Matty comes on the line.

"Reggie it's me, there's been an accident, we need you to go to Dan's office and get his laptop." Her voice is distinctly calmer and far more strident than Jack's and the demand without any explanation snaps my patience.

"Give me a minute to get dressed and I'll call you back." I ignore her groan of frustration and hang up so I can focus on getting myself out of the hotel room as quickly as possible.

I hurry back into the bedroom, sacrificing stealth for speed as I throw my clothes on.

Charlie turns over once, but otherwise doesn't wake up while I finish zipping up my jeans, slip my feet into the silver ballet flats, put all my jewelry back on, grab my purse. I eye his prone form with envy. I wish I'd slept through the notifications on my phone.

In less than a minute, I'm walking out of the hotel room, and calling them back.

Matty answers on the first ring. "I can't believe you hung up on me Regan, this is an *emergency.*" Her voice is edging to the same level of hysteria as Jack's was and a renewed sense of urgency propels me away from the elevator and toward the stairs.

"Tell me what is going on. I heard a gunshot."

There's a beat of silence and I know she's annoyed that I ignored her complaint. When she speaks her voice is taut with annoyance. "Dan was hit in the leg."

I come to a complete stop in the hallway, my hand cover my eyes as horror and confusion kick my heartbeat into overdrive. "By who?" I shout when I find my voice again.

"It was an accident," Matty says as if she can't believe she's having to explain herself.

"What the hell are you doing with a gun?" Anger dislodges my shock and I start walking again.

"It was just in case. He was supposed to have his laptop on him, but he didn't. Then, he wouldn't tell us where it was, so I waved the gun at him. It went off and he was hit in the leg. He said it was in his office."

"Why are you at his house? What in the world do you need his laptop for?" I fly down the stairs two at a time.

"He was supposed to come straight from the airport. We were going to take his laptop and get him to sign a confession and take it to the police," Matty explains.

"A confession about what?" I ask, in a guarded voice. I grab the railing of the stairs and sink down on one of the steps. This is so much worse than I thought.

There are a few seconds of silence, and I know that she's counting to five, the way she does whenever she's trying not to lose it.

Dan has been my grandfather's right hand for the last twenty years. He's the most upstanding, straight-laced person I know. Whatever they think he's done, they're wrong.

"This isn't the time to explain. He's okay. It's not even bleeding anymore. But we need that laptop. Please just go and get it."

"If you want me to do anything *other* than hang up and call 9-1-1, you better start explaining why you were at Dan Harrison's house in the middle of the night waiting for him to come home." I'm not bluffing. I never do. And she knows it.

A tense silence yawns between us and I wait for her to decide what happens next.

"We think he's the John Rebecca mentioned at Wilde."

"Please tell me you are *not* fucking serious. What in the *hell?*"

"I know you think it's bullshit, but it's not." Matty's voice is just as insistent as mine.

"Oh my God. What have you done?" I groan, despair lodged in my throat like a tumor.

"You said you didn't want anything to do with it. So, we didn't tell you. But we kept digging Regan and we *know* it's him. But we need that laptop. Please, help us. I promise this isn't a whim. We have proof."

"Then why'd you break into his house and hold a gun on him?" I ask acidly.

"Because we need his laptop. There's evidence on there."

"Then, *call* the police. I don't want to be in your little circle of trust *now* that your harebrained scheme is blowing up in your faces." I growl.

She's quiet for so long that I start to relax, maybe I've finally gotten through to her. Her next words shatter that hope.

"There are *pictures* of Jack on that laptop. She saw them." Her voice is full of meaning I wish I could pretend to misunderstand. Jack hasn't let anyone take her picture in 6 years. Not since that night. A shiver runs over my body and my mouth goes dry. I close my eyes against the wave of nausea that comes out of nowhere. I double over and take a deep breath to try and stem it. I know I won't throw up. I never do. But it still feels like I need to.

"Are you there? Regan?" Matty calls.

"What kind of pictures?" I ask, dread making my voice hoarse.

"From when Silk had us," she says it with deliberate brevity.

At the mention of Weston Silk, my insides turn to water and my legs threaten to give out underneath me. I slide down the wall and land with a thud on my rump.

"How? How? Pops got rid of all of them," I say as I stare at the floor unseeing, my fingers pinch the bridge of my nose.

"He must not have been able to. Or, maybe other people got them before he did. He was *looking* at them during a meeting and she was sitting right behind him. She's worked with him for five years and that fucker has never looked at her longer than it's taken him to complain about his coffee not being sweet enough." Her voice breaks with angry tears and leaden weight forms in my gut. "We followed him. He went to this place all the way out by the Ship Channel. It looked like a club, but there was nothing but a neon light in the shape of a thunderbolt over the door."

I close my eyes and take a few shuddering breaths to try and calm my racing pulse and fight back the nausea that threatens.

"Maybe it's a coincidence?" I'm desperate for this not to be true.

"Regan. *Stop*. It's not. And you know it. Go get that laptop. His office is locked but I know you have the master. I'm texting you his address. Bring it." Then, she hangs up in my face.

I can't even find the will to be angry with her.

This is all my fault.

When we got back to campus to start our sophomore year, our friendship was just a shell of its former self.

Jack moved off campus with her boyfriend.

Matty and I signed up to be roommates at the end of our freshman year, but I could tell when we moved in that she was having the same regrets about that as I was.

They never said it aloud, but I knew they must blame me for what happened, and I was plagued with guilt for taking them there.

We barely saw each other.

We never spoke about what happened.

One night, less than a month after we'd been back at school, we'd been working in our room with the news in the background when Matty screamed. I followed her slack jawed, wide-eyed expression and turned to the television. And nearly fainted when I saw the face on the screen.

Her hair was a different color and she had two black eyes and a swollen nose but those dark brown, haunted eyes—so much like mine—were forever burned in my memory.

She was the only other person we saw while we were held at Weston's house. When we were rescued, I begged her to come with us.

She just stared up at me with terrified eyes, tears running down her face, her lips were pressed together like she was holding back a scream. And then, one of my grandfather's security men came and whisked me out of there. I couldn't stop wondering what on the outside could make the hell of that house seem like a safer option than leaving.

When my grandfather told us that Weston had been killed by one of his men and that there had been no one left in the house when his team left, I told myself that she'd found a way out.

But now, she was under arrest, and was being charged with all of his crimes. Just the way my grandfather said we would be if we talked to the police.

Weston's mother was interviewed on the broadcast. Her hair the same red as her son's, her eyes full of malice as she talked about their son like he was the victim. *"He was going places until she got her hooks into him. Now, she'll always be a footnote on the pages of his history. Like the Jezebel she is."*

"That's bullshit, right?" I demanded of Matty. But she didn't even want to talk about it. She and Jack were both international students with families who sacrificed everything to send them to school. They were terrified of doing anything to jeopardize their futures.

So, I sat alone and watched the story unfold on television. And as I did, I started to fear for my future, too. But for very different reasons than my friends.

In all of the news reports about the girl in the house, they never said her name. She was always just "Weston Silk's female accomplice."

Soon the story ceased to be worthy of even an inch of copy space in the local papers and she dropped out of mention all together.

In the weeks following the broadcast, it wasn't visions of the men who violated me or the terror-stricken expressions on my friends' faces that haunted me.

It was her face, those terrified eyes of the nameless woman.

She consumed my thoughts.

I wanted to know who she was and how she ended up in that house.

I found her name fairly quickly—it was in the police report. Rebecca Harvey. I found clues about her life—from her Myspace mainly, but she'd seemed like a happy, normal young woman. Not someone you'd expect to find in a place like that. But as I dug deeper, I found more. Her father was an eight-time felon serving a life sentence. Her mother was listed a missing person and had been since the early 90's.

On paper, Rebecca and I couldn't have been more different.

Except in one frightening and fundamental way.

I too, could only be distinguished by my relationship to other people. If I had died in that house, *my* footnote on history would be full of other people's accomplishments and misdeeds.

I was Remi's twin, Tina's daughter, Liam's granddaughter.

It was like living on the dark side of the moon—invisible, predictable, not worthy of distinction.

In a stroke of genius, I figured out how to save us *both* from obscurity. With my conviction in place, I went to my two best friends and asked them to take a leap of faith in me.

We were all desperate to find a way to get back some of what was stolen from us that night. And, they both said yes.

We scrapped our individual submissions for the editor position and created a feature called *"Herstory"* that we would collaborate on under the byline "The Jezebels."

We would focus on misunderstood, forgotten women in popular culture and traditional history.

We spent weeks preparing our pitch. We were buzzing with excitement the whole time. Working together didn't just save our friendship, it gave us all a sense of control and purpose.

We felt like revolutionaries—righting past wrongs, giving credit for stolen achievements, adding nuance, and giving a voice to women who had silenced or erased from moments in history that they helped usher forward.

We were going to change the world and knock the editorial staff off their feet.

They rejected our submission.

But we weren't daunted. They just weren't ready for us.

We started a blog with the same mission. When we launched *The Jezebels*, our first story was about women who'd been made accomplices simply because they shared a bed with a criminal.

It gained enough traction to build a following and healed our fractured friendship. We even got matching tattoos that read *Jezebel* on our lower backs. It didn't become the cultural zeitgeist we hoped it would.

Practical things like careers, and relationships intruded and by the time we graduated it had become our collective labor of love.

When Rebecca contacted us a few months ago and said it was the blog that helped her find us, it became my most bitter regret.

Under the cloak of darkness, the deserted lobby of the building my grandfather built almost 50 years ago looks like a house of horrors. The plants and light fixtures cast grotesque shadows that crisscross the large ceramic tiled floor. But I've got real shadows and fears to fight. My heart seems to beat harder with every step I take toward the door marked "Strictly Forbidden."

My grandfather, my mother, my brothers and I are the only people who have a copy of the master that unlocks it. That same key gives us access to every floor and office in the Wilde World's headquarters. If my grandfather finds out that I used it to get my hands on evidence that could incriminate his long time and most trusted employee, he'll be furious.

But Matty and Jack aren't just my friends. We walked through fire together. We *survived* it together. And we wouldn't have been there if I hadn't led them there. I owe them this.

With that final thought spurring me forward, I hold my breath and say a silent prayer of thanks when the light on the access panel turns green.

I step onto the elevator that is reserved for the exclusive use of my grandfather.

My heart is in my throat by the time the doors open on the 40th floor.

The quiet is eerie. Normally, it's buzzing with people who are either waiting to see my grandfather or working on something on his behalf.

Dan's office is to the left of his. As I approach it, I feel like a traitor. I've known him my whole life. I know why they *think* they're right. But they *have* to be wrong. Dan couldn't be involved. He helped my grandfather rescue us.

His laptop is on his desk and I hurry to pick it up.

I'm back at the elevators in less than a minute. Just when the call button signals its arrival, all the lights come on.

The elevator doors open, and I find myself face to face with my grandfather.

One Week Later

HOUSTON, TX

Chapter 8

ANYTHING

REGAN

"Come in," my grandfather's voice carries out into the hallway outside of his bedroom. He sounds irritated and weary.

I glance at my watch and note that it's five minutes after we were supposed to meet.

That the most anal-retentive timekeeper on the planet kept me waiting does not bode well.

I plaster a confident smile on my face and straighten my spine as I walk into his room. My heart is beating a mile a minute and the speech I'd spent all morning preparing is now just a jumble of words that sounds idiotic as I start to recall them.

He glances up and there is a storm in his eyes that calls to mind the way lightning crackles before thunder shakes the world. I remember how he'd comfort me during the hurricanes and tropical storms that are ubiquitous with life on the Gulf of Mexico. "Don't worry about the thunder, baby. It's just noise. It's the lightning that'll kill you."

All of the questions I've had during the week of silence between us are answered by that look.

There will be no forgiveness.

"Pops, I am so sorry."

"I don't want you to say another word, just sit down." I do as he says but can't meet his gaze.

"Your friends won't be getting the courtesy of a meeting. The least you can do is look at me."

His voice is a machete that slices through the last strands of my control and a tear rolls down my cheek. I wipe it away hastily and lift my head. I flinch at the complete lack of emotion in his eyes. He's never looked at me with anything but tenderness, even when he was angry with me. I can't bear to see the warmth extinguished in those wild blue eyes that used to be my refuge.

"I tried to help you all out of the mess you found yourselves in all of those years ago. I gave you jobs, I protected you from scrutiny and I helped you all move on. This betrayal cuts too deep. The consequences will, too."

My stomach lurches and I have to swallow the dread clogging my throat before I can speak. "What—what's going to happen?"

"As we speak, your office is being emptied. Your keycards have been deactivated and if I have any say over it, you will never work for Wilde World again."

My eyes bulge at his words. "Pops, you can't mean that."

"I do. You chose your side, and now you will stay there."

Panic assails me and I stand, my hands pressed together, I bow my head in supplication. "I had to help them. They're my friends."

"And we're your family. First it was that Rivers boy. Now, this. It's too much," he responds.

I gape at him "You know about Stone? How?" I'm reeling and the dread that was in the pit of my stomach flows, concentrated and unchecked until my entire body is weighed down by it.

"I know everything Regan. Those people are our enemies. And *you* welcomed him into our place of business for months."

"He's only a boy," I exclaim, that crazy instinct to protect Stone flares before my sense of self-preservation can stop me.

He snorts in disgust. "A *boy* who's smarter than most men twice his age and a *Rivers*. That negates anything else he might be." he grates, his cheeks flush with anger.

Tears stream down my cheeks. I brush them away furiously. If there is one thing he hates more than disloyalty, it's crying.

My entire body is quaking with fear and my legs are unsteady as I walk over to his side of the bed.

I drop onto my knees, barely noticing the bite of the hardwood against them, and grasp his hand and press it to my face. It's soft, covered in a sea of age spots, and gnarled. But it's still strong and big as it had been when I was a little girl. This is the hands that checked my brow for fevers, held handlebars, bandaged my knees, and wiped away my tears. Now, it sits limply in my grasp and the man it's attached to is looking at me with a dispassion that reaches the center of my greatest fear—losing *his* love.

"Pops, please. I'm sorry. I love you. Forgive me." I beg numb with shock. He can't mean it.

Who am I, if not his? Who will love me, if *he* doesn't? Despair, the likes of which I've never known casts a shadow over my heart. I tighten my grip on his hand. "I'll do *anything.*"

There's no affection, or indulgence in his pale blue eyes when he looks pointedly at my left hand. "Marcel Landel is coming to dinner on Saturday. Look pretty."

Two Years Later

Chapter 9

AN ECHO IN TIME

REGAN

When I met him, Marcel was a larger than life public persona. From his wife's sudden death, to his brother's arrest for solicitation to his ascendancy to head of his family's business empire—his name was constantly in the news. And he was ready to get married again.

He's brilliant, rich, successful and was considered a most eligible bachelor—by women closer to my mother's age than mine. But I was who he wanted.

The night we met, he made his intentions clear. "When I look across the table and see an old face, it reminds me that I'm old, too. I want to gaze at youth and be reminded that I'm as young as I feel."

My husband may have inherited his good fortune, but he was no brainless, wasteful heir. He'd been working as his father's right hand for years and had already helped transform Landel into one of the largest multimedia companies in the world. They own film studios, television networks, Cable and satellite channels, radio stations, restaurant chains and luxury resorts all over the world.

Marcel was a shrewd and pragmatic businessman. He treated the negotiation of our prenuptial agreement no differently and had a checklist that he wouldn't stray from.

He wanted a woman who was well educated, but not too well. No younger than twenty-one, but no older than twenty-five. She must have wealth of her own and no criminal ties, and most importantly, she must be fertile. And he wanted proof of all of those things before he'd sign anything.

For a woman who had decided that marriage and children were not in my future, it was a very bitter pill to swallow.

But, I did. I slept with him until a blood test showed I was pregnant. And then, we set a date. My grandfather called me the morning the announcement was made and invited me to lunch.

It was a knife in my heart when he had a stroke an hour after he called me. It left him paralyzed and robbed him of his speech. But the die was cast. We'd signed a prenuptial agreement, I was pregnant. There was no turning back.

I smiled through every fitting, every thinly veiled insult from his mother, and did what I knew my grandfather's love was conditioned on. I never complained or hinted at my unhappiness.

Until the week before our wedding when he announced that we would be living in Paris. In a house we would share with his fork-tongued mother.

It was the drop that made the well of rage inside me overflow. I threatened to call off the wedding. I'd sobbed and screamed and drained that emotional well dry. Then, I did my duty.

Marcel jokes that he pulled off the heist of the century getting me down the aisle. Everyone laughs but me. It's no joke at all I gave him everything he wanted in a bid to regain my grandfather's trust and affection and never knew if I'd been successful.

That phone call inviting me over was the last time I heard his voice. I like to think I saw approval in his eyes when I sat by his bed in the months followed his stroke. But when he died, my banishment from employment at Wilde World was still in effect.

Yesterday, we laid him to rest. Burying my grandfather without making amends is something I'll never recover from and it was one of the worst days of my life.

Somehow, the glutton for punishment in me decided that meeting Matty for lunch today, would be a good idea.

It's the first time we've seen each other since the day we all got fired.

Jack married her college sweetheart and moved to California and we haven't been in touch since.

Matty stayed in Houston, but I know she's struggled to find work. Nerves, excitement, and hope lighten my stomach as I stop at the valet stand.

"Welcome to Ruggles on the Green, Mrs. Landel." The young man who opens my door, leans down. I return his obliging smile and accept the hand he's offering and let him help me from the car. After a whole year of marriage, I'm still getting used to my last name and the deference it brings.

I follow the hostess through the restaurant and stop every few feet to respond to greetings from people I don't know.

By the time I reach the table where Matty is already waiting, I'm desperate for a familiar face and give a giddy wave when we make eye contact.

Her less than lackluster smile is more of a grimace and dashes my hopes that I'll be able to relax with her.

She looks different. It's not just the close crop of curly hair that's replaced her ever-present box braids. She looks…older and tired

"So, how's married life?" she asks as soon as I sit down. Her voice is expectant and snide.

"It's fine, thanks. How are you."

She ignores me and nods at the waiter who drops menus off and picks one up, opening it so that it completely obscures her face "So, have you told your husband about Weston?"

Her question catches me off guard and I frown at the back of the menu.

"No, of course not. And can you put the menu down?"

After a long-suffering sigh, she closes it, and eyes me with disdain.

"Well, as selective as your memory has become, I couldn't be sure if you'd forgotten the promise we made. You certainly forgot that we were supposed to be "sisters" when you sold us out."

I can't hide my shock, but quickly school my expression. With a pleasant smile in place, I lean close enough so that she can hear my harsh whisper.

"I sold *you* out? You lied to me for *months*."

Her expression remains completely emotionless. But her fingers curl to form fists on the tabletop and her chest heaves with several deep breaths.

"You know what? I'm gonna go." She puts her menu down and stands up in one smooth movement. Without another word, she turns and strides away.

I'm stunned and by the time I've managed to collect myself and stand to follow her, she's already at the door. I ignore the people who call after me, I don't think about the gossip that will surely follow, and I storm out the door after her.

She's standing at the valet stand, handing over her keys. I step into her line of sight and cross my arms. She looks over my shoulder as if I'm not even there.

"Why are you leaving?" I snap.

She shrugs, still not looking at me. "I'm tired."

"*You* asked to meet for lunch. I just got here. We haven't seen each other for almost two years. I'm married. I have a baby. We've missed so much…. don't you want to catch up?"

She laughs and finally deigns to meet my gaze. Her dark gaze is blazing with anger that belies the careless smile on her face.

"Yeah, sorry my unemployment check didn't stretch far enough to allow me to attend your fancy ass wedding. Oops sorry, I forgot you didn't invite me."

"I *couldn't,* Matty. You know that." I search her face for a hint of the friend I love, the one who loves me too. From the flat lifeless dark eyes, to the scorn that curls her lips, there's nothing of her here.

"Well, while you were getting married, I was just trying to figure out how to stay alive."

"I was doing the same, Matty."

Her indifferent mask cracks and her eyes flare anger, grief, and damning disappointment. "No, you weren't. You turned your back on everything you swore you believed in to protect your precious *family.*"

"That's *not* true," I take an involuntary step back.

"Yes, it is, you didn't even *try* to help her," she bellows, her control gone, tears stream down her face.

A cough from beside us draws my eyes to the group of people watching us with voyeuristic relish.

I grab her arm and pull her away from the waiting area and into a covered walkway leading to a parking garage. I stop and whirl to face her mutinous glare. "I paid her legal fees; I wrote to the parole board. What else could I do?" I remind her.

She yanks free of my grasp and puts a hand on each of my shoulders and shakes me. "Do you *hear yourself?* She told you she thought one of the men who raped her was on *your family's payroll.*"

I shove her hands off and glare at her. "And *I* told *her* that was impossible. No one who worked at Wilde World could do that and you know it. Which one of your colleagues did you believe was a *john?*"

"We left her in that house. We started a blog instead of speaking on her behalf. We owed her more than that. But your perfect grandfather and his company couldn't possibly have done anything wrong."

"It's not just his company. It's my family's." I remind her.

"What about Rebecca's family, Regan? What about the fact that she didn't have powerful friends to turn for help? Oh wait, she did. And *you* told her to go fuck herself."

Her jab sticks in my craw because after what they did, I'm not the one who should be on the defensive here.

"If it wasn't for my grandfather, you would have gone to jail!" I remind her none too gently.

She rolls her eyes. "You know what I think? I think that *you* know that if we'd kept digging, *he'd* be the one in jail. I think *he* knew that they were organizing entertainment for the other pervs who work for him and he didn't mind sacrificing his granddaughter to cover it up."

"I love you, Matty. But that is bullshit. You *know* what it did to my life." I say, my voice hoarse and thick with guilt and clogged by my unshed, angry tears.

She is completely unmoved by my anguish. "If you had any balls, you'd take all those papers your grandfather's people stole when they raided our office. *If* they didn't destroy them already. If you would just look at them, you'd see what we did. And you'll feel like shit that you didn't help her."

"I *knew* she was wrong. And, it's my family," to my shame my voice breaks, but I can't help it.

"Your *family* turned their backs on you. And you *still* defend them." She points a finger in my face, her anger building with each word. "*You* had the power to make a difference. Instead you used their pain to make your disgusting poverty porn and when you got bored you moved on."

I rear back. "Matilda, how can you say that? You know how untrue that is. We all went through hell and we *all* wanted to do something with our pain." I stare at her, fully expecting remorse and apology to be the next expressions I see on her face. Instead, her scowl deepens.

"A hell you led us to. All because you were so caught up in your little fantasy of rebellion, you didn't notice he was a *pimp*. And then, you stabbed your friends in the back, you put on your cloak of respectability and got on with your life."

Matty's words are heavy hands flying, full strength, through the air intent on total destruction. They wound all the tender places I'd left unprotected around her. Because I thought she was my friend. How wrong I was.

For a moment, we stare at each other.

I'm reminded of that moment in Thelma and Louise, where they sat with trouble on their rear and a cliff to nowhere at their front. When her chin tilts upward and her eyes harden, I know that just like the infamous duo in the movie, she's decided that there's no going back. She hits the gas and drives our friendship right off a cliff.

"When it came time for you to put some *actual* skin in the game, you chickened out so you could save your grandfather. Because deep down, you know what he is." Her eyes glitter with the kind of satisfaction that comes from the relief of a burden carried for far too long.

The depth of the malice in her voice steals my breath. The absolute gall of it, though, floods my veins with ice cold contempt.

I straighten my spine and let my hands uncurl from the tight fists that formed while I listened to her speak. I put my pain away. I will not give her the satisfaction of seeing me unravel.

We face each other, twin thunderclouds. High pressure, full beyond bursting, and spitting down lighting and thunder like it's what we were born to do.

"You are right about one thing. My grandfather did shape me. If it wasn't for him, I wouldn't have had anyone." I jab a finger sharply at her. "And yes, I married Marcel to get back in his good graces, but it was also, at the time, what *I* wanted."

"Because it was going to make him happy," she charges.

I stiffen at the intonation of her word. "Why is it wrong for me to want to make my grandfather happy? Because he's a man? He was the only person in the whole world who hasn't *ever* let me down. Can't say that about *any* of the women in my life." I say with a pointed look of my own.

She flushes and looks like she might want to say something. But I don't let her.

"I know I failed you. But I was trying to help. Because I *love* you, Matty. But what you just said … I'll *never* forgive." My voice is even and steady, but there is no mistaking the rage behind them. I feel incandescent with it and if my words were flames borne of it, they would be hot enough to flay the skin off her bones.

I see a flash of remorse in her eyes before she lifts her chin upward defiantly. "Well, at least we're finally on the same page."

I can't hide my regret; I'm nearly drowning in it. I wish things had been different.

At one point in my life, she'd been my best friend.

But now, all of that is done. Friendships live and die by the choices we make. She's made hers and now, I'm finally making mine.

Without another word, I turn and walk back to the valet stand, get in my car and drive away.

Eight Years Later

CABO SAN JOSE, MEXICO

Chapter 10

FEMME FATALE

STONE

I glance around the packed shuttle with dismay. On my way to town I'd been alone. I don't mind people, but this kind of proximity to a bunch of sweaty, sand covered strangers is less than ideal. Especially because whatever the opposite of resting bitch face is, I have it.

On planes, in grocery stores, and even at funerals, people look at me and decide that I'm the person they're going to unburden themselves with.

So, even though the sun was setting by the time the shuttle pulled up, the crowd of people waiting to board with me meant that I'd need my sunglasses to continue to act as my small talk deterrent.

It's rude, I know. And normally, I'd just close my eyes and pretend to sleep during the thirty-minute ride back, but I don't know when I'll be back here again, and I want to see this city at night.

I came into town planning to get my business sorted with plenty of time left to sightsee. San Jose, the other side of Los Cabos, is not as rarified as San Lucas is—and definitely more my speed.

It's where my friend Pedro told me I could find someone to help me plan a multi-day excursion on the Baja Peninsula.

The first part of my day went off without a hitch. But instead of sightseeing, I spent hours listening to my ex-girlfriend curse at me as she left my apartment with a box full of things she kept there. After that I was on the phone with locksmiths, utility and security companies, and all of the other places where we had joint accounts.

Then, my brother called to tell me that he'd forgotten to get his passport renewed. So, I found an expedited service for him and made sure it would be there before he left for Mexico on Friday morning.

By the time I was done, the alarm I'd sent to remind me that the last shuttle back to the resort was leaving in twenty minutes had gone off.

Now, a fat, glowing moon sits low on the horizon taking the sky from light blue to shades of deep indigo and violet.

As the dark transforms the sky, it also transforms the city.

The produce markets and street vendors selling tourist friendly relics that were omnipresent on my way through San Jose this morning are gone. In their place are musicians, magicians, soothsayers and doomsday prophets. A line snakes around the corner from a food stall that's selling parcels of piping hot bread stuffed with strips of meat, tomatoes, onions, and a red sauce that runs unchecked down the fingers of the happy people stuffing their faces with it.

The sliding windows of the vehicle are open, and the cool Pacific breeze carries the mouthwatering aroma of it all. My stomach grumbles and I wish I'd at least had a chance to eat.

If I didn't have a call with my boss in an hour, I'd get off right now and worry about how I'd get back to the resort, later.

I'm here for my brother's wedding. Well, his *first* wedding. He's having another wedding in Houston complete with church, and a huge party in a few months.

I'll be starting my three-month stint as part of a medical staff on site at a refugee camp on the border of Colombia and Venezuela in a month and can't get away.

So, his fiancé, Confidence, decided to have this surprise beachside ceremony, because she knew how it was important to Hayes that *all* his brothers be there when he says, "I do." As much as I hate resorts and weddings, there was no way I'd miss it.

When I went to add the date to my calendar, it coincided with a lunar event I added months ago. One of the best places to see it, according to my astronomy sources. The Baja Peninsula.

I was ten years old when I stopped believing in luck. But every once in a while, there's an alignment of moments and events so perfectly timed that there's no other explanation.

The stars aligned on this trip and I've got a really good feeling about it. Besides getting to see my favorite planet, the excursion I planned is the stuff of my adrenaline junkie heart's dreams. I've got four days packed with things that make my heart race just to think about.

"Is this your first time here?" The woman next to me asks and I stifle a groan. I was doing so well. Resigned to my fate and raised better than to ignore anyone who speaks to me, I respond.

"In Baja, yes," I say conversationally, but briefly. I don't smile or even make eye contact.

I pray that she'll take a hint. My prayers fall on deaf ears.

"Where are you staying at the resort? We're up in the hills. We're here for our anniversary, and I told *him*," she jerks a thumb at the man on her right. "I wanted five stars and nothing less. Didn't I honey?" She slaps the arm of the man next to her.

"Sure did, honey." He gives me an apologetic smile and pats his wife's knee less out of affection and more in warning.

She pushes it away and turns until her back is to him.

"I'm Carol and this is my husband, Ron, we're from Oklahoma" she says and sticks her hand out. I give up trying to pretend I'm sleeping and shake her hand.

"Hi, I'm Paul, from Texas," I say, using my middle name the way I do to make reservations, or order coffee, or anything that requires someone to write down or repeat my name back to me.

"That's our daughter Bailey and her son, Emmet." She points down the row at a young woman with a small toddler on her lap.

"That's Eric, he's Emmet's' father," she says with a small frown before she sits back.

The man she's gesturing to is staring straight ahead like his life depends on it. He doesn't say a word or look in our direction. His ticking jaw is the only indication that he heard her.

"They're just friends." Carol conspiratorial whispers aren't remotely discreet.

"We didn't bring her up like that. Don't get me wrong, we love the *baby*," she says *baby* like it's a bad word. "We would have liked her to get married first, of course, but kids these days do things their own way. In my day, a man like you wouldn't be all alone on a shuttle, Are you single?"

"Mother, *stop!*" Bailey snaps.

"Why? *Look* at him." She gestures at me with a wave of her hand.

Her husband's groan is one of long suffering.

"Honey, please," he pets her arm.

Carol is undeterred. She leans over him and points a finger at her daughter, "If I was your age and single, I wouldn't need my mother to make a move for me."

Bailey leans forward bypassing her mother's glare and looks at me.

"I'm gay. Eric is, too. We had a baby together *because* we're just friends. I'm sorry my mother accosted you. She's going to leave you alone, now."

"Don't worry. I'm used to it. Congratulations on the baby." I smile with empathy. Then, I pop my earbuds in. If it's rude. Oh well, these people are giving me a damn headache.

Traffic slows to a crawl as we approach San Lucas and my eyes drift closed.

I'm roused by the squeaking of brakes and the jostling of the vehicle moving off the main road "I thought this was a direct shuttle." I say to the driver.

He laughs boisterously. "Direct shuttle doesn't exist, and we always stop for the ladies," he says and waggles his eyebrows at me through the rearview mirror.

I glance toward the stop. Two women stand one facing us, the other with her back turned. The sea breeze pulls the floral-patterned sundress she's wearing snug and I can't help but notice the very nice ass she's sporting. I give her an appreciative once-over. She's wearing a huge hat on top of a long dark, curling mane of hair that moves with the wind. I get a flash of Deja vu. But it's gone as quickly as it came and next to me Carol fidgets. "It's full already,"

I'm glad she said it so I'm not the one who sounds like an asshole. The driver ignores her.

He flings the door open and jogs down the short staircase. "*Buenos noches, Señorita*s. You were told about our occupancy issue, correct?" His voice is booming, and theatrical.

"Yes, we know. It's fine," one of the women responds in a much more subdued tone. I pick up a hint of a French accent in her English.

He claps and jogs back up the upstairs, calling to the women over his shoulder, "Then climb aboard and pick a lap. You will find several willing. Am I right?" The four men on board, including the previously mute Eric, all give their fervent agreement. His chuckle is diabolical as he takes his seat again.

I'm glad they're so eager.

The last thing I need is to have a sweaty stranger's ass on my lap. No matter how nice it looks in her very pretty sundress.

The odds of escape aren't in my favor.

I'm the biggest man on the cart, and closest to the door. One of them could sit down before the four eager beavers even get to make their offer.

Recoiling in dread, I pull my hat down over my eyes and slump in my seat as they climb up the short staircase. I hold my breath and pray they walk past me.

"Thank you for stopping," the other woman, speaks. It's one of those voices with no identifying inflection. Not Southern, not east coast, not Cali, not Midwest. Just perfect diction. The likes of which I've only encountered once before.

My heart skips a beat, and everything freezes.

I haven't heard it in fifteen years, but I know, as sure as I breathe that voice belongs to Regan Wilde.

And there's no way in hell she's sitting on anyone's lap *but* mine. I lift my cap up and put an arm out to stop her just as she's about to pass me. "You can sit with me." I use my arm as a barrier that keeps her from going any further.

I peer at her from under the rim of my hat, her full lips pressed together. Her eyes are obscured by her sunglasses, She huffs in annoyance and turns toward the driver. Her husky voice full of dismay. "The dispatch said one of us would have to sit on each *other's* lap. Not a total stranger's."

"No offense," she adds with an apologetic smile in our general direction. "Could you send another shuttle for us? We'll wait. We don't want to inconvenience you all. "

"This is the last shuttle. You can get you a taxi," the driver says.

The seconds that pass before she answers feel like hours. I hold my breath. But I'm sure that if she gets off I will, too. Her friend groans, behind her. "Oh, come on, Reggie. It's fine, it's late and we're all going to the same place. I'm exhausted and I don't want to try to find a cab right now."

Regan bites her lip and looks around the shuttle.

She glances back out at the street and then sighs in resignation. "Fine."

She draws her shoulders back and turns to face me. "Thank you for offering your lap. It's very kind," she says with all the dignity of a duchess.

"No problem. Make yourself comfortable." I pitch my voice an octave lower than my normal baritone. I don't know why I'm disguising it. It's not like she's heard my voice before. At least, not this version of it.

The brush of fabric against my bare knees and a muffled curse are the only warning I have before a body with distinctly soft feminine swells lands in my lap

My hands instinctively come up to grab her hips. The force of her fall pushes me back into my seat. Her thick cascade of hair covers my face like a pillow. I'm assailed by the smell of lemon and ginger scones and the memories this smell is attached to—our bakery in Rivers Wilde.

Nostalgia hits with a one-two punch to my gut and my groin.

My heart starts to race, and it takes all my willpower to stop myself from grasping her by that cute chin of hers and forcing her face around to tell her who I am.

Her back is pressed to my chest, her ass to my groin and her soft thighs rest against the hard muscles of mine

"Is everyone okay? Can I get back on the road?" The driver calls.

"Everything is great." This jovial declaration comes from the man directly across from us, who is providing a seat to her friend.

"Which building on the resort, please?" the driver asks.

"We're going to the main hall," Regan answers.

"Your wish is my command," the driver says. He closes the doors and the overhead lights go off, plunging us into semi-darkness as the shuttle eases back into traffic.

"I'm so sorry for landing on you like that, I'm not used to wearing flat shoes and I've been tripping since I put these on," she says.

"It's okay," I say but it comes out like a groan because I can feel my body starting to respond to hers. I shift my hips back to hide my hardening dick but find that I'm as far back as the seat will allow.

She shimmies and mutters to herself, starts to lift her leg and stops suddenly, groaning under her breath.

"Is everything okay?" I ask.

"Yes. God, this is ridiculous," she mutters, without turning back to look at me. She rests one hand on the small plexiglass shield between the driver and us. The thin gold band on her ring finger draws my eye.

"My ankle bracelet is caught on the lace of your shoes."

She bends over, pushing her soft ass even deeper into my groin and my dick does the unforgivable and starts to get hard. She's moving back and forth, and even though I know she doesn't mean to, it's like giving me a lap dance.

Her fingers flex on the plexiglass, and I imagine that hand on my headboard, her hair pushed aside so I can see her back while I drive into her soft, wet, heat. Lemon must be an aphrodisiac. It has to be. I've got more self-control than *this.*"Almost… got it…" she croons shifts her weight back.

I push my hips far back as they'll go, but I can't do anything to stop her from feeling the heavy hard length between my thighs.

She stiffens and I stop breathing, braced for her to turn around and slap me.

I lean in to speak close to her ear to avoid the possibility of anyone hearing me. "It'll go away if you stop moving,"

Then, to my mortification, I realize I'm still holding her hips in a tight grasp, essentially holding her in place. I let go, abruptly. But instead of sitting still or moving away, she rolls hips

My sharp exhale of breath disturbs a lock of her dark loosely spiraling hair on her shoulder and a shiver, subtle and short, runs through her.

I glance at Carol. She's turned away, talking to her husband.

I look back at the unexpected seductress on my lap and then roll my hips up, just slightly, too. I move my hand slowly inch by inch until it's back on her hip and dig my thumb into the soft flesh there.

Her body relaxes against me and she moves her hips in a seductive circle that brings the head of my dick in contact with her pliant but stiff clit. But for the subtle rocking of her pelvis she doesn't move.

I don't either. I close my eyes, let my head loll back to the window while the gently swaying vehicle sets a slow rhythm.

"So, where are you from, dear?" Carol asks and I freeze.

But Regan doesn't. "Texas," she says, her voice a little breathless but otherwise, normal.

"Oh, that's nice. We're from Oklahoma. We come here every year. It's gorgeous, but you have to be careful in that surf. If you get too far in…" Carol warns in a grave voice.

"You mean, at the resort?" Regan asks in a voice that is slightly breathless but otherwise normal.

"Yes, dear, we heard the most awful story on our first day here…" Carol starts to drone on.

I ease a hand off Regan's hip to tap my AirPods on. Just My Imagination by the Temptations starts to play. I chuckle to myself. She used to sing this all the time. In fact, I only know this song because of her. It's almost enough to make me believe in fate again.

I grip her hip again and squeeze the supple flesh hard.

Maybe it's because I'm living one of my many teenage wet dreams, but she feels damn incredible. My palms itch to slide up and cup her breast. I imagine her nipples hardening against them. I wonder if they're hard already. If she likes them pinched or sucked. If they're pierced.

I tighten my hold on her hip to stop myself from throwing caution into the wind to find out.

She reaches up to pull her hair over one shoulder, exposing the side of her neck and her shoulder. I want to sink my teeth into that smooth fragrant skin and suck.

Her thighs spread, making just enough room for me to sink into the plush heat at their apex.

I lift my hips and rock them, slowly, up.

Her legs quiver and her hand grips my thigh briefly, her fingernails dig into my skin and bite my lip to hold in a groan.

God, I can *smell* her.

Then, she turns and looks over her shoulder at me Her eyes are hidden by the dark opacity of her sunglasses. But I know what's behind them.

Almond shaped, wide set, thick lashed eyes that are as dark, deep, and unknowable as a moonless, starless, midnight sky.

Her lips part, as if she's about to speak. Instead, she bites the plump flesh at the same time that she rolls her hips, slowly but deliberately. Her moan is soundless, but her back arches and her lip slips from the greedy grip of her teeth as she mouths "coming" before she faces forward again.

But for her thighs trembling on top of mine, and the shallow, sharp breaths that lift her shoulders, I wouldn't know anything was happening to her.

By the time the driver pulls into the resort and turns on the overhead lights, I'm rock hard, my balls ache, my mind on the edge of fevered. I want to roar for everyone to get the fuck off so I can pull my dick out and fuck her senseless.

But, neither of us move, not even to breathe, as Carol and her crew climb off.

What happens now? Do I tell her who I am?

And then what? Apologize?

"Reggie, are you asleep?" My eyes fly open at the sound of her friend's voice. She's sitting across from us, smirking. "You can stop using that man like a throne. There are plenty of seats."

"Oh, god, sorry," Regan says as she looks around the now empty carriage. She scoots forward so that she can stand.

I let go of her and grab my hat off my head and drop it over my erection.

My hair is the only thing about me that hasn't changed since the last time I saw her, but it's cut so low that none of the natural waves are visible.

I tense as she looks me over and I wait for her to gasp in recognition. It doesn't come and I'm disappointed rather than relieved.

"Thank you," she says and there's a stiffness in her voice and in the set of her insanely voluptuous mouth as she sits next to her friend.

"I'm glad you got your bracelet free," I say with as much equilibrium as I can manage. I nod toward her foot.

Only the tips of her toes are visible beneath the flood of her dress, now, but I'll never forget the feel of her legs against mine. I can't believe what we just did.

"Your bracelet got loose?" Her friend probes.

"Yeah," she laughs and wiggles her delicate foot, wriggling her pretty light pink-painted toes. "My anklet... It got caught on his laces, but I freed it."

She crosses her arms over her chest, and leans her head against the shuttle window, effectively dismissing both of us.

"We're pulling away, one stop left," the driver informs as he closes the doors and sends us back into darkness. The bright overhead lights are on and I glance over to find the driver watching me through the rearview. with a knowing look on his face before he turns his eyes back to the road.

Shit. Did he see?

Well, as long as his mind was the only thing recording it, I don't care.

My eyes drift closed as we ride along. The warm wind is a soft caress that carries the scent of flowers and the ocean as we zipped along the winding path cut into the side of this cliff. But I can still smell her citrus on me.

With my eyes closed, I could almost imagine that I'm back in that bakery.

Almost.

She's got a hint of her flavor, but the woman sitting across from now is not the girl I spent six months falling in love with when I was ten.

I'm not the boy who was willing to plunge his knife into someone's back to save her.

For more than one reason, she's totally off limits. I should be praying I never see her again, *not* willing the shuttle to go slower.

When we reach the stop where we're all getting off, her friend is on her feet before we come to a complete stop. She's standing at the door and rushes off the shuttle as soon as the doors open.

"No rushing at Pueblo Bonito," the driver admonishes her rapidly retreating back

Regan doesn't move. With her sunglasses on, I can't tell if she's asleep or just lost in thought.

The high-pitched peel of my alarm startles us both and she lets out a small cry and turns her head sharply toward me.

I hold my phone up, "It's just my alarm, sorry," I say quickly.

It takes one blink to replace the dazed weariness in her expression with indignant affront. "Oh," she relaxes slightly and drops her arms to her side.

My phone chimes again and I grimace as I turn it on silent.

She gives me an awkward nod and then she's up and heading off the shuttle, too. It's impossible not to notice the way her shapely ass moves for *just* a fraction of a second after she's stopped walking. Would it do that if I slapped it?

My dick stirs again. Which will not do. It's one thing to keep my hat on my lap on the shuttle, I can't walk around the resort like that.

So, I drop my eyes to the part of her dress that brushes the ground.

"Señor," the driver calls when I'm halfway down the shuttle steps.

I turn back to him.

"Te perdiste tu parada" *You missed your stop,"* His grin is pure mischief.

I give him a good natured, slightly abashed smile. "Lo sé" *I know.*

He nods in Regan's direction, his expression teasing still, with a touch of wistfulness. "No te culpo" *I don't blame you.*

I wish him goodnight and head in the direction of the red brick paved terrace that leads to the reservation desk.

Regan is a few steps ahead of me and I keep a respectable distance between us. I don't know why I'm following her or what I'll do when I catch up, but I can't just let her walk away.

I can still smell her on me. I turn my head to draw in a breath and catch a sweet flowery scent mingled with the tart citrus and spicy ginger. It's intoxicating.

"Are you following me?" She comes to an abrupt stop and pivots on her heel to face me.

"Yes."

She whips her sunglasses off and even though it's dark, this walkway is well lit, and I can see that her eyes are red-rimmed, like she's been crying.

Guilt curdles in my gut. "Oh shit, I'm sorry, I thought—"

"About what happened—"

We speak at the same time.

"Ladies first. Please." I insist when she bites her lip

"I've never done anything like that…" she says in a halting voice.

I step closer to her, close enough that I can smell her again.

It makes my mouth water.

"Did you like it?" I ask.

"Yes," she replies in a husky voice. She bites that sweet lower lip and my eyes drop to her mouth. She lets go of it and clears her throat. I drag my gaze back to her eyes. Her gaze is dark and inscrutable, but the energy between us is frantic and charged.

I reach for her slowly, to give her a chance to step away. When she doesn't, I brush a lock of hair off her shoulder and run the tip of my forefinger down her arm.

"Are your panties wet?" I ask.

She draws in a sharp breath and shifts her stance; her lips part and she licks them quickly before nods.

"Go in there, take 'em off and bring them to me." I demand, nodding at her pelvis.

She cocks her head at me, her wary eyes heavy lidded with arousal. "Have you… done something like…that before?" Her voice is full of anticipation, and when I shake my head no, she seems to relax a little.

"Good, you're my first, too."

Lord, how I wish that was true. She can't hear the thundering of my raging pulse, but when a small smile tugs up the concerns of her mouth, I would almost swear she knows that I'm unraveling on the inside.

"Reggie, come on already, they need your credit card to change it," her friend yells from the door. Her eyes widen in alarm and she slips her sunglasses on before she turns pivots in a smooth circle and turns her back to me.

I want to call after her, I don't know what else I'd say.

Instead, I watch the girl of my dreams, who has gone from pretty young thing, to flesh and blood siren, walk away.

Chapter 11

DRUNK MAN DI TALK TRUTH

REGAN

Good Lord in Heaven what have I done? If you'd asked me to list a thousand things I thought might happen to me in this lifetime, dry humping a stranger on a shuttle full of people until I came wouldn't have ever, *ever* been one of them.

When he volunteered his lap, I was grateful. I'm in great shape, but I'm heavier than I look. I hadn't missed the way his long, athletic body filled the seat.

When I sat down on his thick muscular thighs, the solid strength of him felt...deliciously sturdy. At least I didn't have to worry about being too heavy for him.

Bonus points that he smelled good. Not because he was drenched in cologne—but the kind of good that comes from soap, sweat, and *man*.

His baseball cap hid his hair and eyes, But God, the part of his face I *could* see was enough to whet my fantasies. His mouth alone... Wide and graced with lips so full they verged on pouty. And for a mad moment, I'd wanted to turn around and press mine to them.

Just to see if they were as soft as they felt.

It took me a minute to register what I was feeling. I haven't had a man's dick between my legs in five years. And then his stiff erection pressed *exactly* where it needed to and flip the switch that turns me from mildly annoyed to wildly turned on. A switch I didn't even know existed.

I was afraid he'd be pissed. I'd practically given him a lap dance trying to fix my anklet. He's a man and his body's response was simple biology.

Or so I thought… Until his big, warm, *sure* hand gripped my hip.

Even that woman's incessant prattling couldn't cut through the lust that fogged my brain. I'd forgotten how different an orgasm feels when it's not coaxed out of me by my own hand. The pleasure from the friction of his body was unreal.

Guilt is glaringly absent from the swirl of emotions inside of me. But I can't muster it when everything about what happened felt so… *right.*

In fact, it's the only thing that's happened since I arrived this morning that has.

I pour myself a glass of water, pick up the small silver container that used to hold Jack's ashes, and step out onto the huge terracotta tiled balcony attached to my room.

I take a moment to breathe in the floral, sea salt-tinged breeze carried in from the Sea of Cortez

I got Jack's letter the day her will was read. The brochure for this resort and the boating company that she'd hired for the ceremony were also in the envelope. "It's where I want a piece of me to dwell forever, and I want you and Matty to take me. Together. Please."

It's heartbreaking to think about her planning all of this. And not just because she was going to die. But because, in the midst of her own fear and grief and pain, she thought about *me.* Jack knew my soul needed space to unfurl. In the twelve hours since I arrived, I've had more time alone than I have in the previous twelve months combined.

The life I've dedicated myself to, the one I built with deliberate care, feels so far away right now. Distance allows me to see it with a clarity I've never had before.

It's not a happy scene. Dressed in loneliness, apathy, lack of purpose, every single brick in its façade is held in place with lies, luck, and far too little love.

From the corner of my eye, I catch a glimpse of the small bronze urn I used to carry my best friend's ashes out to sea last night. I'm gripped by a sense of foreboding. That could just have easily been me.

And God, what a waste of a life it would have been.

The loud ring of my room's phone is a welcome interruption and I dive for it and pick it up before it can ring again. "Hello?"

"Hey, it's me. Can we talk?" Matty's tone is clipped, but civil.

My heart gives a little hopeful leap. "Sure, maybe we can have dinner?" I glance at the clock, it's only 4pm, but I'm starving. I came here hoping that Matty and I could repair what was broken between us. I've spent the whole day in my room waiting for her to call. Trying to work up the courage to call her.

"Okay, dinner would be good. Are you ready now?"

"I need to shower, but I'll be quick," I say.

"Don't rush, I'll come up to your room and wait. See you."

"I look so tired," I lament to my reflection and skim my fingertips over the shadows under my eyes. I haven't slept well since Jack died.

"No, you don't. You always look beautiful," Matty calls in a monotone that smacks more of obligation than sincerity. She's waiting in the small sitting area of my suite waiting while I put on a little make-up.

I can't see her in the reflection, but I know that from her perch in the bedroom, she can see me. So, I look directly in the mirror. "Well, *you* don't always look beautiful. In fact, right now, you look as terrible as I feel," I say with a smile that's as sincere as her tone was.

A few seconds later she's standing beside me at the small vanity in my bathroom, scowling at me.

She rolls her eyes and lets out a long, exasperated sigh. "I was trying to be *nice,* Regan," she repeats.

I mimic her eye roll. "You don't have to be *nice*. It's okay to be honest with your friends."

"Here we go." I mutter and turn my attention back to my make-up.

She glares at me, hands on her hips and fierce frown on her face. "What does *that* mean?"

"It *means* that without Jack as a buffer, we were bound to argue." I keep my expression neutral, but I stop trying to make my trembling hands work and put my mascara away and meet her eyes in the mirror.

I regret my quip about her appearance. She *does* look worn out. It's more than fatigue and emotional toll of this trip. What had the last ten years been like for her? I didn't even know where she lived until Jack told me she was in Maryland. She's never met my children. Evangeline's middle name is Matilda.

"I'm going out the balcony to smoke. When you're done, come join me." She turns and walks away before I have a chance to respond.

I watch her retreating back. She's ranged from barely civil to hostile since we met in the lobby to ride out to the boat Jack hired for the ceremony.

When I tried to talk to her, she said, "I'm just here for Jack." And nothing else.

She brought a bottle of wine on board and drank half of it, straight from the bottle. When the captain of our little boat asked us about Jack, Matty said, "We used to be friends, but now, we hate her."

Matty and I…we've always butted heads. I used to love that about us. It felt like our relationship flexing its muscles when we fought and made up.

I counted myself lucky to have such an authentic, honest friend.

We're worse than strangers now and I can see clearly, the role I played in that.

What they did was wrong. But, no one forced me to help them. It's wrong of me to punish them for my choices. It took Jack's call asking me to come visit her in hospice to see that.

I spent ten years thinking she was angry with me and she spent ten years thinking I was angry with her. But when she called to tell me she was dying, all I felt was grief. I caught a flight the very next day and went to her home Sacramento.

Jack was barely a shadow of the woman she'd been last time I saw her.

Her husband told me that she was having a good day and it broke my heart to think what the bad days must be like. But I only smiled and sat in the seat they offered me.

I began with my regrets. "I was going to call… Six months went by and I didn't know what I would say. So, I just…never did. I'm so sorry." It was such a pathetic recitation of excuses

She'd just smiled and patted my hand. "I love you. I'm so glad you came." That was all.

The rest of the time, we reminisced, I read her passages from her favorite book, Love in the Time of Cholera and we cried together when Florentino left after Fermina spurned him.

When I finished the book, she'd grabbed my hand with more strength than I'd felt from her since I arrived. Her eyes were clear and grave. "Don't waste any more time wondering what if. You'll regret it. And it will make the end of your life, whether you see it coming or if it happens in an instant, *feel* like a death sentence instead of a transition. You were my last regret. Make up with Matty, don't let her be yours."

She died that evening and I cried bitterly. Thinking back to it, I feel ashamed that her husband had to find space in his own grief to comfort me.

Shakespeare said that love is an ever-fixed mark that looks upon a tempest and isn't moved. And it's proven true. After all this time and all the muddy water that's passed under our bridge, I still love Matty.

Even if she doesn't feel the same, I want her to know that I didn't just come here for Jack.

She's leaning over the rails, staring out at the majestic panorama of beach, ocean and sky. I watch her for a moment. In so many ways, she's unchanged. High, sculpted cheekbones, full lips, a regal nose and braids piled high on her head like a crown make a striking profile. Her dark brown skin gleams in the moonlight. Her yellow sundress is too big, and even though she's the same size as she was in college, she looks frailer.

I feel sick at the thought she might be sick, with something that will kill her, like it killed Jack. I shake off the melodrama and shake myself. I *know* what's wrong. It's the same thing that's eating me alive. She just doesn't have the budget for make-up and facials that stave off the signs of the internal rot that comes with making your soul a vessel corrosive secret.

I take a cautious step outside and wait to see if she reacts before I take another. After three creeping steps like that, Matty's head drops and she groans.

"Why are you being so weird? It's a balcony not a minefield."

"Are you sure? I feel like if I put one foot wrong, you'll blow up and not speak to me for ten years."

"I don't know where you could have gotte*n* *that* ridiculous notion from," she sing-songs and my nerves are instantly soothed. Feeling a little more balanced, and like myself, I dive in headfirst.

"I should have called you after we fought," I blurt.

"You couldn't have, I blocked your number," she says with a sheepish grimace.

We sigh in unison and look at each other for a long moment. The crashing waves and the strains of music fill the silence that falls between us.

Her expression mirrors everything I'm feeling.

Apology.

Love.

Hope.

"I'm sorry about what I said on the boat, I didn't mean it. I just had too much to drink." She finally breaks the quiet.

"Drunk man talk di truth," I mimic my mother's lyrical Jamaican accent. She always suppresses it in public and even at home. But when we were younger, before she became *the* Tina Wilde, she used to speak almost exclusively in her Patois when she scolded us.

"It's *not* true. It never has been. You *know* that. We've been mad at each other and we've got stuff to work out, but the only thing I feel for you is love. I just didn't know how to bridge the gap."

There's so much advice and common wisdom about what to do when romantic relationships hit road bumps. But you know what's just as devastating? When a real friendship ends for reasons that make it impossible to repair.

"If I'd been a guy you'd fought with would you have blocked my number?" I ask her, curious more than anything.

"Probably not," she admits and cringes at her admission.

"Why do we work harder for the men who hurt us than for each other?" I ask in consternation at the truth of it.

"Because a great dick is hard to find," she deadpans.

I snort a laugh and she gives me a grudging smile. Sharing a laugh with my other best friend, puts a small seal on the crack that the loss of Jack created.

It hurts like hell to know we'll never laugh together again.

"Unless of course, you happen to stumble across one on a shuttle," she quips, and my face goes up in flames.

I slap my palms on my cheeks to hide the flush and turn away. "Oh my God, you saw?"

She bursts out in delighted laughter. "Not that I blame you. He was hot. God, I haven't seen a man like that in person since in a long time."

"Do you think everyone knew?" I ask, mortified at the thought.

"You were very subtle, but we were roommates in college and… sometimes when you were with Charlie, I'd watch. I know your O' face," she says with a sly, but embarrassed smile.

"No, you *didn't,*" I gasp and lean away from her, but I'm not upset. In fact, there's something…intriguing and hot about being watched. But I could never admit that to her.

Marcel is the only man I've been with in ten years and sex was never anything to write home about. He's conservative and anything beyond missionary was sinful. He made me feel dirty the first time I asked him to eat me out. So, my sense of shame about the things I desire is too ingrained for me to share it even with my best friend.

"I'm married." I remind her and hold up my wedding ring adorned hand, as if she's the one who needs reminding.

She pushes my hand down and eyes with a probing expression. "I know what the paper you signed says. What does your *heart* say? There's a difference."

I forgot how insightful and direct Matty could be. It's what made her a crack interviewer. She's good at reading people and she's got great instincts that she always listens to.

I've kept my own council when it comes to our marriage. Tyson only knows the true state of things because he was visiting us when everything fell apart.

Matty and I may butt heads, but I trust her with my life. After the way I left things with Marcel, I would kill for someone to talk to.

Someone removed from my life and someone who doesn't think the sun shines out of Marcel's ass.

I look down at my hands. I've never taken my ring off. But I do tonight. What's next, I don't know. But I need to figure it out.

I sit up and clap my hands together. "For this, we need a drink."

"Well? Spill it." Matty prods when our server walks away.

I can't look her in the eye, so I keep my gaze trained on the drink in my hand. "We haven't had sex in five years. Not since I discovered Marcel's affair. It wasn't his first, but it was the first one he was careless enough for me to find out about. She's pregnant."

"Are you serious?"

"Yes." I turn to meet her gaze. What I'm about to say isn't the kind of thing you confess without the courtesy of eye contact.

"She's eighteen. *And* our nanny. I hired her last summer, and she ended up staying when school started. The kids love her. And so does my husband, apparently."

Her eyes bug out. "He's *leaving* you for her?"

I laugh humorlessly. "Oh no. Marcel wouldn't leave me. His pride will never let him admit that he failed at anything. He won't even acknowledge they had an affair."

She frowns in confusion. "But…then, how do you *know* she's pregnant?"

"She told me. After I caught them together, I fired her. I asked her to pack and leave and then I took the kids to the beach so they wouldn't see her leave. She came down an hour after us and sat down next to me and told me that she was pregnant. She said he asked her to get rid of it, but she wants to keep it."

"How do you know it's his?" Her question is one I know I'll get a lot, but it irritates me.

"I don't. But why would she say it was?" I ask and wish I cared more.

"Because he's a billionaire and she's trying to get paid," she returns easily.

"Not everyone does everything for money, Matty."

She purses her lips and glances away, "Time will tell. What did you say? Did you slap her?"

"No. She's a kid. I said I'd help her whatever she decided."

She snorts a surprised laugh. "You seem awfully sanguine about all of this. Has he gotten someone pregnant before?"

"No, of course not," I say right away and then slump in my seat. "At least… I don't think so. I mean…I don't know. He's had other entanglements." I admit.

"So, he's a serial philanderer." In typical Matty fashion, she gets right to the heart of it.

We sit in silence for a minute and I wonder what she's thinking. This is hardly how I imagined my life turning out.

"I know I can't stay with him. I just don't know where to start. Also, he will fight me every step of the way…and if I'm honest, it's that brawl I'm avoiding more than anything." I groan and run a hand through my hair.

"I wish I could say that the last ten years had matured me emotionally, but ending relationships *still* isn't my thing."

I glance at her and shake my head in fond exasperation. "Don't tell me you're still doing that," I say. She used to ghost on men all the time when we were in college. I thought it was funny, until she did it to me.

She ignores my jibe. "*But...* I can tell you that hot, anonymous sex in a city where you don't know a soul, is a really good place to start. Unclog those pipes so you can think clearly, first."

"God, you make it sound so easy. That was the craziest and most reckless thing I've ever done. I could have gotten caught. He could have been anyone."

"Regan, We're stupidly hot women in our mid-thirties. This is the easiest it's *ever* going to be. And that guy, he's beautiful, *and* you'll never see him again. You should find him and finish what you started."

"I was thinking about it… but what if he saw my wedding ring?"

"Well if he did, it didn't stop him. Not everyone cares about that. Did he seem like an asshole? When you were talking to him?"

I grab a handful of hair as the wind blows it around and lean in so I can speak quietly.

"Does asking for my panties make him an asshole?" I ask and then slap a hand over my mouth when her jaw drops. "Forget I said that."

"Regan, there is no TMI between us," she says when she recovers from her shock "It's just…that's hot. And he's hot. He talks dirty and made you come without even touching you. Go find that man right now. If you don't, I will. Did he have a big dick?"

I throw my head back and laugh, I don't answer the last question, but my body tightens at the memory of his thick length.

I haven't even considered an affair. But if I were to pick a man to do it with—that stranger, with his sharp, strong jaw, his full pink lips and the quiet, calm strength he exuded from every single part of his incredible body—would fit the bill.

My thighs clench at the thought of having that big, muscular body between my thighs. I haven't had a man like him, *ever.*

My phone buzzes with a text and I look down. "It's Marcel," I say and read his text.

"Why aren't you answering my calls? This is ridiculous."

I delete it.

Matty's hand covers mine and squeezes. "Play it cool and don't be obvious, but the guy from the shuttle is here and he's watching you," Matty says under her breath.

I look up and pretend I'm looking around until I see him.

He doesn't look away when he sees me notice him. I smile and wave.

After a beat, a smile tugs up one corner of his mouth and he waves back.

Matty nudges me "Go! Take him back to your room. Have fun."

Why not?

It's been a long time since I've wanted anyone, much less been able to act on it. And this is the perfect place. He doesn't know me. I don't know him. And there's no denying the chemistry…

My phone buzzes again. I look down and frown when I see my mother's name. Her timing is impeccable, as always. I turn away from Mr. Hot God, stand up and walk to a quieter section of the restaurant before I answer.

"Mommy?" My stomach lightens and my heart skips a beat when I hear my son's teary voice.

"Henri, what's wrong honey?"

"Where are you?" His little voice sounds so far away and yet I'm sure that if I closed my eyes I could reach out and touch him.

"Didn't you get my letter today, baby?" I left each of them a note for every day I'm gone. My mother called it overkill, but it's the first time I've been away for this long without them…and so soon after I went to visit Jack.

"Yeah, I did. But you didn't say where you are," he complains.

"I'm saying bye to a friend," I remind him, gently.

"You can do that on the phone. I want you to come home." I stiffen at his demanding, petulant tone. He sounds so much like his father. In fact, I'm sure he's repeating something he's heard his father say.

I keep my voice even and free of my internal irritation. "Of course, I miss you. And I'll be home soon, Henri. Aren't you having fun with your grandmother?"

"Not at *all*," he declares, and I can just picture his frowning pink-lipped pout. "Uncle Tyson took us to Truluck's *again*. He knows they don't have a kid's menu and he eats all this raw, slimy stuff. *And* he wouldn't speak French with Martinez and that made Eva mad. Nana can't work any of the TVs and she makes us practice our handwriting every day. I want you to come home." He's out of breath and fully in the grip of his misery when he's done listing his grievances.

"*I'll come home early*," is on the tip of my tongue. But it's stilled by the promise I made to myself that guilt over being away from my kids wouldn't intrude on this trip.

I miss them, but I need this time to myself desperately. "I'll talk to your grandmother about your handwriting, and I'll be home on Sunday afternoon. We'll spend the whole day together," I promise.

"Will Uncle Remi be back soon, too?"

"I think so," I say and pray I'm right. Remi has done this before—taking off without a word. But never for this long. My kids love him more than just about anyone else. He's more present in their lives than their father and his extended absence has been felt keenly by them. Especially by Eva.

"Where's your grandmother and does she know you're using her phone??"

"She's in the bath. Eva stressed her out, so she needed to *relax.*" He affects my mother's voice and I chuckle. He's an excellent mimic. I normally chastise him for his impersonations - I don't want him poking fun at people. But he's so spot on and it's more of an homage than a mimic and his answering giggle feels like a perfect place to say goodbye. "Alright, honey, I'll call you tomorrow, okay?"

"Wait, can you help me turn on Paw Patrol, first? Evie's locked in her room and she's got that keep out sign on her door."

My ten-year-old is on the cusp of tweenhood and her patience for her twin brothers' antics is virtually nonexistent, and the last thing I want is to be refereeing fights over the phone. "Of course, darling, but let me go somewhere quiet and I'll call you back." With a sigh of longing and one last look across the pool, I head inside.

Chapter 12

CHASING VENUS

STONE

The view of the horizon from my poolside table is breathtaking. That kiss of sea and sky is a siren song extolling the vast and limitless adventures I've yet to take. Proximity to water is the thing I miss most living in Pamplona. It's a stunning town set deep in the valley of a mountain range in Eastern Colombia called Valle del Espiritu Santo. It's a humble, charming community that settled in the 16th century. It bustles with commerce by day and vibrates with revelry by night.

But the excellent food, the welcoming people, and the endless promise of adventure that can be found within a day's drive of the city, can't compare to the crash of waves and the cool, constant breeze that wafts over me like a Sea of Cortez's sigh of contentment. This water is always where I find equilibrium. I could stay here forever.

A loud shriek pulls my eyes to the other side of the pool just in time to see a woman fly through the air and land in the water with a splash so big that several cries of complaint rise up around us.

When I turn back toward the horizon, I scan the dining area and see Regan Wilde sitting across the pool in all her windswept, golden-brown glory.

She leans back in her chair and I get a view of her upper body that makes my mouth water.

Her white romper opens from her neck to her navel, exposing just a hint of the rounded full breasts beneath. A gold chain glints against her exposed chest and snakes a trail down her flat, toned stomach and disappears into the waistband of her shorts.

Beautiful is too tame a word to describe her. Even when I was just a boy who didn't know my ass from my dick, I knew she was something rare and special.

I take a swig of my beer to wash down the nostalgia that's clouding my judgment. All of that was a whole lifetime ago; In *this* lifetime, Tyson Wilde, her younger brother, is one of my best friends and one of the few people in the entire world that I trust.

I met him when I tried out for the track team at U of H. He brought a box of Shipley's glazed donuts to practice and offered them around. Everyone reacted like they were nuns being asked to suck a dick.

Except me. We paired up for team workouts and discovered that a weakness for glazed donuts was just one of the things we had in common.

When the team workout was done, everyone else was laid out, legs turned to jelly, lungs ragged with exertion. I headed outside for a run. Tyson, who's competitive streak asked if he could join me. I humored him and said yes but warned that I was setting a six-minute mile pace."

"Why? You tired?" he asked before he took off. At the end of a fast, hard, flat out run that left us both gasping for breath he extended his hand, a grin of respect on his face and said, "I'm *the* Tyson Wilde, not to be confused with my less handsome, much older brother Remington."

My heart was already racing from the exertion of the workout, but like a deer who sees the headlights too late, I blurted my name and said "I think we're supposed to be enemies"

"Well, I don't know about you, but I'm thinking a feud that has nothing to do with me is a dumb reason to not work out together. I won't tell, if you won't."

We laughed, but I've never told my brothers about our friendship and I'm pretty sure he hasn't either. But when he talks about Regan, I feel guilty pretending not to know her at all. He's as protective of her as I am of my brothers. If *he* knew that she has been the inspiration of every wet dream I've ever had, he'd probably kick my ass.

I don't want to risk my friendship with Tyson. We don't talk often, but when we do, this trip will come up and how can I pretend I had no clue his sister was here?

Determined to do the right thing, I grab my phone and shoot him a text.

"Just saw Regan at my resort."

"You're in Cabo?" His answer comes back instantly.

"Yup. Just saw her."

"Is she okay?"

I recall her tears

Why wouldn't she?

"Her marriage is over.".

" I pump my fist at that. *Hell, yes.*

"What happened?" I text back and hold my breath for his answer.

"He's fucking the nanny." He responds.

"Woah." What kind of idiot has sex with other women when they're married to Regan Wilde?

"Yup. Buy her a drink and help her get laid."

If only he knew just how much I'd like to do that, he wouldn't ask.

*"By anyone *but* you. You dirty fucker,"* his next message reads. I laugh nervously

Duh. And I think she can buy her own drinks and get laid just fine if she wants. I'll just say hi." If she happens to climb on my lap and ride my dick again, I most certainly won't say no.

"I'll text her, let her know so she doesn't think you're some random hitting on her and kick you in the balls before you can introduce yourself."

"I'm looking at her right now. Tell her to look up and she'll see me."

"Cool. Getting a call, later."

I watch her intently now. She and her friend are still laughing and talking. I wonder what she'll think when she realizes Stone is me. She looks down at her phone and frowns.

I hold my breath when she looks up suddenly and scans the pool area. Tyson must have texted her. I stay stock still and wait for her to find me.

Her gaze moves past me and then comes back suddenly. She lifts her sunglasses up and a smile spreads on her lips.Her smile is so bright, I feel the heat of it from all the way over here.

She looks…*excited* to see me. Maybe she's forgiven me for stabbing that dude and cussing her out that night.

I wave.

She lifts her hand and waves back.

Her smile disappears abruptly, and she looks down at her phone, again.

Her expression becomes a frown, and as she lifts it to her ear, speaks briefly and then with a quick, but heated glance in my direction, she stands to leave and that mouthwatering body of hers comes fully into view. The crocheted hem of her shorts skim the tops of her supple, shapely thighs. The sight of which set my palms tingling. I stand, intent on following her, and nearly collide with the server standing at my table with a tray of food balanced on one hand.

"Oh, shit," I mutter, as I lose sight of Regan. I sit, a frustrated sigh slips past my lips before I press them together and give the woman a halfhearted smiled. "That's mine?" I ask.

Her brows furrow and her smile flattens as concern creases her eyes and she reaches for the small pad of paper in her shirt front pocket. "You are leaving? Or, maybe I have the wrong table?"

"No, no, this is right. Sorry, go ahead." I gesture at the table.

She nods, but there's a bemused smile on her face, as she lays my food out on the table and the aroma of sweet roasted garlic, caramelized onions and sizzling Carne Asada makes my eyes roll back in my head, and my empty stomach growls its demand.

I start building my fajita and plan my assault.

Even if Tyson's intel about her marriage is right, Regan Wilde is still out of my league.

But being close enough to touch the one horizon I've always wanted to explore, the adrenaline junkie in me can't resist. It's a long shot; she might not be so keen now that she knows I'm not a stranger.

I attack my meal with gusto and eat every bite.

It's said that fortune favors the bold. I'll need all the stamina I can get because the next time I see her, I'm going to put that theory to the test.

Chapter 13

HEAD START

STONE

I'm sitting at the bar, watching the entrance of the restaurant for her, when the intangible, but unmistakable sultry citrus scent of her fills my lungs. I stop typing mid-sentence and lay my phone down, just as she slides that fine ass of hers onto the bar stool next to me.

"Long time, no see," Regan drawls, in her smooth as cream, sexy as fuck voice. Her impossibly dark eyes glint like obsidian coins, as she drags them over my face in a frank, possessive appraisal.

"Have you come to bring me your panties?" I drawl.

She shakes her head no, but a slow smile lifts the corners of her lush mouth, before she leans in, so close, that her lips touch my ear when she speaks.

"I wanted to see if you were recovered. I felt guilty leaving you in such a state of obvious need when I got off...*on* your lap."

She draws back, and the twinkle in her eye is as intoxicating as her scent and as captivating as her smile. God, the things I want to do to her...aware of where we are and of the rapidly withering integrity of my restraint, I lean away from the temptress and sip the warm, bitter dregs of my beer, so that I can speak without clearing my suddenly parched throat.

"It's nice to know there are still women out there who don't just hit and quit it. Thank you for your concern, unfortunately, I'm far from recovered."

"I *could* take your word for it, or you could come to my room and let me *see* for myself." Her gaze is unflinchingly direct, the invitation in them, unambiguous.

I'd been prepared to wear her down. That she's the one, propositioning *me*, slackens my jaw and scrambles my wits. I look from her face to the card and back again, as I try to force my brain to work.

At my hesitation, doubt clouds her dark eyes, and she glances down to my lap. Her frank gaze lingers there, watching my hardening dick demonstrate what's trapped on my tied tongue.

Like the proverbial cat eyeing her bowl of cream, the tip of her tongue strokes her gloss-slicked lips. *God, how I want to fuck that mouth.*

As if she heard me, her gaze snaps to mine, her eyes hooded, luminous, and clear of the uncertainty that flashed in them, a few seconds ago.

"*You* may be something of a tease, but your dick certainly isn't," she drawls.

I lean in until I'm close enough to smell the juniper on her breath and the brush of her soft exhales tickle my lips.

"Those are fighting words. I must defend my honor. My dick challenges your mouth to a duel."

Her eyes widen, her chest heaves, but her smile is sure and sensual as she reaches into the back pocket of her tiny shorts. "I accept." She pulls a keycard out and slides it over to me. "Give me ten minutes. Room 3260. At the top of the hill." She steps off the stool and with a wink, she saunters away. I watch her until she leaves the restaurant and try to catch my breath.

My pulse quickens the same way it does at the start of a difficult race. I know she's not a thing to be won or a mountain to be conquered, but damn if I haven't wanted to do both since the day she wrapped her arms around me and changed the course of my entire life.

When she got married, my hope of catching my Venus stopped being a deferred dream. At sixteen, on the cusp of manhood, I discarded it as the fruitless fantasy of a boy too young to know better.

Today, there's too much between us for anything more than a tryst.

I live on a different continent.

She's married.

She's my best friend's sister.

My brother is fighting like hell to rebuild our family's tattered reputation and I promised to help him. Getting involved with the wife of a man he does business with would shatter that oath.

I signal the bartender and order two fingers of whiskey, throw it back and set my timer for ten minutes.

When the alarm trills, I settle my tab, drop some cash in the tip jar, and make my way up the hill. I wave away the shuttle that slows to pick me up. I need the walk to clear my head. At this point in my life, the kind of trouble she spells is the very last thing I need.

I churn the same arguments while I make way to her room. Yet, I never consider turning back because for each argument, there is a single, compelling rebuttal that resounds until it becomes a refrain; The woman of my every dream just offered herself to me.

So, tonight, I'm finally going to have what I want, *how* I want. And I'm going to enjoy her *very* much.

Chapter 14

I WANT MORE

REGAN

"If you didn't know me, would you want to fuck me?" I prop my iPad against the bathroom mirror. I step away, place my hands on my hips, throw my shoulders back and wait for my friend Charlie to give his verdict.

His dark eyes bug out of his head. "If my wife walks in right now, which she might 'cause she gets twitchy when you call, she would flip out. Put some damn clothes on." His volume progresses over the course of that sentence and by the time he's done, he's shouting. He winces. "Please?" he pleads in a hushed voice.

I open my mouth to argue. His wife's jealousy is annoying as hell. But the last thing I want is to make it even more difficult for Charlie to be my friend. I position the camera so he can only see my face and flash him an apologetic grimace and perch on the edge of the claw footed tub. "Sorry, I'm just freaking out because I'm about to be naked in front of a man for the first time in five years and I don't want to make a fool of myself."

His expression darkens. "You're letting Marcel back into your bed? I hope you've got extra strong condoms because there's no—"

"It's not Marcel, someone I met on vacation." Normally, I'd let him pillory my husband for being a manwhore, but he's the last person I want to talk about.

"Wow. Okay." He lets out a low, long whistle of surprise that raises my hackles.

I narrow my eyes. "Don't you judge me. You know I've never even considered anything like this."

"Woah, you know I would never," he admonishes me with a glare. "Look, I believe in the institution of marriage. But you and Marcel—what you have isn't even close to that. I'm just praying this is your first step to finally leaving that son of a bitch."

Relief and gratitude swell simultaneously. "I hope so, too. I can't regret him because of my children, but I don't want to live like this any-more," I confess.

He smiles, but it doesn't reach his eyes. "Excellent. It hurt like hell to lose you to him and I've been waiting for this day for more than ten years."

Guilt that lives right below the surface simmers. "Charlie, I—"

"No, don't apologize," he snaps and then softens his rebuke with a tender smile. "I've got my girl and we're happy. And you're one of the best friends I've ever had, Regan. When I got fired from V&E and not even my brother in law would have lunch with me, who invited me to be her plus one at every single event and paid my legal fees when I thought they were going to cost me everything I'd managed to hold on to?"

Giving Charlie the benefit of my social credit when he was fired was one of the few times, recently, that I've felt useful. I roll my eyes and flush at the naked gratitude in his eyes. "What good are friends if they're not there for you when you actually need them?"

He grins. "Exactly. I'm just glad you're ready to make *you* the most important person in your life. And let me add that your body is one of the great wonders of the world. *Everyone* wants to fuck you. Even a few straight women I know."

I laugh out loud, "Oh shut it, flatterer." I chide through a fond smile. Charlie's a better friend than I deserve.

"I only speak the truth. Call me when you're back in Houston. We'll get the kids together, throw some steaks on the grill, and catch up. And since I *didn't* get caught, I'll thank you for a peek at that very fine ass."

He winks and then hangs up.

I turn back to the full-length mirror on the back of my bathroom door and my humor fades as I give myself a critical assessment.

My mother jokes that we hail from the same gene pool that pro-duced Naomi Campbell. It's true that genetics have been kind and spared us cellulite and stretch marks, Naomi didn't test the bounds of that generosity by carrying and giving birth to three children.

When I told my mother I was pregnant, the first appointment she insisted I make was with a plastic surgeon. Between him, my personal trainer, and my Weight Watchers sponsor, I've managed to keep my stomach flat, my tits perky, and my ass firm. I believe Charlie when he says it's generally appealing.

But there are places on my body that haven't been restored to their original glory. I run a hand between my thighs and wrinkle my nose at the soft, plump, looser than it used to be, flesh I encounter.

My handsome stranger's not co-ed or anything, but he doesn't look older than thirty.

Has he ever seen a vagina that's given birth? Much less three times?

I sigh and draw my hand away. Does it matter that my pussy's not so pretty anymore? He's going to fuck it, not look at it.

I wash my hands and startle at the unfamiliar sight of my ringless left hand. Taking it off for the first time in a decade was fraught with a whole host of emotions. Not one of them is shame or regret.

I pour myself a shot of the exceptional clear tequila and throw it back without any ceremony. I glance at the clock. It's been more than twenty minutes since I left that bar. What if he's not coming.

Like a divine reminder that everything is happening exactly as it should, my pang of doubt is followed by the sweet sound of knuckles rapping on my door

"Remember, you deserve to feel good," I tell myself as I reach for my robe. As soon as I slip my arm in, I hesitate. Why am I bothering? I look good and if this turns out to be my one chance at something like this, then I'm going all in.

I lay it across the back of the chair, stride to the door, and fling it open. And feast my eyes on the sexiest man I've ever seen. He's leaning against the frame—looking like he just walked out of a magazine called "Men Who Make Women Thirsty: The Dick Trap Edition."

There's too much character in his face for him to be described as classically handsome. His mouth is too broad, his lips full, the top slightly more so than the bottom. His beard is close cropped but fuller than a five o'clock shadow. The smirk tugging up the left side of that sinful mouth widens.

"Are you gonna come in?" I ask him after the third time he opens and then closes his mouth without saying anything.

He nods but doesn't say anything. But if the bulge in his pants were a word, that word would be "yes."

We stand there like that, like a couple that just ended a dance with a dip.

I grab the front of his shirt and give him a firm tug. He kicks the door closed and loses his footing, and we both teeter momentarily. He recovers his footing and wraps one strong arm around my waist and cradles the back of my head with the other.

"You okay?" he asks.

I nod. But I could be falling through space and wouldn't care.

I'm riveted by eyes that call to mind the brown sugar, butter, and cream pralines I gorge myself on at Christmas—golden brown and endlessly tempting.

I'm enthralled by the heat of his palm on my bare back, the slide of his strong fingers as they curl around my ribcage and the tips of them brushing the sensitive underside of my breast.

"I'm so clumsy," I say with a breathy giggle and coquettish voice that I know for certain has never passed my lips before.

"No, you're *so* unbelievably beautiful." His eyes darken accentuating the flecks of gold around his pupils. He pulls me up to standing straight, and cups one of my bare ass cheeks, squeezes and pulls so that the cool air of the hotel room touches the hottest part of my body.

He growls, his eyes narrowing to slits when I whimper at the swirl of his thumb over my clit.

A thousand pinpricks of pleasure ignite when his exquisitely clever fingers stroke and probe my pussy for the first time. I rock against his hand, seeking, and desperate.

His touch goes from reverent to ravenous—prying, prodding, plunging.

"Did you ask me here to fuck you?" His voice is urgent, rough as gravel, and sends a ravishing shiver through me.

I shake my head and pant through a grin when he grits his teeth in frustration. "I invited you here so that *I* could fuck *you.*"

His chuckle is wicked with satisfaction and it makes my toes curl. "What are you waiting for, then?"

"I want to do something," I whisper as my eyes follow the trail of my hand over the contour of his broad shoulders, fascinated by the velvet smooth skin and its perfect concert with the muscle, sinew and bone it's wrapped around. I explore his trim, muscle girded waist and lean hips with wonder and avarice.

I've never touched a body so finely formed. For the first time in my adult life, I understand why women make fools of themselves over men. I say a quick prayer of thanks that my tryst is going to be with someone who could have been ripped from the pages of my fantasies and who I never have to see again. This must be that good karma I've been hearing about my whole life. Like the grateful sinner that I am, I drop to my knees on the soft cream-colored carpet.

My unpracticed fingers fumble with the buttons of his jeans but get them unfastened just as I see his hands twitch impatiently at his sides. The zipper parts to reveal more smooth skin stretched taught over exquisite muscle and a network of veins along with a dusting of golden hair that's like a roadmap leading me to pleasure.

I'm treated to the mouthwatering sight of the crown of his penis pushing past the elastic waistband of his briefs. The rest of his thick, rigid length strains against the black fabric.

"May I put my mouth on you?" I ask and gaze up at him through my lashes. He's panting and when he speaks his teeth are clenched.

"Anything…you can have anything you want."

The knowledge that I made a man like this breathless with need, takes my breath away. I lean forward and circle my tongue over the hot, smooth skin… *Dear Lord*, he tastes *so* good

He throws his head back, exposing the strong column of his throat and the defined line of his jaw. His plump lower lip is caught between his perfectly straight, white teeth. Every single inch of him is wildly attractive.

It's only when my hand comes into contact with the unbelievably soft skin of his rock-hard erection, that I manage to pull my eyes away from his achingly handsome face.

I lean in and pull the tip between my lips and suck softly. He releases a shuddering breath and mutters something I can't make out. His hand curves around my head, his fingers tangling in my hair, coaxing me forward.

I take my first taste of him, with just the tip of my tongue pressed into the small slit at the top of his dark head.

I slide my lips down and pull him in, as far as I can relaxing my throat when my gag reflex threatens. I can't take him all, but I wrap my fingers around his base. He hisses and his fingers spear into my hair and curl into a fist. He covers my hand with his and thrusts into my mouth, making my eyes *and* pussy water.

"Fuck yes, that is the *shit*," he growls. His hand tightens its grip on my hair when I cup his balls.

"I *love* that. So damn much," he croons, his hips pump faster and his salty precum beads on my tongue. I suck his dark, throbbing crown harder and his big body jerks.

"It's too good, too much," he groans. Then, suddenly the tugging pressure of his hand is gone from my hair and when my cry of complaint loosens the tight sucking hold I have on him, he slips out of my mouth.

"I wasn't done," I pout and reach for him again.

"I don't want the first time I come with you to be in your mouth." He steps out my reach and gives me a grin so wicked that my toes curl.

He pulls a condom out of his pocket and sheaths himself within a matter of seconds. "Get off that floor and let me get in that pussy." He growls and leans down, cups my elbows and hauls me up to standing.

His hands are back at my ass, cupping this time when he lifts me. I use the same resistance that stymied him last time, but he doesn't let me down.

"Woman. Wrap your legs around my waist," he growls.

"I'm too heavy," I protest.

"Not for me, Goddess." He slaps my ass and I yelp and wrap my legs around his waist, and he nods in satisfaction and grins as he walks us over to the bed. He sits and scoots us back until he's against the head-board.

He leans toward me, his mouth aimed at mine. I close my eyes, and my lips tingle in anticipation.

Instead, he presses that sinning mouth to my neck. Any disappointment I feel at not kissing him disappears when the moment his unbelievably soft lips part and he feasts on the sensitive, heated skin of my throat I clutch his head, holding him there while pleasure courses through me.

"I'm *really* ready to fuck you, but I've been dreaming about tasting your pussy after you left the delicious smell of it all over my shorts."

I can't help my bark of surprised laughter. My stomach flips at the easy, sexy smile he gives me in return.

"I guess it should be a balm to my wounded pride that I at least made you laugh…it's like the horizon—the edge of something… your laugh sounds the way a sunrise looks. I could probably listen to it all day."

"My god, you're a total Casanova. Are you a professional seducer of women?"

It's his turn to laugh, but it's a devilish laugh if I've ever heard one.

"Nah, I'm an amateur. I do it for the love of it. But it's nice to know that I'm good enough to be mistaken for a pro."

He grins like the wolf who thinks no one can see him behind his sheep's clothing. But nothing, not even that charmingly roguish smile, can hide the overtly male confidence that comes from knowing that you're good at pleasing women.

I like that, very much.

"You look like an angel…but you're such a bad boy."

"There's certainly nothing "boyish" about my bad. And in the heaven I'm about to take you to, angels aren't allowed."

I groan in exaggerated pain. "That was terrible. But at least now I know you're not perfect."

His eyes narrow in good-natured challenge. "I'm about to make you take those words back."

"How—woah," I yelp when he spans my waist with both hands and lifts me up over his head while he slides down until he's lying flat.

He sets me down so that my knees straddle his head. His face is inches from the one place I was sure he wouldn't look.

Instinct and insecurity have me drawing my thighs closed.

"Don't move, Goddess." He grabs my thighs to hold me in place.

I close my eyes when his fingers spread me open.

"Fuck, your pussy is *spectacular*." His words come out in a rumbling groan and I glance down. His ravenous gaze devours me. He wraps his big hands around my thighs in vice like grip and pulls them apart, spreading my knees until my pussy hovers right over his parted, plump lips.

"You don't have to…." My words dissolve into a guttural exhalation when his hot, slick mouth opens over me.

I let out a cry of pleasure when the stiffened point of his tongue finds my clit and flicks it. I close my eyes against the exquisite surge of moisture and delicious coil of tension in my core as his lips suck and tug and his tongue strokes and fucks. He's so sweet and so filthy, all at once.

His mouth was made for this kind of worship, nothing I've experienced in my entire life has ever felt this good.

When he pulls my clit into his mouth and sucks, my entire body buckles. I fall forward, held upright only by the headboard and tight grip of his strong hands

A titillating pressure builds inside me and my other senses seem to wrap themselves around it so that *all* I'm capable of is feeling. I come on a wave of blistering ecstasy that draws a cry from me that's been building for years. It's a lush, layered cacophony of celebration, sur-render, and serenade.

The sex god between my thigh gazes up at me with heavy lidded adoration. My thundering heart stutters on the flash of Deja vu that's gone as quickly as it came.

I trace his brows with a trembling hand and his eyes flutter closed and the furrow between his dark slashing brows relaxes under the pads of my fingers…as if my touch is relief.

He pulls my throbbing, stiff clitoris back between his lips and sucks it. I shriek at the sharp spike of pleasure. He's relentless, his tongue and mouth insatiable.

I lose count after my third orgasm. My sweat drenched, trembling body has been rendered boneless after being battered by the waves after wave of pleasure.

"Please, it's too much, I can't," I pant, my voice hoarse from the screams his talented mouth coaxed from me.

He presses a kiss to my inner thighs and pulls me down so that I'm resting on his chest. Without the headboard to support me, my boneless body lists forward. He sits up and takes my weight and our foreheads rest against each other.

His eyes are closed. His lips are slightly parted, slick, and as red as the center of a ripe cherry. I want to know what his mouth feels like and what I taste like on his lips.

"Is kissing allowed?" I ask, my pride taking a backseat to my hunger for him.

His eyes pop open, and the gold and brown in them glitters as a wide, wolfish grin spreads across his face.

"It's fucking mandatory," he growls, and then enforces his edict. His lips are softer than I could imagine, mine seem to sink into them. I groan, and he slips his tongue into my mouth. The rough scrape of it, tinged with the taste of me, makes me crazy. He moves us until his erection is pressed hot and heavy against my inner thigh. His kiss is exploring and consuming all at once. I rock my hips and his dick glides through the desire-soaked lip of my sex. I cup his face in my hands and hold him still while I feast on his sweet mouth.

I lift my hips so that the broad blunt crown of his dick, breaches my body. His groan rumbles in his chest, but he doesn't break our kiss.

He wraps one arm around my shoulders and then he drives into me with the ease of a hot knife slicing into butter- filling me, deeper in me than anything I've ever felt.

The friction of our bodies coming together sparkles, shimmers, and burns. It is nothing short of sublime. He breaks our kiss and presses his face into my neck.

"You feel better than I could have ever imagined." His breaths are harsh and hot against my skin, he drags his open mouth over my shoulder and bites

I arch my back, let my hair spill over the arms that hold me in place while he fucks me hard and fast. I'm on top, but he's driving and setting a punishing, desperate pace that is everything I needed this to be.

That coiling heat inside of me expands and starts to burst. He loosens his hold on me and dips his head to my chest. His mouth closes over my nipple, and sucks.

There is a tempest building inside of me and this man is in command of it. When it breaks, it's only the arms he's wrapped around my waist that keep me from flying away.

When the mist of lust starts to clear, I realize he's moved us. He's sitting pressed on the headboard with my body draped over his. His fingers trace lazy patterns on my back. His lips pepper kisses on my shoulders.

"Oh my God, I think I nearly died," I pant.

He brushes a lock of hair out of the way and presses his lips to my ear. "I'm not done with you."

The dark promise is in his rasp that makes my *everything* curl.

He moves us so I'm on my stomach, my face pressed to sheets that smell like us. Hair sticks to my face and my muscles feel spent, but I lift my hips in shameless invitation. I moan when he answers me with one long, hard, glorious thrust.

He's so thick. I've never been so full, and I'm dizzy with pleasure and excitement as he pistons his hips. His heavy balls slap my ass with each thrust.

His hand glides up my sweaty back and splays into my thick, unruly hair.

The blunt scrape of his nails against my scalp as he gathers a fistful of my hair and yanks my head up with a tug that skirts the edge of vicious. The bite of pain only intensifies the bliss that is him moving inside of me.

"God, I wish you could see what I'm seeing. Your gorgeous pussy taking my dick like it's hungry for it," he sounds like he's witnessing a miracle.

I twist my head and look over my shoulder and am riveted by the vision that greets me.

His body is perfect, his broad sculpted chest glistens, and his washboard abs flex and ripple with each thrust of his hips.

His eyes are closed, his plump lower lip caught between his teeth. His unbelievably handsome face is flushed with exertion.

He's a walking wet dream.

His eyes fly open, spearing me. My whole heart flies into my throat at the unmistakable, and intense flash of Deja vu returns. But before I can process it, he leans over and takes my mouth in a ravenous kiss that sends my pulse into riots.

He breaks our kiss and presses his lips to my ear, his hot breath tickling my neck.

"Am I hurting you, Goddess?"

In answer, I reach around to grab his thigh and growl, "More."

His nostrils flair and he grinds his hips against my ass, pressing deeper than I knew was possible.

He drapes his big body over mine, presses one hand to the mattress, and wraps his other arm around my waist and drives into me, fast and hard.

Each thrust makes my toes curl. His hand glides down my stomach and slides between my thighs,

His fingers find my clit at just the right place. "Right there, oh my god," I cry out and he heeds it.

In just a few strokes of his magical fingers, I'm there.

This time, he comes with me.

He groans out his release and fucks me relentlessly until he's spent. And then he falls on top of me and I savor his heavy, sweaty, hot body for the few seconds he stays like that.

He flops onto his back and I muster the strength to roll to my side so I can take him in.

He's glorious in his male perfection. The corded muscles that cover every inch of his body glisten with a light sheen of sweat. His penis is still partially erect and bobs between his thick, hairy thighs.

Without opening his eyes, he reaches over and slaps my ass. My surprised cry turns into a moan at the possessive caress that follows it. "I hope you're going to let me fuck this ass next," he drawls lazily.

"Next? You want more?" I ask in delight and surprise.

"Uh, yeah, Captain Obvious."

I freeze and draw back to look at him.

Only one person has ever called me that and he was small and scrawny and wore glasses. Or at least he used to be. I turn over and peer at the man in my bed. I didn't ask his name because I didn't want to know. And he hasn't asked mine…because…maybe he already knows it?

"St—Stone?" I whisper and watch in horror as his eyes open, all hazel and beautiful, and so very familiar. My heart skips several beats as I see what I should have the instant I looked at him.

This cannot be happening.

I draw a pillow over my head to muffle the groan I can't choke back.

"Regan, are you okay?" He lifts the pillow off my face and peers down at me, his eyebrows raised in amused curiosity. When he sees the expression on my face, his amusement turns to concern.

"You're *Stone*. Stone *Rivers*?" I ask slowly. Each word weighed down with incredulity and disbelief.

"Uh…*yeah*." His eyes narrow in confusion, like we've talked about this a thousand times already.

Panic grips me and I scramble off the bed and grab the robe I so recklessly discarded earlier. I grab the phone from the bedside and hold it in front of me like it's a weapon.

"If Marcel set this shit up, I swear to God, I'll see him in hell before I let him use it against me."

"Wait…*what?*" He lurches back like I've slapped him. His eyes widen with shock.

I glare at him. "Last time I saw you, you said you hated me. Now, the first time I travel anywhere by myself in ten years, *you're* here?" I snarl.

He sits up slowly, his expression completely blank, and his guarded eyes not leaving me for a second. He opens his mouth and then closes it. His throat convulses.

"Who sent you here?" I shout in a voice strangled by dizzying panic. How could I have been so colossally stupid?

"This isn't what you think. Just let me get dressed, okay?" He eyes me like he might a dangerous animal as he stands and reaches for the jeans on the floor.

I turn away from him and pace in an agitated circle and try to find something sensible to cling to inside my racing mind.

"Regan?"

I whirl to face him. The hesitancy in his voice is reflected by the dubious cast of his gaze.

"Well?" I demand with an impatient wave of my hands before I cross my arms over my chest.

"I thought you knew it was me—"

"How? You were a *stranger* on the shuttle." I point my accusing finger at him.

He narrows his gaze and rolls his shoulders, and his nostrils flare. "Do you remember *anything* about me from Rivers Wilde?"

"Yes. I remember that you stabbed my boyfriend, told me you wished you'd never met me and ran off."

He closes his eyes, pinches the bridge of his nose and exhales a harsh breath. When he looks at me again, one corner of his mouth lifts in a sardonic, scornful smirk. "And you think that I've been, what? Plotting revenge because you broke my ten-year-old heart?"

"Well, what else could you be doing here? There's not enough coincidence in the world for *this* to be one." I demand and he raises his eyebrows.

"Didn't Tyson text you?"

The shock that hits me couldn't be more potent if he'd dumped ice cold water on my head. "Tyson? How do you know Tyson?"

"From college, U of H. We were texting while I was by the pool. He said he was going to send you a message, so you'd be expecting me to come and say hi. You *waved.*" He adds in frustration when I just stare blankly.

"You *told* Tyson? Oh, shit. What did he say? Is he on his way here?" I cover my mouth hand to muffle the scream that's building as the full implication of this disaster starts to sink in.

"Why would Tyson be on his way here?" he asks one eye squints at me as if he's not sure I'm completely sane.

"To kick your ass. He doesn't play that shit with his friends and me. He would take this as the height of disrespect. He's *very* protective. If he knows we…whatever…he's going to want to kill you."

"I didn't tell him I was here *with* you. I just told him I saw you. He doesn't know about our history. And Tyson may be protective, but we're adults and no one is kicking *my* ass." He grabs his shirt and pulls it over his head in a rough motion.

His expression when he looks at me again is…oh my God. How could I have *not* seen it?

It's *him. Of course,* it's him. Even his anger is exactly the same, filling the space between us as it grows.

He holds his phone out to me. I take it and read the exchange between him and Tyson.

I flush. "Tyson is such a blabber mouth. He shouldn't be telling you this stuff," I grumble as I read it.

But when I'm done, the smile I offer as I give the phone back is both sheepish and relieved. "You could have told me. How in the world would I have recognized you, Stone? All this time I've been looking for a guy who's 5'5' max with glasses that won't stay on his nose and skin that's pale from being in a lab somewhere all day," I sputter. I sound stupid and I know it, but I'm flabbergasted by the way he's changed.

He *grins*. "You've been looking for me?"

I scowl "I mean, not actively but I thought maybe I'd run into you *somewhere*, maybe." I give him an appreciative once-over. "I wouldn't have ever imagined you'd be so…built."

His grin spreads as he flexes one of his impressive biceps, kisses it and winks. "I had a growth spurt. Glad you approve."

He's really gorgeous when he smiles like that. But even that smile can't make me forget what a disaster this is.

Whatever he sees in my expression sobers him up. He sighs and walks up to me. "Honestly, it didn't occur to me that you'd be inviting me to your room if you didn't know who I was."

I throw my hands up in exasperation "Hello? I rode your dick on the shuttle?" I remind him.

"It's okay, we—"

I whirl away from him and head for the door. "This did not happen. You have to leave."

His hands close over my shoulders before I take two steps and move to stand in front of me.

I squeeze my eyes shut, but even with them closed, I can't reconcile this big, fine man with the small boy that's lived in my memories.

"I'm sorry Regan, but it *did* happen. And it was pretty fucking hot."

"I'm married." I blurt and then feel stupid.

"Well, you better tell your vagina. She doesn't seem to remember that anymore," he says and then smiles.

"Are you *smiling*? Why? There's nothing funny happening here."

"I didn't say anything was funny. And I can't help it that I'm finding quite a lot to smile about. You thought I was a stranger. You wanted to fuck me because you think I'm hot. Not because you thought I was safe. I thought Tyson—"

"You *cannot* tell Tyson, and I just… If my husband finds out…"

"He won't," he says as if it's that easy to dismiss Marcel, but some of the nonchalance in his expression fades.

"He *can't*. I won't make excuses for myself. But I haven't been with him or anyone in more than five years. I'm going through a lot right now and yes, I thought you were a handsome stranger who I could take home, and then…"

"Never see me again?" He finishes for me.

"Yes. Exactly. And that…it was amazing. If you hadn't turned out to be…you, I'd ask you to stay."

"Then pretend I'm not me and give me those seconds you promised." His hands slips off my shoulder and starts to move down my back. I yank out of his reach and raise a hand in warning, and he steps toward me.

"That was *before* I knew who you were. Stone, this shouldn't have happened. And I'm sorry, but you have to leave, now. Please," I urge when he looks like he wants to argue with me.

He nods, his expression neutral but good natured. "You need time to get your head wrapped around everything."

"No, I don't. I already regret it," I inform him with all the resolve I can muster.

"Why?"

"Because it was wrong."

"Why?"

"Stop saying why," I say through clenched teeth.

"Stop making me say it." He remains completely unruffled.

"You don't have any regrets?" I ask, confounded by his lack of remorse.

"None. How could I? It's you."

"But, you don't…hate me still?" I ask.

His brows draw together in surprise. "I was *ten*, Regan. I didn't mean it and by the time I got my head clear enough to apologize, you'd left for college. I wanted to apologize for what I said. I was jealous because *I* wanted to be your boyfriend. I was too young to understand how ludicrous that was. But I have never, ever hated you. I'm here because I want to have sex with you, in every way it's possible to have sex, as many times as you'll let me."

This is too much, I am caught in a maelstrom of confusion and horror and to my surprise, lust.

He touches the tip of that wicked tongue to my mouth and smiles. "And I love the way you taste. I want more. And I know you want to give it to me."

I want to deny it, but it is pointless to try. So, I just walk to the bathroom and stay there until I hear him say, "See you tomorrow, Goddess."

I crawl into my big empty bed, and I lie there, wishing he was there.

Chapter 15

CAN I KISS YOU?

REGAN

"What did you do to him, Reggie? He's been watching you all night." Matty nudges me.

I grimace and shake my head, "Nothing that's ever going to happen again, and he knows it." I take another sip of my ginger beer and vodka, but I hardly taste it.

"Are you sure *he* knows that? He's sure not *looking* like he does," Matty teases in an amused, singsong voice.

"It doesn't matter. *I* know." I skewer her with a challenging glare.

She nudges my shoulder with hers. "Oh, come on. It's at least a little flattering that he's looking at you like he wants to throw you over his shoulder and carry you out of here."

"Not at all," I say and Matty gives me a knowing side-eye, but doesn't say more.

She knows I'm lying. How could I not be flattered? I've felt his eyes on me since we walked in. Once I met his gaze, thinking he'd look away when I did, but he just smiled.

I haven't looked again. I don't want to encourage him to come over and start talking.

Between spending time with Matty and running into Stone, it's like my past is trying to make itself relevant again. That is the very last thing I need.

My present is enough to deal with.

I've been beside myself with mortification. But when a memory of the night before randomly intrudes into my thoughts, it leaves me hot, panting, and wet.

My body is still on fire from what he did to me with his mouth and his gloriously thick dick. God, whoever said size didn't matter had never come across one like Stone's. I've seen dildos less perfect.

Since he left my room, I've been swinging on a pendulum of indecision. I spent half the day thinking about how to make sure we don't find ourselves alone again. The other half was spent hatching frantic schemes to ensure we did.

Which is crazy. Last night shouldn't have happened.

It was so wrong. But I'm *very* attracted to him.

If I'm honest, my body isn't the only part of me that's responding to him.

There was something about the little boy who I found hiding in the back room of the bakery that summer. He was so sad and so brave. And the harrowing experience we shared the last time he came to the bakery re-shaped the trajectory of my life.

Last night, when he looked me in the eye and said, "See you tomorrow," I saw it. The determination that filled the glittering depths of his eyes was the very same I saw in his expression right before he stabbed Weston in the back.

But, that's the only thing about him that's the same.

In every way, he's a new person.

"Well at least you won't be all alone when I leave tomorrow."

I turn to her, my expression pleading. "Can't you stay a few more days?"

She purses her lips and shakes her head. "I gotta be at work on Tuesday. But I'm sure he'll be happy to keep you company," She tips her head to the side where I know he's sitting.

"I'll be fine. I brought a book."

She laughs. "You know what? He looks like the guy from *A Fault in our Stars,* but ten years older because of the facial hair."

"He doesn't look anything like that kid. He looks like… James Norton."

"Who?"

"The hot priest in Grantchester," I explain, knowing that she'll get it then.

"Oh my God, you're right. I was gonna say no because Grantchester is blonder and not as bootylicious, but yes…I see it and definitely that mouth…."

"Ugh, stop drooling over him," I elbow her.

"Why? You said you're done with him, right? Why do I have to play nice just because you can't? And if he's into older women—"

"Shut up, okay? I'm not *that* much older than him." The words ring true. Eight years might have been a big deal back then, but now, there's nothing to indicate the difference between his age and mine is anything but a number.

The way he touched me wasn't the way a man *without* experience would. He can't be older than 28 or 29. But from the way he looks and how sexually relaxed he seems to be, he's more experienced than I am.

I didn't know sex could be like that. I wish I could enjoy just one more night. But I've played with fire. So far, I've gotten away unscathed. I shouldn't take any more chances. This can't be a simple affair we just walked away from when we were done.

He's Tyson's friend and his brother, Hayes Rivers, is a friend and business partner of Marcel *and* Remi's. Hayes is getting married soon and Marcel is flying from Paris so we can go together. What will happen when I see him there? Just picturing it makes my stomach queasy.

"Oh shit, he's coming over," Matty says in a low voice.

My stomach drops, but I straighten my shoulders and take a deep fortifying breath when he slides into the seat on the other side of me. I smell the same verbena, coconut, and clean I did last night. I squeeze my thighs together to ease the ache blooming there.

"Hello Goddess," his voice rumbles low and hot in my ear. Just like that, I'm wet. Annoyed at my traitorous, I stiffen. "Don't call me that." I keep my eyes on the bar.

"*Hello,*" Matty croons jovially and reaches across me to wave enthusiastically at him.

His smile brightens. "Hi. Matty, right? Stone." he reaches over to take her hand.

"Ah, you have a good memory," she coos. I ignore the small flare of irrational jealousy when their hands touch. I sip my drink and the cold and spicy effervescence settle my bubbling nerves and cool my overheating head.

I feel his eyes on me and I dart a dark glance at him without turning my head.

"Hasn't anyone told you it's rude to stare?" I say and take another sip of my drink.

"Yes, but I can't seem to help myself when it comes to you."

"That's not a huge endorsement for your self-control then. You should try harder."

"I'd like to try doing obscene things to your mouth and pussy with my hard dick instead," he whispers. A bolt of white hot, unmitigated pleasure hits me squarely between my thighs and I can't bite back my groan.

"And… *that's* my cue to leave," Matty slides off her seat and looks back and forth between us before she smiles. "Reggie, The dick I was talking about yesterday? The kind that makes good women into fools? Be sure you wear a condom on your heart, cause this one is gonna fuck your feelings." she pronounces with a grin before she melts into the crowd forming on the nearby dance floor.

"You were talking about my dick yesterday?" he drawls in my ear.

I turn to face him; My chest, thighs, and nipples all tighten at once.

His eyes are full of his wicked intent. But his strong, sharply defined jaw is relaxed. His lips are spread in a delicious smile that makes me want to lean forward and bite them. I scowl at him and turn to face the bar again. "You drove my friend away."

He lifts one of his large, surprisingly elegant hands and signals for the bartender and then flashes a brilliant grin that makes me *ache.* "Good. Three's a crowd when it comes to sex."

I give him glare. "Stone."

"Regan." He says in a mimic of my warning tone.

To my surprise, I *giggle.*

He grins and presses his advantage. "You promised me seconds."

I watch him from the corner of my eye, while he orders a neat glass of scotch. He's in jeans and a white dress shirt that looks custom made to my well-trained eye. He's wearing a thin gold cuff on his right wrist.

Otherwise, he's completely unadorned. And he doesn't need anything more. Stone is man candy. The kind that should come with a warning label that reads, "One bite won't be enough"

Several women at the bar have given him the once-over. One of them is actively trying to catch his attention in the mirror. I give her a venomous smile when our gazes meet, and her eyes widen slightly before she turns to talk to the women on her left.

That was small of me.

Ugh, if I had any sense, I would point him in that woman's direction and go back to my room and call my kids.

The waitress sets his drink down and refills my shot glass without even asking. I give her a grateful smile and throw the shot back.

"Rough day?" Stone asks conversationally.

I huff out a laugh. "Something like that."

"I've got something for that, Regan. Let me make you feel good." He's laying it on thick. There's no ambiguity in his approach; he's not being presumptuous or coy.

It's been a long time since I've been pursued by a man and it feels… good. But…

"I shouldn't do this."

"Why not? Doesn't this feel good, like no time has passed at all?"

I scoff, but my drink turns bitter in the back of my throat. I pivot so my whole body is facing him and meet his eyes. The amusement in them annoys me even further.

"Listen, you're holding on to nostalgia. You had a crush on me then, right? I'm not that girl anymore," I warn him.

"Well, that's good. I don't date little girls. I date *women*. Because I'm a man. Not that I need to remind you, since I spent a good bit of effort making your whole body aware of that fact yesterday."

I throw the rest of my drink back and let out a tremulous sigh. "Stone, no one on this planet would ever mistake you for anything other than a man. And I'm not worried about your age."

"Then let's leave the past in the past. Let's talk about right now." A hand comes to rest on my thigh.

"Did you like what we did last night?" he whispers in my ear.

I should push his hand away, but it feels *so* good.

"Do you want me to do it again?"

I shiver and close my eyes.

His fingers slip under the lace of my panties. I gasp, casting an anxious glance around the bar.

"No one is watching, Goddess," his voice is a silk lure and my thighs part.

I finally look at him and the hunger in his gaze quickens my pulse.

"All you have to do is tell me to stop, and I will," he says.

I couldn't tell him to stop if someone was holding a gun to my head.

I never want him to stop.

His fingers skim up, and up, and up. I can't tell where the heat is coming from—him or me, but from the very center of my body to the tips of my extremities, I'm ablaze.

"Let's go back to your room and spend the entire night together. I have years and years of fantasies to live out with you. I want to suck your toes, and fuck your ass, and watch your lips stretch around my dick." he whispers.

Oh my God, I have never wanted any of those things, but now I feel like I need them all.

"Will you let me?" he coos, his fingers trail up and he rubs my clit through my panties. My head lolls forward and he cups my neck and presses his lips to my cheek, kissing his way to my ear while he continues his sensual strokes.

"Fuck the rules," I breathe.

He pulls his hand away and lifts it to his nose and inhales. "Your pussy is so delicious, Regan."

My name on his lips is even more erotic than the words that preceded it.

"I knew you couldn't say no, it was too good between us."

He's not wrong, but I can't help but feel like I've made this too easy for him. He walked over assured of his conquest. This man is all alpha and I know that he'll be at his best if he's got to work for it. Last night was amazing, but tonight I want him in a lather. I want him to leave me sore and bruised so I can hold on to these feelings for as long as possible.

"I haven't said yes. You want me? You'll have to catch me first," I hop off the stool and wave for the bartender. "Settle the tab first will ya'?" I chuckle at the bemused expression on his face as I turn and hurry away.

When I exit the restaurant, I glance over my shoulder to see where he is. He's further away than I thought, but he's following me. His eyes alight with a determined glint that thrills me.

I hurry across the lobby and head down a hallway that ends with a bank of elevators.

I don't know where I'm going or what I'll find on the floors above the lobby and its bar, but I don't care as long as I can get him alone.

I wait until I hear his footfalls behind me before I press the button to call the lift.

The doors open immediately, and I step inside.

"Hold that door," he calls and starts to jog.

"You'll have to be faster than that," I say teasingly when the doors start to close.

He breaks into a sprint, and just when I'm sure he's not going to make it. His fingers slip in between the two doors just before they slam shut. They bounce open instantly and he steps inside.

"Regan," he says my name like it's a promise he's making as he reaches up and presses a button that stops the elevator from its ascent.

"Hi, Stone."

He slips a hand around my waist and turns me so I'm facing him, too.

My hands have a mind of their own, because despite every last shred of good sense I have screaming for me to stop, they slide up his muscular shoulders and drape themselves around his neck.

Everything about this—from attraction itself to the reckless behavior it's spawned—is a bad idea.

But my fingers dance up his collar and twirl in his hair. It's so soft. I wonder what it smells like.

He walks us backward until I'm pressed against the mirrored glass of the elevator and he lifts me by the waist and sets my ass on the narrow handrail.

His hands rest on either side of my head and he spears me in place with his eyes. "I wasn't chasing you…this was a lure. You're an excellent hunter."

I nod in agreement.

He drops his head and presses his nose to my throat. "Can I kiss you right here?" he asks. I don't understand the tears that prick sting the back of my eyes at his question. But it makes me want to give him whatever he asks for.

At my nod, he presses a feather light kiss to my throat.

I arch my neck, pressing closer, my head spinning already.

The sharp edge of his teeth scrapes along my jawline. He nips my chin before he kisses and sucks his way back down my neck.

I'm balanced precariously on my perch with Stone pressed between my thighs, devouring me like I'm his to consume.

His touch is driving me wild.

The loud buzzing is like a needle scratching a record. We jump apart, both wide eyed and panting.

"Hello, this is security. We're getting you out," a loud voice comes over the loudspeaker. It sounds vaguely familiar and it sends my panic into overdrive.

"Oh my God, this is a disaster," I cry and start wiping my mouth and fixing my hair and straightening my clothes.

"It's just security." I snap a glance at him in the mirror and see the irritation in his voice furrowing his brow.

"I think I *know* that voice, "I whisper urgently, cursing my stupidity and swearing to be good if I get out of this.

"So? We're in an elevator both fully clothed, it's hardly suspicious," he says, and his calm voice annoys me. The elevator whines and my heart hammers against my breastbone.

"Let's just get off like we're strangers, you go first, and I'll call you when I get to my room, okay?" I mutter and then put my game face on.

The man on the other side isn't anyone I've ever seen before and the rush of relief I feel almost makes me nauseous.

Stone thanks the man for his help, bids me a civil good evening and strolls away. I walk with the maintenance man back to the lobby and make small talk until we part ways at the huge fountain that sits at the center of it.

I walk on trembling legs to the nearest bench and sit. The fear I'd felt in that elevator, when I thought I knew that voice had been unreal. What would I have done if it had been someone I know?

I've held on to my marriage by Faustian bargain. Marcel has broken faith with me more times than I can count, and I don't owe him my fidelity or discretion.

But there are more than just our reputations at stake.

Buried somewhere in our prenup there are all sorts of morality clauses tied to alimony and more importantly, custody.

Charlie was right, what we have isn't a marriage. We'll never be intimate again. But, Marcel has made it clear that leaving him would be nothing short of a battle. If I'm going to do it, I don't need to give him any ammunition.

Cursing my choices and my husband, I start for my room. I was lucky just now, but this is a popular and public place. I was crazy to think I could have an affair with him here. I'm not going to call Stone when I get back to my room. And since I have no idea when he's leaving, I'll be spending the rest of my time there. It sucks, but I always eat my vegetables. Even when they're covered in shit.

Last night will have to be enough.

My stomach tightens and disappointment lodges in my throat.

Discipline, Regan.

I am the most disciplined person I know. I don't say that as a point of pride but as a matter of fact. It's what has pulled me back up every time life has forced me to my knees.

It's my superpower.

And that makes Stone Rivers… what? My kryptonite? Because the minute I breathe the same air as him, I find myself confronting bullies, breaking decades of family code, fornicating in public, and shattering rules that I have never even been *tempted* to bend.

He knows where my room is, but certainly he can't come in unless I open that door.

And tomorrow, I'll request a room change.

And I won't leave my room until it's time for me to go home early next week. I have my books, my laptop, my phone and a killer view. I could go home early, but…I don't know when I'll get a chance to be alone like this again.

The steady stream of room service will be a boon for the staff— they'll get tips each time they bring me something—so that's a silver lining.

God only knows what kinds of germs I'm avoiding by not using any of the six pools on site. I have a hot tub on my balcony, and that's going to be *amazing*.

By the time I'm stepping off the elevator, my resolve is firm and I'm feeling like maybe this won't be so bad after all.

Until I see Matty sitting on the floor outside my room.

Chapter 16

BREAKING

REGAN

"Hey," I call as I approach.

Matty looks up and gives me an awkward smile. "You're alone?" She lifts up to standing in front of my door and crosses her arms tightly over her chest as if she's warding off the cold. She smiles, but the tense set of her jaw puts me on edge.

I mimic her stance and don't return her smile. "Yeah, we had to go our separate ways"

"So…are you going to see him again?" she asks, and I get the distinct impression she's stalling.

"Probably not. It was reckless. What's up?" I add to preempt any more beating around the bush.

She purses her lips and clears her throat. "I just wanted to say bye. It was nice to see you."

I nod my head slowly, my expression one of exaggerated expectancy, as I wait for her to say whatever she's clearly holding back.

When she just looks up and down the corridor, and doesn't say anything else, my discomfort grows.

"Well, my number hasn't changed. If you're ever in Houston, let me know." I pull my keycard out of my pocket.

"Wait, uh—do you still have the bakery?"

I quirk my eyebrow in bemusement at her out-of-left-field question, "It's still there, but we sold it to a new owner."

"We? Are you back at Wilde?" Her expression is neutral, but her cryptic question feels far from benign and I'm beyond ready for her to get to the point.

"No. Nope. My grandfather's banishment stuck."

She relaxes her shoulders a little and her jaw loosens, as if she's relieved to hear that. "So, what do you do, now?"

"I raise my children and raise money for causes I believe in."

"You don't work at all??"

I tense. Years of Mommy wars and my own dissatisfaction with the state of my life put me on the defensive.

"Marcel thinks it's a negative reflection on him as a provider if his wife works to earn wages." I mimic my husband's French treatment of the word wages, imbuing it with all of the disdain that he does.

Matty raises an eyebrow in surprise, "And you don't mind that? The Regan I knew—

"Is gone," I make light of my heavy predicament and force a resigned smile.

"That's too bad. I…" Matty's gaze falls away, almost shyly. "I miss her."

A spark of hope kindles in my chest. "But, maybe we could…I don't know… get to know each other again?"

Her dark, inscrutable gaze snaps to my face. She scans it with a grim frown thinning her lips. "Do you believe Rebecca?"

I blink, her sharply delivered question like water flung in my eyes.

Her dark eyes flicker with disappointment before they shutter again and my hackles rise. I straighten my posture and cross my shoulders. "You couldn't leave with us in a good place. You had to pick a fight."

She throws her head back in a humorless cackle. "I wish one weekend and a few conversations was all it took for us to be in a good place." She fills the words with scorn and her lip curls. "I'm not surprised you think so, though. You've been keeping up appearances so long, you've forgot what real relationships look like."

My patience, already brittle, starts to splinter and crack. I cross my arms over my chest and uncross them quickly. I'm not the one who should be on the defensive. "And you do? Who are your friends? Who's waiting for you when you get home?" I spit.

The flash of sadness that crosses her face makes me wish I could take my words back. But Matty recovers her sadness and gives as good as she gets.

"At least I didn't *sell* myself for the sake of a man who hung you out to dry."

I gasp in affront., "My grandfather did not—"

She leans in. her chin jutting upward. Her eyes blaze with anger has me taking a step back. "He *Hung*. You. Out. To. Dry. Just like you did us. For something that wasn't our fault."

"It was entirely. *Your*. Fault. You're *lucky* you didn't go to jail. My grandfather did his best for you." I stab a finger in her face.

She shoves it away and leans in, so we're almost nose to nose. "He did his best for his granddaughter and himself. And you can't see that he was involved because you were so *enamored* with him." she says in a voice deepened by anger.

I'm shocked by the way this escalated. I just want to get into bed. I dig deep to find enough restraint to be the bigger person.

"Listen, we're obviously never going to agree on this."

She steps away from me, her lips turning down in disgust. "Oh, one day, you'll find the courage to look at your family and yourself honestly. *Then* we'll agree. But until you prove yourself better than the men who hurt us, I don't think we have anything left to say."

This is it. After that awful fight we had last time we saw each other, I've still thought of Matty as my friend. But it's clear that was a hopeful delusion. It hurts to see that so clearly. There's nothing of the heartbreak I'm feeling in Matty's expression now. In fact, her eyes are completely unreadable.

I can't hide mine and I don't want to give her the satisfaction of seeing how much she's hurt me.

"Good luck, Matty. It was nice to see you. I hope you have a safe trip home." Then, for the second time, I turn away from the sister my heart chose. This time, I don't look back.

I walk into my suite and shut the door behind me. I press my back to it, draw in huge a lungful of air. I press my hands to my heated cheeks and pull them away in surprise.

I stare at the moisture on my fingers in confusion for a few minutes before I realize there's more running down my face.

I haven't cried since the night I found out my husband had made a mockery of my entire existence. Before that was five years prior when my grandfather died.

Nothing had ever hurt as much as those things had, not before or since. But to hear myself cast like that and to know that there were some truths laced in with the ugly accusations she made. My eyes fall on the small box that we brought Jack's ashes in. Oh my God, my best friend is dead and the other one might as well be.

My emotions, so long pushed down, ignored, smothered swirl inside of me like a thousand tornadoes looking for a way out. They are tearing me up inside, but I don't know how to free them.

The door to my suite opens and I spin around, wide eyed with fear that Marcel is here.

"Hey, I used my key…" Stone trails off in mid-sentence when he sees me. "What happened?" He glances over her shoulder and then moves into the suite, his eyes scanning the room.

I open my mouth, but nothing comes out. So, I reach out and in the space of two breaths, his warm hand is gripping mine.

"I've got you." He wraps a strong arm around my shoulders and pulls me into him. I nestle into the warm, clean smelling sanctuary of his chest and cling to him

"It's okay. Let it all out, and when you're done, I'll be here. You won't have to do it alone," Those words are an echo in time. So is the absolute comfort I feel letting my guard down with him.

I've never felt delicate—not once in my whole life—until this man made me his lover. He's strong enough for both of us. So safe in the harbor of his arms, I let the storm raging inside of me loose.

Chapter 17

COME WITH ME

STONE

Regan isn't crying. She is grieving. Her sobs are laments punctuated by hiccups, and sniffles. Her fingers clutch the front of my shirt. Her hot tears soak through the cotton, and she trembles like she's freezing.

I was sixteen when she got married. I hoped she'd be miserable. But, the man I am today hates to think that she has been. I'm glad I took the gamble and came up when I did.

I've never seen anyone pale as fast as she did when she heard that voice on the elevator speakers. She looked like her life had flashed in front of her eyes. She said she'd call me, but I knew she wouldn't.

If I was going to see her again, I'd have to make it happen. I went to the bar to weigh my options.

I'd be off on my road trip in the morning and would likely not see her again. But… she was so ready on the elevator. I could smell it on her. She wants me as much as I want her.

When I went to settle my tab, I found her keycard in my wallet. It felt like a sign.

I passed her friend in the hallway and the wrathful expression on her tear streaked face gave me pause. If Regan was as angry as her friend looked, then this would likely be a short visit.

I opened the door slowly, expecting to find Regan in a lather. Instead, she stood in the middle of the room, her eyes full of regret, her trembling mouth moving wordlessly. She looked like someone dropped a bomb on her.

I carried her to the couch and we've been sitting like this, with her in my lap crying like someone died.

Her crying subsides to soft sniffles. I run a light hand down her back and brave a question. "What happened?"

She sighs wearily, like the weight of the world is on her shoulders, "Matty and I had a fight. Nothing new,"

"Are you on vacation together?" I picked up on a touch of tension between them on the shuttle.

"We were here to spread our friend's ashes. We used to be close, and then…well, life happened, and we lost touch. But I hoped… it's not going to happen. And I'm sad. And tired."

She groans and sags against my chest. She gasps and leans away her wide eyes on my shirt.

"Oh for heaven's sake, I'm sorry. I've cried all over you. I'm…" With another groan, she jumps off my lap.

"No, hey, it's okay." I stand, but she mumbles stilted "excuse me," and rushes to the bathroom, and shuts the door with a slam.

I miss the warm weight of her in my lap, but I'm also glad for the chance to clear my head.

There's a reason our paths are crossing now. She's in need of someone; Like I was the night she found me in that bakery. The words she whispered that first day come back to me. *"I water you, you water me."*

A light comes on and excitement gets my brain back online. I can't do anything to bring her friend back or to mend her relationship with Matty.

But I can give her something happy to take back from this trip. I'll have to make a few changes to some of my plans and it will mean I'll have to forgo my annual howl at the moon.

But, if she's game, this might be even better than that. Having another shot with the girl who hung the moon was a pipe dream. Having the chance to do something to pay her back, something more than just fuck her senseless, is a moonshot. I can't pass up the chance to at least try.

The bathroom door opens and she strides out. "Sorry to keep you waiting." Her voice is cordial but her smile is tight with discomfort, and she doesn't meet my eye.

She cuts a brisk path to the mini bar. Her rigid back to me, she busies herself pouring drinks, but doesn't say a word.

"You okay?" I ask.

"Yeah," she says and turns to face me. Her eyes are clear and dry and the dark flush of emotion is gone, she looks like nothing happened. But her hand wobbles when she lifts one of the glasses she's holding to her lips and down the entire thing in one sip.

"What was that?" I wince at her pained cringe as the liquid made its way down.

"Tequila." She puts the empty glass down, grabs the bottle from the bar and walks over to sit next to me. She gulps half of the second glass and drops wearily onto the couch.

" I never cry," she sounds bemused.

I take the bottle of tequila and glass from her pour myself a shot and throw it back. The burn is good and bracing.

"I don't know what's wrong with me," she takes the glass back and I pour her another finger.

"Well, you've had a pretty shitty trip so far. Except for the parts you spent with me, of course." I grin when she sputters on her swallow. "How long are you here?" I ask.

"I'm leaving on Sunday."

Perfect.

"I'm leaving tomorrow," I announce.

She stills, her eyes widen with surprise and disappointment. Maybe it's not such a moonshot after all. "Oh, so soon?" She tries to sound casual and sits back on the couch, her hands gripped together on her lap.

"I'm going on an excursion for a few days."

"Oh, that's nice. To where?" She asks, her voice tinny with false cheer.

"A road trip to Isla Espiritu Santo. Stopping where we feel like between here and there."

She blinks, frowns. "We? You're *going* with someone?"

I nod. "With a woman friend."

Her eyebrows lift in surprise and then her expression shutters. "Well, Stone it was really nice to see you. Hope you brought enough condoms to last the rest of your trip." She gets up from the couch.

I grab her and yank her back down. "You're gorgeous when you're jealous." I lean forward to kiss her.

She shoves me away. "Are you out of your mind?" she growls, her dark brows furrowing and look like the wings of an avenging angel. Her eyes glitter like stars and her face is flushed with sun and emotion.

I smile, innocently. "Now that you've mentioned it, I don't think I have enough condoms. Do you know where I can get some around here?"

She gives me an acidic, contemptuous smile. "No, I don't, asshole." She yanks out of my grip.

I bite back a cackle and take hold of her arm again.

"What's wrong?" I ask, feigned confusion drawing my brows down.

She doesn't buy my act for one second and her lips curls in disgust. "I hope you and whoever you're taking with you get a flat tire in the middle of the desert and have to walk for miles while coyotes chase you. And, I hope your dick falls off."

I can't hold my laughter any longer. It's shitty of me to be so giddy about it. But I am. She's *jealous*. And I've teased her long enough.

"It would be a shame if that happened because we'd miss swimming with the dolphins, bungee jumping, me eating your pussy when the sun rises, fucking it while it sets…"

"Wait, what?" She stops squirming and puts two hands on my chest and shoves me away.

I grin at the skeptical suspicion on her face.

"Are you *teasing* me?" she asks, clearly affronted.

"Yes. Captain Obvious," I say.

She narrows her eyes and frowns in disapproval.

I drop a kiss on her sweet, puckered mouth. "You're coming with me. Unless you want to stay here, staring out at that amazing view, instead of becoming part of it."

I pull her into my arms, and she struggles, but when I nuzzle the soft skin of her neck with my nose, she melts a little before pulling away again.

"It'll be great." I press a kiss to her cheek, and she scowls.

"I haven't said yes." She stares at her linked hands resting in her lap.

"If you say no, you'll regret it as soon as I'm gone."

"Maybe, but I'm very adept at living with my regret," she says.

She needs the trip worse than I thought. And my attempts to cajole her aren't going to work, so I drop it and give it to her straight. "Listen, you have a lot going on. I'm not saying that I have the answers. But I think you need to really get away. Not just to bury your friend and lay around this boring resort. Let's have an adventure."

Her eyes dart to me and then back to her hands.

"It'll be fun." I nudge her, keeping my voice casual and free of the hope growing in my gut.

"When would we be back?" she asks. It's only tinged with tentative exuberance, but a smile curves the corners of her full mouth, and I have to stop myself from pumping my fist in the air.

"On Friday, when the rest of my family is due."

Her eyes bulge. "Your family? Like…your brothers? They're coming here?" Each sentence is louder than the one before it.

"Yeah. My brother's fiancée is throwing a surprise wedding here, and so, my whole family, except my mother, thank God, will be here on Friday."

She covers her face with her hands and groans into them.

I knew this was coming. "They'll be here Friday, and we'll be discreet. It'll be fine."

She moves her hands from her face and eyes me with a skeptical frown.

"So, let's say we do this. Then, what?"

"We go our separate ways," I answer with the obvious.

"And, what happens when you move back to Houston, and we run into each other, and I'm with my husband.

I envision the moment she's just referenced, and it makes me feel like my skin is too tight.

"It'll be fine," I say, ignoring the sensation.

She winces and looks away. Her shoulders hunch. "Maybe… we shouldn't have sex while we're away."

I shake my head in vigorous disagreement. "I think that is a terrible idea, and I'm sure your vagina would agree."

She doesn't smile. "I think we should be clear about what this is. I may or may not leave my husband. I don't want us to get confused… and, I would hate to hurt you, Stone. The way I did back then."

It pricks my ire to have this compared to that. "I'm not that boy either, I don't think I've got one foot in the grave, but relationships aren't my thing. I used to think you'd be mine—"

"You did?" She asks wide eyed with surprise.

"—when I was too young to know better." I finish.

"And now?"

"Now…" I turn my gaze away, caught off guard by the direct question. I run a hand through my hair while I pick my words carefully. "Now, there's some nostalgia for the past. But 99.5% of this is just a man who is insanely attracted to a woman who speaks his language in more ways than one. Your pussy feels great, tastes great too. I want more of it. But I'm not going to fall in love or anything... so, you don't have to worry that I'll stab your husband."

Her bark of laughter seems to surprise her as much as it surprises me. "I was thinking more like uncomfortable silences and dark glares."

"Not my style." I assure her.

Her lips twist. "Well, then let me speak for myself. I don't want to end up with *my* feelings fucked. Clearly, I'm not in the best place emotionally. Maybe…we should just play it by ear. See how we feel once we're all alone."

I couldn't disagree more, but I'm not going to pressure her about this.

"It'll be great, either way, and I'll take my cues from you." I say and I mean it. Maybe when this is over, we'll walk away friends again. At the very worst, she'll be excellent company. And I know that we don't need sex to connect.

From our time in the bakery and that shuttle ride, I *also* know that Regan will break all sorts of rules when she thinks no one is watching. And we're going to have plenty of alone time in the next few days.

"I was going to leave at 9, is that too early?" I ask.

She looks at me, her dark eyes twinkling, her smile wider than I've seen it since we've been here. "Right *now*, it wouldn't be too early." She declares and then jumps up.

"Oh my God," she screams suddenly and flops onto her back, clutching a pillow to her chest and kicking her legs wildly.

"Woah!" I lurch back in surprise when she pops back up in a flash of dark hair and gleaming white teeth.

"I'm so excited. I've never done anything like this. I can't believe it."

"It won't be luxurious like this. I don't even know where I'm staying in Balandra."

"But it'll be an adventure," her enthusiasm in unflagging.

"Do you speak Spanish?"

"A little?" She says with a nervous grin.

"Okay. Just don't buy anything without me haggling for you, okay?"

"Okay. So, we're going? Really?" Her expression is hopeful but tinged with fear. Like she's just been given the chance to have something she wants desperately and she's afraid to believe it. It's the most vulnerable I've ever seen her, and it takes my breath away.

In a flash of certainty, I know that I'd move heaven and earth before I let that hope on her face do anything *but* flourish.

"Yes, really. It'll be fun at the very worst and at it's very best, it will be life-changing," I say.

She laughs and rolls her eyes. "I'll be happy if it's not a total disaster and I come home with all of my limbs intact."

"Oh, then you're going to be ecstatic. Because you're going to learn things about yourself you can't know until you go to a place you've never been before."

"Wow. You're really good at selling the idea of travel."

"I'm an evangelist for it."

She starts to dance around

Maybe living in Houston won't be so bad. Especially if we can find a way to keep this going.

No. I can't let myself start thinking like that. When I move back to Houston, it won't matter. There, she's so off limits, it's not even funny.

No, what happens here is going to stay here.

But as I watch Regan Wilde's sexy ass twirl around her hotel room with that horizon at her back, I get a glimpse of another unknowable destination—one where my future and my past collide, and then click into place.

Chapter 18

SOCIAL BUTTERFLY

REGAN

"We're here," A warm hand on my shoulder jostles me out of the most delicious nap I can recall taking. It takes me a moment to remember where I am. I glance over at Stone and the tender smile on his face makes my toes curl.

I stretch and glance around at the collection of beautifully preserved buildings and the bright colors of the flags that adorn the main street we're parked on.

"Where are we?"

"Todos Santos, I thought we could stop and grab coffee and take a picture outside Hotel California."

"Like the Eagles Song?"

"Yeah, but the Eagles swear it's not. Wait there." He hops out of the car and I take the opportunity to admire his loose, ground eating stride as he comes around the front of the car to my side.

He opens my door with a bow and offers me his hand and murmurs, "Goddess."

"You're silly," I giggle and let him help me climb out. He twines our fingers together as we walk down the street toward a cluster of restaurants. And, I don't mind one bit. I haven't held hands with anyone but my children in decades. I forgot how intimate it is. Even though I just rediscovered him two days ago, it feels just as comfortable and easy as it did all those years ago.

We left just after sunrise and I didn't even ask where we were going. I found I didn't care. I trust him. And I want this experience, with all the handholding, beautiful views, and unscripted stops it comes with.

I breathe in deep and catch the salt of the ocean and the sweet of the flowers and the spice of the aromas floating out of the restaurants, and my empty stomach grumbles.

Todos Santos is one of Mexico's most popular destinations. And not because of the hotel. It's home to the burgeoning artist community who have come to set up shop and make a name for themselves.

"This place is gorgeous. Can we eat and hang out for a bit?" I ask.

Stone lets go of my hand, to sling an arm over my shoulder and pulls me close to his side. "We can do anything we fucking want," he drawls.

And we do.

We sit and check Trip Advisor and decide on a place called Art and Beer for breakfast. It's a quaint little outpost that can't decide whether it wants to be an art gallery or bar and so has decided to be both. The chalkboard menus boasted everything from shellfish appetizers to whole lobster. We sat out on the reed covered deck that overlooked the spectacular wild blue of the Sea of Cortez.

In all that time, we barely said a word. Normally, I'd feel compelled to fill silences with small talk. But as always, nothing with Stone is as it normally is. I thought the lack of structure in our plans would make me nervous. It hasn't.

I'm more relaxed than I can remember being. Ever.

When we were just kids, and our relationship was based on a very different kind of feeling, we spoke a language that didn't have words. It was accented by a mutual enjoyment of food, music, and trust. Now, I can add adventure, desire and safety to things we can share without saying a word.

When we're done eating, we walk out to an outdoor market set up on a narrow cobblestone street. It's lined by vine covered haciendas that had been converted to tiny artisan shops. And they're filled with glorious creations I wish my children were here to see.

Stone is a social butterfly He smiles at and greets nearly everyone we pass. He asks so many questions about everything, then plays devil's advocate with the answers. When we stopped at an art gallery, he drew one of the other patrons into a boisterous argument about the influence of 20th century Mexican muralists on the Chicano Mural Movement in the United States. At one point the man looked like he wanted to drop kick Stone, but the conversation ended in a fit of uproarious laughter and they parted ways after exchanging hearty slaps on the back.

He kept pausing to translate for me, until I told him that I was enjoying just watching the body language and facial expressions. He's as animated, curious, and mischievous as he'd been as a boy, but he's got all the grace and athleticism of a man who pushes his body's limits and takes a genuine interest in people. He's a joy to watch.

We sit to watch a group of old women, their heads covered in black kerchiefs play a wickedly competitive card game he said was called Conquian. Stone leans in and whispers in the ear of the woman closest to him.

He's been watching her hand from over her shoulder and whatever he says makes her eyes light up. She's grinning when she puts her cards down, drawing groans from her friends. She and Stone share a high five. And they all kiss his cheeks when he tells them we're leaving

"How do you know how to play that game?" I ask we walk on, still hand in hand.

"One of the other fellows in my program is Mexican, he taught me on the flight down.

"And of course, you mastered it instantly," I swing our joined hands and smile up at him.

Suddenly, he presses me against a wall, cups my face and kisses me long and sweet

"I used to dream about kissing you whenever I wanted," he murmurs.

My heart hammers, wild with the thrill of this reckless, spontaneous passion. "Then do it," I breathe and wind my hands around his neck. He presses open-mouthed kisses on my chin, my cheeks, my jaw, my ear, my neck, my eyes.

And I revel in it. The Regan he knew is long gone, but he makes me remember and miss her. More than I have in a very long time. Maybe while we're here, I can pretend that I'm her, still.

His lips come back to mine and he cups my ass and grinds his hips against mine. "I want to fuck you right here. Right now, Regan. Can you feel how *badly* I want to?"

A loud burst of laughter from an approaching group of tourists pierces our bubble. He casts them an annoyed glance, presses one more hard kiss to my mouth and whispers, "later".

We walk hand in hand, but I swear my feet never touch the ground and neither does my soul. The city is beautiful, the weather is amazing, and there's contentment welling in my chest, tickling me, stretching my heart, healing it, too.

I glance over at Stone as we walk along and marvel that this man is *that* same little boy. From the chiseled, stubble covered jaw, to the sleek, bold lines of his high cheekbones, and the strong slope of his aquiline nose, he's a walking work of art.

But the thing I've enjoyed most is seeing him interact with other people and watching all that intellect and charm converge. He doesn't seem to realize how everyone falls in love with him. Because he's too busy enjoying the moment

He turns his head and I wish I could see what's behind the reflective lens of his aviator sunglasses, but the sensual smile on curving his lips is one of pure, male satisfaction.

"Let's have lunch, I'm starving." He says more than asks, and I find I don't mind one bit. I'm like a kite being carried on the wind, without a care in the world because Stone Rivers—strong, kind, and daring—is my tether.

We pick a place called La Molina based on reviews on TripAdvisor… "This is even prettier than the pictures, right?" I remark as we're shown to a table in their courtyard that looks like something out of a fairytale. Lush green plants bursting with huge colorful blooms fill the space. And rustic wooden tables canopied to shield us from the afternoon sun are arranged so that you can spread out. We order fresh shrimp ceviche, octopus carpaccio and pork ribs and settle on a pitcher of their house mojito.

"So, tell me Stone, what have you done for the last eighteen years," I ask as soon as the waitress is done flirting with him and leaves.

"Gosh, how strange that I haven't once mentioned what I consider the biggest part of my life. I'm a doctor. An obstetrician gynecologist, but lately, I've been focused almost solely on obstetrics. I'm finishing up my final year in fellowship in Global Maternal Health in Colombia."

My eyes bug out of my head. "You're a doctor, on top of everything else? How are you single?" I quip and he laughs. He leans back in his seat, letting the sunbathe his face, and links his hands behind his head.

"I'm actually only recently single. But it wasn't serious. And I haven't seen her in almost a year."

It's irrational to be jealous of someone who's name I don't know. Especially when this man isn't ever going to be mine. But, I am. Fiercely.

"I was almost fifteen when I finished Blackwell. I enrolled at U of H for both undergrad—where I met Tyson, incidentally," he winks. "And then medical school. I was twenty—two when I graduated. And by then, my brothers were old enough to move with me to New York, where I was doing my residency. I was there for four years. I got this fellowship with Baylor and this is my last year."

"And after that?" I am blown away by how casual he is about all of the incredible things he's done.

"I have an offer for a position at Baylor College of Medicine as Associate Professor. I'm excited. It's kind of my dream job, but you'd think I was applying for the secret service or something."

"So, you're moving to Houston?" I ask, as casually as I can. Our waitress brings a pitcher and two highballs already full of mojitos and I drink half of mine down in one gulp.

"Yeah, in Houston and so, when I'm done in Colombia in about six months, I'll be back in good old H-town."

"Wow."

"So, what about you? I know you got married, but like I know nothing really more than that. What happened after I left that bakery? And that guy I stabbed? You ever seen him again?"

I choke on my drink.

Chapter 19

I REMEMBER EVERYTHING

STONE

I stand to whack her on the back, and she holds a hand up to stop me. She clears her throat and pulls her sunglasses off to wipe her tearing eyes.

"Are you okay?" I ask when she finally takes a deep breath.

"Yeah, something went down the wrong way," she says, and I frown because she only sipped that mojito, but let it go. I rushed through my retelling of the last eighteen years. Left out details that I'd rather forget. But she looked like a deer who'd heard the cock a hunter's rifle when I asked her the same question.

"So, tell me."

"Not much to tell, really." She rests her elbow on the table and leans forward to rest her chin on her linked hands. She turns her gaze skyward and presses her lips together in a thin pensive mien.

In the light of the late morning, with no make-up on, her mass of inky curls and coils piled on her head, I could be looking back in time. Time hasn't touched her. The spray of freckles on her cheek, the soft dusky pink center of her perfect cupid's bow mouth, the way she sways while she's thinking—it's all the same. And yet also brand new and exhilarating.

She's got on this little white camisole and tiny red shorts that I've been imagining pulling off with my teeth.

"Well, I went to SMU, got a degree in journalism, and went to work for Wilde World's communications department. And then, I got married. And that was kind of the end of my career because I had my daughter right away and we moved to France right after. I moved back home five years ago because honestly, I hated living in Paris. I hate that everywhere we went people thought I was my children's nanny. Someone even asked me "where I got them," once. Oh, and my husband had a new mistress every so often, she'd come to dinner with her husband. I got tired of all that shit and left." She picks at a half-eaten tortilla, and shrugs like she's telling me about her sewing circle. "Now, I'm basically a single parent and an unofficial brand ambassador for Landel Corp and Wilde World, and that's about it."

I take a sip of my beer to hide my frown. Clearly that was the Cliff's Notes version. I don't press for details she doesn't want to give, but I ask questions that I really want answers to.

"So, besides your kids, what are you most proud of in the last eighteen years?"

"The Jezebel," she says quickly and unequivocally.

"Like the tattoo, the one of your lower back?" Heat floods me as the memory of my hand running over it while I fucked her.

She narrows her gaze, but not in annoyance and her smile is wistful. "Yes, we all had one." She shakes her head as if to clear it and her eyes brighten. "And, The Jezebel is a blog we named after the Biblical woman."

"She was a prostitute, or something? Or... not?" I amend when her smile turns to a scowl.

"She most certainly was *not*," she lays a hand over her chest and leans away, as if in personal affront. The look on her face that makes me feel like this is some essential knowledge that I should have learned along with my ABC's.

"So, who was she and why did I think she was a prostitute?" I ask and her face lights up as if she's been waiting to be asked this her whole life.

"Jezebel was the daughter of a Phoenician king. Then, when she married, she became a Queen in her own right. She was a highly effective ruler and she and her husband ruled co equally. The story of her is framed as one about religious intolerance. But really, it was that she dared to be as ruthless and cunning as the men of her time. And for that she has been branded by history as an immoral, wily, seductress who got men to do her sinful and wicked bidding by fucking them into a stupor."

I nod, not surprised to hear that. "Well, The Bible was written by and for a long time, only for men to read. They got the first crack at interpretation. So, that sounds about right."

Regan gives me a grin that borders on giddy. "It's been a while since I've had this conversation with anyone, But I usually get more pushback than that."

"So, what is The Jezebel?"

The twinkle in her eye dims. "A blog I ran with Matty and Jack. A piece of Jezebel was what brought us together. We were all studying journalism and were fascinated by how history treats women. Walk around any major city. Nearly all the historical statues are of men. History only mentions that can't be ignored, Jezebel, Joan of Arc, Yaa Asantewaa, Boudica, Margaret Thatcher, Benazir Bhutto... They were leaders of countries, or armies, or their people's hearts. But there are so many more women whose contributions and accomplishments are completely ignored. The three of us wanted to tell their stories. We paid homage to who's contributions, leadership, sacrifices had excluded, erased and misappropriated. It was the best thing I've done." The passion in her voice is discordant with the sadness in her eyes.

"Why'd you stop?"

She shrugs, sighs and smiles. "Career, life, my children." Her eyes gleam at the mention of her kids. "What are their names?" I ask and surprise myself. But whatever makes her look like that is something I want to know more about.

"Evangeline is my daughter and my oldest, she's ten going on twenty. And my twins, Martinez and Henri are five. They're wonderful and so different from each other, but very close. Martinez only speaks French, which drives a lot of people crazy."

How lucky they are to be loved by her.

She pulls her phone out of her little bag and scrolls through before she hands it over to me. "Here, this is a selfie we took the night before I left."

Her daughter is her spitting image, but with hair the color of nutmeg and eyes that glimmer like honey colored gems. Her boys are dark haired with the same cherubic smiles as their Uncle Tyson wears. Their eyes are a startling blue. And I want to ask if those are her husband's eyes…but I don't really want to know.

"They're gorgeous," I say and hand the phone back. She flushes with pride, and nods. "And so *smart* and incredibly determined. I'm so proud of them." She puts her phone away and leans back to stare at the sky in wonder.

I grab my beer and do the same. I can't believe I'm here. With the woman who made me wish I could bend time so that she could be mine.

But I realize that I never really expected it to happen. Now that it has, it feels like we've been leading up to this forever. I couldn't imagine a more perfect day.

I take a swig of my beer. The ocean breeze is cool and constant. The waves slap, crack, and crash just feet away. In front of me, is the woman of my dreams. And she's turning out to be so much more than I even imagined.

Chapter 20

A CULT

REGAN

"You full?" Stone asks, his smile wistful as he reaches between us and slips an arm over my shoulder and pulls me into his side. It's so natural that my arm winds up around his waist before I think about it.

He smells like heaven—wind, smoke, sun, salt, and man.

He parked the car under a tree to try and keep it from turning into an oven, but when we open the doors, waves of trapped heat escape.

"God don't close the doors until we roll the windows down," I groan when the bare skin of my thighs and lower back touch the blazing hot seat and stick uncomfortably to the leather. He cranks the A/C down to the coldest temperature and up to the highest speed, but the few minutes I roll the window down a crack as we pull back onto the freeway.

"You haven't even asked where we're going next," Stone says.

"I don't care. As long as I've never been there, I want to go," I say lazily as the breeze blows and starts to dry the hair that was sticking to my neck. It feels so good…

That's the last thing I remember thinking before my ringing phone wakes me up.

"Your phone has been ringing for a while," Stone says, shouting to be heard over the wind and road noise the open windows are letting in.

"Oh shit," I say. My mouth is dry and has a sour taste. And my head hurts.

I fumble on the ground for my bag and pull my phone out. The ringing had been muffled by the leather in my bag, but the volume is ear splitting and I curse my uncoordinated fingers when I drop it.

It stops ringing before I can pick it up from the seat between my thighs where it fell. I flip it over and see my mother's number. My heart drops.

I roll the windows up and grab for my phone, my heart hammering as I press "call back" on the missed call notification.

My mother answers on the first ring. "I was just leaving you a voice-mail. Why does Evangeline have her own phone?" She asks in her no nonsense, direct way.

"So that we can reach her when we need to. Marcel's idea," I add because I know that always shuts her up.

Stone's fingers drum the steering wheel, just once

"What's up, Mom? Is everything okay? Have you heard from Remi?" I ask cutting to the chase.

"No. And that Rivers woman who saw him last won't say what it was all about. Anyway, your husband just called, and he says you're not answering your phone." My stomach lurches at the mention of Marcel's name.

"I have bad reception," I lie and cut her off. I can't deal with her right now.

"Everything okay?" He asks.

"Yeah, everything is fine. My mother doesn't have my brother to boss around, so she's turned her attention on me," I say and then feel a surge of guilt at how ungracious I'm being.

My mother is a lot of things, some I don't understand or like. She and my brother Remi have been at each other's throats for as long as I can remember. She and I not so much because I pick my battles and the ones she's waged against me haven't been worth it. She's cold, detached, and she finds disobedience intolerable. But she's a great grandmother and my children love her. And if I didn't have someone who I knew loved them back, I wouldn't have been able to make this trip.

I sigh wearily and correct myself. "No, I didn't mean that. I called my daughter and I didn't call Mom, and she doesn't like that. But everything is fine," I say and pat Stone's leg before I put my phone away and turn back to watch the dessert zip by.

"Hey, I thought we were headed away from Cabo," I say when I see a sign that gives our distance from the city. I sit up and frown, a flare of worry that this adventure is already over.

"We will. I changed our itinerary again," he says cryptically, and it eases some of my concern, but I want to be as far away from anywhere that people might know us.

"Where are we going instead?" I peer out the window. Not that I would know this from any other part of the Baja Peninsula, but I suddenly don't feel so blasé about not knowing what's next.

"Thought you didn't care," he says with a laugh, but his vague and cryptic answers do more to ratchet up my nerves than anything else.

"Yes, I know that. Obviously, since I said it. I don't need you to remind me. I've changed my mind, and now I want to know." I sit up straight. We turn off the road at a sign that reads Wild Canyon.

"What is this place?" I ask, reaching for my phone so I can google it.

"I was going to stop here on our way back, but I thought it would be the perfect way to kick off this adventure. I'm about to show you how easy it is to let go."

Chapter 21

TRANSFORMED

REGAN

"Your guts turned to water yet?" Stone squeezes my hand and I glance over at him to find him grinning wildly. I grip the metal side of the small basket that's currently transporting us several hundred feet above a canyon in the middle of the desert. I have never been more scared in my life. I'm nearly paralyzed by fear. But Stone's grin and the delight in his eyes snaps me out of it.

"Don't fuck with me Stone. I'm really scared. If I shit my pants up here, I'll never speak to you again." I warn him.

"If you shit your pants, I'm not sure I'd mind a little distance."

I slap at his arm and then scream when my movement sends the basket swinging.

"You're safe, I swear," he says. I just stare straight ahead at the gondola that's perched on wire over the yawning mouth of the seemingly bottomless valley and suddenly I feel sick. To my stomach.

"This is a mistake. This thing is a death trap, Stone. And so is that." I point at the gondola parked on the cable ahead of us. The one we're supposed to bungee from. It looks like a perfectly sturdy gondola but, this high up, there's no such thing as safe. There's only lucky, or dead. I squeeze my eyes shut and wrap my arms around myself as tightly as I can. My breaths come fast, but I can't seem to get enough air. "Did I actually agree to this? I would never do anything so reckless. I must have been in a trance.?"

He laughs but puts his hands on my shoulders and massages them. "Take a deep breath, Goddess. And then look at me."

"I'm afraid," I whisper, my eyes still closed tight.

"Look at me," he repeats and squeezes my shoulders. I turn my head to the left before I open them. He's looking at me with a tenderness, so fierce and vast that it makes me want to cry.

"This is your biggest fear, right? Dying young? It used to be mine, too. Until I met a giver who watered me, so I grew into a person who was more afraid of not living than I was of dying."

"Who was that dumbass?" I grumble. He chuckles and shakes his head at me, but his smile is like a break in the clouds and takes the edge off my anxiety. "You said you wanted an adventure. Well, here it is. Or was that just talk?"

"No, I just didn't realize I'd be jumping to my death today. I mean,"

"And just imagine what it's going to feel like to do it, and not die. What could you possibly be afraid after that?"

That resonates. I want that back—that fearlessness that was innate to me once.

As if he read my mind, Stone hugs me and presses his lips to the top of my head. I look up to ask him This time when my stomach lurches, it's not fear that it's reacting to. I forget that I'm about to throw myself out of this gondola with nothing but a rope tied to my ankle.

Because even surrounded by all of this beauty and all of this danger, none of it is as compelling as him. His adventurous spirit is contagious and he's so damn gorgeous.

But he's also really annoyingly relaxed.

"Aren't you scared?" I ask him.

"Hell yeah," he answers with a nervous smile. "But I also know my fear is unfounded. I have more to fear getting on the plane back to Colombia than I do bungee jumping. Besides, I've done it before and it's the closest I've ever come to flying, the closest I've ever been to the sky. It's transformative."

His smile radiates excitement and confidence and I find myself smiling back.

"Okay, I'll follow you."

"Good girl, one step at a time," he says and then turns toward the gondola. I give an apologetic smile to the guide who brought us out, "Sorry for the hysterics."

He waves it off and gives me a thumbs up. "You did good, I've had people start speaking in tongues and shit." I laugh at the visual and use that moment of levity to force myself to step onto the gondola.

It's even worse than I thought it would be. Windowless and glass bottomed with a six-inch-wide opening that divides into two separate compartments, it offers no refuge from the view of the surrounding expanse. My fear takes a backseat to my awe at the wild blue yonder above and the craggy faced valley that surrounds us. It's like being at the top of the world. I can see all the way to the Sea of Cortez and the horizon has never been so far away; it really does look like the edge of the world.

I peer over the side just as Stone says, "Don't look down."

It's too late and I get a glimpse of the 300-foot drop. I yelp and slam my eyes shut and try to catch my breath but all I see behind my closed lids is the seemingly bottomless drop to the river below. There's absolutely nothing between me and the canyon floor.

"Fuck, fuck, fuck," I mutter, and turn away and head back to the cable car. My trajectory is stalled by a pair of warm hands cuffing my forearms in a comforting but firm grip.

"Hey," his voice is deep and melodious, but my nerves are skittish, and I just want to get off.

"It's dangerous," I offer my feeble explanation to the dark grey cotton stretched across his chest. I can't meet his eyes. I'm afraid of the disappointment I might see there. It's clear that he's a born adventurer who only needed a small push to discover that. And here I am, having another meltdown.

Stone leans down and presses his lips to my ear. "You do not have to jump if you don't want to. I won't give you shit if you change your mind. You aren't a coward if you don't. If I had any doubt that this wasn't safe, I wouldn't have brought you. And this is your chance to rewrite your own history. Prove that the story you've been telling yourself about what you're capable of, is incomplete. Fear doesn't rule you, Regan." I lift my gaze to his.

His eyes are a calming swirl of molten dark earthy brown, flecked with gold that have a look of such certainty in them that even before he starts speaking, my anxiety slows down. I'm safe.

"If I die, I'll haunt you."

He laughs. "I'll hold you to it." He grabs me by the shoulders and turns me around to face the door again.

I'm actually going to do this. Buoyed by the first real flare of exhilaration I've felt since we got in the Gondola to ride up, I walk over and get strapped up.

The patient instructor makes quick work of putting me in my harnesses and binding my ankles. He shows me all of the safety protocols and explains each of the ropes, and clasps as he fastens them. "No one will push you and you can't just fall out; you have to jump."

"Leap of faith, Goddess," Stone calls, clapping like a sports fan getting worked up as his team takes the field.

I turn around, press my fingers to my lips and raise them in the air in a salute of solidarity and a wish for good luck. Stone lifts his hand, palm open. "I'm pretending you blew me a kiss." He mimes catching it and pressing the closed fist to his chest.

I burst out laughing. The door creaks open and I know it's time. But when I turn to face them, it's giddiness, not fear, causing a riot in my heart.

"You're all set. Don't close your eyes on the way down. The view is part of the experience," the instructor says as I line my toes up to the edge of the door.

I've been so afraid of dying, of failing, of being alone that I haven't taken a risk in ten years. While I was busy being careful, the whole world has passed me by. This feels like making up for it all at once.

The countdown begins, and I clear my mind. When they get to 1, I launch myself off the gondola, and the whole world rushes up to embrace me. *Is this what it's like for newborn babies taking their first breaths?*

The thumping pulse of my steadily increasing heart rate becomes one with the wild symphony of rushing water, bird calls, and the roaring wind. I fall and fall; it's a smooth weightless plummet. And yet, I could swear I'm flying.

And then, it's over. I bounce a few times as the cord loses velocity. I stretch my arms wide, letting the breeze rush through my splayed fingers, as I take in the swaying palm trees, the lazy lapping river, and the seemingly endless stretch of stone that I'll remember as the place of my rebirth.

I close my eyes on the way up and savor the exhilarating fullness of triumph. I've only had a glimpse of the glory waiting for me on the other side of my fear, and I'm already ravenous for more. The rush of pure adrenaline is instantly addicting. I want to do this all day so I can hold onto the euphoria and pride, I'm feeling. Stone was right. If I can do this, I can do anything. Including divorcing my terrible husband.

The sample-sized bites of happiness I've survived on won't satisfy this new hunger.

I want everything.

Now.

Starting with Stone.

The instructors pull me back on to the gondola and give me a round of high fives as I crest the opening. Two of the crew members help me climb back on and for a minute, I just sit, catching my breath.

"Come on, let's get that off," Stone's big hand cup my elbows and he helps me to my feet. As soon as my legs touch the glass bottom gondola surface, they tremble and send me swaying. Stone's grip tightens on my arm and holds me steady. "Woah, got you," he murmurs in my ear. One of the guides drops to his knees and starts to loosen my harness and Stone and I exchange a grin.

"You made that look easy. And I know it's not. I've done this twice before, and it gets easier. But my first time I almost bailed. And it wasn't anything as badass as jumping from a gondola. You were afraid and you did it anyway." He strokes my arms with his thumbs, his eyes telling me before he mouths. "Proud of you, Regan."

My smile, so wide my cheeks hurt, it's the highest praise anyone could give me. "Me, too," is all I can manage. I'm tongue tied under the weight of his praise and don't know what to say.

But when he asks, "How do you feel?"

I find my voice instantly. "Transformed."

Chapter 22

JEALOUS

STONE

"Come dance with me, Stone," Regan calls from the dance floor, her smile brighter than all of the oil lamps burning around our camp.

"No, go ahead. I like watching," I force a grin and she pouts. I hold the smile in place until one in the seemingly endless stream of geriatric men who are our fellow campers grabs her by the waist and whirls her around to her irritating shriek of delight.

I force myself to watch him, twirl and fucking dip her. It's punishment and conditioning exercise all at once.

I thought I was doing *her* a favor today.

I thought it would be fun to coax her into my bed tonight. That I'd had this wild fantasy with the woman of my dreams and go back to life as I knew it.

Then, I jumped off that gondola.

As I've done every time I've bungeed, I focused on one thing I want more than anything else as I stood at the ledge. The thing that I'm going to never take for granted again if I survive. Because, no matter what I said to Regan, I know that anything could happen. Not just here, but anywhere. I've seen babies go from looking perfectly healthy to being dead in minutes. I don't take anything for granted.

The first time I bungeed I thought of my brothers. I'd been slacking on calling them regularly and vowed to remedy that. The second time, it was my fellowship.

Today, I expected my thoughts to be focused on the job I'm waiting to get a confirmed start date for. This wasn't just the culmination of years of sacrifice and hard work. This job, and the prestige attached to it, will also go a long way to proving myself worthy of my stepfather's priceless gift—the last name he gave us when he adopted Dare, Beau, and me. He also left us each a small fortune in annuitized trusts and college tuition funds.

I've only touched that money to pay for school and to put a roof over my head. But until I could be a credit to his name, I lived on what I earned. This job is my chance to make him proud and to show that we were worthy of his gift. That I'm nothing like my mother.

But as I stood at the open door, poised to jump, all I could think about was her. I plummeted down thinking that if I didn't get to hold her hand all day again, kiss her in an alley again, bury myself inside her again, that I might as well die now.

I rode back up to the gondola, exhilarated by the knowledge I had her all to myself for the next few days. And when they pulled me back inside, I pounced; kissing her until we both couldn't breathe. Any reservations she'd had before we came seemed to be gone. She kissed me as ardently as I kissed her. On the two-hour drive to Balandra, she spread her thighs so I could finger her while I drove. I leaned back when she lowered her head to my lap to suck me off. We held hands like our lives depended on it.

But, by the time we were walking down the pier to catch the boat that would take us from La Paz to the Island Isla Espiritu Santo, reality started dropping reminders.

We were halfway to the boat when we heard a woman's panicked voice calling out "Regan!" over and over from the dock. She dropped my hand like it was on fire. And we turned toward the shout. It was coming from a woman standing by the food stalls on the dock. Regan watched her, eyes wide with fear, until a little girl broke through the throng of people and ran into her anxious mother's arms.

We laughed in relief, but we didn't hold hands while we walked the rest of the way. She sat on my lap for the short ride over. With the wind whipping our faces as we flew through the water, and her warm body burrowing into mine, I started to relax and think about all the ways I'd have her tonight.

Then our boat captain started singing a song I'd never heard before, and she said, "That's Marcel's favorite song."

That brought reality back into focus in a way that I didn't like.

A lot has changed in the time since we last saw each other. But one thing is as true as it was when I was ten—no matter how much I want her; Regan Wilde isn't mine to have.

By the time we got to our tent, all I could think about was the way she'd looked on her knees the night I stabbed that asshole.

It's not that I don't know if she wants me. She's been giving me come-hither looks all night. But I think she's still buzzing on the adrenaline from her jump and those looks aren't enough to convince me that she wants me as much as I want her. It's self-preservation more than pride. It's going to make me crazy if I walk away from this wondering if she wasn't just rolling with it. I don't just need her to say it. I need her to initiate it.

"Excuse me, sir," A soft hand lands on my bare shoulder. I turn and look up into the smiling, but anxious face of a young woman. "I'm so sorry to bother you, but my sister and I are having some trouble with our tent flaps." She trails off, biting her lip and watching me with expectant eyes

"Okay, did you ask the Jorgens for help?" I ask in as patient of a voice as I can manage when she doesn't say anything else. The camp is staffed with a husband and wife team who are supposed to be available twenty-four seven.

"We can't find them. And... you're the only other person not dancing," she grimaces in apology. I glance around and give a groan of self-loathing when I realize she's right.

"You look so upset, I hated to bother you—" she begins again. I stand up, shake off my self-pity and smile in apology.

"You're not bothering me and I'm happy to help." I stand, relieved to have a reason to end my self-flagellation. "Give me a second," I say and jog out to where Regan is holding court on the dance floor.

I tap one of her shimmying shoulders and she turns around, a wide grin already on her face. Delighted surprise brightens her eyes when she sees me, and she flings her arms around my neck. "You came," she croons. Her soft body is warm and slightly damp from sweat.

"This is so much fun, I've made all these new friends and I'm so happy." She squeals and tries to draw me into a dance. If I hadn't been beside her at dinner, I'd swear she was drunk.

I pull her hands loose and hate myself a little when her smile dims. I glance back in the direction I came from. The young woman's watching us with a fretful expression. I hold up a finger to signal that I'd be right there.

"Who's that?" Regan's voice has lost all of its glee and her eyes are narrowed in suspicion and trained over my shoulder.

"I don't know her name. She needs help with her tent."

One of her dark arched brows lifts in question and she turns her gaze back to me. "Isn't that what that couple's for?" She crosses her arms and taps her foot.

"She can't find them. I'm going to help."

"Well, that's nice of you I'll see you back at the tent, then?"

I frown at the tight smile she gives me. "It won't take that long. I'll be back."

"Why?" She is still smiling but her eyes broadcast her irritation.

"For you," I say, biting Captain Obvious on the tip of my tongue back.

"Don't bother, you're not interested in dancing and that's all I want to do. I'll see you at the tent."

She dismisses me with a shout of "*Muevolo!*" before she twirls away from me. A loud cheer erupts from the gaggle of men she's got in her thrall and the sound grates on my nerves like sandpaper. I don't give a shit if they're all old enough to be her father, I want to break every single one of their jaws.

I debate throwing her over my shoulder and carrying her to the tent, and using my mouth on her until she's begging me to fuck her

But I'm not going to make a fool of myself for her again. Each step costs me a sliver of sanity, but I leave walk away without looking back.

I follow the girl, who introduces herself as Riley, to her private campground, which happens to be the one right before ours. She talks the whole way, she and her sister flew to Cabo from Silver Spring, Maryland and are on a road trip that'll take them all the way back home.

It takes less than five minutes to help them fix their tent flap and when Riley invites me to stay for a shot of the tequila she and her sister bought from some place that's supposed to be legendary, I don't say no.

Her sister is starting medical school in the fall and when I tell her I'm in the middle of my fellowship, she peppers me with questions I'm happy to answer.

By the time I leave their tent to make the short walk to our tent., it's almost midnight. I've had enough tequila that I'm in a good mood again.

The light glow from inside alerts me to Regan's presence. A flash of memory from the glimpse I had of her—teeth flashing, hair flying like a flock of ribbons, her hand in someone else's - eviscerates my tequila induced enthusiasm. Uncertainty sends my nerves skittering, and I hold my breath as I pull back the flap and peek inside.

She's laying on one of the plushily dressed twin sized beds in our tent. Her legs are crossed at the ankles and propped on a stack of the blue throw pillows. I stare at the bare soles of her slim feet. They're the only part of her body I've never seen and just like the rest of her, I find them remarkably well formed. A dusting of white sand clings to her heels and toes, but her high delicate arches are clean and smooth.

I walk to stand next to her. My eyes trace the outline of her long legs under the clinging floral-patterned fabric of her dress, the curve of her hips, the delicate, ringless hands that rest on her flat stomach, the swell of her breasts, the small dark mole that sits in the hollow of her left collarbone calls my name.

I bite my lip to hold back a groan and reach down to turn off the small solar lamp on the table beside her bed.

"Don't." Her hand covers mine, and I nearly jump out of my skin.

"Shit. I thought you were asleep." I say, dumbly.

"I bet you did." Her voice is flat, and she studiously avoids meeting my eyes.

"Are you okay?" I ask, taking a step back to avoid being whacked by her legs as she swings them over the side of the bed.

"I'm going to take shower," she announces. Without any warning, she pulls her dress straps down and tugs it off her body. She's completely naked underneath it.

I think about all of those old men who touched her tonight, and see red.

"Were you like this… all night?" I ask, my voice tight with irritation.

"Yup," she chirps and then bends over to rifle in her bag giving me a full view of her naked ass and the lush dusky flesh between her legs.

"Regan, *what* are you doing?" I growl.

She stands with her light pink silk robe in one hand a bemused frown on her face. "Oh, I figured since you'd seen it all before you wouldn't mind. Sorry." Her voice is clipped with irritation. She slips the robe on strides toward the front of the tent.

"Regan—"

"Don't wait up," she calls just before she disappears through the flaps.

I sit on my bed, feeling like I just got hit in the head with a two by four. What the hell just happened and why the hell is she mad at me?

A few seconds later, the sun shower that's right to our tent comes on. For five torturous minutes, I listen to the sounds of water splashing and imagine her hands moving over all the places I want to touch.

When the shower cuts off, I pick up my book and pretend to read. When she walks back into the tent, I manage a casual, "How was the water?"

"Hot," she sighs with deep satisfaction and it takes all my willpower not to look at her. The flutter of fabric my periphery draws my gaze to her. But I keep my eyes on the floor where her discarded towel lies in a sodden heap at her feet.

Only when she turns so I'm looking at her heels instead of her pretty pink-painted toes, do I let my gaze roam up.

Her pink silk robe is belted tightly around her body. Before I can appreciate the way it hugs her still wet skin, she loosens the belt and shrugs it off. It slides down her lean, graceful back in a torturously slow unveiling of her delectable figure.

It molds to the curve of her hips and ass, right below then the twin dimples at the base of her spine and the tattoo that sits in between them. It hangs there for a few seconds before gravity flexes its muscle and the rest of her body is revealed.

When she bends over to pick up a bottle of lotion from her bed, I want to howl from the effort it's taking not to reach for her.

And, as addled as my brain may be, I know better than to even try it. So, I close my eyes.

But it's no good. The scent of lemon fills the tent. The whisper of her hands sliding over her bare skin only makes the torrid images in my mind more vivid. I imagine her fingers gliding over her jutting dark nipples, cupping her supple round breasts, sliding between her thighs, running over her shoulders, smoothing the rest of the lotion over the curve of her neck… By the time my fevered imagination has worked its way over her body, my balls are aching.

I open my eyes just as she steps into a pair of white lace panties and pulls a white tank top over her head.

She turns around, and I look back at my book, staring unseeingly while I pretend not to feel her eyes on me.

"Thank you for today. It's the best day I can remember having, ever," she says quietly before she dims her lamp and climbs into her bed.

I lay in the dark, hard as a rock and confused as hell. I don't know what the fuck is going on, but I know that I'm blowing this, badly.

"Uh, you know… I—I'm going for a swim," I say, hop up, and hustle out of the tent. I pretend not to hear her call my name and ignore my impulse to answer her. I need distance and I need to get rid of this erection so that I can fucking think.

I wade until the water reaches my waist, and then dive, headfirst, into the waves. The water is cool and calm, and I cut through it quickly, pushing myself until my shoulders ache before I turn back to swim for shore. When the water is shallow enough, I stand and face the horizon and try to catch my breath.

The exercise didn't do a thing about the boner in my shorts. I slip my hand past my waist band, fist my aching dick, and groan at the first stroke. It feels good, but there's no relief in it. This should be Regan's hand, or mouth or pussy. I don't know how I managed to blow things so badly.

"Stone!" Her shout carries over the wind and my heart nearly jumps out my chest. I yank my hand out of my shorts before I turn toward the beach.

She's right at the water's edge, sitting close enough that the tide laps at her shins. She's resting her chin on her knees, her head cocked to the side. From this distance, I can't make out her face, and I hope she couldn't tell what I was doing.

The thought is humiliating enough to do what my swim couldn't. By the time I reach the shore, my dick is as limp as the clumps of seaweed that dot the beach.

I drop down on the sand next to her, prop my body up on my elbows and drop my head back to stare up at the dark purple sky and try to order my thoughts.

Neither of us say anything as we sit, stuck in whatever quagmire of misunderstanding we've found ourselves in.

"The moon looks like a pearl sitting on a throne of diamonds, doesn't it?" She says, her pensive voice breaking the silence after a few minutes.

I follow her gaze to the horizon. The moon is low and glowing and the glittering stars that spangle the sky around it, do look like a congregation of courtiers paying homage to their sovereign. But if we're going to talk, it's not going to be about the fucking sky.

"You called me back, are you okay?" I ask, my patience fraying badly.

"Why did you ask me to come with you?" There's a gravity in her husky voice that belies her casual tone and matter of fact inflection.

"Why are you asking me a question you know the answer to?"

"Humor me," her voice is clipped.

I sit up, but keep my eyes facing forward. "Because, you needed to get away."

"I see." Her voice is barely audible, but the hurt in it resounds.

I turn to look at her.

Her jaw is clenched tight and her throat works as if she's swallowing down something thick and dry.

"Regan, what's wrong?"

"Why don't you want me anymore?"

Her question is as shocking as an ice bath after a hot shower. I stare at her, dumbfounded for a few seconds.

"You've got to be kidding me," I growl and stand up.

"Where are you going?" she gazes up at me from her perch in the sand.

"Nowhere, come on," I stick my hand out to help her up, too.

"Okay," she drawls before taking my offered hand and rising to her feet.

I let go of her hand, and peer at her, trying to see if she's serious. Until I see the frustration I'm feeling mirrored in her dark eyes.

I lay a hand on her neck, and she sighs in pleasure, but that hurt expression is still there. "I'm going to forgive you for asking me that because I can tell something is wrong. But you *have* to know, that me not wanting…that's *not* a thing that could be."

Her eyes snap open, the sadness and confusion is gone, and she glares daggers at me. "I practically waved my pussy in your face just now, and you didn't even look up from your damn book," she snaps, and arches her neck to evade my grasp.

"Oh, I looked…but you took your dress off to shower. I would never presume you wanted—"

"Did that girl you walked away with, the one you were helping with her *flaps*," she puts air quotes around the last word, "did you *presume* she wanted you to stay and hang out or did she ask you to?"

Her jealousy, misguided as it is, is *delicious.*

I frown in feigned bemusement. "Hmmmm, I'm surprised you noticed given how engrossed you were with your harem of geriatric perverts."

Her lips curl into a scowl. "I was trying to have *fun.* You turned into a moody grinch as soon as we got here, and *then* you left me to go off with your little band of man stealing whores."

I laugh out loud.

"It's not funny, I walked right past their tent and I could hear you talking, them laughing," she snaps and arches her neck to pull away from me. I slide my fingers into the damp tangle of hair at her nape and hold her still.

I lean in and draw in a lungful sea salt and citrus and press my lips to her ear. "I don't even remember their names. I only ever see you."

"Stone," my name leaves her lips on a gust of warm breath, and my body responds to the plea in it, but I need to hear her say it. My fingers fist around her hair and I tilt her face up to mine.

"Tell me what you want, Goddess." Her eyes glimmer like twin stars set into the beautiful moonlit face that I always find poetry in.

She slides her arms up my shoulders and lifts onto her toes so that her lips are scant inches from mine. "I want you to touch me. I want your hands on me. I want your mouth on me. I want your dick in me. I want to sleep in, swim, eat, and squeeze every last drop of joy and happy out of the time we have here. I want you. So badly. No one but you. Is that clear enough?"

I almost come on the spot.

No rush of adrenaline I've ever felt can compare to the sweet, dizzying thrill of *finally* catching my Venus.

"Perfectly." I drop a kiss on her mouth and then step back so I can see her entire body.

I catch the hem of her tank top and drag it up slowly to reveal the velvet soft skin of her stomach, then the rounded underside of her breast. And up until I pull it over her head.

"You are spectacular." I cup the warm weight of her full breasts and stroke her stiff nipples with the pads of my thumb.

Her breath hitches, but she stands perfectly still, letting me do what I will. And I intend to.

"Where shall I kiss you first?" I ask. My heart thuds in anticipation and my insides coil tight like a bow drawn and ready to fly while I wait for her to speak.

"My neck," she says after a beat and arches her throat for me.

I drop my head and open my mouth on the spot where her neck meets her jaw and press my tongue against the pulse that races there.

Her citrus scent mingles with the moonlight and salt tinged air and she tastes like perfection. The slow march to seduction I planned takes its last breath. My restraint goes up in the blaze of heat. I lick, graze devour like the frenzied, insatiable, greedy beast she alone turns me into.

I dip my head, drop kisses down her throat, her chest, nibble the soft swell of her breasts finally pull that sweet, plump nipple into my hot mouth. Her back bows and she lets out a ragged little moan. Her hands delve into my hair and she bucks her hips.

I suck even harder and find her other breast with my free hand and pinch that nipple, hard.

She goes wild.

Her hands, her mouth, are fevered and frantic as they move over my face, my shoulders, my back. She's scrambling against me, like I'm a tree she's trying to climb.

Her arms twine around my neck and she moans, "Please kiss me," in my ear.

Our lips crash together like meteors that were destined to collide. Her mouth is hot, and sweet. Her tongue—bold and hungry as it slides against mine.

I walk us toward the tent, kissing her like my life depends on it. I lose my footing and we fall. We land on the soft, gritty ground, that could be a cloud for all I feel it.

All of my senses have melded into one that only knows the fragrance, flavor, and feel of Regan.

We lay face to face, our breaths mingling, our eyes supernovas burning with lust and locked on each other.

I run the tips of my fingers over her face, tracing her cheekbones, her broad, full mouth, the pert slope of her nose, the sweeping wing of her brows -augmenting and updating those age-old memories with this new one. When my finger slides into her hair, she moans and closes her eyes.

I cradle her head and hold her in place while I pull my shorts down. I reach between us to push her panties aside and slide two fingers between her lips. She's softer, hotter, readier than I could have imagined.

"Regan, dammit, you're so wet," I groan into her mouth and her thighs part and make room for my conquering hips as I plunge into her without another word.

"Stone," she moans. Every single syllable is imbued with pleasure. I rock into her, never pulling out fully. Now that I'm inside her, I can't bear to leave. Not even for a second.

With an impressive show of strength, she rolls us to my back, her hand pressed to my chest while she rides me. Like a warrior who just saddled her latest conquest, her dark eyes glitter with exhilaration and lust as she takes her pleasure.

"Yes…Stone, yes…" she calls my name over and over as she starts to fall apart.

I thrust up hard and pull her hips down. The rhythmic clenching of her orgasm sends me over the edge.

We collapse in a heap of sweat and sand, panting and groaning until my dick softens and slips out of her.

When I can finally muster the strength, I gather her in my arms and carry her to the shower. We rinse all the sand off, stumble back to our tent, and collapse onto my bed.

I lay in bed with her until she's asleep to slip outside to set up the telescope. I hurry back to bed, wrap my arms around her and fall into a dreamless sleep.

Chapter 23

VENUS AND MARS

STONE

I wake with a start, slapping away whatever is buzzing by my side. My hands brush my cell phone, and I turn off the alarm and squint at my phone and see nothing but a blur. I forgot that I took my contact lenses out last night because the sand wreaks havoc on them.

I grope for the glasses I only wear first thing in the morning. I slip them on and check the time. It's only 4:30. I lay back for a few minutes. I have two more alarms set for 5:00 and 5:30, but I won't need them.

I'm too excited to sleep.

This is the entire reason I planned this three-day trip. For the next couple of days Venus will be visible in the morning sky.

My desire to see this rare sight has only one rival for my attention. And she's lying next to me. I wasn't going to wake her. Most people could care less about this shit. But now I want her by my side when I see it; And, I want her to see it, too.

"Wake up." I nudge Regan with my foot and switch on the lamp beside the twin bed we're sharing.

"What? What's wrong?" she asks only barely coherent as she pushes tangled locks of hair out of her face and peers around the tent.

"Nothing's wrong, I want you to see something," I assure her.

"We just went to sleep," she groans and covers her head with the sheet.

"No, we didn't. And you have to get up." I pull it back down.

"The sun's not even up," she glares at me and snatches the covers back over her.

"That's the whole point." I nudge her shoulder.

"I'll pass," she snuggles deeper into the bed.

"Fine, but you're going to miss one of the galaxy's most underrated party tricks." I slip my arm from under her and sit up. I glance over my shoulder. "And of course, there'll be sex at sunrise."

"You should have led with that," she quips and throws the covers off revealing a vision more beautiful than any fantasy I've ever conjured. My throat feels tight and my balls ache just looking at her. She crawls out of bed and slips a pair of cut shorts and her tank top on. We walk hand in hand out onto the soft white-sand beach.

Like my companion this morning, the predawn sky is too beautiful to be real. It covers us like a blanket of indigo and sapphire. Out here, with no artificial light to disrupt them, the stars look like a million jewels sewn into a velvet canvas.

The moon is low and so bright that its reflection turns the sea below it into a mirror of liquid silver. The water laps at the shore in gentle licks and it feels like we're standing on a planet that's part of the solar system, and not just a beach in Mexico.

"I'll never get over how beautiful this place is. Thank you so much for bringing me."

"You haven't seen anything yet," I promise and guide her to the spot where I set up the telescope.

I was eight when I got my first telescope and I fell irrevocably in love with the sky. For a child whose curiosity felt insatiable, the possibility of unending questions and endless discovery was like finding the Holy Grail.

To this day, no matter how many times I see it, the scope and breadth of the galaxy never ceases to amaze me.

"What are you looking at?" Regan's question snaps me out of my drifting thoughts. I finish focusing my viewfinder and step away.

"Come see," I beckon her over.

She smiles excitedly at me before she looks into the viewfinder and then back at me, and the delight in her eyes, clear even in the dark of dusk, makes my stomach do a flip.

"Wow it's so beautiful. What is this?"

"It's pointed at Venus. If you just look, you shouldn't have to adjust it to see."

"Oh my god, for real? Like the *planet*, Venus?" She puts her eye back to the scope and gasps and her back arches a little.

I wish I could look at the same time; I want to see what she does.

"This is the most amazing thing I've ever seen, tell me about it, please."

"For real?" I ask, surprised. My friends and family humor me and the wonder this holds for me, but they never ask me to talk about it.

"Yes, I want to know everything. God, I wish my kids could see this. This is mind blowing." The awe in her voice is gratifying and the imagery her words conjure, rather than feeling like a pesky reminder of our outside lives, is endearing. "Well, tell me!" she demands.

I smile and oblige my goddess "Venus is the most unique of planets. After the sun and moon it's the third brightest star in the sky. But it's positioning makes catching sight of it rare." I explain.

"Wow …I just can't get over how small we are. Do you think that somewhere out there, someone is looking through a telescope and seeing us on one of those tiny stars, too?"

"Absolutely," I answer right away.

She glances back at me with a mischievous grin on her face. "*You* believe in aliens?"

"Yes," I say unequivocally and her jaw drops.

"You're a doctor, a scientist of sorts, right? You can't really believe in little green men."

"We have no idea what lies at the edge of this galaxy and beyond. We can't be the only intelligent life in the entire universe. They may not be human, but I think they're there.

"I guess. Why haven't they made contact then?"

"Same reason we haven't. It's fucking hard, no matter how smart you are, to travel through space to reach other galaxies. It would take three hundred years to reach the edge of our galaxy—well at least as it's defined. No one really knows where the edge is. There are different measures, even within NASA."

"Wow. It's a wonder you're a doctor and not an astronaut," she says in awe.

I laugh and shake my head ruefully. "Until the year I decided to become a doctor, it was what I wanted to be. I had this book called *Cosmos* there was a time I thought it held the answer to everything."

Including my future with her.

"Huh, so, what happened? You lost interest?" she asks.

I sit down in the sand, gather a fistful of it, and let it sift through my fingers. Like she will in just a few days.

"No, I love space, but I couldn't spend my life chasing something I could never catch." I'm not sure if I'm still talking about space…or if I'm talking about her.

She walks over and sits next to me.

"You okay?" she asks. I hate the concern in her voice. I smile and toss the sand away, forcing my mind back to the conversation.

"Space discovery isn't a challenge, it's a quest without end. Voyager 2 launched in 1977 and forty years later, it's only just reaching the edge of the heliosphere. Most of the people who launched that mission are dead. Imagine if there was a human being in there right now. Alone for forty years. Even if we could supply him with enough food and water to last that long, human beings are social creatures."

"Why aren't you an astronaut?" she asks in a whimsical, but still awed voice. Seeing her so relaxed and present, relaxes me, too.

I stare up at the endless sea of stars. I understand why human beings looked at the heavens and imagined it could only be the work of gods and goddesses.

"I used to want to be. But I want to spend my life answering questions and doing work that has an impact now. I admire the universe but ushering new life into the world…for me, beats it every time."

"So, Venus lost you to babies?" she asks with a good-natured, ribbing smile.

"My Venus will never lose me."

"You talk about her like she's a person," she remarks, and I have to force my shoulders not to tense. She can't know, because I didn't give her that book, how close to home she's hitting.

"She is, kind of," I admit.

"Tell me more about her," she murmurs. And as if her voice was her body or lips, the words wrap around my dick and wake it up. But I wasn't kidding about sunrise sex and we've got time to kill before that. So, I force my mind back to the topic at hand and sift through my mental encyclopedia of knowledge.

"She's named after the Roman goddess of love. Myth says Venus was born from seafoam. She's the goddess of love, victory, fertility and beauty. And even though she was married to Vulcan—she was in love with Mars, the God of War."

"What happened?" Her voice is rapt with curiosity. I glance at her from the corner of my eye and have to bite back a groan. She's stretched herself out in a pose similar to mine, and her breasts spill out of the sides of her tank top tempting orbs of smooth brown skin that makes my mouth water.

"They were lovers, in secret of course. Until her husband became suspicious and set a trap for them."

"A trap?"

"He built a net out of a bronze chain so fine it was nearly invisible and hung it over the bed where they met to make love. When they were naked and joined, the net fell and ensnared them. They were trapped. Caught in the act and he invited all of the other gods on Olympus to come and bear witness to the couples' humiliation."

An awkward silence descends, and I could kick myself. Of all the parts of Venus's mythology I could have shared, why did I pick the part about her husband and lover?

"So, is that why Mars and Venus are synonymous with male and female? Because he was the fire and she was the foam?" she asks.

Grateful to her for keeping the conversation moving, I do my part, too, and it's not hard. I love mythology as much as I love science.

"Mars and Venus really represent one whole person. In the myth, they had a daughter named Harmonia, Greek goddess of…"

"Harmony," she offers when I trail off.

"Bingo." I wink. "In particular, she oversees the harmony of marriage and partnership. She's the soother of controversy in all things. In mythology she tells us that the union between War and Love is cosmic balance. But when you think about them… they're, in essence, polar opposites that couldn't exist without each other."

The flash of her bright, effervescent smile is all it takes to make my heart skip a beat. "Is there anything you don't know?"

"I don't know anything with certainty, but the sight of the stars makes me dream," I quote Vincent Van Gogh in response because what I want to say is that I watched her fall asleep and wished I could know what she was dreaming.

I laugh when I recall her friend's joke about *me* fucking *her* feelings.

I'm the one she should have warned.

She has completely and utterly ruined me and being this close to her, when Venus is right there makes me desperate to sink into her body and claim her like I'm the pillaging god of war himself.

Like she can read my thoughts, she says, "These clothes are stupid.

Let's take them off." She stands up and slips her shorts off and pulls her tiny tank top overhead. She pulls her hair free of it and a cascade of dark ringlets spill over her shoulders. With nothing between her and the view, she appears to be rising out of the foam of the waves crashing behind her. Just like Venus in Botticelli's famous paint—but so much more beautiful than a mere mortal could capture on a canvas.

The underlying gold of her brown skin is set ablaze by the moon's adoring light. I make quick work of shedding my shorts and grip my dick and stroke it. "Come here, my Venus."

"I like that," she murmurs and then sinks down, so her knees straddle my thighs. She cups the back of my neck and she plants a soft, wet kiss on me. The scent of citrus whipped with sea and sky fills my nostrils and shreds my equilibrium.

I grip her hips and pull her down, impaling her with my rock-hard dick. She unleashes a moan so guttural, I'm afraid I've hurt her. "Goddess, are you okay?"

"I have never been better in my life," she pants against my lips. We find a rhythm that's as timeless as the universe and is ours, alone.

I wrap an arm around her waist, cradle her head in my free hand and hold her flush against me while I lose myself her most exquisite pussy. She's a tight fit, but so perfect. We barely move, but the rapid roll of her hips causes explosions of pleasure to every nerve ending in my body.

"Regan," I call her name

"Call me Venus… be my Mars…"

"You want me to go to war for you, baby?" I demand and she groans into my mouth as I grind my hips against her, pressing as deep, but not as deep as I'd like, into the softest wetness I've ever felt.

She has always been my Venus. But instead of her cool easing my fire, every second I'm inside only makes me hotter, hungrier.

While I worship her from the front, the rising sun crowns and veils her in the light of its first rays, from behind.

Her expression is fierce with lust. Her hair is a wild mane of sable coils and curls. The vast sky seems to exist solely to canvas her untamed beauty.

I don't recognize the growls and grunts she pulls from me.

I barely know my own name.

I am undone by the sunlit goddess who just took me like she owns me.

I know we're just fucking.

But damn, if it doesn't feel like flying.

I know we're not supernatural mythological beings.

But when we're together like this, I'm certain we could make the whole world bend to our will.

I'm a fool. I know this deep in my bones because if my life depended on it right now, I'd say this kiss was flavored by portent and the promise of so much more.

She drapes her sweaty, sexy body over me. And instead of pulling away, I let myself sink deeper into the quicksand and wrap my arms around her.

"That was perfect. You are perfect," I whisper into the crook of her neck.

She sighs and nestles closer. "You're a sweet talker."

"Can't be helped. I've been kissing a goddess with a mouth made of sugar."

She peeks up at me through the thick tangle of her glossy lashes.

"Don't say things like that…you'll make me want to keep you," she says in a dreamy voice before her eyes drift closed.

I laugh and ignore the way my heart gets a full blown hard on hearing those words.

It wants to mate her as much as my dick.

Thank God for my job and my unbreakable commitment to spending the rest of the year in Colombia.

Otherwise, I'd be tempted to follow her home.

Chapter 24

FRIENDS

REGAN

"How did you end up in Colombia?" I prop up on one elbow, reaching over him, to grab a slippery, tender slice of mango from the small plastic container that was part of the lunch our guided tour provided.

"You know, for someone who actually studied journalism, you ask imprecise and vague questions." He shakes his head in amazement.

"And here I was, just thinking how wonderful you are. Thanks for reminding me what a know-it-all you are."

His eyebrows shoot up, a cocky grin spreads from ear to ear, and his eyes dance with relish. "You were thinking I'm wonderful?"

I scoff and curl my lip. "You have selective hearing. I said you're a know-it-all."

"Ah, Regan," he says, tssking in mock disapproval. "But you *like* know-it-all's, remember?" He leans forward and nips at my bottom lip. They're swollen and kissed nearly raw, and I wince, even as I open my mouth for his kiss. He swipes his tongue along the inside of my tender flesh, and I groan against his lips.

"I only said that because you were ten years old and sad, but, really, I hoped you'd grow out of it."

He holds his hands up in the universal sign of surrender, as if this fierce, fearless man would ever give up on anything. But it's sexy that he'd pretend to for me. "You're right, it's a bad habit of mine. I know I started it, but let's not fight. I'm sorry."

God, why can't he stop being perfect? I wrinkle my nose at him. "Okay. But only because you asked nicely."

He blows out a breath as if he's relieved. "Now, let's get back to the part of the conversation where we talk about how wonderful you think I am."

Effervescent laughter bursts from a wellspring deep in my soul. I am awash with delight. Being with him, laughing, arguing, teasing, it's like stretching my legs after hours of riding in the cramped third row of an overcrowded minivan.

He reaches one of his long, thickly muscled, arms over my body. He smells like me and mangos, and for a second my wits scramble.

He plucks a slice of mango with his deft fingers. It's perfectly ripe, the succulent flesh barely taut enough to contain the juice. My mouth waters.

I reach up and take a tiny bite of the fruit in his hand.

"I don't think I've ever tasted anything so good," I groan at the perfect balance of sweet and sour.

He swipes at my lip, catches a dribble of juice on the pad of his thumb and sucks it into his mouth. "Hmmm, It's good," he muses. "But your pussy's sweeter."

I bite my lip, and heat suffuses my cheeks. I fan myself. "You could start fires with your mouth." The smoldering unabashed hunger in his eyes makes my whole body tingle.

"You could start wars with that face," he says.

I roll my eyes at his over the top praise. I have zero make-up on and haven't tried to brush my hair for two days. I know I look a fright. But Stone looks at me like I walked out of the ocean like Venus herself.

And I love it.

Being with him is like having a decadent dessert for every meal. Indulgent. Expensive. Impossible to resist. "It's a shame we're not alone, hmmm?" I nudge his calf with my foot.

He scans the riverbank that the rest of our excursion party is spread out across. We're a small group made up of other couples and we've all retreated to private, shaded spots to eat lunch.

"All I see is you." He picks up another juicy slice of mango and lifts it to my lips but before I can bite it, he drags it down my chin, down my chest and draws it around my nipple through the dark green fabric of my bikini top.

And then his mouth follows the sweet, sticky trail with hot open-mouthed kisses. I clutch his head and sink my teeth into my lip, to muffle my moan of delight when his lips close over the throbbing tip of my breast.

The already aching peak swells, the heat of his mouth scorching even through the fabric. My core contracts in delicious anticipation.

But we're not even close to being alone and now that we're off the island and making our way back to Cabo San Lucas, real life doesn't feel as far away as it did yesterday.

Reluctantly, I let go of his head, push at his divinely muscled shoulders and manage to snake out of his hold and scrabble backwards just in time to evade his lunge.

"Stone, stop, not here!" I try to wriggle out of his grasp, but he's so strong and he pulls me into his lap. The urgent press of his arousal nestles against my backside. His lips brush my ear and I giggle.

"Promise you'll sit on my lap on our way back, and I'll let you go." he draws and my shudder in anticipation.

"I promise," I whisper and press a kiss to his temple and draw in a lungful of his delicious sweat, and fresh air scented skin before I climb off his lap and sit cross legged next to him. I cross my arms over my chest when his gaze drops to the wet spot over my nipple.

He straightens and mimics my pose. "Fine, let's talk."

I chuckle at the way he says *talk* like it's an expletive. "Okay. So, you were telling me why Colombia," I refresh his memory.

I'm impressed with, but not surprised by, my ability to refocus on the conversation when my body is still so distracted by aftershocks of his attention.

Stone stimulates the most erogenous zone on my entire body—my mind. And when he's talking to me while he's inside me, it's like having a full-body orgasm.

He takes his cues from me and leans away a little, his eyes darting the banks of the mangrove lined river.

"I went to med school thinking I was going to be a trauma surgeon. Then I had my rotation in obstetrics. My very first delivery made a believer out of me. Babies are the only people in hospitals who aren't there because they're sick."

"Do you like kids?"

He frowns and looks skyward, as if he has to ponder the answer to that question.

"Ummm, that's a pretty easy yes or no question," I tease, but find my laugh constricted by the breath I'm holding.

His chuckles. "Yes, I do. They remind me that there's hope for humanity. As long as they keep coming into the world, we have a future. You know?"

"So, you want children one day?' I ask, genuinely curious but acutely aware of the flutter of apprehension in my gut. I don't know why his answer should matter to me. But it does.

"I don't know…. From the time I was ten until I was twenty-two, every decision I made was based on what was best for my brothers. I was in medical school and too busy trying to survive that to do anything I wanted. Now that I'm finally living just for me, I can't imagine going back to being responsible for getting little people to school, and doctor's appointments, and all that shit."

I feel so many things at once; Disappointment—because it's another reminder of how discordant our pairing is. Admiration—that he not only survived an absent mother, but made sure his brothers did, too. But most strongly, I feel a sense of nostalgia.

"I used to not want kids," I admit.

"I guess you got over that?" Stone says and I don't begrudge him the teasing quirk of his lips. I often laugh at the irony of it myself.

"Getting pregnant kind of forced me too." wince at how that sounds. "I love my children, desperately. Having them is without any doubt the most selfish thing I've done."

He narrows one eye and frowns. "Selfish?"

"Yes. It's selfish. They don't ask to be born. It was purely for me. But I'll admit, when I found out I was pregnant, I thought my life was over."

"Why?"

"My mother is brilliant. From what I heard; she could run circles around my father in intellect. When they met, she was working the concession at the basketball stand, waiting for her moment. She found it when my grandfather offered her a job. Then she fell in love with my father. She forgot her goals, forgot her ambition and got pregnant."

"With you and Remi," he reminds me.

I roll my eyes. "I mean, I'm just saying. I love my mother, but I spent most of my childhood thinking she didn't love *me*. And, from my great grandmother on down, they've all fallen in love with a man who left them - whether by death, divorce, or prison—they spent their whole lives alone and brokenhearted. And even when I wasn't sure what I wanted to do with my life professionally. I knew that I didn't want to repeat that cycle."

"So, you were going to outrun your legacy by making different choices," he says knowingly.

I slant my eyes his way. "I see you're familiar with this particular type of self-medication?"

He smiles. "Oh yeah. I think most people who don't have rosy happy childhoods grow up trying to avoid reliving their nightmare."

"My life isn't a nightmare, just very different from what I used to hope for. But I chose it all." I say.

"Because Marcel swept you off your feet?"

I laugh dryly. "Hardly."

"So why did you marry him?"

It's a Pandora's box of a question. I can't tell him the sequence of events that flowed from the night in the bakery and how it set the wheels in motion that led me to the altar. So, I settle for the bare bones, but still awful truth.

"To make my grandfather happy."

"That's a big decision to make just to please someone else."

There's no judgment in his eyes or his voice. But I know what I sound like and no one can hear that without thinking it's stupid or reckless or pathetic, or all three.

"He raised us after my father died. Well, with my mom, but he was more maternal than she is. And he was such a dynamo." I smile at the memory of him bounding off to work like he was twenty-five instead of seventy. Every day until his stroke stopped him.

"Old Man Wilde was a legend, man." His voice is heavy with admiration.

"Really? Even in the Rivers household?" I eye him skeptically.

"I don't know about that. But I know he toppled the powers that be and upset the social order. That's why the Rivers hate him." I remember as a boy he made the distinction between the Rivers and the brothers he considered family. I wonder if that will change now that Hayes is back and in charge.

"Yes, he was totally unpolished but rich enough to pay the cost of entry to their country clubs. He used to go to parties in off the rack clothes. And the old money set he was so desperate to be a part of would laugh behind his back," I remember with a fond little laugh.

My grandfather said he didn't mind that they'd laughed at him. Now that he was too rich to ignore, it delighted him to see the same people who snickered knocking on his door to borrow money. He never said no. In fact, he was generous with his new friends—he shared everything, his cars, and boat and properties.

And once, me.

I'm so startled by the intruding thought that I bite my tongue hard enough to draw blood.

In the ensuing pain, the thought disappears as if it had never been there. And I'm glad because it's not true. He didn't share me—yes, he encouraged Marcel, but in the end, I married him because I wanted to.

"So, what happened with you and Marcel?" Stone nudges my shoulder.

I peer at him, doubtfully. "You really want to talk about this?"

He nods, his expression earnest. "Unless you'd rather not. But I want to know everything about you."

We share a smile that makes my heart do something strange and my pulse race.

"So, it's over?" he prompts.

I realize I'm just staring at him. I touch my flaming cheeks and blink to refocus my mind on the conversation.

But I can't remember what we were talking about.

"Is what over?" I ask and slap his arm when he bursts out laughing.

"That's flattering as hell, Regan…and makes me wish we weren't talking about your marriage."

That sobers me up and I sigh. "Oh yes, it's over. In every way, but on paper."

"You guys don't have…" His inability to say sex after all the dirty things he's said to me in the last few days is endearing. Just like every-thing else about him is.

"No, we don't have sex. And haven't since before I had the twins." I finish his sentence for him.

"He's crazy." Stone's voice is full of bewilderment

"Not really. Marriage, family —— it's not for everyone, as you know." My laugh is hollow, and I don't want to give him the chance to agree or ask me anything else about it. So, I change the subject.

"So, you went to Colombia to find yourself?"

"Yes and no. I used to think I could save the world,"

"And now?"

"Turns out the world is saving me. Traveling has taught me more than any classroom I've ever been in. And I'm having the time of my life in Colombia." The smile that lights his face makes me a bit envious. There's so much I haven't seen.

'What's it like?" I ask, hungry for details that I can use to paint a picture of it for myself.

"It's like everywhere else on earth—families, single people, old people, public parks and traffic. But it's got this…tenacious spirit." His hand clenches into a fist. "There is so much misery everywhere and yet, they hold on to every scrap of joy, make use of every resource and take such pride in their town's history. It's turned me into an optimist."

I huff an amazed laugh. "I'm so used to hedging my bets, so stuck on cynical, I can't imagine that."

He nods, a pensive light in his eyes as he gazes out at the river. "I get that. It's safer to not expect anything. But then I see the hope on the faces of the women who come through our clinic. Their lives are incredibly hard. Poverty, political unrest, lack of food security, disease, you name it. And yet their aspirations for their children are unmitigated. It's hard to look at them and not feel like anything is possible." His eyes blaze with passion and fondness.

My heart blazes with affection and respect. His empathy and his conviction inspire me.

"Will you be sad to leave?"

"Yeah, especially for the flat, endless sea of suburbia also known as Houston, TX."

"What?" I sputter, incredulous that anyone could feel that way. "The only true thing in that sentence is flat. Are you kidding? Houston is America's melting pot."

His shrug is noncommittal. "It's fine, but I haven't lived there in a long time and when I did, I didn't exactly get to enjoy it."

"Maybe it's because I call it home. Besides my time at SMU and the five years we lived in Paris, it's the only place I've spent any decent amount of time. But I think it's an amazing place to live. When you're back, I'll show you all the things you missed on your first stint."

His smile dims a little and I could smack myself.

"Don't worry, I haven't forgotten what we agreed, I just…" I trail off not sure how to explain myself.

His expression loses all its levity and he takes my left hand in his. He strokes my bare ring finger. "I know you haven't, but this is…nice. We could be…friends, right?" his eyes bore into mine. I don't know what to say, and I can't hold his gaze.

How could I pretend that he's as much of a stranger as his brothers are? But how could I do anything else?

He lets go of my hand and the first uncomfortable silence I can recall us ever sharing, descends.

"Okay, it's time to paddle back to the beach," our guide calls. It's a welcome interruption and neither one of us tries to prolong the moment. We clean up and get ready without any of our normal banter.

When we're back on the paddle boards, we wade out, side by side.

"You're a natural at this," he says, his tone free of the tension that seemed to rattle us both a few minutes ago.

I'm relieved and flash him a grin. "I can't believe it. I was so sure I'd fall off. But I'm afraid to look away," I admit completely amazed at how easy it's been to stay upright.

"Say cheese," he calls.

"What?" I turn to face him again. He's got his paddle tucked under one of his arms and his phone aimed at me.

"Trust me, you'll want to see yourself like this," he says

"Okay, let me pose," I lift my arms into the air, my paddle gripped in one hand and bare my teeth like I've just vanquished a foe.

"Perfect," he declares with a smile. But then, he drops his paddle into the water and pushes himself ahead of me. I'm sorry for the strain between us, but grateful for the distance, too. I need to make sense of what I'm feeling.

"To your left you'll see a flock of Black-necked Stilts," our guide calls.

The mangroves are fascinating—a wetland in the middle of this otherwise arid region and the tangle of trees is a lush ecosystem bursting with a wide variety of fish and birds. But my eyes are fixed on the back of the man who reminded me of all the things I've missed.

I always heard mid-30s were peak time for a woman's sexual drive, but I didn't believe it. I thought my plug-in vibrator and I had already reached it ten years ago.

But it's not just the mind-blowing sex that's gotten under my skin over the course of the last few days. It's his wonder, his compassion, his conviction, his tenderness. It's the way he wears his heart on his sleeve and the way he listens. He brought me here so I could go home with happy memories. I can't remember the last time anyone did something just to make me happy.

This was supposed to be fun, and sex.

But it's gone far beyond that. I've attributed all of my flutters and skipped heartbeats to adrenaline. But after a lazy day of swimming in the crystal-clear water with sea lions and sunbathing on sparkling white-sand beaches, those flutters and skipped heartbeats are more intense than ever. And, there's no doubt as to why.

Which is too bad for me.

Even if I wasn't still tangled up with Marcel, he's just told me he wants to live footloose and fancy free. Which is nothing like my life is now.

I don't doubt that one day, he'll change his mind. Then he'll find someone who can be more than just a holiday fling. The knowledge that my dream man will one day give all of this to someone else, turns the sweet aftertaste of our kisses, bitter.

I banish the encroaching self-pity.

This was never meant to last. Which is fine, because I don't need it to. I just need it for now. But as I follow him down the river, I know I'm in for a world of hurt when we say goodbye.

I may be keeping myself upright on this board, but Stone has brought my heart to its knees.

Chapter 25

EVERYTHING

STONE

It's our final night together. We got lucky and the hotel we picked has a hot tub on the deck. I climbed in while Regan called her kids and changed. I gaze up at the star-spangled cosmos. Every star, every planet, every speck of dust has a role to play. The universe looks like beautiful chaos, but it is in fact, perfectly precise and predictable.

"Is the water nice?" Regan appears in the doorway, dripping wet and wrapped in a towel.

"Yeah, come join me," I hold up the two bottles of beer resting in the cup holders.

She wrinkles her nose. "I just showered…"

"Thank goodness there's more water so you can do it again. Come on. It's our last night."

She sighs, but nods. "Okay, let me put on a suit, I'll be right out," she smiles, slides the door close, and disappears back into the suite.

The tension from our conversation on the banks of the mangroves is gone, but the question that sparked it, is still unanswered.

And for now, it'll stay that way. We've got this one night left in this perfect dimension we've carved out of nostalgia and attraction and I want to spend it happy. Tomorrow, we'll go back to the real world. And no matter how much I wish it, no matter how bright and shimmering this thing between us, we'll go our separate ways.

But there's no way I can go back to a life that she's not part of.

Cosmos taught me that the universe is an impeccable timekeeper, every single thing happens as it should. Us meeting here like this wasn't an accident.

In my line of work, brilliant women aren't rare. And almost all of them can claim something that makes them physically attractive. But, as cerebral as I am, I'm even more adventurous and thrill seeking. I know it's a rare combination, and I've yet to meet a woman who can hang with me on a hike and then talk to me about all of the things that interest me—movies, books, food, travel, family, politics.

Until I met Regan Wilde. She's adventurous, beautiful, bright, and kind. But she's not the kind of woman you win with a few nights of sex and flattery. Nah, if I want it all, I've got to earn it all.

I need to be in the same city, and I need a plan. But until she wants me more than whatever she's getting out of staying married to a man she doesn't like or live with.

I might fail. She might trample my heart again, but to be able to finally claim her as mine, is a hell of an upside.

The door slides open, Regan steps out onto the balcony, and my eyes nearly fall out of my head.

I've seen her naked and it shouldn't make me nearly swallow my tongue. But as she walks toward the hot tub, bathed in silver moonlight, I see Venus,—my ultimate woman—come to life.

She's got on this tiny silver bikini. Her dark hair is swept back and off her face and sits piled on top of her head. It gives me an unobstructed view of her exquisitely symmetrical face, and her long, graceful neck. Her wide, thickly lashed eyes look bigger. Her kiss swollen lips are slick with the coconut lip balm she bought from the small gift store in our hotel lobby.

"Where'd you go?" she asks as she climbs in and sits next to me.

I reach over the side and lift up the tightly rolled joint. "To get this, our tour guide told me where I could."

"I didn't know doctors smoked weed," she looks scandalized when I lift it to my lips.

"And, now you do. And it's not something I'd do if I had to work in the morning," I say, light it again, and hand it to her.

She gives the joint a dubious side-eye, her pert, sunburned nose wrinkling. "I've never tried it. I don't want to be hungover."

"You won't be hungover. But, no pressure." I pull it back to my lips.

"Wait." She lays one of her small, neatly manicured hands on my forearm.

"Change your mind?" I ask with a knowing smile.

She nods, but instead of taking it from me, she leans forward. "Show me how?"

There's meaning layered in those three words that gives them a gravity that I'm helpless to resist. It pulls me to her the way the moon and the sun pull the tide.

She puckers her lips to make a tiny 'O" for the joint, I put it to her lips, my heart hammering wildly when her lips touch the backs of my fingers as she draws in the heady smoke. I slip my other hand behind her neck and pull her forward, so that our lips are almost touching. When she exhales, I pull the curling white smoke into my mouth.

Her eyes dart to my lips. I trace small circles on the soft, damp nape of her neck. She sighs and a wide smile spreads on her face, her eyelids droop as the joint starts to take effect.

I take her hands in mine and lift them to press a kiss to each of her palms.

What started as a casual caress turns into a genuinely interested inspection. Her nails are short and painted in a glossy color that reminds me of Marble Slab's sweet cream ice cream. They're elegant and with not a single chip in sight. But her fingers and the back of her hands have faint scars that are completely at odds with the rest of her.

"Don't look at my hands," she says and pulls them out my grasp and tries to tuck them under her thighs. I grab her wrists and pull them back up and after a few seconds she stops resisting and lets me look at them.

"Why not?" I ask.

"They're terrible. My kids are picky eaters, and most nights I make three different meals, and my hands take a beating, nicks and cuts, oil splatters, whatever. I draw as little attention to them as possible. Nude nails, no extravagant rings."

She curls her fingers inward and I lower my head to press kisses to her knuckles as I uncurl them one at a time so that I can press our palms together. My hands dwarf hers.

"They're beautiful. And your kids are lucky. Even before I went to Blackwell, I don't remember my mother cooking a single meal."

She turns our joined hands over and examines mine. "Tell me about her. Where is she?"

"Right now? In College Station. Hayes came back to town and she scampered. She doesn't need money since my stepfather left her an annuity. We've all been estranged from her for years, except Dare—my youngest brother."

"Wow. I'm sorry." The pity in her eyes makes my skin feel one size too small.

"Don't be. I'm not. Like you said, family isn't for everyone." My mother didn't completely abdicate her role. But she didn't do much more than was required to keep Child Protective Services off her back.

All the things a parent is supposed to guide you through—friendships, falling in love, learning to drive, getting applications in on time—I taught myself, and then tried to teach my younger brothers. I did the best I could, but it wasn't always enough.

"Yeah, but still, I'm sorry," she repeats, her expression not at all what it should be. I don't want to talk about my mother and tarnish the shine off this last night with the bitterness just talking about her evokes.

"Come here and I'll show you how you can make it feel better," I say with a lascivious grin and a waggle of my brows. She laughs, and glides through the water toward me.

Chapter 26

ADIEU

REGAN

We've been quiet most of the morning. Stone's family has already arrived, and we've agreed that when we get back to the resort, he'll drop me off and go drop off the rental. We won't see each other again until the night before we're both set to leave.

I'm bereft of him already.

This trip has been like finding my way home. I was a planet on the verge of extinction, saved by this man's divine light. I may not get to keep him, but that light, the perspective, the feeling that I can do the hard things I've been avoiding—I'm taking those home with me. It's time to figure out who I am. But God, I wish we had more time.

"I don't want to go back." I give up trying to hold it in and sit on the bed, the T-shirt I was folding gripped in my hands.

He joins me, sitting so our thighs touch, but he doesn't put his arm around me. And I need him to, so desperately.

"I know," he says, his voice is as hollow as my heart feels.

"Are you okay?" I ask, running my fingers along the soft scruff on his jaw.

He nods. "For now," he whispers. He leans in and my eyes flutter closed. My lips tingle in anticipation of his touch. Instead of his mouth, the firm pads of his fingers stroke my lips.

My eyes pop open in surprise, and the conflict and misery in his eyes make me want to scream and cry at the same time.

That tortured gaze follows the path of his hand. He runs his fingers up the center of my nose, over the arch of brows, ghosts them over the tips of my lashes and then finally he cups either side of my face.

"You're so much more than I could have imagined, Regan. I…" His voice is strangled, his eyes full of desperation that makes me tremble. He opens and closes his mouth a few times before he seems to abandon the idea of speaking.

Instead with a groan that sounds like surrender, he swoops down and claims my lips in a searing kiss.

His magical mouth thrills me to the edges of my senses and sends my imagination scouring for a new word to describe what we're doing.

Because to call this a kiss, is akin to calling pearl, sand. It may start that way, but when pressure, passion, and fate collide—simple, small things become extraordinary, fathomless treasures.

With every breath we share, we are creating something so priceless that we'd be fools to let it go.

I'm falling in love with him.

God help me. How could I be so stupid?

It's only been a handful of days, but Stone Rivers has already made me feel more alive than I thought possible. I feel connected to the earth, grounded to the moment. When I look at the night sky, I don't notice the dark. I just see an endless spray of brilliant, blazing possibilities.

We make love one last time. There's a rhythm, a natural push and pull between us that is at once cadent and capricious.

We are wanton, wild, wicked and so fucking happy.

My lips may say this isn't real.

But my heart beats with the secret truth…and there it shall have to stay.

Chapter 27

CRASH LANDING

REGAN

"Oh, dear Lord, I feel almost human again," I groan and lever up to sitting.

I can't quite meet the eye of the woman who just finished washing my hair. It felt so delicious that I closed my eyes for a few minutes and pretended she was Stone. I might have come if she hadn't stopped right when she did.

"You've got such incredible hair. It's like the wigs everyone wears; these curls are to die for."

It's not vanity that makes my eyes roll. It's boredom. My hair is unique, but then…so is everyone else's.

But I've learned that attempting to dissuade or explain my resistance to accepting compliments is far more painful than just saying thank you.

I hear a commotion from the front of the small salon. Never one to ignore a fracas, I leave the flabbergasted hairdresser and stroll out front to see what is happening. A very familiar blonde is arguing with the extremely discomposed young receptionist. It's Hayes Rivers fiancé. Stone's soon to be sister in law and the very last person I should want to see.

But she's pregnant, and clearly in distress. The woman at the counter isn't even looking at her anymore.

"Confidence?" She spins around, her eyes wild with panic before recognition flickers and then fades. She gives me an assessing once-over and a confused frown mars her incredibly pretty face and then her jaw goes slack.

Her shocked expression makes me feel like I'm standing there naked.

"Regan Wilde? Wow, your hair...is amazing and...I've never seen you look so...*young* before," she says after tripping on her words.

"Good to know I look like an old hag normally," I say in a dry voice before I can stop myself. I forget that my RBF means that my jokes tend to go over not so well.

Her ocean blue eyes widen in horror and then, she laughs out loud. *Hmmm, that's unexpected.*

She puts a hand on my arm, "And you're funny, too. You know what I mean, girl. You look like you're sixteen years old. I can see your freckles. You're stunning all the time, but right now, you look like you're a sun goddess or something. I can tell you've had a great trip."

Her congratulatory smile makes my stomach dip.

If only she knew. I wonder what she'd say if I told her that I drove a nail into the coffin of my oldest friendship. *Before* I spent four days fucking, feasting and finding my religion with a man who isn't my husband, but seems to know me better than anyone else ever has. Oh, and I think I fell in love with him, but it doesn't matter because there is no hope for us.

Since I can't say any of that, I focus on trying to help her with whatever I just walked in on.

"I wish I could say the same for you. You look downright distressed. What did I interrupt when I walked up here?" I arch an imperious eyebrow at the young woman behind the counter.

Confidence's smile dims and she purses her lips. "Oh, I was being a little bit of a diva," she admits with a sheepish smile. "I wanted to get my hair done. I didn't make an appointment and they're booked. I'm terrible at doing it myself."

"You have an event?" I feign ignorance.

She darts forlorn azure blue eyes back to the young woman behind the small desk before she nods tentatively. "Yes. A beach wedding. At sunset. It's a surprise, though. So, if you see Hayes please don't say anything."

"Don't you worry," I assure her. If I see Hayes, all I'll be doing is moving in the opposite direction.

"I'm so mad at myself, I've never been to one of these places, I thought I could just walk down and get a quick blow out." She bites her lip fretfully. Her hand rests protectively over the small rounded swell of her belly.

I was a pregnant bride, but there was nothing romantic or whimsical about my nuptials. Even in her distress, it's clear that this is a woman who is in the full flush of love.

My pang of jealousy is tempered by my secret fascination with the idea of happily ever after. It wasn't in the cards for me, but I love watching it happen for other people, so I make a snap decision.

I eye her cut off denim shorts and white t-shirt with a conspiratorial smile.

"It won't do for you to become the new Mrs. Rivers with your hair looking like that. Leave it to me."

Her pretty face is full of confusion. "Leave what?"

I turn back to the counter. "Excuse me."

The girl who'd been ignoring Confidence smiles genially at me. "Yes Mrs. Landel, how can I help you?"

"This woman is getting married tonight, surely you can fit her in,"

She pales, her eyes widening and darting over my shoulder before returning to me full of dread and apology.

"I'm sorry, but we aren't taking walk ins."

I quirk a brow at her and frown, confused. "You took me."

She flushes bright red and her eyes dart around as if she's looking for help. When none of her coworkers meet her pleading eyes, she looks back to me with resignation. "Because you're... *you*. VIP. And now, we don't have any bowls available."

"It's okay, Regan. Really," Confidence puts a hand on my shoulder.

"No, it's not. She can have my bowl. I don't have anything more than a good book waiting for me. If you can make me an appointment for tomorrow?"

The girl turns to her coworkers and speaks to them in a rapid fire, authoritative voice that sends them scurrying.

"Of course, Mrs. Landel, what time tomorrow?"

"Oh no, I couldn't," Confidence protests.

"You must. I insist." I smile at the young woman. "I'll call in the morning to see what 's available. "

I turn to Confidence, "I'll just go get my things, so you can get started."

"Thank you so much, Regan." She's bubbly with giddy relief and before I see it coming, her arms go around me in a hug of gratitude.

I'm so surprised, I stiffen. But only for a moment.

In the group of people I call friends, air kisses are the greeting of choice.

But boy…does she give good hugs.

Almost as good as Matty's.

I've been so mad at her, but I wish I'd hugged her like this before she left. I roll my eyes at my own silliness. As if a hug would have healed everything between us.

I miss having girlfriends.

I'm tempted to nestle my head on her shoulder and tell her everything.

I pull away before I do or say something I'll regret.

Confidence is smiling wide, and in a louder voice she says, "Is your husband here? We'll be at the beach at 6pm. We'd love to have you."

At the mention of my husband, Hayes and his brothers in the same sentence, my panic flares.

"He's not here. And I've got a video call with my kids at the same time. I haven't talked to them for a few days, so as much as I'd love to…" I lie. I wouldn't love to. "Good luck tonight. It's quite a feat you're pulling off."

"He's my forever, and I just want him to be happy." she says with a dreamy sigh that makes my dry husk of a heart wheeze in longing

"Oh, I'm sure he will be."

She shakes her head in self-rebuke. "It's ridiculous that you and I had to come all the way to Mexico to have our first conversation. Let's have lunch when we're all back home." she says with so much sincerity that I can't suppress the girlish hope that maybe, she means it.

"I'd love to," I say but when she goes to hug me again, I lean in and press a kiss to each of her cheeks. Hugs are nice, but so are these, when you mean them.

She's marrying a man very much like Marcel—a titan of industry, powerful and from an old, classist family that disinherits its heirs the way the Catholic Church used to excommunicate heretics.

But in all the ways that matter, he's also very different. Every time I've seen them together, it is clear that he is beside himself with love for the little blond bombshell he's marrying. And she returns his affection.

Yet, empire building is not for the faint of heart. Marcel and I might not have fared better if we'd had love on our side. Without it, we never stood a chance.

Confidence waves and disappears around a corner with the now fawning receptionist. I wave back and send her a silent wish for better luck with her billionaire titan than I had with mine.

Chapter 28

OH, BROTHER

HAYES RIVERS

"Why the fuck are you smiling like that?" I nudge Stone with my elbow.

He immediately stops smiling. "I don't know what you're talking about," he says, and I eye him in the mirror but drop it. He's always been a private person and I know that pushing him is the surest way to shut him up.

I turn back to the mirror, but I feel him watching me and dart an inquisitive glance in his direction.

"I can hear you thinking...." I drawl.

"How do you *know*, Hayes?"

"Know what?" I run my fingers through my hair one last time and turn to face him. He looks uncharacteristically unsure of himself.

"That you want to spend the rest of your life with her."

"Because in general, I'm a selfish asshole. But I'd rather swallow hot lead than see disappointment in her eyes."

Stone laughs, and I freeze.

"I haven't heard you laugh out loud in at least three years," I say.

"That's not true," he scoffs, and a smile plays on his lips.

"Has there been an invasion of body snatchers? Who the hell are you?"

"Fuck off, Hayes."

"I saw you two weeks ago on FaceTime, and you looked like the same miserable fucker you've always been. Last time you looked like this you were eating one of those lemon scone things you used to be obsessed with."

He purses his lips in a self-satisfied smile and nods. "You don't say…"

"Are you two peacocks done hogging the mirror?" Beau shouts and I stick my head out of the bathroom. He's lounging on the bed, and Dare is nowhere in sight.

"Where'd he go?" I ask and eye Dare's bed. It's strewn with more clothes than he could possibly need for a weekend, hair products, his laptop, two cell phones, and several wads of cash. I push away the unfair flare of suspicion as I take in his things. Dare has been home from rehab for two months. He's doing well. I can see the change in him. I just need to accept that his lifestyle is less traditional than mine.

I clap my hands together both to refocus my thoughts and to get my brother's attention. "Listen, whatever C is up to, I want you guys to promise me you didn't let her rope you into anything crazy."

"Too late. That little blonde Napoleon you're engaged to can't be reined in," Beau says cryptically and grins. He hops up and saunters to the small bar by our balcony door.

He hands me a glass and another to Stone and raises his in a toast.

He makes a lewd joke about marriage and balls in vices. I laugh even though it's not really that funny. I'm happy. I've missed my brothers.

We're scattered all over the place, and it's been too long since we got together outside of the holidays.

Confidence never ceases to amaze me. They told me she made it clear that she wouldn't take no for an answer when she called them to plan this get away. Even though I've missed her this afternoon, it's been nice to spend the afternoon with them. I feel bad that I didn't thank her before she went off on her mysterious errands.

A simple and easy day is the best gift anyone has ever given me.

In my family, those kinds of words—simple and easy—were met with suspicion.

"Okay, let's go. Everything is ready."

Beau's abrupt declaration startles me. "Ready for what?" I ask.

"For you, dumbass. That's all I'm allowed to say," he adds when I start to press him for more.

I turn to Stone, who is distracted by whatever he's looking at on his phone.

He's smiling again.

This time, with teeth.

My curiosity about the evening is forgotten. I give him a suspicious once-over. "Don't get me wrong, I'm glad to see it. But why the fuck are you smiling so much?"

He flushes, and his eyes get an almost dreamy look, one I've never seen.

"I think… I'm falling in love." He sounds like he can't believe it himself.

"Wow." I can't hide my surprise.

He smiles wryly. "I know. It's a little complicated, though."

"How so?"

"She's married. Don't say a fucking word. Not to anyone," he whispers.

Then, he claps me on the shoulder and follows Beau out the door. I put my shoes on, grab my wallet and hurry after them.

The elevator doors open on our floor, just as I'm catching up with them.

"Good timing," Beau mutters, as we step onto the crowded car.

Conversation is impossible, but I catch Stone's eye and give him a look that he knows means I'm not done with him.

He smirks and shrugs.

I smirk back and plan my attack as we descend.

When we step off the elevator, I pounce.

"I forgot my phone upstairs," I lie.

"Aww, shit. Hayes. If you're late, Confidence will fucking kill me," Beau whines.

"Then you go get it. And Stone can escort me to whatever this is."

"Good idea. I'll be five minutes behind you," he says, and turns back for the elevators.

"That's not a *little* complicated." I fall into step beside a speed-walking Stone.

He scoffs. "It is. She won't be married for much longer. Now that I know for certain she could be mine; I'm just going to wait for everything to align and make my move."

"I thought you had a girl in Houston?"

"That was nothing. This woman, she feels like my endgame."

"Not if she's already somebody else's. You're whipped. You'll get over it." I assure him.

When he doesn't respond, I glance at him and find his attention is on something on the other side of the lobby.

I follow his gaze and glimpse someone… who shouldn't be here.

"Is that…Regan Landel?" It's a rhetorical question.

Of course, it's her. No one besides her twin brother, Remi, looks like that.

"Yes, that's her," Stone says. His voice has an odd tone, and I turn away from where Regan is standing to look at him.

He's watching her the way I watch Confidence. Devouring every detail like his life depends on it.

A terrible foreboding makes my chest tight. "Stone—"

He shakes his head and points at the restaurant we're standing in front of. "We'll talk later. We're here. It's showtime."

I force myself to let it go for now. But only for now.

My brother looks besotted, but every man over the age of sixteen is half in love with Regan Landel; she's incomparably beautiful. So, I can understand why Stone, if he's spent time with her or maybe even had a fling with her, would look at her and think he's found nirvana.

But that way only lies trouble. She's married one of the richest men in the world. He's a business acquaintance. We play golf when he's in town. And I know his wife is his most prized possession. I can't believe she'd risk something like a tryst with Stone.

Even if she wasn't married, when she finds out what our family did to hers, she won't want anything to do with us, much less become intimately involved. If I can cut it off before whatever they've started takes root, then maybe, just maybe, I can stop the nightmare our parents started from getting any worse.

Chapter 29

I NEED HER

STONE

Hayes' wedding went off without a hitch. It was beautiful and his new wife, Confidence looked like a fairy queen in just her floor length sequined white dress. A *pregnant* fairy queen whose belly shimmered like a disco ball when she took to the dance floor during the party that lasted well past midnight.

The moon was full, fat and low in the sky, and cast a silver gilt on everything.

Hayes took his bride to bed hours ago, but Beau, Dare and I decided to stay up and watch the sunrise together. Something we used to do when we lived together in New York City a few years ago.

I was finishing my residency, Hayes was studying for the next round of CPA exams and working for Kingdom in their New York office. Beau was in college and Dare was in high school. The only time we were all up and home at the same time was in the very early morning hours. And so, this became our ritual.

We'd catch up, talk shit, and laugh over a cup of coffee while the sun ushered in a new day.

I miss that, because despite how different we are from each other, we've always been friends.

But, I'm not as young as I used to be. Too much scotch, not enough food or water, and dancing until we were drenched with sweat is starting to catch up with me and I'm struggling to keep my eyes open.

Dare is already asleep on one of the lounge chairs. Curled up in a fetal position, the way he used to when he was a kid. When I see him like that, I can almost recall a time before his name became synonymous with trouble. It's not his fault, he was only three when Jason died, and Hayes left. He got the short end of the parenting stick.

"You dumped her because she got a cat?" Beau's question interrupts my reverie.

I glance at him and my lip curls in annoyance. I reach across the space between our lounge chairs and snatch my phone out of his hand. I have pictures of Regan on that phone and the last thing I need is for him or anyone to see them.

"Why are you reading my texts?"

"Because you keep secrets and you're not allowed to have secrets from me. Remember?" He spears me with an annoyed glare.

"No, I don't remember." I grumble and open my phone's security settings. I change my password; the same one I've had for the last ten years.

"Are you changing your passcode?" he asks in surprise.

"How'd you guess?"

He laughs. "Stone, come on. You read my texts all the time."

"I *used* to. You were a minor and I paid for your phone."

"You were two years older than me and being young doesn't mean I didn't want my fucking privacy, man."

I roll my eyes.

"People in hell want ice water. I stopped checking your messages when you started paying the bill. And yes, I dumped her because she got a cat," I answer his original question. It's not the whole truth but it's a pretext for it.

"Jesus, Stone. She got a cat to keep her company while you were gone. God, you're an evil fucker, man. No heart at all." He shakes his head, his face pinched in mock disappointment.

I quirk my lips in a smirk and roll my eyes, dismissing his teasing.

"We didn't want the same things. And I'm allergic to cats. She knew that. Felt like a natural end to me. How was I to know she'd be upset?"

Beau drags his sunglasses down the bridge of his nose to reveal his red-rimmed, glassy-eyed glare of disbelief.

"You know, I promised Cadence I would get through this week without lecturing you about your lifestyle choices. She said you'd be feeling enough pressure as it was with Hayes getting married and you being next in line."

I roll my eyes upward in annoyance. "I feel zero pressure to do anything. Any choice I make is one I want to. But tell Cadence thanks for trying to use her dark powers for good. That's a first."

Normally, I'm a lot less civil about the vise grip his girlfriend has on his balls. She's overbearing and in general, bad for him.

Last Christmas she announced that she'd had a dream about starting a stingless bee apiary in Mexico. She and Beau bought some land in a town called Playa Encanto and went search of a simpler way of life,

As far as I can tell, the year he's spent in Mexico with Cadence has involved developing an intimate knowledge of hallucinogenic plants and herbs having sex on public beaches and playing his guitar while she dances in circles around a small fire.

At least that's what all the videos he posts on IG make it seem like.

He says they're happy, fulfilled and relaxed.

I think she's just spending his money, pulling his chain, and using him to live a life of leisure.

But there's never been any getting through to Beau when it comes to her. And if I know anything it's that my objections only make him more determined to prove me wrong.

"Don't you worry that you're going to end up alone?" Beau's voice is contemplative.

"It's not the worst thing I can imagine, I think it would be worse to be with someone who made me miserable," I answer and give him a pointed look.

He's been with Cadence since he was seventeen and I've never been convinced that it's love that binds him to her. He doesn't want to be alone. Being raised by Eliza scarred us all equally, but differently. He's afraid of being alone. I've always been afraid of committing to the wrong person.

"What if you've already met Ms. Right, but sabotaged the relationship before you had a chance to find out?" he presses me.

I shake my head. "I've never been indecisive. I know what I want. It's not fair to keep dragging something out because you hope the person will change. Like you've been doing for the last 8 years of your life?"

He groans and drops his head into his hands. "But Stone…what if the pussy is so good, so deep, that you know you'll never have anything that good again and you're kind of addicted to it." Beau asks in a rush of pained words.

I gawk at him.

"Beau, you can get good pussy anywhere."

He shakes his head in emphatic disagreement. "No, not like hers."

I groan and run a hand over my face. "Dude, how do you know? Wasn't she your first?"

"Yeah…but it's so good. I know nothing could feel like her. But, fuck, I don't think I even like her anymore."

"And you can still get it up?" I look at him, incredulous.

"I'm a man. It doesn't take much; and when her mouth is full of my cock, she doesn't annoy me at all."

"I forgot how charming you can be." I give him a disapproving frown.

"Learned it all from my big brother," he says with a wink.

Beau leans back in his chair, tips his face up and drinks in the first rays of the rising sun. "I'm so glad you insisted we stay up for this."

I nod in agreement and enjoy the quiet peace that descends as the sun rises.

Beau taps the table. "I know Mom did a number on us and that you deserve the chance to do whatever you want. But, don't let searching for someone who doesn't exist—some perfect woman without any flaws— keep you from missing out on something special."

It's the tip of my tongue to say I've found her. But, that's crazy. Sure, we had a great week together. But…our lives are incompatible for anything more than friendship. And even that seems to make her uncomfortable.

Beau nudges my chair. "I'm going to swim," he declares and stands up to head to the water.

I throw a fist full of sand at him as he ambles off towards the water.

Beau is soul searching and unsettled. But the fact that we're here together and that he's got enough security in his life to have space to daydream, makes me feel less worried about him.

I missed a lot of my adolescence, and sometimes I lament that, but it feels so worth it to see my brothers whole and happy.

The way I felt when I was with Regan.

Just thinking of her makes my heart thud and my stomach flip.

I want to punch myself.

For a man everyone calls smart, I've been incredibly stupid.

She's married with children, I live on another continent, I've never even come close to falling in love. And whatever I felt for her when I was ten, was gone. But when I jumped off that gondola, I knew.

And still, I persisted.

I thought there was safety in the fact that we would have to say goodbye. I should have recognized that for the wolf in sheep's clothing that it was.

But, there is no safety net you're ensnared by a femme fatal. There's only free fall.

We agreed to wait until tomorrow but, I miss her and it's not like anyone's paying attention.

I scribble a note for my brothers on a cocktail napkin and go in search of my goddess.

Chapter 30

HOT STONE

REGAN

There's a light knock on my door and I put my book down and just stare at it for a minute. It's barely 9am and Stone is fast asleep next to me. He showed up a few hours ago, and I was too happy to see him to mind that he was breaking one of our rules. He crawled into bed, wrapped an arm around my waist, pulled me so my back pressed against his chest and fell asleep.

The knock comes again, a little louder this time. I disentangle myself from the warm weight of his arms and slip my robe on before I pad over to the door.

I look through the viewfinder and my heart drops to my toes when I see Hayes Rivers standing there.

I gasp, my heart racing and jump back from the door like it's on fire.

What in the world does he want? Maybe I can pretend I'm not here. He knocks again, more insistent this time.

"One second," I call out and run to shut the bedroom door, then scan the room for any signs of Stone's presence. Seeing none, I take a steadying breath, and open the door.

Hayes Rivers is an entire mood. He looms large and imposing in my doorframe, smiling pleasantly, but his eyes tell an entirely different story. They're cold and intent and his severe brows give his handsome face an austerity that is intimidating.

"This is a surprise. I expected you to be keeping the new Mrs. Rivers company," I say in a lighthearted tone that is as transparent as his disapproval. I draw my robe tighter around me.

"Yes, my wife told me that you were responsible for her having her hair done. I wanted to thank you." His smile is nothing close to grateful, and my chest tightens.

"You're welcome and it was my pleasure. But you didn't have to come all this way to tell me that." I give him a tight smile.

"Actually, I did." His pleasant smile falls away.

"Oh?" I raise an expectant brow.

"We're having a post wedding brunch. Confidence thought since Remi wasn't able to make it, and you just *happen* to be here, it would be nice if you came."

I jerk backward and frown. "Wait, you were expecting Remi? Don't you know he left town without a word?" I'm surprised because they became good friends last year; Bringing a very public end to the rivalry between our families.

His inscrutable gaze flickers with surprise before he looks away like something down the hall caught his attention. I stick my head out; there's nothing there. But that would mean…he's nervous. Hayes Rivers and nervousness don't go together. *Ever.*

He narrows his eyes as if he's trying to remember. "No. I didn't, I guess. I just, it's been a crazy couple of months and Confidence being pregnant and Gigi getting shot and recouping, you know. So, I have no idea what's up with Remi. We sent him an invite, but…yeah, no."

None of that makes any sense. The hairs on the back of my neck stand up. He sounds like a guilty man talking to the police

What in the world is going on?

I narrow my eyes at him.

"And your wife, who *works* for him, didn't mention that she hasn't seen your best friend in two months?"

He shrugs. "She doesn't work for him anymore."

The rush of resentment I feel toward him is unwarranted

"Your wife was aglow with love for you. Don't force her to give up on her dreams, so she can be your perfect little trophy. Trust me when I say that if you do, one day, you will regret it."

He leans away as if I slapped him and then his expression darkens.

"I don't appreciate the insinuation, Regan. I can assure you that I can't force Confidence to do anything."

I flush. "I see, sorry. I'm projecting. Bad habit."

He ignores me and glances over my shoulder, looking into the suite. My heart leaps in my throat.

"Can I help you?" I ask, moving to block his view.

He turns his intelligent eyes back to me, an almost charming smile on his face.

"I thought I saw something."

"Well, it's just me."

He bites his lip, and nods his head, as if agreeing.

"Sorry. It's a bad habit. In fact, I was just telling my brother, Stone, how easy it is to see things that aren't there. He's spent his whole life working toward this opportunity that's waiting for him in Houston. But an *illusion* is about to ruin it all. I'll do everything in my power to make sure that doesn't happen." He looks perfectly civil…but he's making his point in a ruthlessly deliberate way.

He knows.

My throat constricts and I take an involuntary step away from him. "Well, good luck with that," I manage to croak out.

He nods. "I'll let Confidence know you had other plans and couldn't join us for brunch." His smile is all grace and charm, but his eyes glimmer with a satisfaction that makes me want to punch him in the nose.

If he was hoping to intimidate or shame me, he failed.

I give him a smile that's laced with pure venom "Oh no, there's nowhere I'd rather be this afternoon. Please let her know that I'll be there."

Anger flares in his hazel gaze, and he closes them for the space of a heartbeat. When he looks back at me, they're ice cold. "I see," his voice is grave and low.

"Glad you do. Now, if you'll excuse me, I've got a hot *stone*…treatment waiting for me." I allow myself a second to enjoy the indignation on his face before I shut the door

And then, I start to panic. My scalp tingles and my whole-body flushes hot. God, he could tell Marcel. And then I'd lose my children. My heart constricts. I make it to the toilet right before I throw up.

I strip, turn on the shower, and climb in. I sit on the floor, my knees drawn up to my chin, and let the hard pricks of cold water soothe me. As the water heats up and my pulse slows down, my panic turns to frustration. When I can breathe again, I force myself to think.

There's only one way Hayes knows about us, and *he's* snoring in my bed.

Whether he told him or said enough so Hayes could guess, doesn't matter.

I was deluding myself thinking we could carry on any semblance of a relationship after we left this resort. Even if I leave Marcel, there's too much shit in our way. And friendship…is laughable.

I'd been heartsick when I saw him laughing with those girls in their tent that first night on the island. And Stone…well, he may have outgrown stabbing people, but that possessive, determined spirit is still there. And, right now, the thought of being possessed by anyone, when I'm just on the cusp of finding myself, terrifies me.

I need to put a period at the end of this sentence.

Today.

I step out of the shower, call down to the salon and pull rank to get an appointment. I gaze at myself in the mirror. Freckles spangle the bridge of my nose. My hair is a wild cloud of curls and coils, some of them streaked by the sun. I love the way I look right now. But, like everything else that feels good about this trip, its time has come to an end.

I turn away from my reflection and start getting ready.

Chapter 31

MAKING AN ENTRANCE

STONE

"What the hell are you looking at?" Dare asks. I drag my eyes away from the entrance of the restaurant and throw my napkin at his scowling face.

"Not you, so why are you worried about it?" I snap.

"Boys, behave." Hetty, one of Hayes' new neighbors in Rivers Wilde, and Gigi's plus one, gives us a grandmotherly glare.

We all mumble apologies, and I turn back to watch the door.

When I woke, there was a note that read, "See you at brunch," on the pillow where her head should have been.

I was confused until I got here and saw her name on one of the place cards. Confidence was bursting with excitement as she told me how they'd run into her and that Hayes went up to invite her this morning. My stomach clenched so hard I thought I'd be sick.

He came to her room this morning?

I glance at Hayes and he smiles briefly and turns his attention back to Gigi. He's been nothing but relaxed and hasn't mentioned her, or our conversation, at all. But Hayes is the master of hiding his emotions, so that doesn't make me feel any better.

"Oh, my damn … Regan Landel is here?" Beau asks in an overly interested voice. I turn to him and follow his rapt gaze to the entrance that leads in from the beach.

The version of Regan that strides into the dining room is one I've never seen in person.

Her hair is blown straight and shines like polished sable when she moves. Her skin glows with something more than the sun kissed warmth I got used to seeing at the beach.

She's dressed in an all-white floor length dress that was made to be worn by her. Two diamond shaped pieces of fabric cover each of her plump breasts, drape over her shoulders and meet at the nape of her neck in an oversized bow that sits on her left shoulder.

The deep "v" created by the scant bodice exposes the long column of her throat and the smooth, sun browned valley of skin between her breasts all the way to right above her belly button. The skirt has twin slits that reveal her legs from toe to damn near the top of her hip with every step she takes in her blush pink, open toe shoes. The heels are needle thin and so high that her lithe and graceful frame is nearly as tall as I am.

Beau lets out a low whistle of appreciation and I grit my teeth. "You know I'd never even think about touching another woman, but she is fucking hot, man. Even her toes are perfect. God, I wish I was a billionaire. I'd lay it at her feet for just one night of—"

"Don't finish that sentence," I snap, uncaring that I sound like a fucking cave man.

Beau looks at me askance and then bursts out laughing. "Ohhh, I *forgot* you had a thing for her."

"I was ten," I snap and look back at my phone. And what I felt then is a mere star, compared to the galaxy of emotions that make up the thing I have for her now.

"Was she always a looker?" Beau asks never taking his hungry eyes from Regan. I want to tell him she's mine. That he can't look at her like that.

Instead, I nod. "Always."

"Hey guys, does everyone know Regan Landel? Her family founded Rivers Wilde and her twin brother is a friend of both of ours." Confidence, her eyes bright as Regan approaches.

Hayes is glaring at me with a warning in his expression. I don't know what came over me yesterday. I know better. If there's one thing Hayes isn't good at, it's minding his own business.

"Well, now I know why Landel never lets her out of his sight. And why he's so damn possessive. I heard some guy lost a finger for dancing too close to his *'crown jewel'* at a fundraiser."

I roll my eyes but inwardly my insides feel like water. "He's a publisher, not a gangster and if she's his crown jewel, why is she here without him?"

Beau scoffs and smirks conspiratorially. "I've heard his family's publishing and real estate is just a front for other stuff."

By "he's heard," he means Cadence told him. That woman has a talent for curating and aggregating gossip that seems to far outweigh her talent for anything else.

"Well, I'm sure you've got reliable insider info, but given that I've spent the last year living in a city where corruption and crime are a way of life for most people, I can tell you the wives of men who are really involved with the cartels don't travel through Mexico alone."

"Okay, well, you go ahead and think that, and I'm going to get a tequila sunrise and enjoy the suddenly much improved view."

Chapter 32

GOODBYE

REGAN

Confidence looks as fresh as a daisy and radiates with happiness. I let down some of my reserve to give her a genuine hug of congratulations. Hayes got an air kiss. When she got to Stone, my inflection and expression were exactly the same with him, as they were with everyone else, she introduced me to.

She sat me across from him, in between Dare and her best friend, Cass.

Cass has been preoccupied with her date. Dare has been preoccupied with his phone. And Stone has been preoccupied with glaring at me.

I haven't looked at him properly since I walked in, and it's killing me. I miss him. The days we spent together were amazing. We took pictures, posed like a couple, held hands as we toured ruins, fucked in the ocean, and for a brief moment, I forgot who I was.

But Hayes' visit sobered me up *really* quick. This brunch is exactly what we both need. A reminder of what life would really be like if we were to try to take this beyond this trip.

Confidence's mother finishes her speech, and I can't take another second of Stone's glaring.

I surge to my feet and turn an apologetic smile toward the newly-weds.

"I hate to cut into your speeches, but my car is leaving for the airport soon." I can feel Stone's body tense. But I still don't dare look at him.

"Before I go, I want to wish the happy couple well. Marriage shouldn't be hard. People who say that are crazy. It should be easy and fun and loving and safe. Anything less than that, you're in for a lifetime of misery, divorce, or jail." A small ripple of laughter surprises me. "I'm not joking. Discovery ID wouldn't have more than two hours of programming, if it weren't for all the wives and husbands who try to kill each other."

Confidence gasps, and someone clears their throat. I grimace in apology. "Not that you're in any danger of that. You two are clearly very much in love." I smile at them both, letting the sincere warmth I feel for *her* show. "Focus on *that*."

Hayes' jaw tightens, but his expression is as civil as mine.

"You're lucky to have found each other. Most people never get the timing quite right."

That is when I look at Stone. His expression is grave, and his eyes are wide with an emotion I can't name, but it makes me want to cry. I hate leaving like this, but it's for the best.

I turn back to the happy couple and raise my glass. "Congratulations. Cheers to forever."

"Welcome Mrs. Landel. Please make yourself comfortable," the woman whose name tag reads "Paulina" greets me, as I walk into the lounge for private charters. I walked out of Pacifico and got straight into the waiting car that brought me to the airport.

Time to head back to my real life, and there was no point in dragging it out because I wanted one more night of feeling good.

My feelings won't change anything, and one more night will just make the inevitable even harder.

I pluck a bottle of water from the table, where an assortment of bottled drinks are nestled in a silver ice bucket, and gulp half of it down, before I drop my sore, soul weary, self into one of the winged armchairs. I free my feet from the heels that, after a week of sandals and bare feet, feel like torture devices, and slip on the flip flops in my tote.

I pull out my phone and check my messages. The first one is from Tyson.

"Oh hey, I forgot. Did you see Stone? I was supposed to text and give you a heads up but got distracted. You need to call me, anyway. Busy here, but we'll make time."

"Just saw him this morning. Headed back. Call you soon."

So typical of Tyson. He's so disorganized and self-absorbed that I'm shocked he remembered to text at all.

I drop my phone in my bag and close my eyes. My head aches. I rub my temples and groan at the shiver of relief the caress brings.

"I could do that for you if you'd like."

I sit up with a start and find myself face to face with the owner of that silky baritone. Stone is standing in the doorway. He looks amazing in his blue linen pants and white linen shirt, the deep tan of his skin setting both off beautifully. But his expression is dark and brooding, and I can't tell if he wants to strangle me or rip my clothes off.

My throat goes dry.

"What are you doing here?"

"I wanted to say goodbye."

He prowls toward me, his long legs eating up the ground between us. He drops into the seat next to me, rests his elbows on his knees and steeples his fingers under his chin, his eyes trained on the huge window that faces the tarmac.

"How'd you find me?" I ask.

If he hears me, he doesn't give any sign of it. "Did you know the Transit of Venus happens just four times every 243 years? It's the rarest of predictable astronomical phenomena. It's how early astronomers mapped the heavens."

I gape at him. "Uhhh. What?" I ask, genuinely confused.

"I've dated, had lovers—"

"This better be going somewhere good…" I mutter, irritated at the thought of him and lovers.

He sits up, turns to me, and takes my hands into his. His touch is heaven and hell, all at once. And even if I wanted to pull my hands free, his grip is so tight, I couldn't.

"But before this last week, I've never really been in love."

Panic and regret form a fist around my heart and squeeze. I clear my dry throat and shake my head. "But you said you didn't want…"

"I know. But you've always been my game changer."

I blink…and try to absorb everything he's told me. "What do you mean?"

"I mean, I want to explore what's happening between us," he says, and I cover my mouth to muffle a scream. I dart around the room, not even sure what I'm looking for.

"Where is everyone?"

"On a break," he says, batting my concern away like it's an annoying fly.

"Did you pay them to leave us alone?" I gape at him.

"Yup."

"Why?"

"So, I could make my Hail Mary."

My heart feels like it's being stretched in two different directions. The side that wants to say yes is pulling as hard as the side that knows I have to say to no.

"Stone, I have a lot to sort out. And…so do you." I lick my dry lips and shudder when I remember Hayes and his knowing eyes… and the career Stone clearly loves that a scandal the size of what we'd cause could disrupt.

"What did my brother say to you when he came to the room? That's what made you feel like this."

My eyes widen in surprise. "How did you know?" I ask.

"Why didn't you tell me?" he asks, instead of answering me.

"Because I didn't want to cause a rift. I know how much you love them. And he didn't say anything I didn't already know," I explain.

His jaw tightens, and he nods, the disappointment in his eyes is unbearable.

"I need to check…something." I grab my bag and stand. I need to get out of here. I walk over to the deserted service desk and ring the bell.

"I told you, there's no one here." His voice comes from right behind me. My already frazzled nerves vibrate, and I yelp and spin around.

"Don't sneak up on me like that, Stone."

He grabs my wrists and yanks me to him, in a move that's rough, but that ends with his sweet mouth on mine. He kisses me, and for a second, I kiss him back. How can I not? He tastes like heaven, and I want to kiss him forever. His mouth is hot and demanding and unyielding on mine. I revel in the cinnamon and chocolate on his breath. I breathe in lungfuls of the most delicious man I've ever tasted.

He cups my ass, and I cling to him, a mere handful of heartbeats away from begging him to please put himself inside me. I rally the last bits of my resolve and shove him away.

He looks bewildered, disheveled, and not even close to daunted.

I jump back and just manage to evade his attempt to grab me. I step behind the counter and glare at him. Angry at him and myself for the half of me that wants him to jump over the counter and kiss me again.

"I know you feel the same way," he growls in frustration,

I gape, goggle-eyed at how savage his expression is. My heart thunders, not from fear, but from excitement. What is wrong with me?

"Less than a week ago, you told me you didn't want anything more than sex. And now, you want me to throw away everything because you've changed your mind?" I demand.

"No, I want you to choose a life you actually want. And I want you to let me be part of it." His eyes soften, and my resolve does, too.

Oh, dear Lord. Why am I being tested like this?

Discipline, Regan. My grandfather's voice cracks like a whip in my mind.

"Did you see what happened at brunch? What makes you think we can keep this going, if you were in Houston?"

"No, I didn't see what happened at brunch because I was too busy trying to understand why you wouldn't even look at me." The pain and accusation in his face makes my heart tremble.

But that's as far as I allow myself to be pulled down. "I'm sorry for that. But, if I looked at you, everyone would have known. And Stone, no one can know about us. If Marcel knows I've been unfaithful, he'll get the kids. It's in our prenup. You have to understand. This has to be where we say goodbye. Like we planned."

He glares at me, hands on his hips, and shakes his head, but the determination in his eyes fades, and he looks dejected.

"I'm sorry, Stone." It feels inadequate, but it's all I can manage.

He nods and doesn't say anything, as I round the counter and walk over to my bags.

I take another breath and press on.

"Maybe next time we see each other, and if we're both free, we can...see."

He grabs me by the shoulders and spins me around, so fast, I scream. He pins me in place with a furious stare. "What if next time isn't for another five years? What will I do without you for that long?" His voice is rough, and his eyes look so damn...pained. I almost believe him.

Almost. I pull out of his grasp.

"There'll be someone else. You'll be fine." The jealousy I have no right to, blazes my chest and makes a liar out of my casual voice.

His knowing laugh is unrepentant and infuriating.

"I'm trying to do the right thing, I'm glad you think it's fun—"

He closes the space between us with one long ground eating stride, cups the back of my neck, and his lips cover my mine, in a hard, fast kiss that curls my toes and fries my senses.

He breaks the kiss as abruptly as he started it, his hold on my neck tightening, his eyes growing dark with need. "I'll never be fine again, Regan. You've ruined me," he whispers against my mouth.

"Why did you do that?" I ask, when I can speak again.

"You said you were trying to do the right thing. And kissing you… it'll always be the right thing."

The sincere hope in his eyes is a battering ram against the walls of my resistance. I groan in frustration and drop my forehead on his chest.

His other arm winds around my waist.

"Don't leave today. Let's go back to your room and spend this last night together. Let me say goodbye to you."

I want to say yes.

And that's why I have to say no.

I cup his face. He's shaved again, but his stubble scrapes against the palm of my hand. I memorize the strong lines of his face, the flecks of gold in his eyes, the lush pink center of his bottom lip, and the way he makes me feel like I can touch the sky.

"Thank you so much for this week. It's been one of the happiest of my life."

"We can have more." His face is so earnest. I know he thinks he means it. But life can't just be one big adventure. It's obligations and responsibility. He's got his whole life ahead of him, and I've got children to raise and a marriage to end. And a life to plan.

"Maybe...But before I make promises to anyone else, I want to try and finally keep the ones I made to myself."

He deflates in the face of my plea. He presses his lips together and puts his hands on his hips. His eyes glitter with frustration.

"You deserve that. And I want it for you," His smile is so sad.

I hate myself for putting that there.

I hate him for making me feel the same.

Then he pulls me into a hug so tight, it's hard to breathe. But I hold on and press my cheek to his and savor the feel and smell of the man who has given me more joy in three days than I've felt in fifteen years.

My eyes burn from the sting of unshed tears.

This is over. Probably, for good. But I won't cast it as tragic. That this happened at all is amazing. After years of feeling the exact opposite, I now know that I am indeed, made to be loved. Even though he didn't say the words; from taking me on that road trip, to bungee jumping, to showing me the wonders of the universe, to the way he's letting me go now, I feel loved.

The doors slide open and the sound of jet engines, the smell of fuel and a wave of hot air roll in and bring reality with them. I look over my shoulder to find a member of the crew waving awkwardly at me.

He hugs me one more time and then picks my carry-on bag and walks with me to the door.

"Take care," I say. A lump made of equal parts grief and gratitude lodges in my throat.

He takes my hand and draws it up to his mouth for a kiss.

"We didn't find each other again for no reason. This may be the wrong time. But we are the right people. And you've always been my favorite what if."

"I hope now that will stop being true." I say with a flippancy I don't feel.

"Why would it?" he looks genuinely puzzled.

"Because now you know that what if is sweet, but messy."

He chuckles and it rumbles hollow and sad against my ribcage. That fierce determination back in his. "Well, you told me once that I was good at cleaning up your messes…when I get back to Houston, we're going to find out if that's still true." He presses a hard, possessive kiss to my mouth. And for one glorious, final minute, I don't give a damn who sees.

Three Months Later

RIVERS WILDE
HOUSTON, TX

Chapter 33

THE PRODIGAL RETURNS

REGAN

"This is what you get for cheating on me Regan."

"It was just one blow out." I shake my head at my hairdresser Tanaka's dramatics and sit patiently while she inspects my hair.

When we moved to Paris, all the stylists my mother in law worked with had no clue what to do with my hair. I started doing it myself, and it showed.

I was at the American embassy in Paris one day soon after we arrived and saw a woman who looked like she could have been my sister. Her hair was glorious, and she gave me her stylist's number. She was working from a rented chair in a shop nestled in the shadow of Sacré-Cœur at the foot of the eastern slopes of Montmartre. My mother in law had nearly had a coronary and told Marcel I was frequenting the *slums* when she found out I spurned her Left Bank stylist.

I ignored her. Tanaka worked miracles with my hair.

The night we hosted our first of what would become regular First Friday socials at our apartment in Rue De Bac, everyone complimented my hair. And I was thrilled to send them her way.

She opened her own salon on the Left Bank a year later. She had a six-month waiting list and was well on her way to becoming a real celebrity when I decided to move back to Houston.

And when I told her I was going, she said "Me, too."

It was at Blush, the salon she opened here in Rivers Wilde, is where she truly skyrocketed to fame. Her clientele list is so rarified that she's become synonymous with the likes of Vidal Sassoon.

She could be anywhere in the world, but she's loyal to the bone and for giving her work a platform that changed her life completely, she always makes time for me.

To have one of her only two salons right here in Rivers Wilde was quite a coup for us. She reminds us of that every chance she gets. Underneath all her blunt talk and brusque manner, she is loyal, kind and brilliant.

She fingers the ends of my hair, her critical eyes stricken. "Well, that's all it takes to ruin a decade's worth of work. And you haven't been in regularly enough. I must cut it."

"No." I pull away and give her a wide-eyed look.

"It's for the best. Your hair grows like weeds, you won't miss it."

"I already do." I clutch my hair protectively.

Her sigh is one of long suffering "This is tedious. I always win. Just accept it."

"Glad to know I'm not the only one she browbeats," a lilting, familiar voice says from behind us.

I turn, a genuine smile of affection tugging at my lips before I even lay eyes on her. "Hello, Mrs. Rivers," I greet Confidence with her brand-new name. Their formal church wedding was a month ago and this is the first time I've seen her since. She's glowing.

"Ah, I should have known you two were friends…stubborn as each other," Tanaka chides, even as she and Confidence share a warm hug.

She turns a charming, shy smile on me. "I came by to drop off a thank you note, and Noe said you two were in the consultation room. I had to say hi."

Tanaka harrumphs. "I'll go deal with him, while you two catch up."

Confidence sits on the armchair across from mine and blows out an exhausted breath.

"Tanaka is so grumpy, right? But I think she forces those pregnancy tests on people not out of an abundance of caution, but because she's secretly a sap. She loves being witness to people getting unexpected happy news. That bad ass, I'll put in you my breakfast smoothie and drink you if you piss me off, is an act."

Confidence giggles. "I know. And she's a genius. In fact, it was here that I found out I was pregnant. She wouldn't color my hair unless I took a pregnancy test and…here we are." She drops her eyes to her stomach and strokes it, tenderly.

A rush of nostalgia compels me to reach over and to touch her stomach. I pull my hand back, and wince in apology. "Do you mind if I touch?"

She rolls her eyes and arches her back to stick her stomach out. "Go ahead, I *love* it."

I place my palm on the top of her belly and her smile widens with pride, "I'm growing a *person* inside me."

"I'm so happy for you," I run my hand down the curve of the cocoon her body has fashioned for her baby.

"He's moving," She grabs my wrist and slides my hand to the left. I gasp as the slide of a rounded body part against my palm.

"I know, right?" She beams with the kind of excitement I'm used to seeing on my children's faces—guileless and unmitigated. *The kind of excitement I had countless moments of when I was with Stone.*

I'm gripped by a pang of longing so sharp that my heart skips a beat, but I push it away.

"Do you want more babies?" Confidence asks and the pain I just dismissed leaps back to life. The pain over Stone didn't surprise me, I always feel something when I think of him. But this… this does. For a woman who spent more than half her life thinking she'd never have children, it's jarring to feel a sense of longing when I already have three more than I planned.

Even if I didn't have my IUD, there's no chance of me being pregnant again. Marcel and I are irrevocably broken. I haven't even seen him since I've been back.

As for Stone… I know we'll never be strangers again. The connection we forged on that trip was real and deep. It's been almost three months since we said goodbye.

When I got back home, everything was haywire. Evangeline got into a fight at school the day after I arrived, Martinez had his fifth bout of strep throat this year, and his doctor decided it was time for him to have his tonsils out. And my brother's disappearing act has become a PR nightmare. But it's only in the last few weeks, as life calmed down, that I've had enough of an emotional bandwidth to think about what.

I've stopped pretending I didn't leave a piece of my heart with him. But it doesn't change the facts of our circumstances. He may be interested in a relationship with me, now. But, once he's here, he'll see how burdensome and unwieldy the baggage I come with really is.

He'll meet someone who can live out his globe-trotting adventures with him.

At least, I hope so. Because if he settles here and I have to see him with another woman on his arm, I might have to consider moving.

I used to find, all of the sentiments like "I know I'll never feel this way about anyone again," silly and fatalistic. But now that that's exactly how I feel—there's nothing silly about it. It took me thirty-six years to find him. Those aren't good odds for it happening again in this life time..

"Regan?" Confidence's slightly raised, concerned voice startles me out of my daydream. I glance up to find her watching me with a furrowed brow.

I flush and pull my hand back from her belly. "Sorry, nostalgia." I flash a sheepish smile.

She doesn't return it. "Are you okay?"

"I'm fine, why?" I hold my breath and pray that I speak my thoughts aloud.

"It's just…you looked so sad." Her frown deepens.

I shake my head in dismissal and force my smile wider. "I'm *fine*. I just got lost in my memories for a minute." I sit back in my chair, cross my legs and relax my shoulders. "You really popped since the wedding, haven't you?" I nod at her belly.

Her smile doesn't quite reach her eyes, but she lets me change the subject and nods. "More like exploded. People keep asking if I'm having twins. I just tell them um, no, his daddy's a giant." She rolls her eyes. But the smile that on her face when she mentions Hayes makes me jealous.

She leans back in her chair and her expression dims again. "So, how *are* you doing? Is it hard with Marcel being gone all the time?" she asks.

My stock answer, "I miss him, but it's best for our kids to be here.", is on the tip of my tongue. But I like Confidence and if we're going to be friends, she'll learn the truth sooner or later.

"Not at all. It's actually easier this way," I answer and instantly feel lighter, even when her smile falters.

She leans forward to grasp my hand, her eyes full of sympathy. "I'm so sorry."

I shake my head to dissuade her. "Don't be. I'm fine."

"But—"

"Confidence?" A woman's voice I don't recognize calls out to her and she sits up straight, and rests a hand on her forehead, her eyes widen with guilt. "I'm a knucklehead, I forgot Gigi was waiting for me in the car," she grabs her purse and struggles to her feet just as a dark haired, willow beauty in silk light grey dress walks into the consultation room.

"There you are, I was—" The woman stops mid-sentence when she sees me. Her mouth falls open, her eyes go round like saucers. She looks like she's seen a ghost.

"Hey, Gigi, I don't think you've met Regan Wilde-Landel." Confidence walks over to her. Her use of my maiden name surprises me. But, it, clearly, surprises Gigi more. The paper cup she's holding slips from her hand and lands with a splatter at her feet. Confidence yelps and hops back. I stand to help, but Gigi stays frozen, not taking her eyes off me.

"Is she okay?" I ask.

Confidence glances at me and nods with a reassuring smile. "Noé?" she calls out to Tanaka's assistant, and slides a protective arm around Gigi's waist before she leads her from the room, without either of them saying another word.

I sit, barely registering when Noe comes in to mop up the spill. Gigi's behavior just now was bizarre. I know very little about her. She's Hayes' aunt, but was disowned, when she ran with a man her father didn't approve of. When her brother died, leaving Hayes an orphan, he went to live with her, and she raised him.

But I've been very curious about her lately. She was shot when a disgruntled employee went ballistic outside of the Rivers' business headquarter. And, as far as I know, the last thing Remi did, before he hauled ass out of town, was visit her in the hospital.

She's rebuffed all of our efforts to talk to her about his visit. And I felt bad harassing an old lady, who was recovering from a gunshot wound, and who probably knew nothing about whatever was up with Remi. But now, I wonder if there's more there.

I get up and walk out to the reception area to see if I can catch them and maybe get her to talk to me. But when I get there, Confidence is walking back into the salon, alone.

"Where's Gigi?" I ask, peering over her shoulder to see if I can catch a glimpse of her.

"I told her to go on home. She's still healing from the gunshot and she's tired..." Her eyes don't meet mine and she swallows audibly.

The hair on the back of my neck stands up. "What's wrong?"

She winces and sighs heavily before finally meeting my eyes. Her eyes are bleak. My heart stops. "Has something happened to Remi?" I can barely get the words out and sag with relief when she shakes her head in vigorous denial.

"No, but I do want to talk to you—"

"Mrs. Landel, your phone's ringing." Noé calls as he rushes over to us, holding my vibrating purse out to me.

I stifle my irritation at the interruption and take it from him. "You didn't have to bring it out here."

"It rang twice already, I thought maybe it was urgent." A new worry blooms. Eva seems to be settling back into school after her suspension, but anyone calling three times in a row can't be good news.

"Sorry," I mutter to Confidence as I fish my phone out.

I let out a sigh of relief when the name Kal flashes on my screen. She's Remi's ex…the one who got away. A few days ago, she showed up looking for him. Last time we talked, she thought she had a lead on him and said she'd be in touch. He's gone off the grid before. But never for this long and never without being in touch at least sporadically. I've been waiting for her to call and tell me what, if anything, she's found.

The call rolls to voicemail before I can answer it. I hold my phone up to Confidence, "I need to take this, one sec." I sit down in one of the waiting room chairs and call her back.

"Did you find him?" I skip the formality of a greeting when the call connects.

"Reggie?" My brother's voice rings in my ears.

Wild relief rushes through me. Fear I've kept bottled up overflows and anger surges. I cover my eyes with my hands and start to sob. "Remi? Oh my god, is that you?"

"Yes. Hey, Reggie. Don't cry. I'm sorry" Remi says in a soothing voice that makes my blood boil.

"Don't you dare tell me not to cry, you asshole. You better be calling me from whatever hospital you've been laid up in—*in a coma*—unable use the phone for the last six months." A bone deep fear that I haven't allowed myself to acknowledge breaks and I yell at him through my watershed of tears.

"Regan. I haven't been to fucking Disneyland, okay?" he interjects impatiently.

My anger pushes me to my feet. "Don't you dare raise your voice at me Remington Wilde. You have no fucking right after what you've done to my heart."

"I know, I know. I am so damn sorry," he groans, but his contrition falls on deaf ears.

"I don't care if you're sorry. Tell me where you are and why you didn't tell me you were leaving. And why didn't you get in touch??"

"I'm in Burton at a ranch house that used to belong to our father and his wife."

I go completely still at his grave, cryptic words. "Why are you saying *his wife* and instead of Mom?" I demand.

When he doesn't answer right away, I start pacing. When I turn to face the front of the salon, I almost jump out of my skin, when I see Confidence sitting in one of the chairs in front of the large storefront window. Her face is creased with concern.

I'd forgotten she was there; I mouth Remi's name and press a finger to my lips. Her eyes bug out of her head.

"Remi, answer me!" I bark when he doesn't say anything.

"Reggie, you should sit down first," he says in a grave voice.

My heart starts to pound, and I grit my teeth. "Stop trying to manage me and just answer me, *right* now," I demand. My finger stabbing the air.

"Mom was his first wife…he had another—"

"What the *fuck* does that mean?" My voice is so sharp that Confidence jumps.

"If you'd stop yelling and interrupting, I'd already be done telling you."

I close my mouth and bite back my retort. "Go ahead."

"Lucas Wilde left Mom for another woman right after Tyson was born. He married her. Moved with her to Burton and started a new life. One day, he left for work and didn't come back. She presumed he was dead and left too."

None of that can be true. None of it even makes any sense. A new fear grips me and I turn my back on Confidence and walk to one of the product display stands across the room.

"Remi. Are you in trouble? Is this code for something? Do you need me to call the police?" I ask in a quiet voice.

He chuckles, but it's devoid of humor. "No. Kal found me. I'm at their house. It's all true."

I press a hand to the wall to steady myself. "How? I've seen pictures of us at his funeral. Tyson was a tiny baby. How could he have gotten married, set up house and died in three months of Tyson being born?"

"Because he didn't die. That's what they told us and the rest of the world."

"Who told you that?" My voice is guttural with anger.

"His wife," he says flatly.

"You *talked* to her?" I screech.

"Yes."

"Who is she? How did she find you?" My head rings like something hard hit it. I reach blindly behind me until I make contact with the chair of the arm and lower myself onto it.

"He left me a letter. All those years ago. He was planning on coming back for us. Regan, they had a child." My hand flies to my throat as if it can stop the gasp of horror that comes.

"Oh my God." I sit up straight, my mind racing. "Who is he? And what happened to the kid?"

"Oh God, Regan. *Wait*," Confidence calls with a frantic urgency that draws my eyes to her. But she's not looking at me. She's typing furiously on her phone, her hands visibly shaking.

"It's Gigi Rivers," Remi answers.

The whole world comes to a screeching halt. "What?" croak. My voice sounds far away. All of this feels like an out of body experience.

"Regan, wait," Confidence cries out again and everything clicks into place.

That look in Gigi's eyes…. That expression I couldn't read…it was *guilt*. She was the last person Remi saw. I stare at Confidence and re-member Hayes almost having a panic attack when I asked about Remi in Mexico.

My stomach falls to my toes.

"Who is their son?" I speak into the phone, but my eyes are on Confidence's bowed head.

Her sorrowful gaze snaps to mine. "Regan, let me take you some-where private, please," she stammers. I glance around. Noé is gone. We're alone. I shake my head to say no.

"Who is his son?" I demand again. Confidence closes her eyes as if she's in pain.

"Who's there with you?" Remi demands.

"Is it Hayes Rivers?" I demand.

His silence and Confidence's muffled sob are all the answers I need.

"Does he know?" It's a rhetorical question. Because his wife clearly does. My eyes never leave Confidence. She's sitting in one of the waiting room chairs. Her hands pressed together between her thighs as she watches me with deep, troubled concern on her face.

"Yes, Regan, He knows. He knew before me. I'm sorry. But I need to call Tyson, too and then we've got to get on the road. I know I owe you a million apologies and explanations. I was reeling from shock when I first heard. Then I had this argument with Mom, right after. She tried to justify it all—"

"Mom knows, too?" My voice comes out in a wheeze. I can't breathe.

"She's known the whole time. Pops, too. Listen, I know I owe you more. But I really need to go."

I take a deep breath and compose myself…My whole life is unraveling. And I don't know what to do next.

"That's fine," I say in the voice he expects me to use—calm, collected, cool.

"I love you, Reggie. We'll be okay. We'll get through this."

I almost laugh at his use of the word we.

Is there a "*we*"?

I hang up and face Confidence.

"You already knew?"

Her nod is slow, her eyes sorrowful and downcast.

"I couldn't say anything because Hayes asked me not to. I'm so sorry," she sounds so sad.

And, it pisses me off. Why is she sad? When it's me who's entire life is a lie. I curl my lip at her. "So, was all of this friendship shit so that you could keep an eye on me for Hayes? To make sure I wasn't planning on fucking his brother, since it turns out he's my fucking *stepbrother*, too?" I yell and Confidence's eyes nearly bug out of her head, and fill with tears.

Guilt deflates my anger. I'm not mad at Confidence. She's not the one who betrayed me. "I'm sorry." I cover my face with my hands and try to catch my breath.

"It's okay. I can't imagine what you're feeling," she says after a minute. Her voice is soft but guarded. I nod, but don't meet her eye. "But I didn't even know about you and… I'm praying it's Stone…until right now," she says.

To my horror, a sob breaks loose and a tear streaks down my cheek.

"Can I call someone or take you home myself? I know it's a lot, but everything is going to be okay."

Nothing will be okay, but I don't have the strength to argue. My whole life has unraveled.

In the days to come, all of this will feel like a gust of warm wind compared to the tsunami that will land on our doorstep.

Chapter 34

OPPORTUNITY

STONE

"I've got some news. Call me when you can talk."

Hayes' text is curt and ominous.

My first thought is that something has happened to Regan. Then, I remind myself that if that was the case, he wouldn't be the one calling to tell me. I'm not surprised she's the first person I thought of, though, there hasn't been a night, since I got back to Colombia, that I haven't dreamed of her.

They're vivid dreams, all set on that beach in the Sea of Cortez. They alternate between nightmares of me drowning or her disappearing and wet, hot fucking where my mouth and dick learn every inch of her intimately. I feel them all like I'm living them. I wake in throes of emotions and physical sensations so strong that either my pillow or boxers are wet with proof of how gripped by the dream I was.

And every day, I leave my bed and force all of those thoughts to stay there. And they do. I go through my day in complete isolation from my emotions.

But three months of trying to pretend that I don't miss her, has left me exhausted.

Something tells me that Hayes' news, even if it's not about Regan, is going to force me to call on the same discipline that saw me through the night the first time I lost a patient.

I put my percolator on the stove and walk out onto the small balcony of my apartment.

I stare out at the fog-covered valley I call home. The sun will be up soon, and the small courtyard of our building is already full of the aroma of coffee brewing and bread baking. The city stretches out in a sprawl of churches, and homes and businesses that mingle to create a vista of soaring stone steeples and the red tiled rooftops that are ubiquitous to this area. On the edges of the city, modern residential skyscrapers sit like sentinel barriers of the town and ominously dark Cordillera Oriental, a discontinuous cluster of are part of the Andes range.

The view never fails to steal my breath. This morning, I barely notice it. My attention is still on Hayes' text. My reluctant spirit slows my movements as I pull my phone out, and with a resigned sigh video call my brother.

He answers on the first ring and his grim face fills the screen.

"Hey, what time is it there?" His dark hair falls in messy waves over his forehead and he pushes it away from his face and rests his head in his hands. He reminds me of the way I felt the first time I had to inform someone that their loved one had died.

"Five thirty in the morning. Sun's almost up, so your timing is good," I make small talk, even though my heart is beating out of my chest.

He doesn't seem to hear me.

"No easy way to tell you this…so I'm just going to say it. Gigi Rivers is my biological mother."

My stomach clenches as if it's just been kicked by the sharp end of a boot. "What? What does that mean? She and your dad…he's her brother." I jump out of my chair, my coffee cup crashes to the floor, shattering against the concrete floor.

Scalding-hot coffee splatters all over my legs and I register the pain somewhere behind the loud rush of blood in my ears.

"Jason Rivers wasn't my biological father. Gigi was married, got pregnant with me, but my father…her husband went missing before I was born."

"What?"

"She was alone, disowned by my grandfather and shunned by her husband's family. So, she gave me to her brother to raise as his own. And she moved to Italy to start her new life." He sounds like he's reading from a script, but the devastation in his eyes is very real.

I barely feel the bite of the ceramic shards digging into the soles of my bare feet as I walk back into my apartment and grab my jeans and a t-shirt from my closet. I don't know why I'm getting dressed but I feel the need to be ready

"I don't…How? When… did you find out?" I stumble around the questions and rifle through my drawers for a t-shirt.

He lets out a long, weary sigh and grips the back of his neck with his hand and closes his eyes. I trap the phone between my shoulder and cheek so I can step into my jeans while I wait for him to answer.

"Two weeks before Gigi was shot."

I stop in mid-motion and the phone clatters to the floor and spins halfway across the room.

"Shit, hold on," I call and run to scoop it up, but my heart feels like it paused at his answer. "Before we saw you in Mexico?"

"Yes." His expression is regretful, but unapologetic. "I couldn't say anything, Stone. Not without talking to Remi first. And until last week, I didn't even know where he was."

A chill of dread washes over me at the mention of Regan's twin.

"What has Remi Wilde got to…." The answer to my question comes to me before I can finish asking it. One of the curses of a quick mind is that nothing comes to me in a soft cloud of thought. Thunderbolts are more my mind's style, and this one packs the punch of a thousand of them at once.

Hayes stares at me and waits for me to say what is so obvious.

"*Not* Lucas Wilde?" I ask it, but it's less of a question and more of a desperate plea for him to say I'm wrong.

He nods and my head starts to spin.

"How is that even fucking possible."

"Stone, I'm not finished, please," he shouts to cut off my senseless stream of questions. But it's not his raised voice that ties my tongue. Hayes, never, ever says please.

I brace myself for whatever could be worse than the bomb he just dropped.

I close my eyes, drop my head into my hands. "Go on,"

"Lucas Wilde *is* my father. Also, he's not dead."

I drop back into my chair and stare at my brother in total disbelief.

"He barely survived an attempt on his life. And when he was found, he had no memory of who he was. He's been homeless since."

"Someone tried to *kill* him?"

He nods gravely.

"Who? Do you know?" I press when he doesn't look at me.

When he does, I wish I hadn't asked. His eyes are wet with tears.

"His father, Stone. His *own* father. Because he married a Rivers. I thought our grandfather was an evil son of a bitch for cutting off his own daughter…Old Man Wilde was a fucking maniac. How Remi and the rest of them survived living with that monster is beyond me."

I blink in disbelief. "That can't be. He and Regan were really close."

"He fooled everyone." His voice is laced with disgust.

"How's Regan?"

He shrugs, his eyes grow wary. "I don't know. I haven't really had a chance to talk to her."

"Well, what about Remi, or Tyson?"

A small smile lifts the corner of his mouth, and it plucks a nerve to see that when he showed no feeling when I asked about Regan. "They're okay. Remi's back in town and holed up with his girl. Tyson is…Tyson. He was pissed, blew off steam, and now he's thrown himself into his work."

"And what about Regan? Or does she not count because you disapprove of her?"

His eyes narrow. "Remi and I were close before this. Regan and Confidence are friends. Maybe, she'll go see her. If you're hoping that somehow this will make me more inclined to forgive her for your little…whatever, don't hold your breath. Marcel is a friend, and he deserves better."

I want to tell him what I know about that man, but I doubt he'd believe me, and I don't want to betray her confidence. "I'm not sure why you think she's done anything you need to forgive her for. And you have no idea what kind of husband he is."

"The kind she's *still* married to," he snaps, his expression hardening with annoyance.

"*For now*," I say and hate how petulant I sound and how clueless I am. We haven't been in touch at all But, I haven't let myself imagine anything other than her getting her ducks in a row to divorce him.

"Stone, think about what would happen if people found out about your… *thing* in Mexico."

"It wasn't a *thing*," I say between clenched teeth.

The damnable pity returns to his eyes. "For your sake, I hope it was.

I don't want you coming home thinking that you're going to take Marcel Landel's wife from him."

His demands make my skin feel one size too small for my body. "She's not a thing to be taken."

His expression grows rigid and his eyes narrow. "You listen to me. I've been busting my ass to restore some of the good faith our uncle squandered while I was away. Your mother is still a pain in my ass. Dare is just barely back on his feet; I don't have the bandwidth for another crisis. Especially not one that has anyone with *my* last name in the center of it. Please, *think* about what it will mean. And not just to me. But to our family. To your career. Stop thinking with your dick," he growls.

His words slip under my skin, rub against my insecurity, my guilt, and my pride. They burn away the final veneer of civility I was clinging to.

"You've always been good at turning a challenge into an opportunity. It shouldn't surprise me that you're doing it now," I sneer.

"What the fuck do you mean by that?" Hayes' eyes narrow.

I mimic his expression and bring the phone closer to my face. "You just dropped the mother of all bombs on me. Yet, the first thing on your mind is Regan and me?"

His anger erupts. "Of course, it's been on my mind. You're my brother. I want what's best for you, and another man's wife isn't it. This isn't an opportunity, Stone. It's a fucking tragedy, and I'm just trying to stem the bleeding."

"And you think asking me to subvert *my* happiness for the greater good of a family that has deceived you your whole life is what's best for me?"

He winces, and color blooms on his cheeks, and he drops his gaze from mine.

"Exactly." I take no joy in being right.

"Stone, that's not fair."

"What is?" I bark, and he closes his eyes in a bid to find his calm.

He sighs and runs a weary hand over his face. "I know you like her. She's beautiful and smart, I get it. But you have no idea the hornets' nest you'll be kicking, if you don't let it be. Please." There's that word again.

I walk back to my room and stare at my bed. I should lie down and close my eyes and just, for once, say fuck it.

But the sun has started to rise, and it's too late to indulge in the confessional of sleep. Self-indulgence will have to wait until the moon comes back. Someone's life depends on me showing up. Even on days when my own life feels like it's up for grabs.

I turn my back on temptation and my ire on my brother. "Beautiful and smart are tame words to describe what she is. And I don't like her, I love her. And I know I owe you a lot, but that you'd call me to remind me of it, pisses me off."

Hayes blinks in surprise "*Love* her? You don't even know her."

"I know her better than I've ever known anyone." And, saying it out loud, I realize how true it is.

Hayes gapes at me. "What the hell did *I* miss?"

I laugh, but it's bitter and short. "My formative years."

He looks like I punched him. "Stone—"

"I have to go. I've got more patients to see than I have hours in a day."

"Wait," he barks.

"Can't. But feel free to continue worrying about who I'm fucking. And I hope you and Remi have an awesome reunion with your dad," I expel the last word like a curse propelled by anger and jealousy.

I wish both of my dads would come back from the dead.

Yeah, and people in hell wish they had ice water.

Nobody cares.

I hear him call my name, right as I hang up.

"*Buenos noches*," I call over my shoulder to the guard at the front of the refugee camp, and then jog over to the white van that's waiting to take me back to my apartment. This is my last week here, and I feel guilty at how glad I am of that.

The conditions here are bleak. This refugee crisis is the worst of its kind in our hemisphere. But for the news coverage it receives, you'd be hard pressed to even know it's happening.

But teams like mine, from all over the world, have come to help serve the people who are caught in the crossfire of political stagecraft. It's easy to feel a sense of helplessness, because there's no hope in sight for an end to the problem.

I climb aboard the van, and before I can buckle up, we're off. It's dark in the van, and everyone else is asleep. I pull out my phone and scroll to my favorite torture devices.

Pictures of Regan—a couple of us, but, mostly, just her.

My screen saver is one of her on a paddle board the afternoon we explored the mangroves. She looks like she's eighteen. Her hair is braided into plaits that run down either side of her head and dangle over her shoulders. Her bikini is a mismatched black bandeau top and bright green bottoms. She's grinning wildly, her hands lifted in the air over her head, an oar clutched in the left one. Her expression is triumphant.

Worry makes my heart skip a beat every time I think about her alone right now. The upheaval must feel endless.

I've started to call her so many times, and each time, I've stopped.

She's so off limits, it's not even funny. And despite lashing out at Hayes, I don't want to make things harder for him.

I gaze out at the scenery as we wind our way through the valley. The horizon doesn't calm me the way it used to. Now, when I gaze out at the place where the sky and earth kiss, all I see is her.

Regan, for me, is what that spot in the distance must have been for the men who were inspired to sail toward it, even though they fully expected to fall off the edge of the world. And just like them, I can't resist that call.

I shouldn't even attempt it. I'm not on a ship by myself. My brother is breaking his back to repair what my mother has broken. If I make a mess of things, I'll take him with me.

And what if Regan never leaves her husband?

Can I risk so much when I'm not sure that the horizon isn't just an illusion?

So, whenever I've had the urge to call her, I write it down in a letter. I've got a couple dozen notes that I never planned to mail.

The shuttle drops me off and I trudge into my apartment. I head straight to my desk and pull out the paper and pen I've been using and start another letter.

When my ink runs dry, I go in search of another pen. I feel around on the top of my bookcase where I keep my supplies and my hand brushes against a book. I grasp it and pull it down.

It's my copy of Cosmos. The one thing that I always take everywhere with me. It's like a Talisman. I open and read the inscription I wrote in my ten-year-old scrawl. "You're my Venus, I'm your Mars."

How true that turned out to be—just not the way I'd hoped. Like the actual planets, it feels like we have the whole world between us.

Yet, she's still my Venus—that out of reach, elusive star. My goddess of love, my ultimate woman.

But am I her Mars? Didn't I tell her that how the god fought for the love of his goddess even though she was completely off limits to him?

In three months, I'll be headed on an expedition that will take me away from any modern conveniences for a whole month. If I didn't come back, wouldn't I regret not telling her that until my last breath, I loved her?

I make a decision, one that feels slightly premature and that I'm certain I'm not prepared for. But that's never stopped me from trying before.

It certainly won't stop me now.

Not when I think that loving Regan Wilde the way she was born to be loved - the way I know no one is loving her now—is also my calling.

There is nothing about a life with her that is as I imagined my life would be—the children I thought I didn't want to raise, the domestic stasis of cohabitation—but after just that week with her, I know I'd live in hell if it meant she was by my side.

So, I package everything up and I make this last note a question. One I hope she'll answer when she's ready. And until then, I'll take a measure of comfort in knowing that she'll have these to remind her that I'm thinking about her.

Chapter 35

WALLS COME TUMBLING DOWN

REGAN

"When you punish a child for telling the truth, you teach them to lie."
That was one of my grandfather's most common refrains. I stare
unseeing at his undisturbed, meticulously arranged desk and wonder
what else he taught me but didn't really believe.

He made me think he loved me. He made me think I could trust
him. And because I was so desperate for a loving father figure, I didn't
ask questions that I should have. I just…followed his rules and gave
whatever he asked of me.

Even when it cost me everything.

In the week since Remi's bombshell about our father's disappearance and the role my grandfather played in it, I've been plagued by
something deeper, more corrosive than guilt. There are huge fissures in
my consciousness.

I can't change any of it. I can't disown my family and as far as I'm
concerned at the most basic level, we're all victims of one person's God
complex. But, if Matty could see it, that means I *chose* not to.

I came to the belly of the beast today, not even sure what I was
looking for. I don't know what, if anything at all, from all those years

ago would even be here.

So far, I've looked through the filing cabinets built into the desk. But there's nothing, at least nothing that means anything to me. My mother has only let the cleaning lady in here to dust and vacuum since he died.

The book he was reading the morning he had his stroke lays open on the wood lacquered side table next to his dark brown leather recliner.

I don't even know what I'm looking for. But there's no one left to ask. Dan, his assistant, retired to Costa Rica, the year my grandfather died and hasn't responded to the email I sent him. I want to have some answers before I call Matty. Or maybe, I'm just putting it off because I don't know how to apologize for the wrong I've done.

I shove away from his desk and walk over to the bookshelf, where dozens of sterling silver frames line the shelves, with as much prolificacy as the books they were built to house.

Most of the photos are of him and me. There's only one of him with my father. I used to think it was because he found looking at him painful. The truth of it makes bile rise in my throat. I pick up the picture and look at it through this new lens. It's from the day of my father's high school graduation. I run a finger over my father's broad, handsome smile. Remi, minus the blue eyes, is his spitting image.

I wish I'd known him. So much so now that I know that he was brave enough to do what I haven't been able to—choose his happiness over everything else. And in letters he left for Remi, ones that Gigi has held on to all these years, he said he was coming back for us. Was it selfish of him to leave us? Yes. But it's not like he left us in a ditch to die. Not the way his own father did to him.

He may have loved Gigi, but he loved us too. And he would have been there for us if my grandfather hadn't seen to it that he wasn't.

I drag my eyes to the face of the other man in the picture.

Emotions batter my chest with the blunt force trauma of a steel-toe boot. I can't believe the man who raised me so gently, who plucked me out of trouble, who literally saved my life, could do the things that we know for certain he did.

His smile is full of a smug pride that he always wore when one of us accomplished something. He saw them as his accomplishments, too.

I start to put the silver framed photo back on the shelf when the shadow of something on his wrist catches my eye. My chest tightens like it's been placed in a vice grip and I grasp the edge of the bookshelf to steady myself.

I bring the picture closer to my face.

There's a tattoo on his wrist….one that wasn't there when I was growing up.

A flaming blue lightning bolt.

Like the ones on the wrists of the men who held me down while my body was used in ways that transformed my very soul. Like the one above the nightclub where his assistant was seen by Matty and Jack.

I barely make it to the bathroom before I lose the contents of my stomach.

In the last few years of his life, when he couldn't do it for himself, I dressed him. I fastened the burgundy leather straps of his Piaget watch to his wrist every single morning. There was nothing but his smooth, freckled, freakishly unwrinkled skin in the space underneath it. It didn't even leave a scar. Or was it just that I wasn't looking?

Because, there it is. Clear as day on the wrist of the arm he has slung over my father's shoulder.

Before I know what I'm doing, I raise the frame over my head and slam it down with as much force as I can gather and nearly howl with satisfaction when it shatters.

I spent my whole life without a father. I was distinctly aware of what I was missing by growing up without him.

And to know that the man who pretended to offer me succor was the one responsible for my sorrow. My rage is going to burn me alive and I want to let it. I want to burn away my old life, my old hurts, my old mistakes and start over.

Blindly, I grab one frame after the other and smash them, too. There isn't a single memory here that deserves to be preserved.

Suddenly, I'm engulfed by a pair of arms and the scent of Chanel No. 5.

I sink into her, let her body cocoon me, and let the frame I'm holding slip out of my grasp and lay my head on her breast, and even though she hates tears, I let them fall. Because goddammit, she owes me.

"Shhhh, Reggae Queen…" she calls me by the name she used to, before she started hating us all. That thought makes her arms feel like restraints, and I struggle to break free of her.

She lets me go with an "Oomph," and I realize I've elbowed her in the side.

I meet her wide-eyed stare with an incendiary glare. "Why didn't you protect me when it actually mattered? It's too late. You knew what he did, and you let him get away with it."

I expect her to slap me. Or maybe even punch me. Tina Wilde does not suffer insubordination, and she certainly didn't let it go unpunished.

She just bows her head and nods in a silent, but clear confession, and shock completely stunts my rage.

But when she says, "I'm sorry," My guard goes up.

My eyes dart around this room. "Is this some sort of set up? Why are you apologizing?"

She props a hand on her hip and spears me with a glare of consternation. "Can't I just be sorry?"

"You never have been before," I point out, my eyebrows raised, daring her to contradict me.

She looks at the ceiling and shakes her head. "Father save me, you are such a pain in the ass, Regan." She stalks to my grandfather's desk and pulls a cigar out of the humidor. I know she keeps them freshly stocked for when she hosts meetings and parties here. She picks up a silver-handled trimmer and expertly clips the end.

"Here," she says and hands me one.

I stare at her. "You smoke?"

She rolls her eyes and presses the cigar into my hand. She takes a curling pull of hers, before she sits down. She tilts her head, as her dark eyes assess me. I have to stop myself from straightening my clothes and my hair and sit down. She hands me the cutter and lighter. As if I'd know what to do with them.

I drop the foul-smelling cigar on the small table beside my chair.

"You can be angry and break things. You deserve to. It was a terrible thing we did to you."

"Are you just saying that because we caught you? You said you never would have told us."

"I meant it. Why would I want you to know the truth?"

I laugh with startled surprise and no humor at all. "Wow… so you think it was *right* to tell us that our father was dead, when you knew he wasn't?" I narrow my eyes at her and wait in vain for a sign of remorse.

"I didn't know he wasn't. It wouldn't have changed anything, and you would have been in danger, too." She takes a pull from her cigar and turns to gaze around the room. And as she does, I gaze at her.

She's made quite a dramatic recovery since I last saw her. She'd been as close to an emotional wreck as we drove her home from Remi's house the day all of this came out. She and Gigi had a confrontation that turned physical. She was nearly catatonic with grief. And in that moment, I forgave her everything.

She may have kept his secrets, but she was my grandfather's victim, too. After her husband left her for another woman. My anguish felt like a trickle compared to the monsoon of it that roiled in her. Without her asking me to, I forgave her for the lifelong lie.

"Actually, I would have done something different," she muses. "I wouldn't have married a man thinking somehow I was going to be the making of him. No one makes anyone but themselves. And people don't change unless they want to." My emotions are in turmoil and I want to shake the cool, unruffled expression off my mother's face.

"I thought you were going to say, I wouldn't have raised my children in the same house as the man who tried to murder their father. How could you live with him? Knowing that he'd tried to have his own son killed? And how could you watch us grieve for a man who wasn't dead."

"Your grandfather was a dangerous, wicked man. But he loved you and your brothers. If I'd tried to take you away from him, he would have killed me. I was worried that if any of you disappointed him, he'd hurt you, too. So, I cracked a whip on your backs to keep you safe."

"Why didn't you let me go to Wellesley?" I ask.

She looks startled and then pensive. She opens her mouth and closes it twice before she finally answers me. "That's where Gigi went to school. It's where she met your father." Mom admits with a deep sigh as if admitting it is a weight off.

"Wow. So, that's why you didn't let me go?" I rear back—surprised how much empathy is mingled with my incredulity.

My mother's expression clears, and she lifts her chin as if I've offended her. "*I* would have let you go, Regan. You kids had already paid so much for his sins. And by then, I knew he'd never been mine to lose, in the first place." She takes another draw from her cigar and blows a smoke ring.

"So then…why?"

"The same reason as everything else. Your grandfather forbade it. He only let Remi go because unlike you, Remi could afford to pay his way."

She leaves out that it's because the men in my family all got access to their inheritance when they were eighteen. I had to wait until I was thirty.

"So, he lied about that, too. And made you take the blame…" That hurts more than it should. Especially, when in the grand scheme of things, it's the least of his crimes against me.

My mother shrugs it off. "Oh yes. You were his pet. He couldn't bear to be the bad guy in your eyes. And even though he never expressed remorse for what he did to Lucas, he thought he'd gain some redemption in raising the three of you. And I let him because I knew that as long as he loved you and as long as you followed his rules, you'd be safe. But I hated how close you were…when you and I were at such odds.

Before I can ask, she starts speaking again.

"I should have turned Liam in. I was barely old enough to buy liquor, with three very young children, a violent and cunning father in law, a broken heart, a shattered ego, and a business to run. And I didn't have a soul to confide in about the worst thing that had ever happened to me."

She takes a puff of her cigar and blows an expert smoke ring. It's like she's speaking from my heart.

In that moment, I see my mother in an entirely new light. She's always been this fearless, unstoppable, resilient, tough as nails, bitchy-as-fuck, hard ass. She's successful, flawlessly composed, so utterly capable that I forgot, that she's also just a woman. Flesh and bone and with a heart as prone to pain as mine.

I've had challenges, but nothing like what she has overcome. I don't think I'd make the same choices as her.

But I can't say for sure.

The night my daughter was born, I lay awake all night with her in my arms, making promises and vows I'd longed to hear my whole life.

I've kept all but one—that I would never lie to her. The first time she asked me about her father's frequent nights away while we were still living in Paris, I lied. And I continued to for years because I didn't want her to know who her father—and mother—really were.

My mother stares sightlessly in my direction. The cigar dangles from her long elegant, bejeweled fingers and she looks every inch the titan she is. Can I really judge her not wanting to tell me her truths? Especially when the stakes were so high.

It's only been three months since I last saw Stone and I can barely breathe for missing him.

She's spent 32 years without my dad. She's dated, being Lucas Wilde's widow is part of her identity. I can't imagine how she'll handle things when his return becomes public knowledge.

"Do you still love dad?"

"You still love your grandfather?" She retorts in a slightly defensive tone, one eyebrow raised in challenge.

"I don't know." It's the closest thing to the truth I can manage. I'm still trying to reconcile my memories of the man I thought I knew with the evil I'm confronting.

"I shudder to think of all of the secrets shared with him and kept from me," she grimaces.

I scoff. "Until I find a way to top 'your father's not really dead,' you might be setting yourself up for a pot and kettle comparison, by calling me secretive."

"Touché. Not much worse than *that*," she concedes, waving one hand in the air, as if she's giving a testimony.

Not much worse, but there are things equally awful. I look over at the pile of glass, chrome, and pictures and think of secrets that brought me here today.

"What was that tattoo on his wrist?" I watch her closely for any flickers of recognition or surprise.

She looks at me askance and that one-sided frown of annoyance is a relief. She considers herself a connoisseur of information and not knowing something *always* annoys her. "What tattoo? Be more deliberate with your words, girl," she snaps.

I point at the pulse point on my wrist and trace a thunderbolt. "Pops had one."

She waves my words off. "He didn't have a tattoo on his wrist. You know that."

I walk over to the mess I made and sift through the glass with the toes of my shoe, until I get to the first frame I smashed. I pluck the photo off the backing and hand it to her. "Yes, he did at one point."

She puts the cigar down and takes the picture from me. She scrutinizes it closely and frowns. "What the hell is that?"

"I don't know. But I've seen them on other…people," I tell her.

She puts the picture on the settee next to her. "What other *people?*" Her voice is hard, but her eyes…aren't. She looks afraid, but there's also a vengeful light, a slight curl to her lips, that remind me of a wolf's snarl.

I know that I'm not the one she wants to hurt. But now that I'm a mother myself, I know that I'm about to break her heart beyond repair.

I haven't told anyone this story. I haven't wanted to relive it. It's the monster that lives under my bed. But I've done my mother a great disservice in keeping it from her. So, I gather my courage and sit down.

"I need to tell you something." I take her hand in mine and start from the night in the bakery when Stone stabbed Weston.

"*Dan?* That sycophantic little *fucker*, I never liked him." She's been stoic, her eyes flickering with rage and anguish, but completely silent. But now she stands, pacing the way I do when I'm agitated.

"Well, he was involved, but he's been gone for ten years."

She stops pacing and taps a finger to her lips. All signs of distress she was feeling have been replaced with intense focus. "What was his connection to this Weston scumbag?" She starts pacing again, talking more to herself than to me. "I mean…how could Liam have known you were there?"

"He said he had a tracker on my car."

"No, he *didn't*." She makes it sound like the most absurd thing she'd ever heard.

"It didn't?" I ask around a hiccup.

"No. He must have known that boy, that house. Where'd you say it was, Palestine?"

"Yes."

She sits back down and cups my face, with achingly tender yet, commanding hands.

"Where is this man? This Weston?" She says his name like it's a curse. Her midnight eyes glitter like exploding galaxies.

"Pops told us he was dead. Killed in the raid that set us free. And when that girl was arrested, the news reports said he was missing, and presumed dead."

She grimaces with disgust and pinches the bridge of her nose. "Well, then we *must* assume that he is in fact alive. And we *must* find him. We'll have to do it on our own, because we can't be sure whoever helped him isn't still on the police force."

Fear and loathing coil in my stomach. I shake my head violently. "No, no, no, I can't do that." I never want to see him again. Not ever. "And if he isn't dead, then where's he been all these years?" The idea of him lurking in the shadows makes me dizzy with fright.

My mother grabs my shoulders and gives me a firm shake. I look up into her dark, terrifyingly cold eyes. "We need to be sure. I can handle that part of the plan. You need to focus on the rest."

I look at her askance. "The rest of what?"

She continues talking, as if she didn't hear me. "I need to find out more about these blue thunderbolts. Whatever he was a part of, we need to make sure it's completely dismantled." She claps her hands impatiently at me and rises to her feet. "We've got work to do. Why are you just sitting there like a bump on a log?"

"Because I don't know what you're talking about." I shake my hands in exasperation.

She rolls her eyes impatiently. "Keep up, child. I'll hunt for this man, and *you* must finally leave your husband."

I choke on the shocked gasp the word hunt drew from me and do a double take at her. "*What* did you say?"

She rests her hands on her hips and purses her lips. "He got your nanny pregnant, didn't he?"

My eyes bug out. "How do you know that?"

She gives me a look that says, "*really?*"

"Yes, he did. That was the last straw."

"And you've been helping her. Why?" she asks, and my back stiffens at the disapproval in her voice.

"Because she's young and scared, and she's about to have a baby that will be a brother or sister to my children."

She sighs. "You don't need to be defensive. It's just very different from what I would have done."

My defenses come up even further. "I know it's unconventional, but I don't know what else to do. What would my children think of me if I sent her out into the world on her own? After all the things I've told them about being decent."

"I wasn't being critical. In fact, I'm in awe. I was faced with this myself. Gigi came here, pregnant and scared and we sent her away without any help. How different would all of this might have been if I'd had a fraction of your grace?"

My heart lodges in my throat and my eyes sting with tears I hold back because I know this isn't the time. But, it's the highest praise she's ever given me and I didn't know how badly I needed this from her until now.

"What would you have done if you hadn't married Marcel?" she asks, taking me by surprise, again.

"I would have been a journalist."

She frowns, her gaze considering, and then shakes her head. "Forget that. I know you had that poison pen thing. Thank God you've stopped, but that's not real experience, so the doors to traditional careers are closed to you. I suggest you start a podcast," she declares.

"Do you even know what that is?" I ask.

She lifts her chin, her smile turning smug. "I'll have you know that I listen to True Crime Daily regularly. It's fascinating. And from what I understand, you can do it from anywhere. You can be home with the children and have something on your own. Even if you don't need the money, you *must* have something that is completely yours. Do you concur?" She looks at me expectantly.

I gaze at her in amazement. I feel like I've learned more about her in the last few minutes than I did in the eighteen years I shared a home with her. "*Okay*, I'll look into it."

"Good. When you've done that, you must find a way to atone for the wrong you feel you've done."

I raise an eyebrow at her choice of words. "The wrong I *feel*? Don't you think it was wrong of me to turn Rebecca away?"

Her expression is as inscrutable as always. "It doesn't matter what I think. If you think so, then make it right, as far as you can. Then, let go of the guilt and get on with your life."

And find my way back to Stone.

The thought comes from out of nowhere but it's not a surprise.

Stone said I ruined him. Well, turnabout is fair play.

"Oh, Regan." Her words are choked by a sob, and her eyes shimmer with unshed tears.

It's like watching a diamond shatter—terrifyingly wrong. I put an arm around her. "Mom?"

She shakes her head with sad, resigned eyes. She twists her lips in a bitter smile. "My mother used to say, *"Bad luck wus dan obeah."* She strengthens her Jamaican accent.

"What does that mean?"

"It means some bad luck is worse than witchcraft…or death." I've never heard her sound so dejected.

"No, that's crazy. If you're still alive, then you can try again. It's not too late."

"Isn't it?" she groans, her composure crumbling. She runs a frustrated hand through the short crop of curls on her head.

"Hey, why are you falling apart now?" I ask, completely disoriented by her vulnerability.

"I'm sorry Regan. Because I know as much as you didn't want to be…you're so much like me. Constant, honest, committed—sacrificing. I didn't want your tender heart to be trampled the way mine was. So, I did my best to steer you in a direction that I thought would prevent that, and all I've done is make all of you as lonely as I am."

"Oh Mom…we all do the best we can."

"No, we don't, Regan, and that's the problem. Liam didn't. I didn't. But you… You're a good girl. Even though your husband cheats, you keep your dignity, and you have never stooped to his level."

I squirm at the undeserved praise. "I would hate for my children to know that side of their parents. I understand why you didn't want us to know. We aren't anything like a family should be. But we're some kind of family. It's all my kids know. And…I don't want to tell them that I don't love their father."

She shrugs. "You knew more than I told you as a child, right? Your daughter is smart, and mature. I bet she knows more than you think."

I nod in grim agreement. She's right. Eva is so observant.

Mother lets out a long-suffering sigh and sits back in the chair. "I wish that you'd found love. Maybe…you can, still. I know you've got this great big life and you're comfortable—"

"I'm not comfortable."

"Then why haven't you left him?"

"I've been busy."

She gives me a disbelieving look, and I sigh.

"Fine, I'm afraid. Marcel is going to fight me." And I don't add that it's too late. That I fell in love with a man I have no business doing anything with. One who doesn't want children or the kind of life I lead.

"Let him fight you, you're not some powerless whelp. You've got me, Remi, Tyson—and who cares about scandal? Now that your grandfather's dead, at least we know he can't kill us." She smiles mischievously.

I guffaw. "So, you're glad that Kal's story is going to be published?" Remi's girlfriend is a journalist, too. She's writing the story about my father and his return. I encouraged Remi to let her, when he was reluctant.

She's quiet and contemplative for a few seconds. Then she laughs. "I'm too old to be living with teenage angst. I'm over it and him. And myself. I'm clearly a misguided person when it comes to love. Remi had it right. Don't listen to me. Maybe you'll end up as happy as he and that useless girl he married are."

"Mother, stop it," I admonish.

She looks sheepish. "Sorry, bad habits die hard. Kal is lovely, I guess. That daughter of hers is a vast improvement on the stock she came from."

"Mom…" I shake my head.

She shrugs, but her eyes lose focus and turn sad, as she stares absently out of the window.

"What are you thinking?" I ask, my discomfort maxed out, after almost two minutes of silence.

She looks startled, like she forgot I was there. "That people are going to call that man bold, brave, and romantic. And I'll be the mother who lied to her children to protect my reputation and business." She draws in a huge breath and lets it out slowly. "Being a woman can feel like a burden. But it's not a burden. It's a gift. It's on *our* backs that every single man in existence has stood to reach adulthood. The burden comes when they expect us to be happy being nothing but their stools." She shakes her head and stares off into the distance.

My mother is exactly twenty years older than me, and I've never thought she looked her age. But the last week has taken a toll on her.

We were all dealt a huge blow, but she's borne the emotional weight for years, and now, she's having to live it all in public, all over again.

She claps her hands and her voice turns brisk again. "Thank goodness I've got everyone we need at my fingertips. And nearly all of them owe me a favor. Cause we have things to take care of."

I sigh. "Remind me again."

She stands and wipes her hands together in relish. "Emancipation, atonement, vengeance, and rebirth."

"Mother, you have a flair for the dramatic."

She nods, as if accepting it as a compliment. "You are a Wilde. But you're also half me. I know that hasn't always pleased you," she draws a finger along my temple and presses it to my lips to silence my protest, "but it has *always* pleased me. You see, I was born a warrior, an enchantress, a leader, a goddess."

I smile at her use of the same word Stone uses as a term of endearment.

"And a flair for the romantic," I tease her. My heart flutters with the novelty of this new ease between us.

She tilts her chin up unapologetically. "New rule—romanticize *yourself*. You are the stuff of fairytales, my Reggae Queen, and it's time you started living like it."

Chapter 36

OF OMELETTES AND EGGS

REGAN

Last week, I baked some scones for our annual Spring Fling, and one of the owners of our neighborhood coffee shop, Sweet and Lo's, had one taste and asked if she could order some to see how they sold. So, I got up early to make this batch. And nearly had a heart attack, when my daughter came bounding down the stairs, a few minutes after me, even when she hates them, and said she wanted to help. Eva has been withdrawn, and the smile on her face as she draped her apron on was like a shot of sunshine.

We listened to music, talked about school, and laughed nonstop. I put her change in mood down to the fact that she's almost eleven, and she sees everything through the lens of her tween angst.

Two hours later, the first two batches are cooling, the rest are in the oven, and I pick a piece off one that didn't hold together well.

"You're not going to *eat* that, are you?" Eva gasps, when I lift a scone to my lips.

"Why wouldn't I?" I ask, before I shove the mouthwatering confection into my mouth.

"You *never* eat bread. That's why," she says.

"It's a new day. And this isn't bread. It's a scone." I speak around the mouthful of food, and my daughter eyes me with something like an alarm.

"Mom, it has sugar."

I chuckle at the horror on her face. "You say it like it's a bad word."

She looks at me like she's never seen me before. "Mom…Are you *sure* you're okay?"

I laugh at the genuine concern furrowing her brow. "I'm fine, baby." I drop a kiss on her head. "Now help me box these up for Sweet." I point at the stack of flat packed boxes on the counter. Instead of the groan of resignation I expect, her expression lightens. "Can I help you next time you get an order?"

I smile in pleasant surprise. "You're going to get up early again?"

"This was fun. You smile and dance and sing when you're baking, and I love seeing you happy." She smiles widely at me before she hops down and walks over to get the boxes I pointed to.

I sit there, my heart in my throat and full to bursting with gratitude that I got *something* right. I watch my daughter bounce around the kitchen, smiling and tossing her head of unruly curls that range in texture from tight spirals to loose corkscrews. I resist the impulse to call her over, so I can braid it up. Because she *loves* her hair. But for its light golden-brown color, it's just like mine. When I don't have it flat ironed within an inch of its life.

I run my hands over my still scarf covered head and scowl at the rows of pins holding it in place and long for the ease of the wash and go style I wore in Mexico.

"So, how are things at school?" I broach the subject gingerly, hoping that I can get her to open up, without disrupting our cozy vibe. She's an amazing kid, quirky and a little shy. But, she's no shrinking violet. The girl she fought used to be one of her best friends. They grew apart, and Eva didn't seem to mind that. But when her former friend joined a clique of bullies and targeted Eva, she defended herself. She was anxious about going back to school after the suspension and very tight-lipped about how she was doing.

To my relief, she shrugs, grabs a scone, takes a bite and grins. "I don't care about those girls, Mom. 'Cause you taught me the rules, re- member?"

"Yes, I do." I tussle her hair.

When she was seven, she encountered her first bully. And I'd given her a list of what I called "rules of friendship" and made her memorize and repeat them every single day.

1) Friends don't hurt us on purpose.

2) Friendship is optional and it's okay to end one.

3) To have a friend, you have to *be* a friend.

"So, if they say something mean, that means they're not my friends, and I don't care about them anyway," she declares. She reaches for my hand and links our fingers and squeezes. "I'm fine, Mom. And I want you to be, too."

Startled by her solemn tone and knowing gaze, I let go of her hand and walk to the fridge to make myself some tea. I've been dreading this moment for, what feels like, her whole life. "Why do you think I'm not, okay?"

"She walks over to me and wraps her arms around me from behind and presses her cheek to my back. I cover her small hands with mine. And she tightens her hold on me. "Mom, I'm young, but I've got eyes. You're alone. And you're bored, and you're sad."

Guilt stabs at me. I hate that she knows and is worried about me. I pat her hand and turn around, so we're facing each other. She looks so determined, and pride swells my heart. "I'll be fine. I've got stuff to figure out."

She purses her lips and puts her hands on her hips, in a terrifyingly, exact imitation of my mother. "Then do it, Mom. Because you're amazing. And Daddy…I love him. But...you don't have to stay like this for us."

"What do you mean?"

"I know about Hanna." She looks at me, her eyebrow raised in challenge, daring me to deny it.

"Whaa—" I grapple for what to say. My mother warned me. Shit.

Raised voices outside the kitchen door announce my mother and Tyson's approach up my back walk. I asked them over to talk about an idea I had, but they're an hour early.

"We'll talk about this later, I promise," I say, and she nods and steps away, just as they walk through the door. They're so deep into their argument, they don't even look our way. They stride to the round dining table and sit, without missing a beat of their conversation.

"Ty—you're not ready and you don't get a thumb on the scale just because your last name is Wilde. In fact, having that last name means you have to earn your place; there can't be a perception of nepotism." My mother's tone is more placating than normal. She hates arguing with Tyson, he's her favorite.

"I can't believe you're doing this." Tyson slaps the table hard enough that the glass top rattles and the blue and gold painted china tea-cups jump in the saucers.

My mother doesn't even blink. "You're the one who's making this difficult. You shouldn't be pursuing this when you're not ready," she tells him, matter-of-factly.

He growls low in his throat and looks like he's fighting to maintain control. He slips into a chair and pours himself a cup of coffee in brooding silence.

I look between the two of them, neither of them seem to notice we're there. "Good morning to you, both." If they hear the sarcastic saccharine tone in my voice, they both choose to ignore it.

"Hey, sorry Reggie. Hey, Eva," Tyson's greeting is caustic and dis-tracted.

My mother smiles warmly in our direction, but her eyes are tight with tension. "Eva, darling, I left my cream scarf upstairs a few weeks ago. Can you go find it and bring it to me?"

Eva glances at me in question, and I nod.

"Of course, Nana," she says, and then darts from the room. She'll be gone a while, and if she comes back, she'll be empty-handed. My mother used to send us on errands whenever she wanted to get rid of us. I wish she'd sent me instead. Their fights are legion and never end well.

I continue boxing up the scones, without comment, and they dive back into their argument.

"Are you kidding? I'm bringing Phil Wolf's new restaurant to Rivers Wilde. We have a waiting list for new residents at all our properties, and this is the third year I've been listed as who's who."

My mother nods, in agreement. "That's all wonderful and you can continue to grow in your role. But until I know you're ready, Erin is my choice. And the board will agree."

"I *am* ready. Right now." He slaps a hand on the table, again, and gives her a look of pure stupefaction.

"No, you're not. I'm not sure you'll ever be," my mother says calmly, before she pops a scone into her mouth and moans in pleasure. "Regan, these are sinful. I think we should start selling these at Eat!"

Tyson's handsome face goes hard as flint. My brothers are both so easily wounded by her. But their reactions couldn't be more different. Remi clams up when he's upset. Tyson is like a wounded animal and lashes out. I want to stop this Battle Royale before it escalates.

I place a hand over one of his, in a gesture of empathy, and as a sign that he needs to cool down.

He shakes my hand off and snatches up his phone and keys from the table, before he fixes my mother with a spiteful glare. "If you're hoping Lucas Wilde is going to get his memory back, realize he made a huge mistake leaving us, and come back to you, it's never going to happen."

"Tyson," I gasp, my voice full of sharp rebuke.

My mother doesn't even flinch. "Don't be silly, Tyson."

He bristles. "It's not silly. You're disloyal. You've always punished Remi and me for looking like him. But this is too much. Are you really going to hire this outsider because you hate our father?" He snarls and then blinks, as if he's shocked by his own words.

"Ty—" I gape in horror. My mother shakes her head at me, a signal to stay out of it.

She pops the last bite of scone into her mouth and chews it slowly. Then, she folds her hands in front of her on the table and regards Tyson with complete aplomb. He starts to squirm, and I have a flash of sympathy for him, because she's about to ether him, without even raising her voice.

She quirks an eyebrow when he scoffs and looks away from her in answer. "I know you're overwrought by the latest turn of events and not yourself. So, I will ignore your callous question," her voice is as cold as ice. "This isn't about loyalty, son. And outbursts like that prove your lack of readiness to lead. Learn to take no for an answer. If you want it, work until it turns into a yes. As talented and smart as you are, no one wants to work for you because you think you know everything. And you don't even know a little bit." Her smile is full of pity.

Tyson is visibly shaken.

"Mom, come on," I chide her and reach for his hand. He yanks it back.

"I don't need you to take up for me, Reggie. That is a lie, and she knows it. I'm leaving." He stands.

"Please stay, I really want to talk about this idea," I implore him, and he turns to me, his handsome face is so pained, I immediately retract my plea. "I'll call you later."

He nods gratefully. "I'm too upset with your mother to think straight."

"Take a number and get in line," she says dryly.

He storms out.

She shakes her head after him. "That boy has always been so dramatic. He'll understand one day. Like you did once you had Eva," she sighs. I want to tell her that's wishful thinking but keep that to myself.

"You could have been kinder," I chide her.

"I could have been born in Japan. But I wasn't." She looks at her watch. "You said you wanted to talk, and I'm here, and I have forty minutes before I need to be downtown, so…"

"Mama?" My son sticks his head into the kitchen.

"Yes?" My mother and I respond at the same time.

She smiles sheepishly. "Some habits die hard," she says, and holds her arms out to my son. My heart swells with affection, as I watch him crawl into her lap.

"What is it, Darling?" I ask him, when he settles into his grandmother's lap.

"Eva said Hanna is having Papa's baby. Is that true?"

By the time I press a kiss to my sleeping son's brow, it's 8pm. He's the last one to fall asleep tonight, and I creep stealthily out of his bedroom. I feel the need for a workout and a good stiff drink. The pandemonium that ensued after Henri asked about Hanna lasted all day. Telling them about Hanna and answering their questions was one of the hardest things I've ever done. They're confused, excited, worried about me, and worried about their father.

But it's done, and I'm glad. Now, I can be, too. I get into the shower and wash my hair, get back out and make two braids for it to dry in overnight. I'm tempted to throw away my flat iron, but that feels like overkill.

Last year, *Time* magazine did a write up on Marcel. They described me this way. "

His wife, the famously beautiful socialite extraordinaire, Regan Wilde-Landel, is by far his greatest coup. Twenty years his junior, she makes him look like he might just know what he's doing. She's not just beautiful and the belle of every ball. She also comes with a very impressive pedigree of her own. It's not the five-hundred-year-old French Duchy of her husband's ancestors, but it's nearly as rich. Regan Landel is the face of the modern American woman. She's the best dressed, most well connected, most philanthropic, and her parties are the most coveted invitation. She is, unapologetically, embracing full-time motherhood, and yet, manages to look like she just stepped off a runway. She's the woman we look at and think, there's no way that's real. The one we all either want to Fuck, Marry, Or Kill."

That, in a nutshell, is who everyone thinks I am. And I was prepared to let them think it, until the day I died, because I was afraid of being without my family. All because I was so afraid, I'd end up like my mother.

Now, I've landed in worse waters than she's ever been in, and they just keep getting murkier.

The chime of my doorbell startles me out of my dark thoughts. I open the nest app and see a small package on my doorstep. It's addressed to me, but I can't make out the return address.

I turn on the flashlight on my phone and peer closely. There's a row of postage stamps that have Colombia printed on the top. My heart does a double take, and I clutch the package to my chest and inhale, searching for a whiff of him. I don't know if it's my wishful thinking, but I catch a trace of coconut, and the ache of longing, that I normally ignore, floods my veins, and I can't do anything but surrender to it.

I hurry through my chores; secure the house for the night, clean my kitchen, and brush my teeth.

And then, I climb into bed to enjoy my dessert.

I tear the package open and pull out a hard-sided book with a dust cover and a stack of letters tied together with a gold ribbon. When I open the book, a piece of paper flutters out and lands on my feet. But my eyes remain riveted to the inscription. Written in a little boy's hand, *"You're my Venus, I'm your Mars,"* with a note that's written in an adult's below it that says, "True then. True now. True always."

I run a finger along the ribbon, my heart thundering in my ears, as I bend down to pick up the piece of paper that fell. I unfold it and start reading.

Regan,

I've been writing you these letters since I heard the news about your grandfather. I didn't intend to mail them. And then, I found this book—with the inscription I wrote when I was ten years old. I wanted you to have it then. And I want you to have it now, just as you have my heart.

I know you're not in a place for more than friendship. But I want to at least be that. So, when you're ready, write to me, call me, send a smoke signal…wherever you are, I'll find a way to answer. Because, as Ralph Waldo Emerson said… "The only way to have a friend is to be one."

In the meantime, here are the letters I wrote you. Read them in order the first time.

Love,
Stone

I read it ten times before I put it down. He couldn't have known that this is exactly what I needed. Or that today would be the day I'd be open to receiving this. But like every other time this man has entered my life, his timing has been uncanny.

I untie the ribbon and start with the next one.

Dear Venus,
Last night, I drank enough to forget my own name. But I can't forget yours. I can't stop thinking about you. You asked for distance, and I've given it to you, even when it's killed me to do so. So, these letters are my entreaty, my fair lady. I will write you, and one day, I'll have the nerve to send them. Until then, I want you to meet me where the gods gather to make love…and we'll build our world there.
Yours,
Mars

Oh my God. I am undone. I keep reading. My heart feels like it's been hooked to a source of electricity and is humming in my chest.

Dear Venus,
You're my most beautiful someone.
Yours,
Mars

Dear Venus,
I had a revelation as I lay awake missing you, reveling in the way it hurts…because that pain means that my heart works. Sometimes life puts you in touch with the people you need to meet—to help you, to hurt you, to leave you, to love you, and to gradually strengthen you into the person you were meant to become.
Yours,
Mars

Dear Venus,
Don't let anyone tell you that your dreams are too big.
They don't have your vision.

They can't see what you see.
Your belief in them, and yourself, is all you need.
Yours,
Mars

Dear Venus,
You can't make an omelet without breaking some eggs. It's such an asinine saying. Surely, the eggs aren't glad to be scrambled and cooked before some asshole eats them? So why do people say that instead of saying…nothing good comes easy? Isn't that clearer and truer? I make a great omelet, by the way. They'd be awesome with your lemon ginger scones.
Yours,
Mars

Dear Venus,
Today, I just miss the hell out of you,
Yours,
Mars
Dear Venus,
If you aren't already mine, why am I so afraid to lose you?
Tell me…
Yours,
Mars

Dear Venus.
I've found that my heart was stretched by its experience with you. Now, it won't go back to its old shape. Can you help?
I miss you,
Mars.

By the time I'm done, I can barely breathe for the happiness that's swelled inside of me.

If the last three months have been a trial, this feels like a reward. Yes, my life, as I knew it, is completely broken. But I have all the tools I need to reshape it.

I put his letters away and email my lawyer, asking for his first available appointment.

When that's done, I pull out my stationary and write Stone back.

Chapter 37

A SURPRISE DOLLOP OF CREAM

STONE

I rush inside and tear the letter open, my heart damn near in my mouth by the time I've opened it.

Dear Mars,

You are spectacular beyond measure or compare. Your letters were like a surprise dollop of cream in the center of an already very delicious lemon ginger scone.

Until we can have that omelet...I would love to take you up on your offer of friendship. I've missed you. And have so much to tell you. If you agree, call me—713-779-5555.

Yours,

Venus

I'd like to take the word friendship, stick it in a self-destructing rocket and launch it to the moon. But it's better than nothing, and it's a start. And, damn, if I don't miss her, too.

I pick up the phone and call her.

"Hello?" Her voice is husky with sleep, and it's the most beautiful thing I've heard in a long time.

"Goddess, it's me."

There's silence for a beat, and then I hear a whimper, and then she clears her throat.

"Stone, is that really you?

"Yes. I got your letter. Thank you for writing to me."

"Oh, I've missed you. So much. Oh my God, thank you for all of those letters. I've read them every day. I'm blabbering. Sorry. I'm just so nervous. And happy. Hi," she practically sings that last word.

My soul sighs in relief. I wasn't sure what to expect, but she sounds good. The knot of dread that's been eating away at me starts to loosen.

"Hi. And I miss you, too. I've been really worried, Regan."

Her sigh is too weary, and I hate that I can't see her. "It's been a rough few months, as I'm sure you know. But, I'm so glad I know the truth."

I don't know which truth she means, so I focus on the one that is at least somewhat my business. "You and Hayes…you're…related." I use the most sterile word I can manage.

There's a pregnant pause before she clears her throat. "Yeah…I guess. I can't wrap my head around that part, if I'm honest. I've been more focused on the other dumpster fire."

"Your grandfather…I heard, so what's happening?"

"Nothing, he's dead. Any accomplices he had are, too. I just…I feel like I need to find a way to make things right."

"Make what right?"

"Everything, my father wasn't the only person he hurt. But…I don't want to talk about the past—not now. I want to know how you are. How was the refugee camp?"

I love that she remembered and that makes talking about it less burdensome. "It was hard, and I was so ready to leave. But I signed up for an extra month because they need so much help."

"And because you love a challenge," she teases

"That I do." *And I love you, too.* The thought comes unbidden. And I'm glad we're not on FaceTime, so she can't see the panic that freezes my face for a second.

"I'm so glad you're making the most of your time there… and I'm learning to love challenges again, too…" she trails off.

"Don't be cryptic, Regan," I scold.

"Don't be impatient, Stone," she shoots back. And we laugh at the same time. Just like that, our grooves click into place and that knot is finally loose again.

"Okay, I had an idea, and at first, I thought it was crazy… but it's actually happening."

"Spill it, Goddess,"

She squeals. "Okay, okay. Last week, I took a large chunk of my inheritance and bought a property in West Houston that used to be a boarding school. And I'm going to turn it into a transitional housing space, with a community center, and courses, and counseling, and even, eventually, a fully functioning outpatient clinic on sight. And guess what?" She gasps, breathless with giddiness, but doesn't pause long enough for me to speak. "I'm going to call it Venus Rising. After the goddess who inspired me so much." She sounds like a game show host announcing that I won the grand prize.

I certainly feel like I've won *something*. "Regan. That's incredible, I'm so proud of you."

She lets out a shuddering breath. "Thank you for the inspiration. And I can't wait to show you everything. It all needs updating, and I'm having three newly constructed buildings added to the property."

"So, are you and Marcel funding it completely? Or are you raising money?" It's a sly move to get the information that's foremost on my mind. If she can sense that I'm fishing, she doesn't call me out for it.

"There is no Marcel and me And soon not in any sense at all. I… met with my lawyer a couple of days ago." She says the words in a rush and I hear them before they sink in.

"Oh…so, like a divorce lawyer?" I'm almost afraid to ask and hold my breath when she takes a second to answer.

She laughs softly. "Yes. A divorce lawyer. Like you said, no reason to stay is a good reason to go. My children are the only reason I've been holding it together and I don't think, no I know that it's not what's best for them anymore. So, I'm doing it."

"Wow, are you okay?"

"I'm great." And she sounds it. Relief and motivation are twin fires lighting in my mind at the same time.

"Yes. Of course, you are. So, what next?" I rub my hands together in anticipation.

"Well…I've got to get my finances in order so I can figure out how to pay for my *proje*ct." Her emphasis on the last word is tinged with light rebuke.

I check my excitement at her divorce. Getting a divorce doesn't mean anything. Her marriage was the least of my worries. I know Regan wants to hit a reset button on other parts of her life. Talking about us, right now, would be premature. She read my letters, so she knows how I feel.

"Oh yeah, tell me more."

"So, I have a trust fund that vested when I was thirty, and I used some of it to buy the property out right."

"But years of fundraising for other people's good deeds was good practice. I paid for the property out right, but I've created a non-profit, with a board of directors, to oversee staffing and programming and to help me raise money."

"Who's on the board so far?"

"Matty, my mother, and Tyson, if I get him to sit down long enough to sign everything."

"Save a spot for me. I want to help."

She shrieks. "Really? Oh, I'm so glad. You can be on the board, or just brainstorm, or help me think through the clinic. Whatever you want to do."

"All of it, Venus. I want to do it all."

One Month Later

HOUSTON, TX

Chapter 38

FREEDOM

REGAN

The slam of my bedroom door jolts me from sleep. I sit up and find Marcel standing at the foot of my bed.

"Marcel, what are you doing?"

I fumble for my phone to check the time.

"Give me that," he roars, and before I see him move, he grabs the phone from my hand and tosses it onto the bed.

I scramble to sitting and command my voice-controlled lights to full power. "What is going on?"

"I was served divorce papers in my office yesterday," he says, in his deep, even toned voice. My pulse jumps. I knew they were being served. I should have expected he'd come straight here.

"Yes. Well, you can't be surprised. We haven't lived together in six years." I keep my voice even, despite my heart beating like a bass drum.

"So what? You are my wife. There is no divorce, unless I say so." He brings his hands together in a clap, as if signaling the end of the discussion.

I scoff. "Maybe in feudal France. But here, in Texas, I don't need you to agree."

He puts one hand on his hip and points at me. "I will not allow you to do this. You will not drag my name and my children's names through the mud because you're *jealous.*"

"I'm not jealous, Marcel. To be jealous, you'd have to have been mine in the first place."

"What does that mean? I am your husband." He throws his hands up.

"Marcel, you are my *spouse.*" I wrap my comforter around myself and smooth my hair and try to look as dignified as the circumstances will allow. "You haven't been my husband in years. I don't want to live with you anymore. I don't want your last name. I don't want…"

The crack of his hand across my cheek comes from nowhere. It's not a forceful slap, but only because Marcel is small and weak and lazy.

His gasp is louder and sharper than mine. "Oh, *mon dieu*…look what you made me do. You know I am not the kind of man to hit a woman."

He starts to pace frantically, pulling at his hair. I take in his day's growth of gray stubble and creases in the houndstooth Façonnable blazer he wears when he travels. He must have come here straight from the airport.

I touch the stinging spot on my cheek and eye him warily.

"I want you to leave. We have a prenup. This shouldn't be messy. And we live separately anyway. The children will visit you, as they normally do, in the summer. When and if you come here, they can spend time with you in your home.

"This is my home. The children will visit me and so will their mother. You cannot do this," he roars.

The last thing I need is for him to wake the children. "Get out. Or I'll call the police."

His gaze turns murderous. "You will not get away with this. You will not. Maybe you can get a divorce, but I will not let you have a life. You will not make a mockery of my family."

"Are you kidding? Who is making a mockery of whom? Our nanny is having your baby, Marcel. You've been having affairs for as long as I've known you. I am tired of it, and I don't need you."

"You've never needed me. You made that obvious from day one. No, you married me because you wanted to be your grandfather's pet again. And I married you because I wanted to own the woman who no one else could afford to buy."

I flinch at his characterization. "But I'm not a fool, I know when a woman is wet and when she's inserted lube before coming to bed. I didn't complain. I just found a way to take care of my needs without making it your problem. Why can't you do the same thing?" he hisses.

Guilt pricks my conscience and blood rushes to my cheeks, but I don't apologize. I'm not sorry, but I didn't realize he knew.

"I want free of this gilded prison. I want to travel and work and not spend my summers in Monaco. I don't want to be your spouse, in any sense of the word."

He pulls the papers out of the inside pocket of his jacket.

He pulls a slim gold lighter out of his pocket and sets the papers on fire.

"Marcel, burning them won't make this go away. This is a no-fault state. You can't stop this. It's over."

His face mottles red with anger. "Not even when I'm dead. We're Catholic. We married in a Catholic church. You are my wife for eternity," he snarls, and throws the burning papers onto my bed, before he storms out.

I grab them and rush to the bathroom, throw them in the sink, and turn the water on to douse the flames.

The smoke makes my smoke detector go off, and I grab a towel to wave the small plume away. The sound stops, but I hear the patter of little feet, as soon as I turn the water off.

"Y'a quelque chose qui brûle ici?" (*"What's burning?"*) Martinez peeks around the frame of my bathroom door. For the last two years, he's only spoken French. He goes to the French school here and is fully immersed in it. I don't mind, because it makes them very easy to tell apart. Unlike Remi and me, they are identical.

"C'était un accident, chéri," *(It was an accident)* I tell him, guiding him out of the smoke stink of the bathroom. I shut the door and then stoop to put myself face to face with him. He looks so much like my brothers, but he has his father's sky-blue eyes. Right now, they're heavy and groggy with sleep.

I run a hand over his mop of curls and smile indulgently at him. My heart is still racing from Marcel's fire and brimstone routine, but just having my hands on my son helps me calm down. "Tu es toujours fatigué?" (Are *you still tired?)*

"Non, mama," he says, and then gives a huge yawn.

I laugh and scoop him up. "Allez viens. Retournons dormir." (*Come on let's go back to sleep).* I plop him onto the bed and pull the comforter off, when I see the spot when he'd thrown the paper. I grab a blanket from the leather bench at the foot of my bed and cover him with it, command the lights off and lay down with my soft, sweet smelling reason for everything tucked by my side. When his breathing evens out and I'm sure he's asleep, I get out of bed and grab my phone and go back to the bathroom to call Stone.

Unlike the wild, consuming love affair we had on that island, our daily phone calls, while treasured, are distinctly dissatisfying.

By tacit agreement, we talk about everything but us or how we feel. Instead, we talk about work, our families, life, politics, anything, but the huge elephant in the room. With so much left unsaid, there's an undercurrent of frustrated tension in every conversation.

But still, there's no one else I'd rather talk to. And I know he feels the same way. As if to prove me right, my phone buzzes with a text before I can dial his number.

Are you awake?

Yes.

My heart skips a beat, and a smile breaks across my face when my phone starts to ring almost immediately.

"You okay? How'd it go?" He sounds like he's holding his breath.

"Yes, I'm fine. It's fine. He was mad, but it's done," I say, with a small burst of excitement.

He lets out a harsh breath. "I wish I could get away." Half of the doctors on his team are out sick with the flu and he's been working double shifts. He's got enough on his plate without adding this.

"Don't worry. The hard part is done. And I'm fine," I reassure him.

"You know the more you say that, the less I believe you, right?"

I chuckle. "Okay, well I'll stop saying it. But it's true."

"I need to know, Regan. Did he call you? When is he coming back to Houston?" He asks each question in rapid fire succession. I can feel his anxiety, and I wish I could say something to soothe it. But given that mine is running high, I can't even begin to.

"He flew to Houston."

"He's there? Shit."

"Yes. He came as soon as he was served. He's not happy. There's nothing he can do to stop it. But he'll try and this this is going to get ugly before it's over."

"But you're strong and when it's over, you won't have to worry about him again," he says this in that assured way of his that makes me believe it's true. Just talking to him makes Marcel's visit feels like it happened in another lifetime.

"God, I miss you, Stone."

"Me too. I can't stop thinking about you. People keep asking me why I'm smiling so much."

I giggle. That's another new thing that being with Stone has brought about. "Let's go back to Mexico," I whisper.

"I wish. I've been looking at the pictures from our trip. I took so many good ones of your sexy ass." His voice is husky and deep, and it makes my knees weak just to imagine his face right now; his irreverent smile is everything.

"Ooh, I found one…I don't know who took it, but you'll love it." I find the picture on my phone, taken by our tour guide when we weren't looking.

"Send it," he says.

"No, I'll show you when you get here."

"Ugh, you're such a tease," he groans.

A deep male voice calls his name, and my stomach drops because I know he has to go.

"I've got a staff meeting in five minutes. We're leaving at first light tomorrow, so I'll try to call you tonight."

"Okay, have a good day." I try to sound cheerful, even though this three-month long expedition of his feels like the sword of Damocles hovering over my neck. And I don't even know why. Other than how much I'll miss him and the sense of safety having him in my life gives me.

We've had this month of late-night phone calls and endless text messaging threads. He's helped me think through my plans for Venus Rising, and I hate that he's going on this trip, just as it's finally coming together.

I know he's going to do things that will save lives and that this is important to him, so I keep my disappointment to myself.

"I'm so proud of you. It's going to be incredible."

"I'm going to miss you, Goddess." His voice is gruff, and I drop my façade of happiness.

"I'll miss you, too. So much." I wish I could hug him.

"I'll write you and mail the letters whenever we stop somewhere that has postal service," he promises.

"I'll text you every day. And email you about Venus Rising. We're breaking ground on the dorms, and I want you to see it all." I force cheer into my voice.

"I won't have service," he reminds me, and I swallow a groan.

"Then they'll be there when you get back."

"And what about you? Will you be here for me when I get back?" His voice is low, sensual, and heavy with meaning.

"Of course, I will be."

"Good. In three months, I'll be back in Houston, and I want more than your friendship."

My heart flails with happiness. I was afraid he'd never ask again. "Really? What about Hayes?"

"Who cares what he thinks?" he says, with bravado that makes me nervous.

"Are you sure you know what you're getting into? Maybe we should test the waters, first. Go slow."

"I'm not testing anything. I know the temperature of this ocean, Baby, and it's perfect. Get your ass in here with me, and I'll show you," he says, in that growly voice of his, that makes my scalp throb for the tug of his hand in my hair.

"So, just three more months?" I check my mental calendar. "And everything is good with Baylor? Are you ready to start?"

"Yup, after the longest background check in history. I'm pretty sure they called my ninth-grade math teacher for a reference," he chuckles.

"Woah, is that normal?"

"Yeah, they've got a major morality clause in their contract, and they do a background check that makes the secret service one look tame. If this wasn't my dream job, the one I've been working for since I was old enough to remember, I'd tell them to eat shit."

I laugh because I know he means it.

"Hey, gotta go. No more what ifs. Only up from here, Venus. I love you." His voice is dark with promise, and he hangs up before I can respond.

I stare at the phone in shock, when I blink to clear my vision, a tear rolls down my cheek. All the seeds he planted with those letters and that book explode into beautiful blooms of joy, gratitude, relief, impatience, and excitement. Oh my God. *This is happening.*

"I love you, too," I say to the dial tone.

I crawl into bed with my son, and he rolls over and throws one of his little legs across my hip and nestles his head on my shoulder and all is right in my world.

Finally.

Present Day

HOUSTON, TX

Chapter 39

ONE MORE DAY

REGAN

My alarm's trill sounds like a starting gun in my brain. I spring up, grab my marker, draw the nineteenth red x on my small calendar and my heart leaps in my throat. One more day. Just one more and I will be free. And when Stone gets back, I'll go pick him up from the airport and welcome him home with open arms.

I glance at the picture I teased him with. I love having it all to myself. I don't even know who took it. It was the last night on the island, and we were dancing. I hate that it looks like I'm bottomless—but I guess that's better than being able to see the wedgie his arm is hiding.

But this is how I remember us…how I want us to be again.

Just one more day…and I've got a lot to do before I'm finally a single woman again.

Two Weeks Later

HOUSTON, TX

Chapter 40

FUCK THE HIGH ROAD

REGAN

"I think I'm going to be sick. Can you press pause?" I breathe through the sudden grip of nausea in my gut. Throwing up in the waiting room of my husband's lawyer's office is *not* going to happen.

My racing pulse moves like an untamed herd of horses and echoes like thunder in my ears as I gaze with dismay at the screen of Remi's iPad where we're watching security footage from my house.

When he doesn't respond, I press pause myself.

"What?" Remi pulls his ear buds out and turns his concerned gaze on me.

I wince as I take in the "me" captured in the freeze frame of the video.

My hair, that was almost completely dry and no longer weighed down by water, had contracted into a dark, unruly mane, so full, it obscured most of my face in the first few minutes of the video, when I was facing Marcel and in profile to the camera.

From that point of view, the bold swell of my cheekbone, the slope and slight, but noticeable, upward-tilt of my nose and the deeply down-turned corner of my mouth are visible.

As I watch it, with no volume, you'd think I was on the receiving end of something mildly upsetting. But in the freeze frame, with my eyes looking directly into the camera, the stark terror I was feeling at the nuclear bomb that was being dropped on me is clear as day.

Watching a replay of the morning Marcel came in to confront me about the photo is harder than I thought it would be. It's like having an out of body experience. All of the feelings that coursed through me that day surge up, creating a ripple layer of anxiety, right below the surface of my skin. It feels tight and hot. Just the way it had the morning everything that kept my life anchored fell away.

It happened in an instant. I should have seen it coming, but I wasn't looking because I was so wrapped up in Stone.

In the space of seconds, I was devastated.

Tears blur my vision, and I squeeze my eyes closed to clear them.

"Regan?" Remi's concerned voice next to me helps me settle down faster. The prospect of another person seeing me cry makes my tears dry up faster than anything else.

"I just needed a minute." I turn to look at him, with a reassuring smile on my face. He's watching me with the same worry that's been in his eyes since this all started.

"Are you sure? I mean, it's only been a week, maybe you need more time."

"It feels like yesterday," I say, wistfully, regretting the toll this has taken on him, too.

My brother scoffs and slides his unamused gaze back to the iPad. "Really? Feels like the longest month of my entire life, Reggie. Watching this, knowing what I know, I want to kick Marcel's ass. I can't believe he made us all feel sorry for him."

I brush a hand over the lines furrowing his forehead, and my sigh is heavy with equal parts regret and dismay.

"He didn't make up the part where I was kissing another man. The pictures aren't doctored," I remind him pointedly.

He scoffs, his lips pursing, as if he can taste something bitter. "I wish you'd made a fucking video, so he could have heard it, too. That's what he deserves. I can't believe he had the nerve to treat you like this when he was doing *all* the shit we found at the same damn time." He shakes the tablet in his hand for emphasis.

I put a hand on his arm. "I need you to be the one who doesn't make a scene, okay? You *have* to keep your cool. We can't let our emotions get the best of us in there."

"Emotion isn't a bad thing," he says, eyebrows raised in challenge.

"I know that," I snap, and cross my arms over my chest.

He smiles, a knowing smile, at my defensive gesture. "Well then, why are you acting like nothing is wrong?"

"I'm not *acting* like nothing is wrong."

"It's okay to not be okay, Reggie." He pats my arm, reassuringly.

I groan in irritation. "I don't know why you think I need reminding of that. I know myself. There's a storm the likes of which I've never known brewing inside me. I used it to get myself here today. Just because my outward reactions are not what you expect, doesn't mean it's an act."

We hold each other's gazes. We may have shared a womb, but we're as different as sea and sand. And just as vital to each other. Right now, the ever-present sparkle in his eyes is dulled by disappointment. I'm not the only one nursing a heartbreak.

If charisma and empathy were divided and distributed between us, then the lion's share went to Remi. He's got the most tender of hearts and is swift to injure and slow to forgive. Because he knows that about himself, he's careful about letting people close.

His good opinion and friendship are hard to come by.

Marcel won both of those, in spades.

We even have a running joke that he liked Marcel more than he liked me. It was said in good humor, but, like every joke, it was peppered by the truth.

He and my husband have much more in common than we ever had. What started off as a distant relationship between in-laws, has blossomed into a real friendship. One that I have never interfered with, even when I wanted to. I wasn't in any sort of danger, and there was nothing about the image we portrayed to the world about our family that I wanted to change. So, I've kept my own counsel about the things that were going on behind closed doors.

When I only had my suspicions about Marcel being the one to have stolen that picture, he dismissed it outright.

Marcel had sent that email to everyone in my family and in our close circle of friends. He's played the cuckolded, devastated husband perfectly.

Remi was only humoring me when he sent his firm's new private investigator, Dina, to follow my lead. He didn't expect to find anything behind that mirror in my room that Marcel kept glancing at.

Who would want to believe their friends capable of the kind of subterfuge and deception I was accusing Marcel of? It even took me a while to put it together.

Last week, when Marcel offered me this meeting, things were very different. According to the terms of our prenup, he was awarded temporary, full custody of our children, pending our divorce and a formal custody agreement.

I didn't fight him because I wanted to spare my children any more drama and publicity. I was desperate, heartsick, and humiliated.

He held all the cards, and he used this meeting, with his offer, to discuss custody as a big stick that he's used to beat compliance out of me. He picked the date, the time, the place, everything.

The fallout from my public shaming wasn't just my reputation. It endangered something that means even more to me.

My podcast, The Jezebel. I started it after my mother suggested it, but not for the reasons she did. I knew that when he got here, I'd have to tell him the truth. But first, I had to hear myself say it all out loud. And that's what I did with the podcast, used it as an outlet. But then, people started writing to me, commenting and sharing their stories, too.

But it turned into something completely different, which makes the timing of this picture's publication, with my tattoo visible for all the world to see, even worse.

Two days before the picture was published, the podcast was mentioned in a news report and was credited as the source of information that led to the re-opening of a case involving a prominent plastic surgeon here in Houston. He'd been acquitted of a sexual assault charge after the woman, who accused him, was discredited during cross examination. The woman, who chose to remain anonymous during the trial due to safety concerns, had been a prostitute and that was enough to convince a jury that whatever he did to her, she asked for. He was acquitted, and she was left to get on with her life.

Then, one day, she sent me an email. Lori, as she called herself, found the podcast, inadvertently. She asked me to tell her story because she'd been so maligned in the press. So, I did. That opened the floodgates. It turns out that since the trial, there'd been more complaints from women who no one cared about. I started getting emails from women, mostly sex workers, who'd been his patients at the free clinic he volunteered at, with stories very much like Lori's.

They had dates, times, complaints they filed, officials who ignored them. I compiled them and used The Jezebel's email address to forward them to a staff writer at the Houston Chronicle.

There was an outcry from Dr. Zimmerman's powerful friends and patients. He was one of them. Their golf partner. Their campaign donor. Their museum patron.

They wrote opinion editorials, claiming he was being "framed, hustled, and schemed on by desperate, broken and deluded women who were angry that he'd spurned their advances."

But, this time, it's not just his word against one vulnerable sex worker who could be steamrolled. A tidal wave of women have come forward to stop him and I think we might just do it.

So far, no one has made the connection and noticed that the name of the podcast is the same as the name emblazoned on my back. But it wouldn't take much for Marcel to figure it out. And I know he'll use it as leverage.

With my reputation so tarnished by this picture that everyone has seen, being associated with me could cast doubt on their credibility, again.

Thankfully, I have a big stick of my own that I'm going to use to bind his tongue.

My hunch the possibility of a hidden camera behind that mirror paid off.

There were also cameras in our children's rooms, and the small library I used for my monthly sit down with my accountant. I was livid.

Until Dina, brilliant woman that she is, called to say she'd struck gold. She hacked the Drop Box where the surveillance videos were stored. He recorded me in that library, but he also recorded himself.

What I saw made me sick, before it made me smile.

When Remi watched it, he insisted on representing me himself. He's one of the country's most decorated litigators. And as relieved as I am to have him on my side, I hate that it comes at the cost of that disappointment in his eyes.

I soften my posture and take his hand in mine.

"I know this is hard for you, too. Let's not argue. I can't change who I am or how I cope with things any more than you can. So, let's just cut each other some slack. Once I have my children back under my roof, I'll curl up in my huge bathtub with an entire bottle of champagne and cry myself dry, okay?"

He closes his eyes and shakes his head. "I'm sorry all of this is happening. I'm sorry I didn't see who he was," he says, in a voice made rough from a week of shouting arguments and late nights, followed by mornings, so early it felt like we hadn't slept at all.

"We only know of other people, what they let us see and you're not a mind reader." I nod at the phone. "Go on, let's watch to the end."

His finger hovers over the triangle on the screen. "You don't have to. It's not like you don't already know what happens," he says, in that way he has of being kind, but managing, at the same time.

I give his hand a resolute squeeze. "I want to watch it. The man in this video is who Marcel really is. I'll need that reminder when I sit across from him today. Press play," I say, with resolve.

The video resumes. I'm prepared for what comes next. But my throat still constricts as the worst day of my entire life replays on the screen.

My heart is tied into a million tiny knots. When we get to the worst of it, I close my eyes. And even with no volume, I can hear the sounds of mayhem and destruction from that day—my shouts, my daughter crying, Marcel's thundering silence.

"What men?" I growl, the fear in my eyes morphing into rage that turns them into slits of fire and brimstone.

I hit pause and close my eyes. Sweat beads my upper lip, and my nails dig grooves into the palms of my curled hands.

I flatten them against my thighs and let the black wool soothe the hot stinging skin of my palms. But it doesn't. Instead, it launches another round of memories that are as painful as the ones I just watched. It was a gift from my grandfather.

When my mother told him Chanel was too extravagant for a twenty-one-year old, he'd laughed.

"She's a work of art. It's my job to make sure she's shown in the best frame and in the best light. And that suit is it." He'd pointed at this black Chanel summer wool. "It's a signal that this is a woman you should not underestimate."

Every time I wear it, I stand a little taller, feel less vulnerable. So, even though my feelings for him are still so muddled, I put it on this morning, because I need to feel those things today. But thinking of him now, only adds to my agitation. I'm supposed to revile him. To hate him. And, I don't. Yet, I can't say I love him, when I didn't even know him.

Like I didn't know Marcel.

Like my mother didn't know my father.

I don't trust my judgment anymore…and as much as I miss Stone, there's a part of me that's glad things ended, before he could disappoint me, too.

"Hey, you okay? You growled." Remi puts a hand on mine and

squeezes.

The tenderness in his voice makes my undeserving heart ache. He's done so much for me this week.

"Yes, I'm fine," I say. And then, I proceed to fake it until I can make it true.

The door opens, and Sylvester Hadnott, the most unscrupulous family attorney in the city, sticks his head out. He's wearing a huge grin. I'm going to enjoy wiping that smile off his face.

I get my focus back, put the smile Marcel isn't expecting on, and walk in to face my fate.

Marcel looks every single one of his fifty-seven years. I take some comfort from the gray scruff on his cheeks. He dyes his hair, as regularly as he needs to, so he can hide all but a few wisps of gray at his temples. I haven't seen him with stubble since our honeymoon. It's gratifying to see him look like hell.

"Are you ready to discuss terms?" The mediator, sitting at the head of the table, speaks.

"Yes. We have ours ready," Remi says.

Marcel huffs in indignation. "Terms? What terms could you have? I have you by those little hairs on your disloyal cunt."

"This is a negotiation," I return evenly.

"You don't get to lecture me. You have broken rules, and now, you will learn the consequences. Cunt," he enunciates.

"Mr. Landel, please. Remember that all oral exchanges will be part of the record I submit to the court. The petitioner can begin. I understand you have a list of terms."

Marcel chuckles. "By all means, let me hear your terms...of *surrender*."

Ignoring him, Remi pulls out the list we prepared and starts to read.

"Regan will continue to raise the children. You can have the summers, as you do now. Regan will retain her residence at the family home she has always lived in with the children. She's willing to buy you out of any equity you're deemed to be owed. She wants you to sign an NDA, agreeing to keep personal knowledge gained during your marriage private, and she is willing to do the same."

"The fuck I will," Marcel bellows. "You must think I'm insane," he scoffs, flouncing back in his chair, affronted.

Marcel's lawyer leans over and whispers something in his ear.

Remi looks at me and raises his eyebrows, his eyes clouded with worry. I smile reassuringly.

Nothing Marcel knows about me is more damaging than what's on that video. Once he sees it, he'll do whatever I say.

I nudge Remi under the table, and he clears his throat and looks back at the document. "Mr. Landel will agree to keep private any information he accessed when he breached Mrs. Landel's account to steal the photograph that was originally printed in *Aussi* magazine."

Marcel yawns. "I didn't steal that picture. Who would even believe that? Why would I want the world to know I'm a cuckold?" He points a self-righteous finger in my face.

"Further, Mr. Landel will agree to seek help for his anger issues and sex addiction in exchange for continued unsupervised summer visitation with his children."

Marcel's face turns red, his lips thin into furious white slash. "You have lost your mind," he speaks in a muffled scream.

I have to bite the inside of my cheek to stop myself from laughing in his face.

"Like the rest of our terms this one is a non-negotiable and certainly more than you deserve." Remi concludes stoically.

Marcel gapes, looking between Remi and me repeatedly, his rage easing into righteous indignation. "*You* are the one in violation of the prenuptial agreement. *You* are the one who made a whore of yourself for the whole world to see. You should be on your knees, *begging* me to take you back. *Begging* me to let you see your children. Instead you are wasting our time."

I nod at Remi. "Send it now."

He returns my nod and hits a button on his laptop. "I've sent you a video. Please watch it and then we will discuss," he informs the three of them.

Then he leans back in his chair, crossing his arms almost leisurely, and gives Marcel a sinister smile. I love my big brother. He's as flawed as anyone, but when he gets it right…he gets it *right*.

Their devices beep simultaneously, and they're fingers moved in seemingly synchronized taps as they open the video.

I glance at Remi, and we share a silent high five. Then we both watch Marcel while *my* grenade blows up in his face.

It's just a highlight reel. Him with Hanna. The conversation he had with the reporter of the magazine, after he'd sent him the picture, which he broke into my iCloud account to steal. Him getting a blowjob from the young man who I *thought* was his physical therapist. Him dragging me out of the room by my hair, while our ten-year-old daughter screamed and begged him to stop.

When everyone is finished watching, there's an awkward beat of silence, before our mediator clears his throat and pushes his glasses up his nose. Marcel's expression, when the tape ends, is nothing short of shell-shocked.

He came in here expecting me to ask him to take me back. To beg him to forgive me.

It didn't occur to him, not once, that I might not stand down. I never minded that he didn't think I was good for anything more than being a sparkly vessel to continue his line.

But I mind *very* much that he set me up and tried to ratfuck me out of my entire life. So, after more than ten years of being married, he's finally getting a taste of the real me. And I can tell he doesn't like my flavor—not one bit.

Marcel finally meets my eyes. He looks like he wants to rip my throat out with his bare teeth.

Or, maybe I'm projecting.

"You are out of your mind," he snarls.

"How do you figure?"

"You want to blackmail me?" He bares his teeth like a rabid dog.

"Not at all. I'm just meeting you where you are. Now that I know you're not naturally inclined toward doing what's right, I'm incentivizing your behavior."

"You wouldn't show anyone those things."

"Before you put that picture into the world, so our children could see it, that might have been true. You dragged my name through the mud. And you are completely crazy if you thought I'd stand by and let you ruin me *and* take my children. *No.*" I flare my nostrils and lean toward him. "And, I have one more term."

Remi stiffens and puts a hand on my arm. "Regan, what is this?"

I ignore him and the guilt that tightens my throat and keep my eyes trained on Marcel, so he can see just how serious I am. "You will not try to identify or reveal anything you may have already learned about the man in that photo."

His lips twitch, and if looks could kill, I'd be taking my last breath. But his glare makes this all even more satisfying. "You know, of course, that's just a trailer, right?" I point at the phone in his hand. "You *will* do everything I just asked, or I'll send the full feature film to TMZ, and anyone else who wants it."

His face grows pale. "But…it would *ruin* me," he cries, in disbelief.

I shake my head and make my smile regretful. "Yes, it would. But as you know, when you break the rules, you've got to live with the consequences."

His eyes go black with rage, and he lunges across the table at me. "Fuck you, Regan. You can't do this. I am going to bury you."

Remi is on his feet so fast, he knocks his chair over. He steps in front of me and leans forward, towering over Marcel like an angry god. "You're lucky I have people who depend on me. Otherwise, I'd tie you to this table and beat you with my shoe for what you did to my sister. And I'd go to jail with a smile on my face," he spits.

Marcel may be burning with outrage, but he's not crazy. He pales and wilts back into his seat. His expression is pleading now. "Remi, you are a man of integrity. This is a shakedown."

Remi scoffs and sits, his gaze burning with loathing and still on Marcel's pallid face. "This is a negotiation. You have choices."

The next few seconds pass in tense silence.

"This is a waste of time," Marcel hisses.

"So, it seems," his lawyer's response is flat and unemotional.

They gather their papers and briefcases. Marcel's expression is stony and frigid, as he stands, buttons his suit jacket and leaves the table, without another word or glance in my direction.

I know I've got him by the short hairs, but I came here with a very specific goal, and I won't let him leave without giving it to me.

"You have until tomorrow afternoon to leave my house. Consider this your heads up," I call to him.

"Fine," he snaps, and then the door slams so hard the windows rattle.

Remi and I walk to his car in tense, stoic silence. I know he's waiting for us to be alone to unleash on me. As soon as I climb inside the cool, dark interior of his car, I let loose the breath I've been holding for the last few days, in a long sigh of relief.

"I'm exhausted," I groan, letting my head loll to rest on the seat.

"That went better than I hoped." Remi's voice is tight with unspoken annoyance.

I cast him a sidelong glance. "Then why do you sound like we lost."

"I don't like surprises." His voice is quiet but seething with anger.

"I'm sorry, but I didn't want to talk to you about it because I knew you'd press me for more."

"Yes, I would." He leans back against his door, his disappointed glare, unrelenting, as he rails at me. "I want to know why, if you care about him enough to protect him from your husband, why the *fuck* doesn't *he* care enough to not let you?"

I drop my head into my hands. "Because he doesn't know what's happened."

"How? That picture was in every single tabloid, including the ones in Mexico. Or does he live on the moon?"

A wave of despair washes over me. "He might as well," I say. Stone is only one month into his three-month trip, and I feel sick to think of what he'll say when he gets back and finds everything so different.

"Then why do you feel the need to protect him?" he snaps, and my heart trembles because, Lord, I hate hurting him.

"Because he's not the one who broke his wedding vows. He didn't do anything wrong, and Marcel would completely dismantle his life. I don't want that on my conscience. It was a fling. And I just want it done." The words leave a bitter aftertaste in their wake. But they do the trick.

"Fine. You're entitled to your privacy, Regan. I just hate the idea of him walking around scot-free, while your name is being dragged through the mud."

"I'm fine, Remi. I'll have to stop some of the bleeding and try to salvage Venus Rising, but that meeting was a huge hurdle, and I just want to look forward." I grab his hand and give him my best little sister puppy dog eyes.

"Fine," he sighs and pulls me into a hug. "Besides, you got everything you wanted today. I'm proud of you."

"Not everything." I banish the thought from my mind. I've been very grateful for the distraction of disaster to take my mind off him. I've also given thanks for the distance between us.

But as his date of arrival grows nearer, my longing only intensified to an insatiable, tenacious growl of demand. One that robs me of sleep.

And one that I know, if presented with opportunity for appeasement, won't be denied.

Two Months Later

PAMPLONA, NORTE DE SANTANDER
COLOMBIA

Chapter 41

MOVE

STONE

I stumble into my apartment and drop everything where I stand. Without stopping, I stride straight into my bedroom and put my phone on its charger. I grab the stack of mail that my neighbor bundled and left on my kitchen table along with his copy of my spare key.

I'm dying for a hot shower and for the soft mattress on my bed. But I need to check my messages, open my mail and call my woman.

I grab my phone from the drawer in my bedside table and plug it in. Three months of lying dormant has left it completely dead and it takes forever for it to even register that it's charging. I stare at it, willing it to turn on.

When I knew I couldn't use it, I didn't once yearn for it. Now that I'm seconds away from being able to communicate again, each minute that I stare at that black dead screen for what feels like eons. I know a watched pot never boils, so I turn away from the phone and walk over to the stack of mail. I see the big envelope at the bottom and recognize Regan's handwriting in the corner reserved for return sender's information.

I've been writing to her every day, sending the letters whenever we crossed paths with a courier or stopped in a village that had a post office.

In the last one I sent, I asked her to send me a copy of the new Tom Clancy. This must be it.

I trace the outline of what is clearly a book through the envelope. I feel the impression of something else inside. My dessert after dinner rule is still in place, I make myself wait until I've opened the rest before I open that.

I open each bill. The only exciting piece of mail there is the letter from Baylor College of Medicine. My start date for the fellowship in Houston has been set. I glance at the calendar on my wall, and smile.

Only two more weeks. A year ago, I was sure that heading to Houston would feel like the end of an adventure. Now, I have Regan to look forward to. Just as I reach for her package, I hear the vibrating tell of my phone powering on. And then, the phone's staccato vibrations turn into one long buzz as my messages start to download.

As a compromise, I walk over to the phone while I rip open the envelope.

I pull out the smaller item first. It's a stack of notecards tied together with a delicate gold silk ribbon like something precious and cared for.

But even before I read the small note stocked into the top of the stack, I know that they are, in fact, the exact opposite of precious and cared for.

The handwriting on all of them is mine.

The sinking sensation seeps all the way to my bones. The sense of loss and doom infuses my marrow.

I wondered if she was getting them. At least now, I know.

I pull the book out of the envelope and the letters were also stuffed into and stare unseeingly at the worn edges of the dust cover.

With my heart thundering like the ominous rumble of thunder before a storm breaks, I open the messages on my phone.

Even in the swirl of all my confusion and panic, when I see her name pop up, I smile.

I start reading her texts. There are twenty-two of them.

The first one reads "I love you, too."

The first twenty are a variation of "I love you" or "I miss you" or both.

The twenty first is a link that opens to a newspaper story. When I read it, I understand everything. Or at least I think I do. It was published two months ago, while I was busy pursuing an opportunity most doctors only dream of, she was waking up to this.

I don't want to read her final message. I can't imagine that whatever it says is going to do anything less than gut me. But I force myself to open it.

Stone,

I'm sorry that you came home from your trip to find that so much had changed.

By now, you've seen the news, and you know what's happened. I'm sorry that my recklessness resulted in that picture being shared with the world. It has completely changed the landscape of my life, and I have got to focus on my children and myself. I won't drag you into this. Nobody knows it's you, and I want it to stay that way. Things are bad enough, without adding another log to this fire. When you're back here, distance would be best. I'm so sorry. You deserve so much happiness, Stone, and I hope you find it. Thank you for taking me on the most glorious adventure I've ever known. I hope one day, we can find a way to be friends, again. We're so very good at that.

Yours,
Regan

Chapter 42

NO

REGAN

My phone buzzes, and I reach to grab it from my bedside table. The sun isn't up, but I'm wide awake.

I knew he'd be back today, and I've been waiting on bated breath for his response to my texts and the package I sent last month.

I take a deep breath and compose myself before I open his text.

I got your letters and your text. And I understand why you feel that way. But I must, respectfully, say no. Because Venus, if I had the power to command blood and bone, mind and spirit, you are the very person I would have created. I told you I loved you. And I meant it. So, no fucking way am I moving on. I'll see you soon.

Chapter 43

HOME

STONE

I step through the sliding automatic doors and inhale the warm petroleum-tinged air that is Houston's calling card. I glance around until I see Tyson's black Escalade down the row of cars. He sticks his hand out and waves, before the trunk flies open.

He offered to pick me up when I called to tell him I was coming home. I hoped it would be Regan. I've called her so many times that I've lost count.

She doesn't answer her phone, and she's only texted me back once to say, "I'm sorry."

I've been caught between rage and despondency for the last two weeks.

I can't eat.

I can't think.

The only details I have are the few that Tyson's given me. I don't know what's going on with her kids or her, and I hate that I'm just a bystander in a disaster I helped cause.

So, I've decided to tell him everything.

She'll be pissed. But I can handle that. And I'm sick of lying to one of my best friends.

But, as I walk toward the car, my confidence that Tyson will understand and support me, flags. She's his sister and her association with me has made her life exceedingly difficult.

He knows what kind of man I am. He'll know that I wouldn't dare move on his sister if I wasn't serious. At least, I hope he does. If not, I hope he'll give me a chance to explain before he goes off.

"Welcome back to Clutch City, Flintstone," Tyson gives me a boisterous hug and a few hard slaps on the back that remind me how strong he is. They called him a pretty boy in college, and he killed himself in the gym to build his body enough that no one could mistake him for anything other than the badass he is.

"I see you've been slacking on your workouts without me around to kick your ass," I tease him while he throws my suitcases in his trunk.

"Slacking? Man, are you nuts? If this line wasn't so long, I'd race you down to that sign and back to show you what your eyes clearly can't see."

"Yeah, long line's the reason," I quip and pick up a box of Shipley's donuts that's sitting in my seat. The crumbs of sugar glaze from the dearly departed pastries cover every surface of his car.

"Man, you are a slob. I know you don't drive women around in this heap," I say as I look at the piles of empty water bottles, plastic bags, fast-food paper bags and books everywhere.

"This is my mobile office and I take the honeys out in my Aston Martin. And stop bitching and be glad I didn't bring my Explorer."

I make a show of dusting off my seat, before I sit down.

"So, where am I taking you?"

"Same place. Kirby and OST," I buckle my seatbelt and turn the radio down.

"Aww, shit. I forgot you live in the cut. Now that you're a doctor, doctor and not just a resident, you gotta move to a better neighborhood. Come to Rivers Wilde, man. The Ivy has everything, *and* we'll be neighbors. And, now that your ass is legal, we can go cause mayhem. There's this new strip joint off Montrose and, man…the pussy is *out-standing*. I am so glad to have a single friend in town. All my friends are being assholes and getting married. They don't know about this bachelor life, right?" He slaps my shoulder and flashes a conspiratorial grin. It's so much like Regan's rare grins and it hits me square in the gut.

I clear my throat, uneasy and not sure that this is the right segue, but I decide to take it and tell him. "So," I say and clear my throat.

His phone rings and his car announces, "Remi, calling"

He holds up a finger, hits the green button to answer it and says, "Hey, what's up?"

"Yo, I was thinking we should cancel dinner at Reggie's tonight." At the mention of Regan, my whole body tenses.

"Why? It's Friday. This is one home cooked meal I eat all week. Why is she canceling?"

"She's not canceling, I am. This is her last weekend in her house and she's grieving a little. She loved it."

"Why's she moving?" I interject as casually as I can.

"Who's in the car, Ty?" Remi's voice drops a whole octave.

"Shit sorry, it's Stone. I should have said."

Remi's silent for a beat. "Yeah, you should have," he snaps. Then he softens his tone. "Stone, hey. I knew you were headed back. Didn't realize it was today. You staying with Hayes?" he asks conversationally, but his voice is more guarded now that he knows I'm in the car.

"No, I kept my place in the medical center while I was gone, so I'm headed there."

"Yo, damn I forgot!" Tyson slaps the steering wheel.

"What?" Remi and I ask at the same time.

"Stone was in Mexico when Reggie was. Maybe he saw the asshole in that picture." Tyson's hands tighten and twist on the steering wheel and his lip curls.

"Man, I fucking hope so," Remi growls. "I want to kick his ass for hiding while my sister dangled on a hook all by herself."

My stomach plummets to my toes. This doesn't bode well.

"Hmmm…What did she say when you asked?" I ask trying to handicap my prospects.

"She says he's some dude she met and had a fling with him…but that's it." Remi grumbles.

"Who was she with? Besides that chick." Tyson asks.

"No one," I answer flatly and turn my head to look out of the window. We're flying down the airport service road and the scenery speeding by gives me an instant headache. My stomach roils. A stranger? She really expects me to go spend the rest of my life pretending that we don't know each other. And I can't breathe

"For real? Damn." Tyson asks, disappointment clear in his voice.

"For real." I spot a cluster of fast-food restaurants and point. "Can we stop? I'm starving."

"Yeah, and if we're not going to Regan's I'm going to get something, too." He slams on his brakes and makes a squealing turn into the parking lot of the restaurant and joins the very long drive through line. Tyson throws his car into park as if he expects to be sitting for a very long time. Shit.

"So, we'll start Friday nights in a few weeks. Let's let her get settled, cool?" Remi asks.

"Hell no, it's not cool. That's the only home cooked meal I get all week." Tyson whined.

"I just told you that Regan is wrecked. Stop being selfish." My stomach clenches to hear that she's wrecked, that she nearly lost her children because of that picture.

"I'm not just thinking about myself. I'm thinking about Regan, too. She needs adult time. Fun adult time. She needs to date again and get over that French motherfucker who I never liked, for the record."

Remi lets out a long-suffering sigh. "Stone, welcome to the family. This is your life now. We don't know each other well, but I'm looking forward to changing that. Since we're kind of…brothers now."

My gut tightens and I can't hide my discomfort as I stammer through my answer.

"Uhh, but not really, though. I mean, he wasn't my dad."

Tyson gives me a surprised side-eye, and there's silence from Remi's end of the line. I grimace and look away. I rub a hand over the back of my suddenly warm neck. "I'm sorry, I just haven't really had time to process this—"

"Hey, hey…no pressure." Remi sounds like he's talking to a skittish animal. "I know this is strange. Just wanted to let you know where I am… You can meet me there, or not. Either way, welcome to the family. You should come to dinner at Regan's one Friday. Ty drive like you have sense and call me when you get home. We've got some business to discuss."

He hangs up, without saying bye or waiting for Tyson's response.

"Older brothers. Bossy as fuck. See how he just ordered me around? He's always sticking his nose in my shit. You'd think I was still thirteen and not thirty-two."

"Hayes is the same. Sticking his nose where it's not wanted."

"Listen, you got any nice doctor friends Regan's age? She needs a regular guy, but you know my sister—she's so image conscious. She'll want someone who, as my mother would say "has the same size door as hers." He gives me a knowing look.

"What does that mean?"

"I mean, she's had a rough time. Since that picture dropped, all the funding for her little center she was building has disappeared. Her little fake housewives clique dropped her, boards she's served on for years asked her to resign. Her kids come home crying because people are talking about their mother's ass. And so, I want to find her a man who makes the bitches who have been kicking her while she's down, choke. I'm thinking chief of staff, head of a department, or something."

"You want me to find her a man?" My head spins at his request.

"Yeah. What did you think? That I was asking you to date her?"

"No, no, no," I laugh, through my queasiness.

Tyson laughs, and the line finally moves. We inch up another few feet and come to a stop. "Regan is a rare vintage. I'm vetting her next man myself. And I don't know anyone with better judgment than you. So, when you get to work, take notes, give me names, so I can start getting them checked out, and we can get her introduced. Okay?" He punches me in the shoulder, and I muster a weak smile.

"You know what, I'm not hungry anymore. So, if you're only stopping for me, we can leave."

"What's wrong with you? You're passing up shitty food?" He puts a hand on my forehead, as if he's checking temperature.

I shove his hand off and give him a critical once-over. "From the look of that gut, you might want to do the same," I quip.

He just laughs and slaps my back. "Stone, my man. I missed you. It'll be good to have you around. If you're not hungry, you will be, as soon as we get close enough to smell the grease."

His phone rings again. The car announces the caller as "Tami."

I pull out my phone and check my messages, while he talks to her. But I can't focus. I keep replaying the things Tyson said.

He crushed my hopes of getting him on my side in my bid to win Regan back. But, I didn't come all this way to let something like Tyson's approval keep me from her.

And, right now, the biggest obstacle in my way is the woman herself.

I'll see her on Friday at this dinner. I'll keep my feelings to myself, until I've had a chance to talk to her. Because there's no way in the world that I'm going to let her go.

Chapter 44

ALWAYS BE UNFINISHED BUSINESS

REGAN

"Come meet us at The Belvedere. Stone's only been in town for a week, and he's already got a girl. You need to take lessons from him."

I re-read Tyson's text, my heart in my throat, as I stare at the picture of my brother with a grinning, gorgeous Stone and a half-naked girl who appears to be sitting on his lap.

I look at my missed calls. Today is the first time this week that he hasn't called. At least now, I know why.

I slip my phone into my purse and close my eyes. "Charlie, I have a headache. Can we take a raincheck?"

His hand cups my forehead. "Are you sick? Do I need to pull over?" He puts on his turn signal and starts looking to his right, for a chance to change lanes.

"It's just a headache. I'm fine," I lie, but the strain in my voice isn't feigned. I'm tired and anxious and scrambling to figure out all of the things that need solving.

Every day, I remind myself that the past is a useless place to dwell. I force myself to focus on my future.

I have a lot to do. Marcel isn't the only bridge to my old life that's no longer passable.

Friends, board directorships, club memberships, and long-standing invitations all disappeared faster than roaches when the lights come on.

When the crowd thinned, I could see clearly who my real friends were, and they're pretty amazing. So, yes, I don't have Stone. But I have my brothers, and Dina and Confidence and Kal. And Hayes, kind of.

He's made attempts to talk about what happened. I went to visit after Phoenix, their beautiful baby boy, was born. He didn't miss the chance to remind me of what Stone stood to lose if his identity was revealed. I know Hayes means well and that he's just trying to protect his brother, but I wish he'd see that I am, too. Even when it's killing me too. And I know I can't avoid him forever. I'll have to see him at some point.

My heart and thighs clench, simultaneously, as joy and desire swirl inside me, and for a moment, I'm lightheaded with giddiness.

I have to shake myself free of it. This is how I got into this mess in the first place.

As a reminder of that, I read Tyson's text again and memorize that picture and all the places he's touching that girl.

"Here we are," Charlie drawls, as we pull to a stop in front of my house. I glance up and see the dark row of windows that line the second floor. My mother has them tonight. The week that Marcel kept them from me was the longest of my life. But I wasn't the only one he kept them from. When she asked for them to spend the night, I said yes. Now, I wish they were here. I need their warm little snuggles and unrestrained affection.

"I'm sorry to be a pain. But at least you're spared an evening of being seen with the notorious Regan Wilde." I reach across the center console and press a quick kiss to Charlie's scruffy cheek, at the same time that I pull the lever to open the door.

He puts a hand on my arm to stop me. "Fuck anyone treating you like shit. Marcel is well-liked, but so are you. And you're family. I'm here for you. I wish I could do more than lend a friendly ear."

I only nod, because I can't speak around the throb in my throat. I press a grateful kiss to his cheek and slide out of the car.

I stand on the sidewalk in front of my house and wave goodbye, until he turns right onto Wildewood Parkway and disappears from sight. I trudge up my driveway, tired and feeling sorry for myself.

"Venus."

For a second, I think my mind is playing tricks on me.

I stop in my tracks halfway up to my garage.

My heart kicks into high gear, and the next breath, I attempt to take, doesn't come as easily as the one before it. By the time I've managed to turn around and face him, I'm nearly panting from the onslaught of emotions running riot through me.

He steps into the flood of light from the security lamp that hangs right above my garage.

He looks…like the answer to every single one of my problems. His hair is shorter than I've ever seen it. In his gray suit, white dress shirt, and a dark blue tie is draped over his neck, he looks more like Mr. Grey than Dr. McDreamy. "Stone, what are you doing here?"

"You've been ignoring my calls. So, here I am." His voice is ragged with frustration.

He stops short of being an arm's length away. I want him closer. I cross my arms to stop myself from reaching for him. "I've had a lot going on with my kids."

He crosses his arms, too, but from his furrowed brow and deep frown, he's restraining something very different than desire. "Regan, cut the shit. Let's just get this over with," he snaps.

I flinch at the bite of steel in his voice and bristle at the accusation in his eyes. "You knew what this would be, Stone. I was very clear in my letter."

"I was very clear in the one I wrote you back. Or did you get it mixed up with your…how did Ty put it?" He snaps his fingers in rapid succession and then dons a eureka expression. "Random s*tranger*," he spits the word like a curse.

My face flames, but I dig my heels in. "What did you want me to do? Announce it? It's not as if anything can come of… us."

His eyes narrow, and his expression grows even harder. "The only way that's true is if everything that happened in Mexico was a lie."

I suck in a breath and look down at the ground. He's, unwittingly, given me the key to lock the door behind me when I walk away from him. If that's the only way, then that's what it will be.

"Well, then, maybe it was. I mean maybe it was nostalgia and pent up lust and a little too much sun."

"Really?" His voice is low and dark and the hair on the back of my neck stands up. I can't look at him and tell such a lie. I keep my eyes cast downward and nod.

I brace myself, waiting for him to say something. I should have turned on my heel and run instead.

His arm moves, fast as a whip, and wraps around my waist, as he drags me until our bodies are flush. He's rigid with anger, and yet, it's the most comforting thing I've felt in months. I drop my head onto his chest.

He grips my chin and forces my face up. I close my eyes. "Fucking *look* at me, Regan." His voice is a rasp of frustration.

I open my eyes, and my heart throbs with regret. I hate the shadows under his eyes, almost as much as I hate the naked pain in them.

"Was it a lie?" he demands, and I'm helpless in the face of his hurt. I don't want to cause any more than I already have.

"I'm trying to do the right thing." My words come out on a whimper.

"Me, too, dammit." The flare of heat in his eyes and the low growl that rumbles between us is all the warning I have before his lips cover mine.

The heat of him, the divine taste of him, the way he kisses me like I belong to him—it makes my head spin.

He drags his mouth from mine and kisses his way down my face. "I told you that when I got here, I wouldn't let you go."

His words are like a splash of cold water. I won't let another man manage me, tell me what to do, possess me.

Suddenly, his arms feel like a cage. I can't breathe. I wrench away from his kiss, and without another word, turn and run for my life.

Chapter 45

OUT OF MY SYSTEM

STONE

It sets my teeth on edge with resentment to watch her run from me like I'm the man who hurt her. I'm not going to let her act like she's the one who's suffering. I follow her, my eyes on the long ponytail that swings as she walks.

And, of course, she looks good enough to eat. Her black slim fitting dress molds to her perfect ass and hugs her long lean thighs with each stride. Below the knee, her bare, shapely legs glow like they've got a spotlight on them. Her strappy gold heels slow her down and let me catch up with her before she makes it to the door.

I wrap a hand around her bicep and spin her to face me. Her face is the picture of agony. But I tighten my hold on her and walk her backwards, until we hit her door. "You act like the world will end if people know that you fucked me. Are you ashamed of me?" I snarl.

Her eyes fly wide, and her full lips part to form a perfect circle. " That's not it," she gasps, a hand to her heart as if she's offended.

"Isn't it?" I ask, shaking my head in disbelief. "I was good enough for an island fuck, but only if no one ever knows?"

"Stone!" she admonishes me in another pearl clutching gasp.

"Then tell me the truth. Because I know it's not that you don't want me." I demand.

She crosses her arms and taps her foot, her expression turning frosty. "I'm surprised you even care. You and your *girl* seemed mighty cozy." She puts the last words in air quotes.

"My girl? What are you talking about?" I feel like I'm in the twilight zone.

"I saw the pictures," she growls, puts her hands on my chest and shoves me hard enough to force me to take a step back.

My jaw goes from slack to rigid in the space of time it takes her to finish that sentence.

"I'm not seeing anyone. And hello? You're *married*."

"Well, *I* never lied to you about anything." she yells, pointing indignantly at the ground.

I throw my head back and groan in frustration. I can't believe what I'm hearing. "You said you loved me. And now, you're standing here ripping my *fucking* heart out without so much as a flicker of remorse, makes me think *that* was a lie. And makes me wish I could stop loving you. I wish I could cut the stupid right out of my chest, Regan. But I can't. And I'm so mad at you for it." I don't know why I'm confessing my feelings to this woman who I know I can't trust them with.

She presses her lips together. Her thick fan of her lashes flutter furiously as she blinks back tears. "It wasn't a lie. But this just can't happen. You should go." She tries to step around me, and I block her path.

I'd come here prepared to tell her to go fuck herself. But I need more than this. I need to understand.

"Regan, are you serious?"

Her dark eyes narrow with anger. "Do you know what will happen if we start seeing each other? I'm not even divorced."

"You will be in six weeks."

She stamps her foot in exasperation. "And the last thing I need is to play another round of Regan Wilde's Love Life with the press. I just…can't have another scandal."

"So, you told everyone you hooked up with a random stranger? That's less scandalous than saying you were kissing your first best friend?"

She winces and shakes her head, "If only that's all you were. "

She steps around me, unlocks her front door, and walks inside.

I should let her go, but the flash of misery in her eyes compels me.

I grab the door handle before she can close it and follow her inside.

"Do you think I'm the kind of man who would let you take all the blame and watch blithely while you burn?" I demand.

"That's not what—Ohhh shit," she yelps and hops on one foot over to the sofa and collapses onto it.

"What's wrong?"

"I stubbed my toe because I wasn't looking where I was going because *you* distracted me," she speaks through gritted teeth and bends over to unfasten her shoe.

I kneel and take her foot in my hand.

"Stop it, I'm fine," she grouses, but I ignore her, undo the tiny buckle and pull the strappy gold high heeled shoe off.

And just like that, I'm touching her. It's only her foot, but it's soft and delicate and pretty like the rest of her. I stroke the tips of her toes. "Where does it hurt?" I ask.

Her breath hitches and her eyes follow the path of my fingers as they stroke her feet. I lift her toe to my lips and press a kiss to each one. With each touch, her tight calf muscle relaxes. I press my thumb into the high arch of her sole and she moans my name.

It's a call to worship, one that I'm heedless to refuse. My reverent gaze collides with her dark, hungry one.

Her chest is heaving like she's been running. Her nipples are hard and pressing through the thin fabric of her blouse and from here, down on my knees in front of her, I can *smell* what she wants.

With our eyes still locked, I press my palms to the inside of her knees and push them apart. And then I surge up to fit my hips in the space I just created.

She opens for me, wraps her arms around my shoulders and sighs in relief.

I press my nose into her neck and breathe in her ginger, lemon scent "You smell so good," I whisper. When I hold her like this…I know she's mine. I wish she'd let me be hers, too.

"You do, too. Like everything I've ever thought was delicious," she says, and her voice is pained, and I draw back to look at her.

She's flushed. Wisps of her hair cling to her face. Her supple lips are parted as her breaths come in short pants. Our gazes lock in a battle of wills that I can't afford to lose. But that I'm not sure I *want* to win.

We stay that way, suspended mid-motion for five, lust-charged, emotionally fraught seconds.

And then, we lunge.

When our lips collide, the whole world breaks open. When my tongue sweeps into her mouth, new solar systems explode into existence and I am home.

Her arms enfold my neck so tightly, I can't move my head.

As if I'm going anywhere. Now that I'm finally here, I never want to leave.

I unzip her dress and tug it down to her waist and lean back to gaze on my bounty.

I almost blow my load at the sight of her. Her dark nipples are rigid and jutting, begging to be sucked. My hungry mouth can't get there fast enough. Her back bows, and her fingers claw at my neck when I close my lips around the stiff, sweet nipple. I flick it until she calls my name, and then, I suck.

Her body bucks against mine. "I want you naked," she growls, and nips my ear.

I relinquish my treat to unfasten my tie and rip my shirt open. Buttons clatter and scatter, and I don't care at all. She sinks her teeth into my shoulder, and then licks and kisses the place she bites, over and over, while her frantic hands work at the button and zipper of my trousers.

My hands are just as frenzied trying to pull her dress all the way off. Her slim, strong hips are banded by nude lace panties that barely cover the lips of her pussy. She's soaked through and left a spot right where she's the neediest.

I take a moment to marvel at how exquisitely made this woman is. How perfectly we fit, how easily we come together. As much as I want to be inside her, I also want to just lay my head on her chest, listen to her heartbeat and savor being with her.

But then she whimpers and scratches my shoulders. "Please, please, please," she chants.

I cup her heat and press the heel of my hand into her clit. She throws her head back, lifting her breasts, their tawny peaks jutting upward, as if in offering. I take it. I suck her nipples and stroke her slick, swollen pussy.

"Stone, baby, oh God," she calls out in a husky, pleading voice that goes straight to my dick. My hands stop pressing and start pulling. Fabric tears and I release her delicious nipple, blow on it and watch it pucker before I kiss my way down her stomach.

"God, I've missed this so damn much," I confess in between kisses and licks.

She's intoxicating—the taste, the smell of her, the way it clings to me…I'm drunk on all of it.

"Stone, I need it…my clit it's so…fuck…" She groans my name and shoves her hands into my hair, grinding her pelvis into my face.

I press the flat of my hand to her stomach and hold her writhing body still. I pull her swollen, stiff clit gently between my lips and suck it while I flick her hood with the soft tip of my tongue.

The muscles of her stomach flex under my fingers and her thighs start to tremble so violently they slip off my shoulders. I spread her thighs wide and press my tongue inside her. She's so hot and there aren't enough hours in the day for me to ever have enough.

I want to eat her until she comes, but I'm so close myself and I need to be inside her more than I need my next breath.

"Have you been with anyone?" I ask.

"Only you," she pants

"Only *ever* me," I reiterate and bite the inside of her thigh. I slide up to nestle into the cradle of her hips, and without preamble or permission, push inside her.

For a moment, my vision blurs and I close my eyes against dizzying waves of pleasure that move relentlessly from my scalp to the soles of my feet.

"I want to slow down, but I can't. It's been too fucking long, Regan. I've been going god damn crazy, fucking my fist, coming on my stomach instead of in this pussy," I confess in breath starved rasps while I press deep, deeper, and yet it's not deep enough.

"Ah, oh my God." She wraps her legs around my waist and presses her forehead to my shoulder. I bind an arm around her hips and cup her head with my other hand. I bury my face in her neck and make love to her for all the nights I've missed.

Every time I drive back into her, I taste something like heaven. I haven't come yet, and I'm already hungry for her again.

"Lie to me, Regan. Lie to me and tell me that you are mine."

"It would never be a lie," she responds immediately with her hot mouth on my ear and our chests pressed together, so tightly, that I can't tell her thundering heartbeat from mine.

She comes fast, clenching around me like a fist, and my control starts to slip and splinter.

"Wait," she pants, and I pull out of her and lift off when she bucks her hips. She rolls out from beneath me and slides off the couch.

"What are you doing?" I turn around, and she puts a hand in the center of my chest and pushes me down onto the couch. My dick bobs, and her eyes follow the motion greedily.

She kneels in front of me, spreads my thighs, and drags her breasts over my erection. "I want you to come in my mouth.

"Then, why are you still talking?" I ask.

She chuckles and licks her lips, before she grabs my hips with one hand and cups my balls in her other. My head hits the back of the couch. "Fuck, Venus, goddess mine," I chant nonsense words in a guttural voice. I tug the gold elastic holding her ponytail free and it falls in sleek sable waves, veiling my thighs. I lift it by the fistfuls so I can watch her suck me off.

Her kiss stung lips stretch around my length and her eyes close when she pulls me into her mouth until the pulsing head of my dick hits the soft back of her throat. Tears roll down her cheeks. I cup her cheeks and tug until she lifts her head.

She yanks free of my hands and glares at me.

"I thought I was hurting you," I explain.

"You weren't. But if you don't put your dick back in my mouth, *I'll* hurt *you*." She yanks me forward. I glide back into her hot mouth. Her groans of pleasure vibrate around my cock every time I thrust into the pleasure palace of her mouth.

I don't last ten seconds.

I come so hard that the rumble that started in my chest leaves my mouth in a growl. I throw my head back and. I shoot off—thick and fast—releasing all the tension, all my need, all my love, all my anger that I've held back like a tightly drawn bow flies out of me, and she takes it all.

She releases me with one last long suck and then falls back onto the rug with a groan. Her arms and legs sprawl artlessly while she stares up at the ceiling, panting.

"Regan, what are we doing?" I reach for her.

She rolls away and stands up, tugs her dress up and looks down at me with her hands folded in front of her like a fucking schoolteacher. "We shouldn't have done that. You…your job, my kids, our families… there's just so much going on." She starts pacing back and forth.

"My job?" What the hell does that mean? I sit up and start straightening my clothes and watch her pace.

"You've got your whole life ahead of you and I live a life incompatible with that. I have kids, you don't want them. I live here. You want to travel. Your job has a morality clause, and I'm married, stained."

She slaps her chest with her open palm.

"Wait, what?" I stand, surprised at her mentioning my job again.

She keeps pacing, almost talking to herself. "I've done everything I can to protect you, but the minute we start dating, people will know. And everything I've done will be for naught. Marcel will ruin you. And for what? For a woman you don't even know?"

"I do know you." I put my hands on her shoulders.

"You don't," she snarls, and bares her teeth at me. "I'm not the girl you fell in love within that bakery or even on that beach. You like fucking me, but you couldn't last five minutes in this *fire* with me."

I lurch away, her words are like a backhanded slap in the face. If she notices my reaction, she doesn't show it. She's ranting, pacing, talking to herself.

"I'm trying to save Venus Rising, I'm trying to keep my children from spinning out of control and I am trying to let you go because it is for the best."

"You'll see. You'll move on. You have to," and then, she walks out and leaves me sitting there by myself.

I don't go after her. I don't trust myself to. I've never been so close to actually breaking something as I am right now. I stalk out to my car.

I can't believe what a fool I've been. Thinking that this woman knew me and trusted me.

There hasn't been a challenge in my life I haven't been able to figure out. And this…this shouldn't be a challenge at all. We are so fucking right together. But here we are.

And here we'll stay.

I could go back inside and tell her I would have given up my job, my passport, whatever I had to, to protect her and what we have.

I could say it until I'm blue in the face.

And she'd never hear me.

I've already handed her my heart on a platter twice, and, both times, she's found it lacking. So, she wants me out of her system. Then, that's what she'll get.

Chapter 46

THE JEZEBEL

REGAN

The Jezebel Podcast: Episode 35

"Hey ladies, I know we're still taking a victory lap after Dr. Zimmerman's downfall, so you'll have to forgive me for being a Debbie Downer. But my life has come a little too full circle recently. You all have heard my story; you know what happened to me in that house. But what you don't know is that I'm a total hypocrite. It took me almost twenty years to tell my mother. I've never told my brothers or any of the friends I made, before or since. Not because I'm ashamed of what those men did to me, but because I know that it was my fault. My best friends lived a nightmare because I thought I was untouchable and led them straight into a trap I should have seen coming. When I had the chance to help one of the women who was there with us, I turned my back on her. All because I wanted to pretend it never happened. I used to be afraid of my own shadow. Then, I met this man—and guys, he's amazing. My dream man. I love him. Things weren't going to work out… because…well, the why doesn't matter now.

My first thought when he left…was, "Thank God, I won't have to tell him about those three days of hell." And I was relieved. I saw that as a silver lining to losing the only man I've ever loved. Can you believe that? I'm a prisoner in a cage I've built around myself.

And I had to ask myself. "What the hell is wrong with you?"

How can I sit on here and preach about shunning shame and ask you all to overcome your fear so that I can tell your stories? How? When I can't do the same. I've been so mad at my family for the secrets they've kept from me…and here I am keeping a whopper of one from them, myself. How can I expect them to trust me, when I don't trust them? How can I help my daughter be brave and speak out if, God forbid, anything like that happens to her, when I haven't been willing to myself? I watch tv. I've seen what happens. From Anita Hill to Christine Blasley-Ford, it's always the women who lose. I was afraid of the scrutiny, and I let that fear keep me in a marriage I should have never entered. It's precluded me from knowing real intimacy with anyone, and now, it's become the silver lining for my heartbreak.

I'm struggling, ladies. I've been telling your stories, setting the record straight for everyone, but I don't know how to do it for myself.

I don't have any answers or a happy note to end this on. I just don't know who else would understand. Thank you for listening. Next week, I'll be back with more stories about women we won't allow the world to forget. This is The Jezebel, signing off."

Chapter 47

VENUS RISING

STONE

"Thank you so much for coming, I know it was a lot to ask," Regan greets me with an outstretched hand and I just stare at it in disbelief.

"It's flu season. Unnecessary touching isn't recommended," I say and climb out of my truck.

"Right," she says, and stuffs her hands in the pockets of her skirt.

It's fucking petty, but three months after that night at her house, the weight of resentment still sits in my gut like a boulder.

"I'm here. So cut the cloak and dagger. What do you need?" I ask, and cross my arms impatiently.

"It's an emergency or I wouldn't have called," she says urgently.

I laugh. "Yeah, I'm aware that you avoid me at all costs." I can't keep the bitterness out of my voice.

She swallows audibly, and her eyes narrow as if she's in pain for a second. "There's a woman here, she didn't have anywhere else to go. And she's in labor. I think. She's been having contractions all day."

"Why didn't you take her to the clinic you partnered with?"

She sighs, her hands flexing and curling at her sides. Her lips barely move when she speaks.

"They terminated our agreement after my divorce. Marcel is one of their largest patrons. I haven't been able to negotiate another arrangement like that yet. I'm working on building my own clinic on sight, but that takes money that I'm still trying to raise. Permits that keep getting "lost" And, as you noted, you are my last resort, because it's a fucking emergency." She pauses to take a deep breath. I know we have issues, but if you could put them aside and please come help this woman who has trusted me with her life." Her voice breaks and her chest heaves, her eyes are pleading and bleak.

But I need to understand what I'm walking into.

"Have you been timing her contractions?"

"Yes, but only since her water broke, and that's when I called you."

"How close?"

"Four minutes, max."

"Do you have a delivery area set up?"

She nods eagerly. "I have everything in place. I found some info in the book about home births...I fitted the room out today."

I grab her arm, "Today? She's been here all day. Why'd you wait so long to call me?"

She bites her lip. "The baby's not due for another month, and until her water broke, I wasn't sure she was in labor. So, I let her rest and went to get stuff from the medical supply just in case."

I'm already moving again by the time she's done talking. I grab my field kit from my car and start walking back to her.

"Take me to her," I say with a curt nod, and wait for her to take the lead. I open the bag to see if I have everything I need and look up to find her standing in the same spot, watching me. "Is there a problem?" I ask in a brisk, but civil tone.

"Thank you so much for this. I know you're angry with me..." She puts a hand out as if she's going to touch me.

I step back with a sharp shake of my head. "That doesn't even begin to describe what I'm feeling, but this isn't the time. Let's go."

She nods and drops her eyes to the ground but not before I glimpse some of the sorrow in them.

I'm torn between heartache and hope. The last month of silence and distance has nearly eaten me alive. Tyson has made it sound as if she's never been happier. But that's not what I see now. It's not what I feel.

Her shoulders sag and my heart mimics the motion.

"Okay, let me show you the way."

"Thanks Rob, appreciate you coming." I shake hands with my retired pediatrician. He was the only person I could think of to call who would come.

"No problem, Son, we're lucky the baby's healthy and mama is, too."

"I know." I glance behind him and frown. "Where's Regan?"

"Oh, she said to thank you and tell you goodnight." He sets down his bag and heads toward the bed where Lucy and her baby girl are getting to know each other.

She's very lucky. Less than two hours of pushing brought a beautiful baby girl into this world, and when I caught her, she gifted us with a lusty, robust cry of displeasure. The miracle of life is a humbling sight to behold. And Regan was a great birth coach and my right hand. We work so well as a team.

The goodwill and optimism that started to grow while we were in the thick of delivery evaporates at Rob's message. She may not want to talk to me, but I damn sure want to talk to her. I leave the patients in the very capable hands of one of the best pediatricians in the state and go in search of trouble.

I walk through the stone-arched walkway that connects the residential facilities with the classrooms and offices. I'm angrier with Regan than I have been with anyone in my entire life, but I can't help the rush of pride, as I survey what she's done with this place.

Venus Rising is nothing short of remarkable. It's everything she said it would be. It's bittersweet to see her doing it all and not to be part of it. We've made an art form of avoiding each other.

I see her twice a week when she joins our CrossFit Team for a workout.

She doesn't talk much to anyone. Even her brothers. She comes, gets her workout done, and then leaves. It hurts like hell to see her and pretend I don't crave her, with every fiber of my being.

The buzzing interest around the picture has subsided—mainly because she keeps such a low profile.

I still wake and experience the same sinking sensation I've felt since I moved back here and realized that she would not be mine. Tyson has invited me to her house every Friday for the last month, and I've said no.

That first encounter, at her house, was still too close to the surface. I'm not ready to socialize with Regan.

Thank God I love my job and that it's demanding and intense. But, at night, when I'm alone with my thoughts, they're all about her.

As I approach the suite of offices where hers is, doubt descends and slows my stride.

I don't know if I'm ready to be alone with her. But I don't know when I'll have another chance, and at the very least, I need her to know that she can't provide medical services here unless she gets licensed. And to tell her that she can't call me like this again.

I steel myself and knock lightly on the door with "Regan" etched into the frosted pane of glass that serves as a window. There's no response, but I see a light on, so I test the knob. I open the door, and I stick my head inside, slowly, and look around the room.

The first thing I notice is the map that takes up one entire wall. It's dotted with different color push pins and sticky notes. I step into the huge space and close the door quietly behind me. It's part office, part situation room.

Regan is sitting propped up, lengthwise, on a small bright blue sofa. Her laptop is on her thighs. Her head lolls to rest on the back of the sofa and her hand dangles off the edge. A soft snore punctuates her exhales.

I walk over and gaze down at her. She looks as wrung out as I feel.

But even exhaustion can't tame the beautiful synergy of her bold cheekbones, her wide-set heavily lashed eyes, or her generously full lips and the soft set of them made even more so by sleep. I would have fought any war by her side, or at her front, if she'd have let me.

I trace the lines of her body with my eyes. Each one on prominent display, beneath her light grey calf length pencil skirt, topped by a form fitting white t-shirt. Her feet are bare; her toes are painted candy apple red. God; I want to taste them.

She is a whole eight course meal, and I'm a man who's been living on beans and toast for months.

My entire body responds with what I can only describe as a full-body hunger pang. My mouth waters. My fingers twitch, and my cock stirs. My gut rumbles, the way it does when I'm hungry.

Her eyes pop open as if she heard it. She gasps and covers her chest with her hand. "You scared me." She closes her eyes and takes a few deep breaths.

"Sorry, I knocked." I step back from my hovering stance and shove my hands in my pockets.

"I was only closing my eyes for a minute… Let me just shut down, really quick," she says, groggily, and taps her mouse to wake her laptop. She lowers her feet to the floor and starts to type in earnest.

Something falls from beneath her skirt and lands on the floor with a thud, and then rolls a few times, before it stops halfway between us. She's immersed in whatever she's doing and doesn't seem to notice.

I stoop to pick it up and smile when I realize it's a vibrator. And it's warm and sticky. I lift it to my nose and inhale. The smell of her, citrus and fucking heaven, fills my nostrils, and I go from disinterested to full on rock hard in seconds.

"Okay, all done," she announces, and reaches over and puts her laptop on the small side table next to the couch.

"Did Rob not tell you I was…" Her words die on her tongue, as her vision clears, and she sees the toy in my hand. Her face blooms with color.

"You dropped this," I say, and smile innocently.

Her lips compress, and she clears her throat.

"Here." I drop it into her outstretched palm.

"Thank you," she says stiffly, and tucks it between the cushions of the couch.

I rub the wetness on my fingers together. Her eyes widen briefly, before she starts looking around, like she can't find something.

"You lose something else?"

"Have you seen my shoes?" she asks, a tinge of panic in her voice.

"What do you need those for?"

Her head snaps up, and she narrows her eyes. "I'm leaving."

I laugh. "Fuck if you are. You owe me at least more information about this reckless thing you dragged me into. If anything had gone wrong, Regan…I don't even want to think about it. Robert Hirsch is a great pediatrician. But I want her to come to my office, tomorrow, if she's up to it, and she should be. She needs a proper exam and blood work. She's healthy, young, and in good shape, so everything went smoothly, but Regan, the hospital is where all of this should have happened."

Her jaw tenses, and her words are clipped. "I know that, Stone. I've explained that this was extraordinary, and she might have been in danger. You're a doctor. And, I trust you."

I snort in disbelief. "As if you know the meaning of that word. I think you called me because you think I'm so pussy whipped that I'd risk my career for you. You needed a chump, and you called the biggest one you knew."

She rears back like I slapped her. "No, how can you say that?"

I take a sweeping survey of the room in an effort to escape the damning hurt in hers.

I glimpse the papers she left scattered on the floor and see one that reads "The Jezebel" in large letters, in the same font as her tattoo. I lean down to pick it up, and she dives to beat me to it. She tucks them behind her back.

"What is that?"

"Nothing," she snaps, but she looks panicked.

A prickle of unease runs up my spine.

"Did you start your blog again?"

"No."

"Then, what is it?"

"Nothing, Stone. Leave it," she snaps, but she's nervous as hell.

"Why can't you tell me?" I advance on her.

She stands her ground, sticks her mulishly set chin out at me and says, "I don't have to tell you anything. No matter what you think, you don't own me."

Disillusionment is like a dagger in my side and I'm so tired of her and this whatever the hell is going on with her. I nod. "You're right. I don't. So, fuck all of this. I'm done asking you questions."

"Finally!" She raises her hands in celebration and exasperation all at once.

"Yeah, fucking finally. I'm done. Whatever you're up to, keep me the hell out of it."

"Oh, no problem there," she quips.

I laugh and snatch up my backpack. "Big fucking problem, actually."

"Enlighten me," she scoffs.

"Gladly," I say walk back over to where she's standing.

Her eyes widen and she backs up and hits the wall after only a couple of steps.

She licks her lips and her eyes drop to my mouth. "What are you doing?"

I place a hand on either side of her head and bring my face close enough to hers for our noses to touch. "Enlightening you, Goddess."

I lift my fingers where the wetness from her vibrator has dried and run them under her nose, drag them over to her lips and press until they part for me. She moans at the intrusion and she sucks them deeper into her hot, soft mouth.

"See how good you taste?" I ask her in a low rasp.

She nods. Her inky lashes flutter like the palm leaves caught on a breeze.

"Have you let anyone else taste it?" I ask, and I wrap one hand around her throat, and she bites her lips.

"Have you?" I growl when she doesn't respond

"No." she squirms against my erection rucking her hips.

I slide my other hand up her thigh, slip it under her skirt and cup her through her panties. She rocks against my hand, grinding into her damp heat into the heel of it.

"I know how bad you need me inside you..."

"Yes, so badly…" she admits in a voice thick with misery.

I brush the tip of my nose against hers, move my mouth just a sliver from hers, but I don't let our lips touch.

I draw in a deep breath and smile. "No matter how hard you try to hide it from me, I'll always know. Even if I never touch you again."

"How?" she pants.

I gaze down at her beautiful face, memorize the look of rapture adorning it. "Because, like recognizes like, goddess. We're made for each other."

I am so in love with her and so damn angry at her. But I don't know how to wake somebody who's only pretending to be asleep.

I pull my hand away from her body and take a huge step back. "It's a damn shame that you fucked this up so royally."

Her eyes flutter and open, dazed and glassy with need. I bite the inside of my cheek to stifle a groan and shove my hands into my pockets to keep myself from yanking her back to me.

She blinks, the glaze in her eyes clears

"What do you mean?"

"I mean I'm sick of your secrets, and your desire to help everyone but yourself."

"That isn't true." She yells, but I am done listening.

"You make me so crazy, like… some nights, I want to set myself on fire for it. But I'm done trying to prove myself to you, …" I wipe my palm on my trouser leg and her eyes grow wide.

I look away. Because fool I am, I can't look her in the eye and lie. "So, you got your wish. You are officially out of my system."

I walk out and it takes all my self-control not to slam the door behind me. I'm so angry I could spit. What the fuck is happening? It just keeps getting worse. I wish I could get her out of my system, but I can't.

I whip my phone out and call Hayes.

"Hey, you home?" I ask when he answers.

"Yeah, what's up?"

"Need to talk to you. I'll be there in five."

"It's late. why can't you talk on the phone?"

"Man, you have a 3-month-old baby. You weren't asleep anyway. Can I come over or what?"

"Uhhh…not when you sound like you want to kick my ass."

I chuckle, surprised that I can manage it when I'm so angry. "No, I just joined a board and I'm fundraising money for the organization."

"That's nice," he deadpans.

"I need you to write a check. Make some phone calls and grease a few squeaky wheels at the city department of health." Regan won't like it, but I don't care. I'll remind her that she offered me a spot on the board the first time we talked about Venus Rising.

He laughs out loud. "Oh, I'm sorry. Did I forget the part where I live in a lamp that you're the master of?"

I sigh, still weary. But I feel a little less defeated just talking to him. "No, you're my brother. I need your help. Help that's in your power to give. So, I'm asking."

There's a beat of silence, but I'm not worried. My brother is an asshole, he'd cut his arm off for me as fast as I'd cut mine off for him.

"Well, shit. Come on over. I'll get the coffee on."

Chapter 48

I WANT WHAT CAN'T BE MINE

STONE

"That is so good, Venus," I moan, and lift the long fall of her hair off her face, so can I see her better. The sight nearly scrambles my senses.

She's lying on her stomach draped between my spread thighs. My dick is as deep as it can be inside the lush heat of her talented, wicked little mouth. One of her hands is fisted around the base of my dick, the other splayed on my stomach. I bend a knee, and she moans around my cock, her eyes flying up to mine. The scorching need in her gaze makes my mouth water.

I sit, grab her hips and rotate her body, until her knees are on either side of my head. Her lips never surrender my dick.

I spread her glistening, neatly trimmed pussy, and she rocks her hips. With a growl, I cover her with my mouth and run my tongue over her in one long, luxurious stroke.

My balls tighten and sparks of pleasure start in my toes and course up my legs. She moans, and it vibrates all around my pulsing dick and—

"Hey, wake up, man. It's time to go," Beau's beefy hand slaps down on my shoulder and startles me out of my erotic dream. I glance down at my lap and I'm relieved to see that my bulging erection is still trapped in my jeans.

Three nights ago, I woke up from a nap in the common rest area during my overnight shift at the hospital with my dick fisted in my hand. I've been afraid to sleep during a shift since. And now, I'm exhausted.

I shove Beau's hand off. "I'm ready. Just finishing up some paperwork," I lie. I spin in my chair to face him and do a double take when I realize he's not alone. A petite pink-haired woman is plastered to his side. She's dressed in a skintight pink bodysuit, with pink framed glasses, and pink tassels tied to pink streaked pigtails to complete the Pepto-chic look she's got going on. She's grinning so widely; I can see all of her teeth.

"My name's Zephyr," she shouts, as if I'm not sitting two feet in front of them and sticks a hand with sparkly pink nails shaped like daggers out at me.

"Stone, nice to meet you." I shake her hand, while I give my brother a subtle wide-eyed, "what the fuck is this?" look.

"Cadence and I are done. You were right." His smile is wide and hopeful. I can't muster the same. I eye the woman next to him. She looks wasted already.

"Where did you meet?" I ask, even though I'm afraid of the answer.

"At the CITGO on Fondren and West Airport," Zephyr answers brightly.

"At the gas station?" I ask, praying that I heard her wrong.

He clearly misreads my dismay, because his smile widens. "Yeah, I know. How lucky was I to be there just when she needed help? It's only been two hours, but Zephyr here's already helping me get reacquainted with all of the fun I've missed while I was locked down with Cadence." Suddenly, he sings out, "She's like the wind, through my trees."

He grins and presses the writhing woman closer to his side. "Get it? Zephyr is the wind? The song from *Dirty Dancing*? You know? By Patrick Swayze?" He presses when I just stare blankly at him.

"Yeah, I know…" I say noncommittally and lean in to sniff him for alcohol. I frown when I smell nothing.

"Satisfied?" he asks, with a knowing smirk. I've been checking him like this since he started driving at sixteen.

I ignore him and glance over at Zephyr. "Are you on birth control?"

"Stone!" Beau yells, and turns her away, as if he can shield her from my words. "You're a buzzkill, brother," he says, with a scowl.

My shrug is unapologetic, and my stare unwavering. "No, I'm a gynecologist. And your reaction to a very straightforward question makes me think that safe sex isn't a priority for either of you. It should be. You're strangers. Who met at a gas station." *Says the pot to the kettle.*

Beau mouths, "Stop." And then turns to comfort his…hook up.

"I'm sorry, Zeph. He takes his work really seriously. Let's go wait in the living room, before we lose interest in sex the way he has."

I roll my eyes.

She laughs. "As if that could happen, stud," she squeals, when he gives her ass a squeeze and rises up on her toes to kiss him.

Decidedly turned off by their display of affection and desperate for them to get out, so I can finish what I'm doing, before my date gets here. "Get out!" I snap.

He rolls his eyes, but in acquiescence. "Yeah, yeah, yeah. I know, you've got work to finish. We'll wait in the foyer."

I give him a curled lip in response, but when he rushes ahead to open the door for her, I smile. At least he knows right from wrong.

I'm not sure the same can be said about me. I'm sitting here thinking filthy thoughts about a woman whose name I shouldn't even say.

Suddenly, Beau sticks his head back in. "Oh, hey. Sorry. I came in to tell you that your date is here."

My stomach dips.

"Oh, shit. Okay, I'll be right out." I glance over my shoulder when he doesn't leave.

"She's hot." He waggles his eyebrows and grins.

"Get the fuck out," I say, when I really want to ask, "really?"

I don't know why I let Tyson talk me into bringing a date tonight.

After our workout, he invited me to dinner at Regan's. Their adult night was a couples evening, he informed me. He said Regan would probably have someone with her, too.

I almost declined. But I decided that if I'm going to live here and be part of this circle of friends, I need to get used to seeing Regan in social settings—no matter how miserable it makes me.

My sleep is fitful at best. I only eat to fuel my workouts. I've picked up extra shifts at work and I can't jack off enough to take the edge off my hunger for her.

At the same time, I'm so angry at her, there are days I can convince myself that I'm better off without her.

Almost.

But I know better. Yes, life is simpler without her. But, I'm not better off.

"Stone?"

I grimace and turn around to face Celine.

She's a friend of Tyson's from the gym. We talked on the phone a couple of nights ago, and she ticks all of my boxes. Sexy, smart—she can hang with me on a hike and climb, and then talk to me about all of the things that interest me—movies, books, food, travel, family, politics.

I have zero interest in her. Because, no matter how great she is, she's not Regan.

"Hey, sorry. I was just wrapping up some work. Did you find the place okay?"

She smiles - it's sweet and sincere and does nothing to stir my interest. "Yeah, this is nice," she says, and tucks a lock of hair behind her ear.

I follow her out to get this first/last date out of the way.

Chapter 49

FLAT ON MY FACE

REGAN

"I've had too much to drink," I whisper to Dina, as she slides into the seat next to me.

We're sitting in the living room by ourselves now. Everyone else has gone through to the dining room to eat. But I don't want to because Stone is there with that woman he brought, and I've never hated anyone, on sight, the way I hate her.

"Uh, I told you that three shots ago," she whispers back, and hands me a glass of water.

"Did you? I don't remember." I take the glass and chug.

"Come on, Remi has dinner laid out, and they're ready to eat." She nudges me when I just shrug. "Let's go. Food will help you feel better."

"I don't wanna. *He's* here. And I don't want to see him."

Her eyes widen with interest, and she slides closer, lowering her voice to a whisper. "Who is *he?*" She glances around the room, as if trying to see someone she's overlooked.

I grab her arm and squeeze, until she meets my gaze, her eyes widen.

"You've got mayhem in your eyes, Regan," she says, but she's far from disapproving. In fact, she looks like she wants in on it. I snicker. I don't know why I don't drink more often. Life is a lot more fun this way.

"He is him. The hand," I hiss and pantomime someone taking a picture.

Her jaw drops. "Oh my God," she squeals, before she covers her mouth with her hands and screams into them.

"Shhhhh." I shake my head in disapproval. Somewhere in the back of my mind, I'm aware that the room shouldn't keep moving once I stop, but I have bigger fish to fry right now. With this liquid courage coursing through my veins, I feel like I can do anything, including draw blood from a stone.

"I thought you said he was a local you met." If the look on her face is anything to go by, she is thoroughly scandalized. I'm delighted.

"I lied," I admit, in triumph.

"Does anyone else know?"

"Yup, his brother."

She grabs me by the shoulders and gives me a shake. "Regan, who is it?"

I groan at the way my brain bounces, but when she shakes me again, I blurt, "Stone."

Her jaw drops. "Not Dr. McDreamy? No fucking way. He's *so* hot. But…*so* tightly buttoned up. No way. Not *him*," she says, her eyes wide.

I snort in disagreement. "He's not even close to buttoned up," I inform her, with pride.

She purses her lips, and her eyes dance with excitement. "So, you two met in Mexico, but nobody knows?"

"Pay attention. I said his b-brother knows." I wave my hand in the air to dismiss him. "But he's never gonna tell because he's afraid Marcel won't play golf with him anymore or something."

Dina looks at me askance, and I roll my eyes. "And also, *maybe*, because he loves his brother *so* much, he doesn't want the big bad adulteress to ruin him," I quip, and then burp loudly.

"Reg, Dina, what are you doing?" Remi sticks his head into the room, and his smile turns into a frown when he catches sight of me. "What the hell is wrong with you?" He gives me a disapproving once-over.

"Well, nice to see you, too, brother," I say, and give him a two fingered salute and reach for my drink.

"I was just getting her some water before I brought her in." Dina stands.

"You're not on the clock; you don't have to explain to him," I tell her, and grab her hand.

Remi shuts the door behind him and walks over to where I'm sitting. "Are you drunk?"

I widen my eyes in mock affront. "*No.* I had a few drinks. In my own house. Is that a crime?"

He rolls his eyes ceiling-ward and groans, before he cuffs my arm and lifts me to standing.

"Come eat. You'll feel better," he says, and starts leading me to the door.

"I don't want to," I whine, I let him pull me because I'm too wasted to fight.

When we get to the closed French doors, leading out to my backyard where the food is set up, he stops and spins me to face him.

"You're so handsome, Remi," I croon and stroke his cheek. He gives Dina a helpless look over my shoulder, and I pat his chest. "Don't you worry. I'm fine."

"You will be, as soon as we get some food in your belly, and more water down your throat. "

"I know how to behave, Remi, and I'm not drunk." I shove him and, promptly, stumble and land on my ass.

He grabs my arm to haul me to my feet and gives Dina a dark look.

I wave a finger under his nose. "Don't you dare blame her. I'm an adult. Go on. I don't need you to drag me. I am perfectly capable of making an entrance without your help." I pull my hand out of his grasp.

"I'll walk with her," Dina volunteers, and links arms with me.

"See, I'm fine." I flutter my lashes.

"Remi?" Kal calls him and with one last, long disquieted look, he opens the door and steps outside.

As soon as he's gone, Dina grabs my shoulders, turns me to face her and peers at me.

"Okay, Lady Chaos. Are you sure you don't want to go to bed? Sleep this off?"

"I'll be fine, as long as I don't have to sit next to him." I assure her.

I mutter under my breath to Dina as we walk out into the warm evening.

The backyard is what sold me on this house.

The huge pool and attached hot tub take up most of it. The summer kitchen with the fire-burning brick oven is spacious and tricked out with everything from a wood burning pizza oven to a Spit large enough to fit an entire pig.

And of course, when I look around the backyard, the first person I see is Stone sitting there without a care in the world.

My heart, so stupid and foolish, does a flying leap like it's trying to get to him.

It hurts when it meets the hard wall of my chest in a painful thump.

That's what you get for wanting what you can't have.

I turn away from him and walk toward the table laden with the meal I spent all day preparing. It's Jamaican fare—Oxtails, curry goat, coconut curry shrimp, Ackee and Saltfish, rice and peas, fried dumplings, brown stew chicken and beef patties I picked up from Cool Runnings in Rivers Wilde's Market Food Hall. And a huge pitcher of Guinness punch.

Remi and Kal are sitting with Hayes and Confidence. Last thing I need is to deal with the smugly happy couples.

"Let's go sit with Tyson," I say, and turn to head to where he's sitting with the newest member of his little fan club.

"Uh, you go ahead." Dina lets go of my hand, and turns to head back, the way we were coming, before I can object.

I'm almost there when I hear an annoying, braying laugh, coming from the hot tub. "That asshole, he has the nerve to sit in my hot tub with a girl who laughs like a donkey. And hasn't even said hello to me? I'm gonna tell him what's *what*," I mutter. I spin on my heel and head toward them.

"Hey, Regan, your seat is over here." Tyson stands and heads over to me. But I don't even look his way. I'm on a mission.

Stone looks in my direction, just in time for him to see me trip over my feet and fall flat on my face.

Conversation comes to a halt, and everyone looks over at me.

Humiliation burns, and I close my eyes, as I hear the scrape of chairs being pushed back and feet crunching grass, as they rush to help me.

A large hand cups my elbow, and I look up to see Hayes, lifting me off the ground.

Oh God, Hayes Rivers is being nice to me. This has to be the lowest point of my life.

"I'm fine, thank you." I tug my arm free of his grasp and brush the dirt off my blouse and shorts.

When Tyson puts an arm around me, I let myself be led away. I grab a bottle of Blue Moon from the cooler. I drop into the seat next to his and chug it.

"Slow down." Tyson pulls the drink out of my hand.

"I'm so sick of everyone saying that. I'm fine. Worry about your damn self." I reach over and grab his glass and down the caramel colored liquid in one gulp. I wince as the liquor burns a trail down my throat.

"This isn't like you," he says.

"You don't even know what that means," I inform him.

He looks at me sideways. "Wha—?"

Stone and his little perfect perky young pretty are out of the hot tub and head our way.

"I need to pee," I announce. "My bladder isn't what it was before three kids." I use the arm of the chair to lever myself to standing, but sway as I do.

"Let me help you," Tyson says.

"No," I whisper angrily. But it's too late.

"She's really drunk," Celine pretends to whisper, as she drops into a chair around the small table I'm sharing with Tyson.

"Aren't you going to call her Captain Obvious, too? Or is that just for the girls you fuck?" I ask. I giggle, but no one else does.

"What did you just say?" Tyson asks.

"Oh, grow up, Tyson," I snap at him, and then spin on my heel with a loud burp.

Halfway across the yard, I kick my shoes off, so I can walk faster.

I get to the bathroom and shut the door behind me and suck in deep breaths. I slide down the door and drop my head on my knees.

When my heart isn't tap dancing on my sternum anymore, I open my eyes and use the counter for support to get up. I reach to turn on the taps, and, for a second, I don't recognize my own hands.

In the months since I started rebuilding the shattered foundation of my life, nothing has changed more than they have.

They tell the story of the new me in a language that's universal, but in a pattern that only I understand. They've become my visual anchor to the present.

The three diamond eternity rings stacked on to my right forefinger remind me that I gave birth to three little lives that will always be mine to cherish.

The tattoos that run on either side of my left middle finger read *"Weh nuh ded, nuh dash weh"* in my mother's Jamaican patois, reminding me that as long as I'm breathing, there is hope.

On the inside of the bare ring finger of my left hand, my name is tattooed. And that reminds me that now, I belong only to myself. That my second chance is only one heartbeat away. I just have to not give up.

Now, if only I could find a way to murder that woman Stone brought here tonight and get away with it.

I ignore the stab of pain, the sense of betrayal, the melody that hurt plucks out on my heartstrings with the reckless abandon of fingers dancing across a guitar's bridge.

I told him to move on.

So, why does it make me breathless with pain to find that he has?

I know that this is for the best. It's just that… Stone Rivers stripped every shred of protection I put around my most tender places. And, my stupid heart hasn't learned any of the lessons I've tried to teach it. It wants what it wants and when it comes to Stone, it has the allegiance of my body, too.

Feeling fortified and strong again, I head back out. I'm not going to sit there and watch Stone with another woman all night. I don't need this shit. Stone can have his stupid little girlfriend.

With my equilibrium back in place, I walk back out to the backyard.

Chapter 50

MEMORY LANE

STONE

Hayes and Confidence left a few minutes ago to relieve their babysitter, and he whispered, "You're *so* fucked," when he hugged me goodbye.

He was right.

Regan's expression as she walks out of the house is a little terrifying. She's grinning, but it's more like a predator baring their teeth than a smile. Her dark brows are drawn low over eyes that look like they're ready to shoot lightning.

I've always known she's possessive and even though I feel a trickle of unease at the way she's watching Celine, it's nice to know that she's jealous.

Because I am, too.

Of her brothers, of her friend Dina—even her clothes have earned my envy tonight. They all get to touch her, talk to her, tease her. And I have to sit here, watch it all, and pretend that's not my girl.

And it's one of the hardest things I've ever had to do. If I could stop looking at her, it might be easier. But I can't. I'm so greedy for the sight of her.

She's wearing this scrap of blue fabric masquerading as a blouse. A delicate gold chain belt wraps around her tiny waist. Her little white shorts are probably illegal in some autocratic countries.

I can't take my eyes off the supple, taut skin of her thighs as she walks right past me to sit next to her brother.

"Did I say you could smoke weed in my yard?" She shoots Tyson the middle finger before she sinks down next him.

"She gets passive aggressive when her feelings are hurt. It's her tell." Tyson says, laughing through a haze of smoke from the joint he's just fired up.

"I am not being passive aggressive. Why are you such a traitor?" Regan asks and splashes him with water.

He just laughs and continues to poke at her. "She'll never actually say that she's upset."

"Tyson, that is a lie," Regan says, her indignation real, this time.

Tyson's grin only grows more mischievous. "No, it's not. I'm not judging you, Reggie. We're all friends here, right, Stone?"

I narrow my eyes at Tyson's cajoling tone. "Right." But without any of the humor he's exhibiting.

"How about everyone tell me how you know each other," Celine says in a singsong voice, taking the joint from Tyson and taking an impressive draw.

"Why don't you start since you're so new?" Regan answers with a singsong that's just a touch shy of being mocking.

Celine's smile widens. "Okay! Well, I moved here to work with Teach for America after I graduated from BU. I'm so glad I joined that gym. I've had the hardest time making friends with anyone but work people."

"What's wrong with work people?" Regan asks, grabbing the joint which had worked its way to Dina.

"Nothing. But they're all so young and sheltered and so obsessed with work. I mean, I am, too. Obviously. This is like, my passion. But it's also just a stepping stone, ya know?" She smiles sweetly. "What about you?" She cocks her head, an eager smile directed at Regan.

I glance at Tyson and glare at him. None of what she just said matches the story he gave me when he introduced us. I look over at Celine and she shoots me one of those sweet smiles, but I don't miss the way she can't seem to hold my gaze.

Who the hell is this girl?

"Oh, I met Stone when he was ten. He stabbed my boyfriend while I was giving him a blow job and then I didn't see him again for twenty years," Regan announces with a smile so pleasant that it's not until after she's done that what she said sinks in. I turn toward Tyson, my explanation already halfway out of my mouth, "It was so long ago. I didn't think it—"

He slaps my shoulder, hard, "You *stabbed* somebody? Man, Stone. I guess that was before you took your whole do no harm oath, huh?"

I wince, and rub my shoulder, eyeing warily, waiting for him to ask why I hadn't mentioned any of this.

"So, did he die?" he asks with a conspiratorial grin, and I quirk my brow at him, confused.

"Who?"

"The dude you stabbed."

I snort in surprise. "I was ten and scrawny. It was a flesh wound, right?" I try to catch Regan's eyes. But she's staring at Celine with barely disguised malice.

"What was Regan like back then?" Dina nudges me and leans forward with an eager smile on her face.

"Exactly as she is now," I answer. Regan's eyes flash to mine before she looks down at her lap, but she watches me under her crescent sweep of her sooty lashes.

"She loved The Temptations and the Love Jones soundtrack. She loved to bake, loved history and politics. She was obsessed with the idea of rewriting history and living like every day might be her last."

"You remember all that?" Her eyes have lost the intensity they held just a moment ago and now are limpid with nostalgia.

"I remember every second, every lesson." I admit.

"What was so profound that you remember?" Tyson asks, breaking the spell and saving me from myself.

I look up at the sky, as if I have to search my memory for an answer. I don't have to do more than blink to be back in the bakery, standing next to Regan at the marble slab kneading dough, zesting lemons, grating ginger and putting butter on everything.

If I let myself dwell in the memory long enough, I'm sure I'll smell the sugar and vanilla, feel the roll of sweat down my back and the ache in my forearms. I can hear her speaking the words that changed my life.

"She told me I was perfectly made." Saying it aloud makes my heart do something strange. I glance up and we share a smile. It's the first time she's smiled at me since I've been in Houston and that twinkle in her eye is like a door to a different time.

I don't know if it's the weed or if it's that Regan is a sorceress.

Because, even with everyone watching and an entire ocean of shit between us, for the few seconds our eyes hold, we're completely alone and back on that beach. And in that dimension, there's only room for the truth.

"I was in free-fall when I met you." I say and she nods, as if remembering. "I was hanging on by a thread and so focused on surviving that I wasn't living. And then, came you. You revolutionized the way I saw myself," I tell Regan the simple, but powerful truth about how much she impacted my life. It's much more than I should say, but I don't regret it.

While I was talking, her expression morphed from discomfort, to surprise, to pained, and now, it's all of those things together and layered with wide-eyed wonder and simple, but unfiltered happiness.

"I said that?" She asks in a whisper

"You don't remember?" I laugh in surprise.

"No, God, but I want to." My laughter dies at the plea in her voice. I don't know what she sees when she looks at me. But when I look at her, my breath feels like it's tangled around my heart. I feel like I've fallen back through time. Back to when I was sure she was going to change my life and was stupid enough to pin my hopes on it.

"Aww," Celine sighs and claps loudly. "And then you grew up and became this man." She wraps a hand around my bicep and smiles suggestively at me. "I'm guessing you've got a huge appetite."

"Uh, I need to get dessert out of the freezer." Regan stands and practically runs back into the house.

Chapter 51

BLEEDING LOVE

REGAN

"Did you eat my ice cream?" I stalk back out to the backyard, an empty carton of Bluebell's Pecan Pralines 'n Cream in one hand, my eyes fixed on the back of Tyson's head.

Like a shot, Remi is on his feet and rushing toward me. Kal is hot on his heels.

Tyson's guilty ass turns around and when he sees me, instead of begging for mercy, he grins.

"Yeah, man, I can count on you to have Pralines 'n Cream on deck—"

As I get closer, and he sees the tears on my face, his smile falls away.

"Reggie, hey, are you okay?" Remi steps in front of me and I slam into his bare chest. I cross my arms and glare up at him.

"I am so sick of you assholes coming over here, eating all my fucking food, and then leaving me with nothing," I bellow. Remi's jaw goes slack and he takes a huge step backward.

"Hey Reggie, what's wrong?" Remi asks in a voice that's too tender, and too patient and too pitying.

"You left and didn't say goodbye. You didn't call me once in almost six months. How could you?" I ask him.

His expression turns stricken. "Oh, Regan. I'm sorry."

I barely hear him before I whirl to face Tyson. "And *you*. This is my favorite. And you ate it all anyway. And then you left the empty carton in my freezer *knowing* that drives me nuts. Do you *want* to see me lose my shit? Will you stop hurting me if I let you see me bleed?" I shout.

Tears blur my vision. For the first time I can ever remember, Tyson doesn't have anything to say.

"You think because I'm calm, I don't have a heart?" I direct this question at all of them.

"I *do*. And it is oceans deep, and right now, so empty I can hear it echo. You *never* think about me. You just do whatever the hell you want." A sob wells in my chest. But I hold it.

I will not cry in front of these people.

No fucking way.

I lift my chin. "I'm going to bed. You can stay as long as you'd like. But clean the fuck up before you leave."

As I turn to leave, my gaze falls on Celine. "And yes, Stone has a *huge* appetite. When we were in Mexico, he couldn't *stop* eating my pussy."

Kal's startled gasp is the last thing I hear before I close the doors behind me.

Chapter 52

DRUNK IN LOVE

STONE

Pandemonium breaks loose in the backyard. Everyone is talking at once and I'm torn between running after her and dealing with the fallout of what she said.

"Oh shit, oh shit, oh shit." Tyson paces with a fist pressed to his mouth.

"What the fuck did she mean about *you* eating her pussy?" Remi's voice explodes behind me and my heart nearly stops. I turn with my hands out to block any sudden swings. "I can explain."

"Save that shit. I already know it all." Tyson stops pacing and rests a hand on each hip, his head tipped skyward as if he's searching for an answer.

"Know *what?*" Remi presses, his entire body turning rigid, his shoulder tense, and his hands ball into fists, like he's ready to swing.

"That Stone's the dude with his hand on Reggie's ass in that picture," Tyson says as if it's common knowledge.

"The fuck you say?" Remi's eyes, so like his sister's, spark black lightning right before he starts toward me. I stand my ground, ready to do whatever. He's got a couple of inches on me, but I can take him.

Tyson suddenly jumps between us and to my surprise, instead of joining his brother, he puts his hands on Remi's chest and forces him to stop. "Stop, man. Stop. Come on. It's Stone fucking Rivers. He's the best man I know. And he loves our sister, man."

Stunned. I walk over to one of the wicker armchairs surrounding the big fire pit and drop into it and look at him. My dazed mind can't make my eyes focus, and I stare unseeingly in their direction."How do you *know* that?"

He walks to sit in the chair next to me.

"You sent her some letters. She left them out and I was at her house one day and I saw them. I'm her little brother. It's like…my job," he adds the last part with a defensive uptick of his chin.

But I'm too bewildered to be angry. I shake my head. "Why didn't you say anything in the car, or when I called you?"

He leans back with a sigh. "Because it was obvious that it was a secret. And I thought you'd tell me your *damn* self." He slaps his thighs in annoyance,

I glance at Celine and turn back to him, suspicion replacing my confusion.

"So, what was all that shit about me helping you set her up?"

He scrubs a hand through his hair, his expression half exasperation, half horror. "I was fucking with you. I thought you'd tell me at some point. I'm sorry."

"And tonight? This whole date thing?" I nod at Celine who's watching us with morbid fascination.

He groans. "Regan is the most possessive female I've met in my entire life. I figured seeing you with someone would get her head out of her ass. She's been miserable. And so are you. And since you *both* wanted to keep your secrets, I left you to it."

"And you used Celine to do that? That's messed up."

"Don't cry for me Argentina," Celine drawls. She drops her sincere, sweet smile and smirks. "I got paid for tonight. And I got to sit on your lap, handsome." She winks.

"Are you serious?" I turn a murderous glare on Tyson.

He has the grace to wince. "I didn't know Reggie was gonna get blotto and fucking cry and shit. I thought she'd maybe throw Celine out and drag you upstairs by the collar."

"Wait, so you're the guy in the picture that Marcel put in the paper?" Kal asks.

I nod.

"So, why did Regan say it was a stranger?" She looks as perplexed as I feel.

"Oooh, ooh, pick me," Tyson says in a high-pitched voice waving his hand like an eager school child.

No one laughs.

Remi walks over and smacks him on the back of the head. "Start talking, Ty. Now."

He rubs his head and sneers at Remi.

Then, he cracks his knuckles as if he's getting ready to exert himself before he starts talking. "Marcel threatened to ruin Stone in every way possible. She was worried Hayes would blame Stone when his struggle to get Kingdom's Foundation out of the shit Thomas left it in didn't work. And she's worried that Stone would lose his job, and she knows how much he *loves* his job and how hard he's worked for it. Last but not least, she was worried what more gossip would do to her kids at school and how they'd feel knowing she'd stepped out on their dad." Tyson pauses to take a dramatic inhalation of breath.

I blink, dumbfounded that he knows so much. And then in realization that I know it all, too. That she told me as much that night at her house. And I was so angry, my pride was so wounded, that I didn't hear anything but her telling me that I couldn't handle the fire.

"Dude, I put that shit together. If you'd get your head out of her ass for long enough, you'd be sitting with her and not out here looking like you just woke up from a bad dream," Tyson scolds me.

"I would?"

"Yeah, bonehead. Now, I'm going to go apologize to my sister," he starts for the doors.

I get up and step in front of him. "No. Stay the fuck back. She's mine. *Mine.* And I'll take care of her. She said you don't have to go home. I'd like to amend that—you don't have to go home, but you gotta get the hell outta here."

Then I run up the stairs and go get my girl.

I find her sitting on the floor of her bedroom, draped in a pink bathrobe, staring forlornly at herself in the mirror. Her eyes come to the door, and she glances up and sighs deeply when she sees me.

"Hey, you okay?"

"I hate you for making me feel like this," she says, her voice dull.

I smile and take a tentative step into her bedroom.

"Would you rather we didn't feel so good together?"

"Yes. Because, maybe then, I wouldn't feel like Venus must have felt when Mars left her. Except, you didn't leave. I sent you away." She drops her face into her hands.

My heart is a shooting star; I walk over and sit next to her, cross legged, and face the mirror. Our eyes meet there, and damn, if I don't want to kiss her. "Mars never left her, without her, he wouldn't exist."

She throws her head back and cries, "Oh God," and then, suddenly, she grabs her side, as if in pain.

Her honey brown skin glows like she's just spent thirty minutes standing face up in the shower. Her hair is wet and hangs in wet clumps down her back.

I lean forward and sniff.

She leans away. "What are you doing? Why are you smelling me?" She scrambles to her feet. "Why are you even here?" She asks, her speech slurred.

"Why are you wet?" I remark.

"Because I just showered, Einstein," she says her chin tilting up and her eyes glaring, "You haven't even said..." she pauses to burp, or hiccup. I can't tell quite which it is.

She blushes prettily and I can't do anything but smile.

She's a fucking mess, but she's my mess.

"Now, go away before I vomit on you," She says and points an imperious finger at the door.

"You wouldn't," I laugh incredulously.

"I would," she says grumpily. She tightens her little silk pink robe around herself. And everything it's clinging to is everything I've been craving that she won't let me have. I need to get to the bottom of this shit so we can start fucking again. I miss that body.

"Tell me why you're angry with me," I demand.

She bites her lip and shakes her head miserably. "I'm not angry with you. I told you to move on and you did. I just hate everything because I want you for myself."

Her misery is palpable, but I'm not sorry to see it. In fact, her words are music to my ears. If she wants me then, we can do this.

"Regan, we're two consenting, single adults. I'm not here to fuck you and run. I want to make an honest woman out of you. I have since I was ten years old. I just had to grow up so you wouldn't go to jail for being a pedophile."

"Don't be gross," she mutters, but a tiny smile lifts the corners of her mouth.

"I did it. I'm a man. I can make my own decisions. *And* live with the consequences of them."

"But you love your job, you wanted it so much, if they fire you, you'll hate me," she moans.

"Hate to break it to you…but if that's the reason you won't be with me, I'll hate *that* more. You don't get to decide that my job is more important than you. And, I don't give a shit what your ex-husband or my brother have to say about it. We have something special. When is the last time you slept as well as you did the nights we spent together? Have you had any conversations as good as those? Has your body ever hummed the way it does when I touch you? Have you ever felt a connection as life-changing as the one we have shared since the *instant* we met 18 years ago?"

I cup her face in mine, tilt it up to mine. She shakes her head, her eyes full of misery.

"You won't. Not in this lifetime. Or the next. Not unless it's with me. But you've got to hold on as tight as I am. Or this won't work."

She stares at me, unblinking, before her face crumbles. "You don't understand. I'm not…right," she blurts.

"What do you mean?"

"*I love you,*" she wails, tears turning her dark eyes to a glittering obsidian. "Being with you is dizzying and exhilarating and exhausting and sublime in a way that I didn't know anything could be. But…you don't know what I've done…what I *am*. I ruined Rebecca's and Matty's *and* Jack's lives. And I can't make any of it right."

I shake my head, confused. "Who the hell is Rebecca?"

"Oh my God, Stone…" she gulps—and then she doubles over and vomits all over me.

I rush and pick her up, grimacing and gagging when the smell assails me before I can hold my breath. I rush us both to the bathroom and pray I'm not sick, too.

She groans and I strip her robe off and hold her up with one arm as I turn on the shower with the other.

"Oh, Regan." I stroke her hair and when the water is warm enough, I carry her in and put her down on the bench. I strip my clothes off and get in with her.

I wash her hair with her ginger shampoo and comb all the snags and tangles out. I prop her in my lap, her back to my chest, and give her a good massage with a conditioner.

She lets her weight rest against me, with her eyes closed, and a small smile tilting up the corners of her soft, wide lips.

I lift her off my lap and sit her down on the bench beside me. Then, I drop to my haunches in front of her, grab her washcloth and douse it with the vanilla soap.

I start with her neck and work my way down. I scrub every inch of her and inhale a lungful of vanilla-flavored steam. I'm methodical, and don't linger. She needs sleep and so do I.

I brush her teeth as best as I can, dry and lotion her, and dress her in a sleep shirt with the words, "No rain, no flowers," scribbled on the front.

Indeed.

I manage to get her hair into one long braid that hangs down her back. She watches me through sleep-heavy lids the whole time. At one point, she reaches up to pat my cheek.

"Just making sure you're real," she murmurs.

I carry her to bed and she's asleep before I pull her comforter up over her shoulders.

I watch her for a moment. "What's going on in that head of yours, Goddess?" I run a thumb over the rise of her cheekbone.

A snuffling snore is my answer.

I leave two aspirin and a bottle of water by her bed, turn out all of the lights, drop a kiss on her head, then go wait for her to wake up.

My clothes sit in a sodden pile of vomit. I rummage through her drawer until I find some socks that might fit, wrap a towel around my hips and go in search of intel that will give me some insight into whatever else is going on with her…and find out who this Rebecca is.

I wander through her house. It's a two-story rambling mid-century modern with more windows than walls. It's decorated elegantly— brushed gold and shade of blue accent white walls, white furniture and the dark wood floors are dotted with white rugs and gold accent tables piled high with books and toys.

The open concept living area has a vaulted ceiling with massive sky-lights that allow the bright moonlight. In between each pair of windows, huge blown glass chandeliers drop down low enough that I can touch them when I lift my hand.

Pictures of her children cover every single wall, and her fridge. They are gorgeous. Her daughter is, but for her big hazel eyes and light brown hair, her spitting image. Her sons have identically mischievous grins on their faces in every single picture. There's a painting of her holding them as infants, one in each arm, a wreath of flowers on her head like a crown. Her daughter sits at her feet, her hair woven through with the same flowers as her mother's.

I can't wait to meet them and see her with them.

I stop at a picture of Regan pregnant. She's on a beach, in profile, standing in ankle deep surf. She's wearing a brilliant blue sarong; her hair is loose and flowing behind her. Her hand cups her hugely pregnant stomach, and her head is bowed as if she's talking to the baby.

I want to see her like that.

I never imagined that domesticity could be as thrilling as globe-trotting, but I'm getting that tingling just thinking about being in that backyard with her and the kids. I wonder if she wants more children.

I walk past her kitchen and enter a short hallway that has a door with a piece of paper with "Mom's Office" written by a child's hand in green crayon, decorated with huge red exclamation marks.

She's got a small recording station set up at one end. At the other is a large, pristine white desk. The only thing on it is a small silver laptop, a cordless landline phone, and a huge computer monitor.

I sit in the white leather chair behind the desk and see a small business card tucked underneath the laptop. It reads simply, "The Jezebel" Herstory with a phone number on it and a URL.

I dial it. It goes straight to voicemail and Regan's voice starts speaking. "You've reached The Jezebel. If you've got a tip, leave it after the beep. If you're calling to try and scare me, you wasted your time."

What the hell is she doing?

I go to the URL listed on the card and start reading. The logo is similar to the tattoo on her lower back, but it's adorned with gold leaves.

"It is a universally accepted lie that well-behaved women rarely make history. The truth is this: Women are only deemed worthy of me-morial when they behave in ways that the men who write our history books find acceptable. The Jezebel is a voice for those of us who want a safe place to set the record straight and know that the person listening believes them. I want you to tell me the truth that's so inconvenient, you've been forced to rewrite it. Release the burden of your untold story. Let's make herstory, together."

There are three dozen episodes. The first one six months ago, around the time I sent her the book and my letters.

The first episode is titled: He Called it Revenge.

With my heart in my throat, I pop my earbuds in, click the link and start listening.

By the time I'm on the last episode, the sun has come up and my world view has been turned inside out. I'm afraid I'm going to be sick. My stomach heaves and my blood feels like it's been set on fire. I'm sweating from the effort it's taking to sit still.

Not just because now I know what happened to her the summer after her freshman year. The other stories I heard and the assumptions and premises they've challenged me to question.

Tyson only knows half of what is wrong with Regan. Now that I know everything, I don't blame her for wanting distance to figure it all out.

I only wish her grandfather was still alive so I could kill him myself.

How could he have done those things to her?

Even through these new lenses, one thing remains true. I wasn't wrong all those years ago when I thought Regan was magic personified. My woman's blood is tinged with mercury. Her spine is fortified by steel, her mind is wondrous, and her heart is a boundless bounty, and I love her without any condition.

And even though she's proven herself more than capable, I won't let her carry this load alone for one more day.

From the day she put her arms around me, meeting my fury with her gentle words and safe sanctuary, she started shaping me. When I saw her last, I swore that one day, she'd be mine. Since then, every decision I've made has been influenced by that goal.

Thank God that the struggles of my youth were a whetstone for my character, my confidence, and my tenacity. Regan's walls are up so high, I'll need all of them in spades to get over them.

I shut the computer down, walk back to the bedroom and crawl into bed with her. I draw her warm, sweet smelling body against my chest and close my eyes and let my mind shut down so I can get some rest, too.

Because when she wakes up, her ass will be mine.

Seventeen Years Earlier

PALESTINE, EAST TEXAS

Chapter 53

HE CALLED IT REVENGE

REGAN

"Right this way, ladies," one of the men from the truck says.

"Hey, let me go, asshole," Jack screams.

"What's going on?" I swivel around to see what's happening, but a rough pair of hands grab me and start pulling me toward the door. My heart is beating so fast and so hard, I'm afraid I'm going to pass out.

"Shut up and keep walking," a man growls and tightens his already punishing grip on my arm. He drags me through the yard, and I stumble, my heels sticking in the mud, twisting my ankles, as I scrabble to keep up with the man.

It's pitch black, and the cabin is completely surrounded by trees that soar, so high, that I can't see the tops of them.

The front door of the cabin swings open, and Weston steps out. "You made it, Princess, and you brought friends."

His expression is twisted in a grin that is so cruel and excited that it makes my blood run cold. I stop and start trying to scurry backward.

"No, you can't take us in there," I yell, as I try to dig my bare feet into the ground. I claw at the hand around my arm, screaming for Matty and Jack. Why are they suddenly so quiet?

The man lifts me, hoisting me over his shoulder, and carries me into the house. Panic is all I know, as he walks through a sparsely furnished living room. The wall-mounted tv is tuned to something loud, but he's moving too fast for me to see anything clearly. My feet and fists strike his back and torso, but he doesn't seem to feel it.

Tears run down my face and into my open mouth, choking my screams and filling me with a terror more visceral than anything I've ever known.

He dumps me unceremoniously onto a mattress in the middle of the room. It's thin, and my head slams against the hard floor, and for a moment, I'm dazed. He tugs my leg, and before I know what's happening, something tightens painfully, pinching near my foot. I sit and wail, in horror, when I see the shackle around my ankle. I kick for everything I'm worth. And yelp, as whatever it's anchored to on the ground makes my joints pop, as I yank to try free myself.

"Men three times your size can't break free. You'll just hurt yourself," the man says, in between grunts, as he wrestles to grab my other ankle. I manage to pull it free, and my foot connects with his face.

He howls in pain and returns my blow with a fist slammed into my cheekbone. Pain and light explode, and I fall back, sobbing as the coppery taste of my blood trickles onto my lips.

"Why are you doing this?"

"Getting paid, bitch. Shut up." He grunts and grabs my arms. He pulls them together over my head and I feel the now familiar slide of cold metal before they're bound together and attached to an anchor in the ground.

I'm trapped, helpless, and staring into the eyes of a man I've never seen before, but who I know, without a shadow of a doubt, that I'll never forget.

"I can pay you more."

"Doubt it. But you'll make us some nice money." His smile makes me want to throw up.

Weston strolls in.

"Welcome, Princess. You like my new house?"

I gape up at him in horror. "Wh-Why are you doing this?" I cry.

He smiles that terrible smile and sits next to me on the mattress. I struggle to catch my breath.

"Do you want money? My grandfather will pay you to give me back. But if you hurt me, he won't."

"You, dumb cunt. I don't want money. I want my pound of flesh."

He lifts his shirt and twists to show me a small scar on his lower back. Tears fall from my eyes, as I look at it.

"Thanks to you and that little shit who called the police, I have a record. I had eight months of community service. So, I'm thinking that once I stab you and then make you spend 8 months getting fucked up the ass by men you don't know and who don't give a shit about anything beyond the nut, they're going bust inside of you, we'll be even."

And then he holds up a knife, one just like the one Stone stuck him with.

"What are you doing?"

I scream as the knife flashes down and slices my shirt open leaving me completely bare from the waist up.

His smile makes my stomach heave.

"Weston. You can't do this."

He lowers his head and draws his tongue around my nipple. It's a disgusting imitation of a lover's caress, and I can't hold back my cries, as he sucks and licks and bites me until I beg him to stop.

"See? All you had to say is please," he says, as he lifts his head.

He cuts every stitch of clothing off my body, and when he finally leaves the room, there's not a single part of me he hasn't touched.

"Turn her on her stomach," he says to the man who carried me in. He's sitting on a small sofa, stroking himself, as he watches me. I've never felt so vulnerable.

"And Regan, you better try to get used to it. I've got three customers upstairs waiting for you."

I start to scream, and I don't stop until Weston sticks a needle in my arm and injects me with something that makes it all go away.

Chapter 54

TRUST

STONE

"Good morning, Goddess." I push a lock of hair that came loose from my makeshift braid, out of her eyes and she blinks, several times, then peers at the clock.

"Oh, heaven help me, why does my head hurt so much?" She presses the heels of her hands over her eyes and moans.

I reach over her and grab the two aspirin and the bottle of water. "Here, take these."

I help her sit up, and she opens her mouth to let me drop the aspirin in and sips the water.

She grimaces and swallows, but sighs and takes a few more sips of water before she lays down—a sigh of relief slipping past her parted lips as she sinks into the pillow.

She swallows hard and grimaces like it hurts.

"Are you okay?" I ask.

Her eyes, narrowed against the light, slide to me—groggy and puzzled. "Why are you still here?"

I'd planned to ease into it, give her a chance to wake up, but I can't make small talk when there is so much we need to talk about.

"I heard your podcast, Regan. I listened to the whole thing."

She makes a sound that's between a moan and a whimper, presses her lips together, and covers her eyes with her hands.

I pry them off her face and weave our fingers together in an imitation of what, I hope, we'll do with our lives.

Then, I press our joined hands into the mattress to ground myself. Her warm, pliant hands serving as a reminder that she's here with me and safe. And that as long as I draw breath, that's how she'll stay. "I'm so incredibly proud of you," I say my eyes on our joined hands.

"Proud of me? For what?"

I glance up to find her watching me with worried eyes. "For being braver than I'll ever have to be. I'm so, *so* sorry you went through that. It makes me sick that he hurt you because of what I did."

She sits up abruptly, and winces in discomfort, but her eyes are clear and direct and laser focused on mine. "Don't say that. You were a child. He was an adult, and what he did was because he's depraved and emotionally broken. And because he could."

"Yeah, but I stabbed him. I pressed the silent alarm and then left you face the music. Shit, Regan. I'm sorry..."

"No. Please. I can't." She tugs the hand to free it from my grasp and I let it go, immediately.

She groans and flops back onto the pillows and flings an arm over her face. "See, *this* is why I didn't tell you. Or anyone else." Her lips pucker as if she's tasting something bitter. "I can't carry the burden of your guilt on top of mine. And unlike yours, mine isn't imagined."

"Imagined?"

She lifts her arm a fraction, and peers at me. "Yes, imagined. Even if you'd shot him and wounded him for life, what he did isn't your fault," she half yells and covers her face with her hands.

"Hey, take it easy," I stroke her shoulder.

She sighs and sits up. "I'm not fragile. Don't treat me like I am. What happened to me shouldn't happen to anyone. But I got out of there. I got my life back. I'm a survivor, not a victim. You should be afraid of *me*. Do you know the kind of strength it takes to put one foot in front of the other after a piece of your soul is irrevocably damaged? I won't ever be the same. But I survived."

I take her hand in mine again and trace the network of veins, smile at the way her fingers curl into my palm. I'm relieved she doesn't resent me. But it's going to take me a little while longer to get over my guilt. I wish I could get my hands on that fucker.

"What happened to him?"

"He's dead." Her voice is sharp and she draws the sign of the cross over her chest. "At least I pray, so."

I chuckle at the gesture, but I'm unsettled. "What was that about? Are you not sure?"

"Please, lower your voice," she moans.

"Sorry," I mutter and take a deep breath. "Well? Are you sure or not?" I ask again, my voice softer, but no less demanding.

"I don't know," she sighs deeply.

"Why would you think he wasn't?" I keep my voice calm, speak slowly to hide the storm clouds gathering in my mind.

"My grandfather is the source of that information and I can't take anything he ever said at face value. The woman, Rebecca, was released from prison five years ago. But, there's no trace of her."

"Have you tried to confirm your grandfather's information?" I struggle to keep my voice free of the frustrated anger I'm feeling.

She shakes her head. "My mother is looking into it. I haven't asked though. Honestly… I try my best not to think about him. And I'm more concerned about finding her and making things right."

I nod, but my mind is stuck on the possibility that he's out there somewhere living his life freely after what he did to her and countless other women.

What I wouldn't do for the chance to stand face to face with him. To show him what it's like to be helpless while someone takes pleasure in hurting you. *Before* I let the law have him.

"I'm sick with guilt," she says, and I blink to refocus my vision and glance down at her.

"About what?"

"*Rebecca.* Are you listening to me?"

"Of course, I am," I stroke her hand and push my thoughts of vengeance away. "Have had any luck figuring out where she is?"

"None. It's like…she doesn't exist."

"Well since we know that's not the case, we'll keep looking."

"I guess," she mutters but her gaze drops to her lap.

I don't try to reassure her of things I can't control. I run a thumb over her delicate cheekbone and hold my tongue until she looks at me again.

"You mentioned people sending hate mail. Have you been getting threats?"

She winces and something like regret fills her eyes, but she holds my gaze and shrugs. "Of course, I have. It comes with the territory of being a woman online. I'm not worried. As long as nobody knows who I am, it'll be fine. And I'll do everything I can to make sure no one makes that connection."

"You don't have anything to be ashamed of," I reassure her.

Her eyes narrow and her glare glitters with annoyance. "I know that. It's not no one's business but my own and I'd like to keep it that way."

"Okay, I'm sorry. I misunderstood," I say.

Her expression softens and she sighs in resignation. "At first, it was because I didn't want to deal with everyone knowing. But now, there's also them..."

Her gaze loses focus, and she presses her lips together.

"Who is them?"

Her eyes come back to mine. "The women who found each other on the podcast and came forward to put an end to Zimmerman's reign of terror. I'm still the lady with the scarlet letter A on her chest. I don't want to do anything to hurt their chances in court. Right now, The Jezebel is an anonymous, but reliable source. If they know it's me, all of those women will be guilty by association."

I scoff in surprise. "But surely not. that's crazy."

"That's *misogyny*, Stone," she says, her voice as bitter as the scowl on her face.

I can only nod in agreement.

"Getting their day in court is going to be hard enough. I want that man to be held accountable for the lives he's altered. And I want to see justice done." She ties up her explanation with that perfectly simple, simply perfect bow.

If I wasn't in love with her already, I would have fallen again, right in that moment. "I want to help."

She smiles, but it turns into a yawn. She groans softly and flops back onto the bed, her eyes drifting closed. "Can we talk about this later? I feel like garbage and my kids will be home in a few hours."

I yawn, too and slide down to lay beside her. "No complaints, I've been up all night." She curls around me, draping one of her shapely legs over my hip, and resting her chest on mine. I cup her head and stroke the thick tangle of curls. I can't believe we're here.

Just like *that*.

"Sleep. Then, food. And I'd love to meet your kids." I let my eyes drift closed.

"Okay." She tilts her head downward.

"You're stretching out my socks," she grumbles.

I crack an eye open and the smile on her face is the best thing I've ever seen in my life.

"I can't sleep barefoot. My toes get cold."

Her chuckle is the last thing I hear before I drift off.

Chapter 55

SO DOMESTIC

REGAN

"Mommyyyyy, catch me," Henri shouts at the same time he launches himself up into my arms. I catch him, but stagger to stay upright when Martinez wraps his arms around my legs.

"Did you miss me or something?" I ask, delighted by their warm hugs and the weight of their small bodies melding with mine.

I hitch Henri on my hip, take Martinez's hand and turn to smile at Eva.

"Hi, angel." I blow her a kiss.

"Hi, I guess I'll get the bags," she grumbles, but with a smile on her face. I lean down to drop a kiss on her cheek. She smells like chlorine and sunscreen. Eva climbs back into the car to get her brothers' backpacks, and my mother hops down.

"You let them go swimming already, you're getting soft." I raise an eyebrow at my mother's mock disapproval.

She shrugs. "They're much nicer than you were." She smiles and walks past our huddle toward the house. I pivot and rush after her as fast my clinging children will allow.

"Are you coming in?" I ask, when I catch up.

She glances at me like I've lost my mind. "Don't I always?"

"Wait. I want to tell you someth—"

"Qui est cet homme?" Martinez digs his heels enough, to bring me to a halt, and I follow the trajectory of the finger he's pointing, and even though this isn't going according to plan, I can't help but smile.

Stone stands in the doorway freshly showered and dressed in the same jeans and shirt he was wearing last night, looking like a dream come true.

"I see," my mother drawls, and looks at me with arched brows.

"C'est un ami et il voulait vous rencontrer tous," I explain to wide-eyed Martinez.

"You made a new friend?" Henri shrieks at my explanation, jumps down from my hip and strides up the walk. "I am Henri Landel. I'm the oldest boy in my family." He extends his hand for Stone to shake.

For all his earlier talk about being nervous, he looks as relaxed as ever. He grins down at my son, "Hello, I'm Stone Rivers. I'm the second oldest boy in my family. Very nice to meet you." He drops to his knee so they're almost eye level and they shake hands.

"Mom?" Eva calls, tentatively from behind me and I turn to face her, Martinez still clinging to my leg.

"Are you okay?" I ask when she just stares at me.

"Is that...your boyfriend?" she mouths.

"Women your mother's age don't have boyfriends," my mother answers loudly and I give her an exasperated glance.

A flushing Eva makes her way toward the door and Stone stands and meets her halfway. "Can I help you with your bags?" he asks.

She cocks her head and considers him, "Would you offer to help if I was a boy?"

"Eva!" My mother chides.

Eva's undaunted, "Well?"

Stone nods. "Absolutely," he confirms.

"Okay, that's good. And thanks, but I got it." She turns around to give me an inconspicuous thumbs up. I drop my head into my hands and laugh. This couldn't be any more wonderful if I'd planned it.

"Well, let's take this little party inside, shall we?" my mother says and starts to herd up toward the open front door.

"Oh, I'm sorry. I came out here because I just called in to work. I'm sorry," Stone grimaces.

We planned on me bringing the kids in, introducing him and having lunch together.

But Martinez's grip hasn't eased, and I think maybe it's for the best.

"Maybe come back for dinner?" I ask.

"Yes, I'll cook," my mother chimes in.

He smiles at her like she just offered him a pot of gold. "I can't wait."

Chapter 56

MAKE IT OFFICIAL

STONE
Later That Evening

I slip out of bed and drop a kiss on her head and leave an invitation to the hospital's biggest fundraiser of the year by her bedside along with a note.

> *Venus,*
>
> *I had to go to work and I've got shifts every night this week. That's an invitation to a Rivers Foundation fundraiser. I'd like you to be my date.*
>
> *I know it's more public than you may be ready for. But I'm certain that after dinner with your mother, we can handle it.*
>
> *I know you love me, but now, I need you to trust me, too. It would be fucking awesome to make a life with my soul mate, so I'm praying you'll choose me over the fear, the worry and have faith in us. I do.*
>
> *Love, Stone*

I walk out of there knowing I've put my heart back in her hands.

What if she decides that as much as she wants me, she wants other things and people more?

I'd like to think that I'd get on with my life.

But hell, I don't want to think about living without my Venus. I'm hers. Body and soul, heart and mind.

We could do incredible things together. I can only hope that in the face of this leap of faith I'm asking her to make, she'll want what's on the other side more than she fears the fall.

Chapter 57

MAKE THEM STOP

REGAN

After putting it off all week, this afternoon, I gathered my kids to tell them that Stone was more than a friend.

He's picking me up tonight, and I wanted them to understand before he arrived.

They were all happy. He's been over a few times this week. And, he's even working on his French and has won Martinez over. Henri likes him because he's tall enough to climb. Eva likes him simply because *he* likes me.

I reassured them that he wouldn't be trying to replace their father. We also talked about how they felt about their father and me not being married anymore. It turns out, because we've lived apart for so long, they were happy just to have some certainty about our situation.

Eva is still not speaking to him after the day he confronted me with the picture. When I encouraged her to forgive him, she said, "You first."

So, I called Marcel.

What he did was so wrong, but he's not a monster. He's just living proof that marriage isn't for everyone. And despite his failings as a husband, I know he loves his kids. I don't want them to have hang ups about love or to look at their parents' less than stellar track record and think that it has any bearing on them.

By the time we were done talking, we'd made a tentative kind of peace.

But that wasn't even close to the most difficult conversation I didn't want to have today. I've saved it for the last possible moment. I glance at the clock by my bed and now I can't put it off any longer.

The kids are all still in my room, the boys playing with their Bey blades, Eva is reading on my bed.

"Okay, guys. Go brush your teeth and get into bed," I instruct them. I indulge the boys' grumbling for a few minutes before I shoo them upstairs.

"Eva, can you wait, please? I want to talk to you," I call after and pat the spot next to me on the small sofa.

"Okay," she bounds back into my room, smiling, because she loves getting to hear things her brothers are too little to.

My stomach cramps, as I watch her walk toward me. What would I do if someone hurt her the way I was hurt? I hope that by telling her, she'll make better choices and understand that silence and secrets don't do anything but fester and make us sick.

This week has been a watershed. Besides agreeing to go with Stone to his event, I finally told my brothers about the podcast and then about what happened. They were both devastated and so angry at Pops when they heard the role he played in all of it.

But even as I help them navigate their anger, grief, and guilt, them knowing isn't a burden. In fact, it's lightened the one I've been holding.

If I can use my considerable platform to shed light on the plague of sex trafficking that's part of Houston's underbelly, maybe I can do some good.

So, I've decided to come out on The Jezebel, to say my name with pride. I want people to understand that anyone can become a victim of it, but that it doesn't have to ruin your life, And I want my daughter to be the first to know.

I won't let her listen to the podcast.

It's for audiences 17+, but I'm also very aware that the girls who are affected are much younger. But at eleven years old and on the cusp of young adulthood, I decided to just give her a very broad overview of what happened.

"So, I want to tell you a story of something that happened when I was nineteen. I promised when you were born that I wouldn't ever lie to you. That I would protect you with my very life, and I meant it."

Her light amber eyes grow wide. "Mom, you're scaring me."

My heart thuds and my gut knots, but I smile and take her hand. "I don't ever want you to be afraid. But I also want you to know that fear is normal. If you're scared, just remember that darkness exists so that we can see the light, okay?" I tell her.

She nods, solemn and brave. My heart swells with love for her. I push my own trepidation to the side and follow my daughter's lead and let my courage propel me forward.

"When I was nineteen, I was taken by men, who sell human beings and force them to do things against their will. All sorts of things. I'm fine. I was rescued after only a few days. And I'm very, very lucky that I had a family to fall back on."

Her face has turned ashen and her wide eyes are glassy with tears. "Someone *sold* you, Mommy?" she asks in a small, high-pitched voice made thick by the tears she's holding back.

"Yes, but I got out and I'm here," I tried to reassure her, but she had been beside herself.

"Can they still do that?" She asks.

"To me, or you? No. They'd have to kill me first, baby. But there are people who still do it, and who hurt other people the way they hurt me," I say and hold my breath and pray she doesn't ask for specifics.

She brushes her tears away and sits up straight. "We have to stop them, Mom. They can't do that," she says, her eyes brighten with anger and for the millionth time, I fall head over heels in love with my daughter.

I pull her into a hug. "No, they can't. And we will stop them. Or die trying."

Chapter 58

AT LAST

REGAN

"I'm so sorry. But she's still crying. I can't leave her like this."

I hit the little blue arrow and send Stone the very last message I wanted.

I'm despondent, as the three dots populate and disappear half a dozen times, before a response finally pops up.

"I understand. I'll call you when I'm leaving. And don't take that dress off…you promised me that privilege, and I plan on collecting."

Oh, that man…he does things to my heart.

"Mom? Are you almost done?"

At the sound of my daughter's voice, my heart leaps and nerves assail me. I came into my bathroom to text Stone when it seemed like she wasn't going to calm down any time soon. Someone reposted that picture of me and Stone on Snapchat and tagged her in it. She was devastated and has been sobbing all night. I had just finished getting dressed when she came to show me the post.

My mother is here, and I know Eva's going to be fine, but I feel terrible going out when she is so upset.

With one last peek at my reflection, I turn off the light and step out of my closet.

Eva is sitting on my bed, her eyes glued to her phone, her fingers flying.

I smooth the fabric of my dress and clear my throat to get her attention.

Her head whips up, and I'm startled by the wide smile on her face. "Holy cow, Mom. You look amazing." Her eyes wide with wonder, her grin one of pure delight. She throws her phone onto the mattress, hops down and rushes toward me.

"Really? You sure?" I ask out of habit, but I can see the sincere appreciation in her gaze as she looks me over from head to toe.

"Yes. Stone is going to love it." She grabs my hands and spins us around.

I force a smile, as I trot, in my precariously high and narrow heels, to keep up with her.

She stops spinning and teeters backward to the bed and flops back, lands spread out like a starfish, her hair framing her face like a halo. I flop down next to her, with as much ease as my skin tight mermaid-style dress will allow. We stare at the ceiling, and I try to catch my breath.

Eva nudges my leg with her toe, and I turn my head to look at her. She's watching me intently, but the storm has cleared from her eyes, and she's smiling.

"Are you okay? Ten minutes ago, you couldn't even speak," I remind her, with a skeptical smile. I trace a dried trail of tears over her cheeks.

"I was sad because I hate them for trying to hurt you. But I'm so proud of you. You are so strong. I know I'm just eleven, but I see you, and I am so glad you're my mom."

Tears sting my eyes. Children love so easily. Even when their parents don't deserve it. I see now how helpless I was to my grandfather's whims. It's not a matter of judgment, we're wired to crave the approval of our parents.

"Aren't you worried about what your friends will say?"

She looks at me like I just said something ridiculous. "Mommy, rule number one, remember?"

I laugh out loud, relief and gratitude mingling and swelling into one. "I'm so proud of you," I say, with a teary smile and pull her into a hug.

"Oh good, you're finished, Tyson's on his way." My mother strides into my bedroom.

I let Eva go and sit up.

"For what?" I ask, as I scoot to the edge of the bed and stand.

"When you said you weren't going out because she was upset, I intervened."

"Mother!"

She shrugs. "Good thing I did, no? You still have time."

"I told Stone I wasn't coming. I glance at my clock and grimace, he's probably already there."

"But I could drive myself, right?" I ask, tentative hope rising.

"Nonsense, Tyson will drive you. He owes you a few favors. He'll be here in five minutes."

I glance down at my daughter. "You feel okay, babe?" I ask.

She nods and smiles. "You look too beautiful to stay home," she urges.

"Okay." I shoot them both a nervous grin.

"You can't wear that," my mother says, eyeing my dress with deep disapproval.

"Why not?" I smooth my hands down the length of my black sequined sheath dress with a mermaid-style train that trails behind me.

"Because it's something anyone would wear." She eyes me with displeasure.

I wrinkle my brow in confusion. "That's the point." It's bad enough that Stone's dating the most notorious adulteress in Houston. I don't want to cause any more of a stir tonight than my mere presence will. It would be nice to make a good impression on the people Stone respects so much.

My mother mimics my confused look and then rolls her eyes in exasperation. "He didn't fall in love with just anyone. He didn't invite you so *just anyone* would show up. He asked *you. You* should go."

The truth about my father coming out, seems to have liberated my mother. She's not a whole new person, but she's definitely a whole new kind of parent.

"Okay, I'll change," I say, and she starts tugging my zipper down and follows me to the closet.

Ten minutes later, with both their stamps of approval, I'm on my way.

"Mom," Eva calls after me, as I hustle down the stairs. I look up and our eyes meet. "Be happy." She grins and gives me a thumbs up.

With those words beneath my wings, I go get my man.

Chapter 59

SCARLET

STONE

"Holy Mother of God, you do not deserve all of that." Dare nudges me. I look up from the email I'm drafting under the cover of the tablecloth.

"Huh?" He's staring, with rapt attention across the room. Bewildered, I glance at Beau, and find his attention focused in the same direction. In fact, everyone at our table is looking at something and whatever it is, it's making Hayes' jaw clench furiously.

I follow their gaze and then, I understand.

It's Regan. The man she's speaking with points in my direction and she looks up sharply. The distress on her face vanishes and is instantly replaced with a smile that speaks of complete satisfaction. When she steps onto the crowded dance floor, a path clears for her.

She's stunning and the meaning of what she's wearing isn't lost on me for a single second. Her dress is a scarlet satin with a neckline that plunges to her navel where it knots in a bow before falling all the way to the floor in a curve hugging sea of fabric that shimmers with every step she takes.

Her hair is pin straight and is scraped back and caught into one long ponytail that I know is going to wrap nice around my fist later.

Her heart-shaped mouth is painted the same siren red as her dress and the smile that lifts the corners of it grows wider with every step she takes.

As she passes them, I notice people's eyes moving to, and lingering on, her back.

Her gaze is locked on me. Her eyes alight with an emotion that no one can misread. She is the tip of Cupid's arrow moving toward her target. I stand, wanting to make sure it's my heart she pierces.

When she texted to say she couldn't come because of Eva, I'd understood. Yet, disappointed didn't begin to describe how I felt.

But here she is, walking toward me, looking for all the world like a woman in love. I start toward her but Hayes' hand on my shoulder stops me. I turn toward him, braced for whatever he's about to say. Even though he did everything I asked of him, he and Regan haven't had a détente yet.

"Give me a chance," he says when he sees my wary, impatient expression.

"Hurry," I bite out.

"I'm sorry I stood in your way and asked you to give up something that is, if that smile on her face says anything, very special. You're the smartest, hardest-working man I know, Stone. And if you get any shit for this, I've got you. Just—"

"Glad you see the light, brother," I cut him off. "But can you save it for later?"

He grins and I turn around just in time to take two steps and close the gap between us. I reach for her, wrap my arms around her waist, and her arms slide up my neck. I encounter bare skin when I lay my hands on the small of her back. No wonder everyone is staring. Her tattoo is on display.

"Hi," I whisper and lean down to drop a kiss on her mouth. She presses her body into mine and I growl into her mouth. But I break our kiss.

"Surprise." She gazes at me.

"Indeed. Come on, let's sit." I take her hands and we walk back to the table I'm sharing with my brother, my advisor and his family. We make introductions and I can't stifle my chuckle at the look of surprise on Regan's face when Hayes stands to pull out her chair. Hayes has always been great at pivoting. But this has got to be a record. Maybe fatherhood has mellowed him out, or maybe he really can see how much I love her, but either way, I'm glad.

She joins us at the table, and I introduce her to everyone she doesn't know. Confidence squeals and jumps up to wrap her arms around her neck, Regan laughs out loud and hugs her back.

It's an amazing evening. She shines brighter than anyone else in the room. We dance all night, except for the one that Hayes cut in for. Dancing is also something he never does. They didn't hug when they were done, but they were both smiling when they came back to the table.

On our way out, we stop to use the Photo Booth and we create our infamous pose—the kiss, my hands palming her luscious little ass, my mouth devouring hers. The Jezebel tattoo is clear as day and this time, we make sure that my face is, too.

On our way home, I post it to my IG feed with the captions. "Call her Jezebel if you'd like, as long as you also call her mine. #Thosearemyfuckinghands."

Later than night, Regan shares my post in her story, and she captions it, "This is us—Wicked, Wanton, Wild and really fucking happy."

Chapter 60

MINE

REGAN

We take our time coming up the stairs. Stopping every few steps to kiss, or nibble, or stroke and when we finally reach the landing, I am in a frenzy of need.

I grab his tie and tug him back until I hit the wall. "Woah," he chuckles, his breath warm on my lips before I take his mouth with mine. His mouth is hot and slick from our marathon of kissing, and I groan at the slide of his tongue back into mine. I pull at this suit jacket and he lets go of me long enough to shrug it off.

"Yes, take off all these stupid clothes, right now," I command and turn my attention to the waist of his pants.

He grabs my hands, pulls them away and suddenly the warm weight of his body on mine is gone. My eyes snap open.

"Don't move, I'll be right back," he calls, his hand slipping from mine for the first time since we left the fundraiser.

"Where are you going?" I ask as the top of his head disappears. He doesn't answer me. Frowning, I peer over the banister frowning when only the sounds of retreating footfalls greet me. And then, my smile makes a miraculous recovery as I remember our makeup session on the way up.

I turn to face the room that takes up the entire top floor of his townhouse. The floor is covered in the gleaming blond hardwood. The windowless walls are white and bare. The ceiling has a huge tray in the center. The walls are completely bare. There's no art, no bookshelves, in fact there's only one piece of furniture in the entire space.

Right in the center of the room, directly beneath the tray ceiling, is the biggest bed I've ever seen. Draped in a simple white comforter and dressed with a mountain of plain white pillows it sits right below the center of the opening in the ceiling. I rush toward it like a shipwreck survivor would swim toward land and dive on, landing on my back in the middle and all the air leaves my lungs.

The tray is a window, opening up to the dazzlingly dark, diamond crusted night sky. The pane of glass set into it so clear, that from here, it's like having an unobstructed view of the heavens. I can't believe I'm going to fall asleep here, tonight.

"What do you think?" Stone asks and I sit up to find him standing at the top of the stairs, a bottle of champagne in one hand and two long stem champagne glasses dangling from the fingers of the other. He's been kind enough to take off his shirt and unfasten his black tuxedo trousers.

His hair is disheveled from my marauding hands and his full lips are swollen from my avaricious mouth, and his eyes burning with a fire that burns hotter than any obstacle ever could. He looks like a fallen angel. And he's all mine.

"I think… I'm in love," I drawl and come up on my knees. I move toward the edge of the bed, my arms outstretched. He puts the glasses down and walks to me, uncorking the champagne as he approaches, the smile on his face that of a man coming to claim his hard-earned bounty.

"Open up, Goddess," he growls, lifts the bottle to my lips and pours the cold, fizzy liquid into my mouth. I swallow what I can, but his generous pour spills down my chin and trails down my neck, seeping into the bodice of my dress.

"I'm going to take that thing off with my teeth," he promises, taking a swig of the champagne and then slamming his lips against mine, wraps an arm around my waist, and pulls me to him until our bodies are flush with each other.

I gasp when a fat drop of champagne lands on my shoulder and spills down my back in icy rivulets. Another lands on my chest and I lurch away from the cold.

"Ah, ah," Stone's arm tightens his hold on me, and his other hand, unburdened by the champagne bottle, slides around the back of my neck. He presses his lips to the tender spot where my neck meets my shoulder. Then he opens his mouth to lick and suck.

My body is burning from the inside out, my head falls back as I succumb to the rapture his mouth is unleashing.

"I want this dress off," I pant, made desperate by the scrape of his teeth against my throat.

"Not as much as I do," he growls and then the world blurs and when I can see straight again, I'm on my stomach and his big hands are planted on either side of my head and his big body casts a shadow over us as he straddles my hips, his knees pressing into the mattress.

"What are you doing?" Anticipation makes my voice husky and low.

"Making you mine and taking my time," he says and then his lips are on my skin. He charts a course of soft kisses and small licks down the center of my back, moving his body lower, too. Between each touch, he whispers, "Mine." I lay completely still, my heart thundering as I free fall into love, moving a million miles an hour toward its final frontier…on a journey that will never end. And there's no fear, or doubt—just joy and transformation.

"*My* Jezebel," he says the name with all the love it was never intended to engender. "I'm so proud of you. And I love you so much." He skims the tattoo with the lightest of kisses and then, his lips move lower.

And ever a man of his word, Stone pulls my zipper down with his teeth. He spreads the fabric, tugs it off my body, and flings it away. I'm completely naked underneath it. He palms my ass, his fingers gripping hard and spreads my cheeks apart. "Let me see the goddess I've claimed," his voice is deep and dark, I squirm under the heat of his ravenous eyes.

"*Fuck* me, you make me weak," he groans before he jerks my hips up and back and puts his mouth between my thighs.

"Oh God," I moan when his tongue probes my tight pucker over and over, his lips sucking, introducing me to a pleasure I didn't even know existed.

"I want in here," he slips the tip of his thumb into my ass and presses. "Does it hurt?" he asks, and probes deeper when I shake my head no.

I yelp at the first icy cold splash of champagne against the tender skin he's just ravished. Then, I moan when his sinful lips suck it up. I groan when his thumb slides back inside me, deeper than before. I bear down, testing how it feels. "I hope you've got lube in your pocket." I grunt when he pressed even deeper.

"It's the only reason I kept them on." He shifts off the bed and I turn to watch him undress and smile when he pulls a foil packet and a tiny bottle of clear liquid from his pocket.

He steps out of his pants and briefs and rolls the condom over his glorious erection and pours half the bottle into his hand and strokes it over himself.

"You ready?" he asks.

I nod and turn my head as he lifts my hips up. He drops a kiss onto my back and then, my god of war mounts and makes me his.

He goes slow at first, sliding in inch by inch until he's fully seated. My body opens like a flower for him, when he starts to thrust, the pleasure is explosive. His hands glide up my back, slide down to cup my breasts, and he thumbs my nipple, pressing in, pinching it until I am on the verge of a cliff so high, I'm not sure I'll survive the fall.

But I'd be happy to die trying. I slip my fingers between my legs and rub my clit, and together we fling my body into a blistering release that pulls a scream from me. He pulls out of me and flips me over. The velvety dark sky glitters above me before his face comes into view.

He kneels between my thighs and rolls the condom off, flings it away and lifts my thighs over his shoulder and slams his rock-hard dick into my pussy, burying himself to the hilt.

My back bows off the bed as pleasure spears me, and his hand slips behind my neck, holding my head up when it would roll back. His gold flecked eyes, narrowed to slits of desire, are more wondrous than any sky could be. My captive heart catches fire, and tears spill from the corners of my eyes. "I love you, Stone. So much. Thank you for loving me, too."

He smiles. "Yes Regan, I do love you. I *live* for you. I'm never, ever going to let you go,," he promises.

"You couldn't. I'm holding on to you forever." I wrap my arms around his neck, pulling him down, so I can seal that promise with a kiss.

Chapter 61

VICTORY

STONE

I look down at the goddess I'm ravaging and smile. There is a wanton abandon in the careless sprawl of her body. The smile on her face is carnal satisfaction incarnate. But it's her eyes that tell me what I want to know. In the dark depths of them there's an eternity of light and love that burns brighter than any star I've ever seen. My heart is home, finally.

Six Months Later

HOUSTON, TX

Chapter 62

HOME BASE

STONE

"Perfect day, right?" Hayes muses, more to me than himself. We're sitting on the sidelines watching Eva's baseball scrimmage. His son, Phoenix, is in his usual spot, curled up on Hayes' chest with his mouth drooping open, and his eyes closed. Blissed out is this kid's most common facial expression. I've never met a happier baby.

He must have gotten it from his mama because his father is a grumpy asshole. Well, except for the moments when he's my bad ass big brother who slays dragons for me.

Beyond the check he cut for Venus Rising, and the calls he made to move her licensing along, he's also brought Marcel to heel.

When he realized that I was the man in the picture, and he went on a bit of a rampage.

He started filing frivolous motions that were dismissed with court costs and attorney's fees awarded to Regan every time.

He tried to have me fired by petitioning the board to enforce the morality clause. I tendered my resignation without waiting for them to finish their review. Even if they didn't find me in violation of their clause, I didn't want to work for an organization that thought they had the right to dictate my personal life.

After that failed, Marcel filed an ethics complaint with the state licensing board. That's when Hayes moved to void all of the contracts they'd signed for their joint project unless Marcel backed down.

Marcel Landel is the biggest whale in the sea. His pockets are deep and his fondness for seeing his name on the sides of buildings makes him a favorite in fundraising circles. And Hayes' charm offensive made feuding with him inconvenient.

So, Marcel waved a white flag and even wrote Regan a note of apology.

"Just ask me…. I can *feel* you thinking," Hayes complains without taking his eyes off the field. I hate how astute he is. It's been a few months and I've always wondered but didn't want to offend him when he'd taken such a huge gamble on my behalf.

"You weren't really going to cut ties with Landel, were you?"

He glances at me, his hazel eyes as unreadable as always. "You think I was bluffing?"

"Weren't you?"

"Never. I would have canceled those contracts. Yes, he's given us a lot of money, but I don't *need* it. You're my brother. If he's hurting you, then he's hurting me. Also, it's clear to anyone with eyes that you two reformed conformists belong together. I knew he'd see sense." He slaps my shoulder fondly and I cough to clear my throat. Damn, if Hayes didn't nearly bring a tear to my eye.

The crack of the ball striking the bat has us both turning toward the field.

"Holy shit, she's fast," Hayes says, and I follow his line sight.

Eva is running like a demon, tagging bases and dodging the grasps of the boys who try to catch her with the ball. She streaks from third to home. The outfielder who caught the ball makes a running leap at her and she evades him by inches, but she never looks back. She's the only girl on her baseball team, but she's the fastest and the most fearless.

I'm on my feet, my camera out to record this for Regan as Eva slides into home to the deafening shouts of the crowd. The twins are having a Bey blade battle a few feet away but tear their eyes away from their game to clap for their sister.

My conversation with Hayes is forgotten and my heart nearly bursts with pride. Her teammates flood the pitch and lift her on their shoulders to carry her to the dugout.

The last six months have gone by in a blink and yet it feels like we've been doing this forever. The kids are off for a summer in Monaco in two weeks. While it'll be nice to have the house to ourselves as we settle into domestic routine, I'm sorry they're going for so long

My phone rings just as I'm about to head to the dugout to take more pictures.

"Hey, goddess, you should have seen your girl—" I answer, out of breath and excited.

"My mother...she's gone after him. She left me a note. She says she's going to kill him. I'm going after her," she says in a clipped, calm voice.

"Who is he? What are you talking about?"

"Weston. He is *Weston.* Remember, I told you that my mother was looking into the connection with him and grandfather?"

I remember vaguely from that night, but we haven't talked about it again.

"Yes. What happened?"

"She found him."

"He's not dead?" A chill runs through me, from toe to tip.

"Not even a little. He's been hiding in plain sight." My eyes dart around the field, would I even recognize him if I saw him?

"Where is he?"

"Well, according to her note, he's at the house in Palestine."

"Her note? I thought you were running errands this morning."

"We were. I went to take a bath and came down to find a note from her. She said she's going to kill him."

"What?" I jump to my feet and move away from Hayes and the kids.

"I know. I'm on my way to try and catch her. She drew me that bath and then left. She gave herself an hourlong head start."

"Do you know where she went?"

"Of course, I have an address. He's been in that house. You have the kids. So, I'm on my way. I was just calling to let you know."

Like hell. I press mute and run over to Hayes. "Can you take Eva and the boys home with you? I'll leave their booster seats on top of your car, okay? Emergency," I add, deliberately making it sound like work calling so that the boys won't worry.

"Sure." He gives me a thumbs up and I turn back to the call.

"Regan, give me that address now," I demand.

She sighs, loudly. "Fine. But if you get there first, don't get any ideas about finishing what you started all those years ago. He is not worth you going to jail. And if anyone is going to have the pleasure of hurting him, it'll be me. Sending you that address now. I love you."

I race for my car. My heart is in my throat and rage is nearly choking me. If I get there first, *nothing* will stop me from finishing what I started.

Chapter 63

FINALLY

REGAN

I pull off the exit and break out into a sweat. I checked my rearview mirror compulsively on the drive over and every time a car appeared behind me; my heart raced. But no one is following me. This is not that night and I am not going to be anyone's victim today.

But telling myself that doesn't make my pulse any slower and by the time I turn up the long tree lined drive leading to the house, I am trembling.

I pull up next to my mother's black Cadillac, breathing so hard I'm practically panting. I need to get out of the car. She's in danger, and I need to help her. But I can't move. I drop my forehead onto the steering wheel as a flood of memories, the sound of screaming, the places on my body they hurt, sting now with phantom pain. The crunch of gravel under tires jolts me back to the present and I almost burst into tears of relief when Stone's silver Ranger Rover pulls in behind me.

"You okay?" he asks when he pulls my door open. He crouches down beside me.

"You don't have to come in. I'll go. I called 911 and they're on their way, okay?" he speaks in a steady, reassuring voice and rubs his big, warm hand down my back.

My breathing grows steadier and I nod.

"I want to go. I need to." I add when he looks like he's about to argue with me.

He helps me out of the car. We walk toward the house of horrors. But, with Stone holding my hand, the cloying fear recedes, and vengeful anger takes its place.

A scream from inside smacks into my consciousness like a runaway freight train. It shatters everything, but my need to help my mother. I break into a run and ignore Stone's shouts for me to stop.

I scream my mother's name and my voice as loud as a raging wind as I cross the threshold into the house. I run through the living room and down the corridor and burst into the room where the sounds are coming from.

I walk in to find a stark-naked Weston cuffed to the bed, his legs spread eagle, his arms bound above his head. His screams stop when he sees me.

"Oh my God, stop her, she's going to get me killed." I look around the room and don't see my mother, and then I hear the sound of the toilet flushing.

I rush over to the bathroom and see my mother dumping bags of brown powder into the toilet, a satisfied smile on her face.

"Mother?" I call and she shrieks and drops at the bag and turns toward me.

"Oh my God, child. Don't sneak up on me like that. I didn't hear you over that man's wailing. Apparently if all of this heroine goes missing, I won't have to kill him, cause the Mexican Cartel will."

I stare slack jawed at her, unable to formulate a response.

"Regan?" Stone bellows my name.

"We're in the bathroom. She's fine," I yell back out to him just as Weston starts shrieking again.

"Oh, Stone is with you. Perfect. I was thinking we could burn this place down before we leave. What do you say?" she asks, as if she's discussing what we should eat for dinner.

"Mother, the police are on their way. Stop flushing those drugs and why is he naked?" I ask her in exasperation.

She reaches into a bag on the floor beside her and pulls out a bottle of honey and holds it up with a smile. "I was going to pour this on him, leave the door open and let the bugs have at him until the cartel showed up."

"You fucker!" Weston shrieks and I dash out into the hall and make for the room.

Stone is holding a knife under Weston's balls and he's got a hand cuffed around his neck.

"I'm a doctor. I know how to cut this so that not even the best surgeon could make you right," he says and Weston howls bloody murder. A trickle of blood drops onto the sheet between his thighs.

I grab Stone's wrist and tug. I might as well be trying to maneuver a mountain.

"No, baby. I want to finish what I started the last time we were all together." His hand around Weston's throat tightens and the man's face turns red, his eyes turn to me pleading for help.

Looking at him is hard. Despite his current predicament, he looks well. Better than Jack did, and certainly better than Rebecca looked last time I saw her. It's not right that he's had a moment of comfort. But I don't want one more entanglement with this man. I don't want to lose one more person, or minute because I gave him more power than I should have.

"You can't. It'll make it easier for him to get off."

Stone growls and closes his eyes, his jaw clenched, his lips flatten in a grimace. Then he pulls his hand away from his throat and Weston coughs and draws in huge lungfuls of air. "I wish I'd shoved that knife deeper into his back when I had the chance," Stone says, and I realize the knife is still pressed to his balls.

Weston's eyes go wide as they dart from my face to Stone's. "You're that little shit who stabbed me? You're *all* fucking crazy."

"Remember what happened last time you talked to her. Keep talking and the police be damned, I will slice it off clean." Stone's voice is calm but cold as ice.

Weston's frantic eyes grow wide and he starts bucking like a wild man. "You gotta help me. He's crazy; you can't do this," he shrieks, tears running down his face. I would laugh if I wasn't starting to twitch the onslaught of memories that are too vivid, and too painful.

I slap Weston, hard and he howls and starts to sob. "God, you are so pathetic. You, who tortured women for years can't bear to be slapped?"

"He's gonna cut off my cock," he sobs, his chest heaving.

"Oh, shut up. He's not going to cut off your little prick. He knows you're not worth it." I put my hand on Stone's shoulder and squeeze. He looks up at me, the sinister look in his eyes morphing to worry when he sees the look on my face.

He drops the knife and stands up. "Are you okay?"

"Please, I need to go." I whisper. I don't want Weston to know how much being here is affecting me.

He wraps an arm around my waist, and I lean my head on his chest. The thundering of his heart against my ear is soothing and muffles the horror of this place.

The wail of sirens approaching fills the cabin. My mother sticks her head in from the bathroom. "Who called the police? I haven't even gotten the honey on him, yet."

"Mom, come on, please let's get out of here, I just want this over."

She looks between me and the bed and purses her lips in disgust. "Fine." She marches out of the bathroom with a big black marker in her hand. "But this time, I'm going to force them to get the story right."

Weston was apprehended, dragged out of the house with the words "PIMP" and "RAPIST" drawn in black marker on his chest. Courtesy of my mother and the news cameras she made sure were waiting when he arrived at the Harris County Court House for processing.

It was only then, as Weston made a plea bargain in exchange for a more lenient sentence, that the full truth of my grandfather's deception was finally revealed.

Weston went to jail for the drug charge he caught the night Stone stabbed him. He might have gotten off with parole and community service, but my grandfather used his influence to make sure he served a full year for possession.

When he was finally released, his father's small drug dealing operation had been disrupted and with the conviction on his record, his job prospects were very slim. He found work procuring women for trafficking ring. He earned extra money by renting out the small cabin in Palestine as one of their dens. Once he had a regular income, he turned his mind to revenge—and thought he'd found the perfect way to kill two birds with one stone.

When he lured me to the cabin, he had no idea that the ring, whose members had tiny blue lightening bolts tattooed on their wrists had been started decades ago, by my grandfather.

After he'd had his way with me and my friends, he sent his demands to my grandfather. He wanted a million dollars in exchange for our return and for the pictures to go away.

What he got instead, he said, was more than he could have hoped for.

My grandfather offered him a way out, a clean slate, and lifetime of income. He didn't understand why the old man had sweetened the pot, but he didn't look that gift horse in the mouth. Once he had the money and identification documents from my grandfather, he skipped town.

He wasn't even in the cabin the day my grandfather's private security raided it and rescued us.

He'd been living in Odessa when my mother found him. She lured him to the cabin by pretending to be one of the women he'd kept there. He thought he was coming to pay off a blackmailer.

The ring was still operational and he gave over the names of the men who'd run it all those years ago in exchange for a reduced sentence.

The weeks of legal maneuvering and court appearances left me mired in resentment and despair.

Those hours my mother had him tied to the bed would be the most severe punishment Weston would ever face for what he'd done.

My grandfather would never face the consequences and reckon of his betrayal and depravity.

Those truths were bitter, jagged pills to swallow. But even worse was knowing that I'd never be able to atone to my friends for the way I thwarted their efforts to bring these men to justice.

But on the day of Weston's sentencing, I walked out of the Harris County court room determined, and finally ready, to try.

Epilogue

LOVE OF MY LIFE

REGAN

"So…are you okay?" Matty's question surprises me. I expected her to be angry, to demand to know more, to ask why I didn't call months ago.

"Uh, yeah. I am. Are you?" I ask, not quite ready to believe smile in her voice.

"Yes. Thank you for calling to tell me. For what it's worth. I'm sorry I was right. And I'm so glad that asshole if finally where he belongs. You should have let Stone cut off his dick."

I chuckle, but it's weary and sad. "That would have been a disaster on top of everything else. But it was kind of fun to hear him scream."

Matty laughs and even though she sounds as tired as I do, it's lighter than she's sounded in a long time. I feel unworthy of it.

"Matty, I'm sorry we can't find Rebecca," I address the last elephant in the room. "I wanted to wait until I had more to say than that, but my mother has been looking for her almost a year." I hold my breath and wait to see if we can cross this hurdle.

"I'm sorry for that, too. It's the reality though, isn't it?"

"Sadly, yes.

"But I think what you're doing in her name over at Venus Rising is amazing. I'd like to help. If you need it."

"We need it, badly. And we have funding for two staff positions." I respond quickly, hope kindling in my heart.

"I don't want to be on staff, I want to be a member of your leadership and I want to be in charge of the newsletter."

"Okay. Sure. We'll make it happen." I know I sound like overly eager, but I am. I want her back in my life and the chance to make up for lost time.

"Your story wore me out," she yawns loudly. I'll call you in the morning. We can talk more, then."

"Okay, sounds good. Thank you, Matty." I hang up and walk out of my office.

Today will go down in the record books as one of the worst and best day of my life. I walk through my house, turning off the lights as I go. I'm bone tired and I walk into the bedroom ready to fall straight into bed.

"They're finally asleep. I'm so—"

My words trail off when Stone stands up. He's palming the erection pressing against his blue and white striped pajama bottoms. "You're so…tired? That's too bad, cause I'm horny as fuck,"

"Oh?" I lean against the door frame, my cheeks hurt from smiling so much today, but I savor the feeling of another one tugging at the corners of my lips.

"But I have a dilemma." He bites his lip as he pulls his pants down his hips and his erection springs free and stands straight between us. He grabs it with both of his hands and starts stroking himself.

"Are you getting yourself off?" I ask.

"Ah, Captain Obvious is in the building," he says with a wicked smile so sensual it makes my toes curl.

"Stop talking shit and come over here," I tease him.

"No can do. I told you, I have a dilemma," he says and sits back on the bed and keeps stroking himself.

"Yes, and I have the solutions between my legs."

"Be careful what you wish for… If I stop this …" He nods at his dick. "Then I'll need to bend your sweet ass over and fuck you. You just said you're exhausted and so I don't think you can handle me tonight. I'm pissed; I might be too rough."

"You are mad at me?"

"Yes. For telling me that you didn't need me today."

"Aww, babe. I didn't mean it like that. I just knew I could handle it by myself."

He grunts as his hand moves faster. "There is no more by yourself. Don't ask me to let you go into battle alone. I never will. Never."

I've never watched a man do this before and it's mesmerizing.

He lets go of his dick long enough to yank off his pants and pull his shirt over his head. And then he stands.

His body is distractingly big, so *perfect*.

And it's all mine.

So, I run.

Straight into my lover's arms.

And right before his lips cover mine, his voice smooth as velvet, he whispers. "You water me, I water you. Together, we win."

To get a copy of the extended epilogue click here. If you have the print version, keep reading.

To read The Gathering, a holiday novella with points of view from all six main characters including a scene from Tina and Tyson Wilde's point of view click here.

To read Tyson and Dina's story, The Daredevil, click here.

Extended Epilogue

STONE

"Rise and shine, lover." Regan's soft, husky drawl tickles me in my sleep. Her warm, lube slick hand wraps around my dick and I come awake in a rush of arousal and confusion. I sit up and wrap my hand around her delicate wrist to still the up and down motion of her fist.

"Why is Stone always trying to spoil our fun, huh Mars?" She gives my hardening length a long, tight, toe curling tug and then, releases her hold on me.

"I wasn't stopping you, just waking up." I murmur. When I reach for her, I grab nothing but air. I peer into the inky dark of our bedroom, willing my eyes to adjust and cursing these black out shades we draw on the weekends so that Regan can sleep in.

"Oh, well in that case," she murmurs.

The rustle of the sheets and the brush of her hair on my thighs is the only warning I have before her hot mouth closes over the swelling crown of my erection.

My back and hips arch up in shock and one hand automatically cups her head as she suckles the sensitive tip, flicking her tongue into the slit just the way I like before she lowers her mouth to take me in deep.

"Venus, holy fuck," I groan and clutch at the sheets with my free hand.

Regan's mouth is the sweetest place I've ever been. Whether she's using it to kiss me, talk to me or suck me off—it's a conduit to love, knowledge, and pleasure. And it's mine, for as long as I draw breath.

A rush of possessive need courses through me and I'm gripped by the need to see her. I call out a gruff voice command and a tiny motor whirs to life.

The massive shade covering my moon window, as Regan calls it, begins it slow retreat and the early morning light spills in from overhead as more of the window is revealed.

First her toned legs, bent at the knee and crossed at the ankles, come into view. Then the backs of her supple thighs glow a soft bronze under the sun's worshipping gaze. I want to linger on those luscious legs and fantasize about how they'll look hooked over my shoulder, but the light's revelations draw my eye up...over the sweet curve of her pert ass to the small of her back.

As always, my heart skips a beat when I see the linked symbols of Mars and Venus tattooed below her Jezebel.

She got that for her birthday last month. The shade draws back and in the full light of day, the undertones of gold and caramel in her dark brown hair are visible.

I gather the long fall of coils and curls that shroud my thighs into my fist and lift it away so I can see her face. I lean back on the headboard and close my eyes, settling in to enjoy the outrageously intense pleasure of fucking my woman's mouth until I come.

It's a very rude awakening when her mouth pulls off me suddenly. My eyes pop open and I growl in frustration when I see Regan is already off the bed and reaching into the small bathroom to grab a robe.

"Where are you going?"

"Matty's here to drop something off. Don't move. I'll be back before you know it," she calls breathlessly, her robe only half way on, as she tears down the stairs.

"I know it already," I call after her, but get no response. I check my phone. It's only 8 am. Matty should be working the intake desk at Venus Rising this morning. What would she be doing here? I slide off the bed, step into my hastily discarded pajama bottoms, intent on ignoring her directive to wait.

I need to get the ring I bought her out of my desk and into the bedside wall drawer. I'm going to ask her to marry me on Sunday morning and I want to have ready.

She's been working from home all week. She hears everything and she's nosy as hell, so I didn't want to risk her catching wind of my plans. I want to surprise her.

I hear Regan's voice, and what sounds like at least two other people, downstairs. Whatever she's doing, it'll take her longer than the minute I need to check on the ring.

I rush into my office, my attention focused on Regan's voice as I reach into my desk drawer and fumble around for the small black velvet box I've had tucked away there all week. When I can't feel it, I lean down and peer into the drawer and see the silhouette of it in the back corner, out of my hand's reach.

I pull the drawer out fully, dump the meager contents out onto my desk and pluck the small box out of the pile of pens caps and paperclips. "There you are," I whisper, and scoop it up. I open it up and my heart comes to a screaming stop when all I see is an empty pillow where the ring I bought for Regan should be.

REGAN

"I can't believe this is happening," I groan to no one in particular. My eyes, and all the horror in them, remain fixed on the empty platter where the meticulously constructed tower of scones—the one on top with a three carat, emerald cut diamond engagement ring baked into the center—should have been.

"Regan, on what planet did you think stealing your own engagement ring and staging a coup proposal was a good idea? It was bound to go wrong." Tyson slaps my shoulder and gazes down at me with pity.

I glower at him, unamused. "It would have been fine if you hadn't been here to scare the hell out of her."

He shakes his head, a cagey frown pulling his lips down. "I locked myself out of my place. I was just crashing until I could call a locksmith in the morning. And if your friend hadn't lost her shit and thrown that entire tray at me and made this mess, you wouldn't even have known I'd been here."

I turn to Dina, who's on the floor picking up the fragments of scone. "Why *are* you here? Matty was making the delivery," I ask her.

She sighs and looks up at me, her expression pained. "Matty called me. Something came up and she couldn't get away to pick up the order and she didn't want to bother you. I'm sorry I messed up your proposal and lost the ring. I didn't expect to see anyone when I came in. I freaked." She tosses a handful of crumbs on the plate with a grunt and eyes Tyson with a contempt-filled glare.

"It's okay, really. This is all my fault, I should have just picked them up myself." I cast my horrified glance at the spectacular mess the projectile scones made. They all look exactly the same, and I have no idea which one had the ring in it.

"Really, though. This was a dumb ass plan, Regan. You should have let him propose when he was ready. No man wants a woman getting down on her damn knee," Tyson remarks as he picks up a chunk of scone from the counter and pops into his mouth. "These are good as hell, though. I can see how you got him so whipped," he chuckles to himself.

"Oh look, Tyson's being completely unhelpful. It must be show your true colors day," Dina taunts over her shoulder.

Tyson chuckles and strolls to stand in front of her. "Oh *look*, Dina's on her knees in front of me, It must be an act out your favorite fantasy day."

"You are a child," Dina snaps and rises to her feet. She's so much smaller than him, the top of her head doesn't reach his chin, but her ferocious glare knocks Tyson back a step.

I step between them before he can compose himself enough to return her fire.

My disbelieving glare darts between them. "Can you please do this later? Stone is upstairs waiting for me and everything is fucked."

Dina curls her lip at Tyson before meeting my gaze. Her smile is apologetic and placating. "Don't worry. We'll find the ring. He'll love the proposal just as much as he would have if you'd carried it in on a pyramid of scones." She pats my hand and then crouches to continue sifting through the mess.

I join her, holding back tears as I destroy the scones to feel for the delicate ring. I cling to the rope of optimism Dina tossed my way. She's right. Stone won't know this happened. At least, not until he comes into the kitchen that I don't have time to clean. If the rest of the morning goes according to plan, neither Stone or I will be coming anywhere near this kitchen until Tyson and Dina have had time to clean up after themselves.

By then, all of this will be nothing more than a funny story to tell our kids and grandkids.

"Aha!" Dina crows and hops to her feet, her hand extended toward me.

"You found it." My voice is half groan, half sigh and I pull Dina into a quick hug before I pluck the ring from her hand.

"Thank you," I press it to my lips and lick off the residue of crumbs left behind while I rush to the sink and run it under the water, relieved to be holding it again.

The creak of the floorboard interrupts my respite and I whirl to face Tyson and Dina. "Shit, I'm not ready. I wanted to look pretty and be clever. Ugh,Ugh" I growl my fists balling so tightly my nails dig into my palms.

"Venus?" The agitation in Stone's voice is palpable and I can't imagine what could have put it there in the few minutes I've been gone. Then I remember what he told me last night. One of his patients had a stroke a few hours after giving birth, and when his shift was over she was still in the ICU. I forget the ring, and a new worry blooms. "I have to go. I don't want him to see all this. Will you leave by the back door? After you're done cleaning up," I give Tyson a pointed look.

Then, I rush out into the large foyer that separates the kitchen area from the rest of the house. I smooth my hands over my robe and drop the ring into my pocket. Tyson was right. It was an idiotic idea. Thank goodness, I'll have time to slip it back into the box before he notices it's gone.

I get to the foot of the stairs just as he's rounding the last landing. I force myself to relax my posture and smile. "I told you to wait for me upstairs, Mr. River—" The bleak expression in his eyes stills my tongue and my stomach fall to my toes.

"Is it your patient? Is she…" I ask, my dread only intensifying when he shakes his head and closes his eyes.

"Regan…I don't know how this happened." He pulls me into a tight embrace and presses his cheek the top of my head and starts rocking me.

"Stone, you're scaring me," My lips are squished by his hug, but he understands my muffled words and loosens his hold, if only a little. It's enough to let me breathe a little easier. I wrap my arms around his waist. "Please tell me," I plead when he just sighs deeply.

"I think maybe it was the cleaning service…they're the only ones who could have. But, I don't understand. I'm sorry, but I need to call…shit."

"Baby, you're not making sense." I pull out of his hold and cup his face in my hands and turn it down so I can look into his eyes.

Pure misery flashes in his eyes, but whatever he's opening his mouth to say is cut off by the clatter of pots in the kitchen draws his attention and he frowns, his eyes trained on the hallway. "You said Matty was dropping something off. Is she still here?"

"It was Dina and she'll be gone soon." I tug his face back to look at mine, and search his eyes. "Tell me why you look like someone died."

He sighs heavily again, his shoulder falls with resignation and he takes my left hand in his, toying with it the way he does when he's nervous. "I was going to ask you to marry me this weekend."

All the breath leaves my lungs. "You...were?" I ask, my voice a breathless squeak, my heart rioting with joy.

"I was waiting for the kids to get back so I could ask them, too. At the same time...well, after you said yes. Assuming you'll say yes, that is." His eyes meet mine and there's a glimmer of doubt in them that would be endearing if it wasn't so misplaced.

I slide my hand into my pocket and curse my impulsivity and impatience. "Yes is all my heart knows when it comes to you, babe. You know that," I tell him while I finger the ring.

He gifts me with a sweet, relieved smile that makes me feel even worse. "I wanted to get down on one knee, to lay my heart at your feet and ask you to do the same. But the ring is gone. I don't know—"

"I took it," I say the words as quickly as I can and slap a hand over my mouth and watch him, wide eyed and waiting.

He steps back like I pushed him and blinks. "You did what?"

I can't look at him. "I thought...I found it...Not on purpose, I was looking for batteries.... And The Breakfast Klub called to confirm your order for tomorrow morning...all my favorite things were on there...so I figured that was when you were going to do it then...And I figured I'd beat you to it."

"You found it? *You* were going to ask *me?*" His voice is monotone, his expression—unreadable.

Tears blur my vision and I stare at our still joined hands. I swallow the lump in my throat and nod. "You know...turn convention on its head. Be the one to make a grand gesture this time. I thought you wouldn't look for it until at least tonight. I had Sweet make this stupid scone tower thing and the ring was baked into the one sitting on top. Dina dropped it off, but Tyson messed it up. I'm sorry. It's not missing. It's here."

I take his limp hand in mine and drop the ring into his palm.

The silence that follows my confession is terrible and I apologize more to fill it. "I'm sorry that I caused you a moment of distress and that I ruined what should have been a wonderful moment for us." I brave a glance up at his face and sob in relief at the radiant smile he's wearing. "You're…not mad?"

He cups my cheek, strokes my jaw with his thumb and presses a soft kiss to my lips. "My goddess…just as everything else that's ever happened to us, your timing couldn't be more perfect." Then, the god whose love for me blazes so hot that nothing could ever stand in its way gets down on one knee and pledges me his troth.

"Regan Naomi Wilde, you are my universe. The place where I was born, the place where long after my body fails me, my spirit will dwell. Us together is the natural order of things. If I could cut my heart out of my chest and lay it at your feet, I would. I hope you'll accept this ring as a tiny token of my esteem. And if you allow me to slip it onto your finger, I promise that I will love your children as fiercely as you do. I will be your castle, your throne, your crown. Yours, and yours alone for as long as I live."

A typhoon of emotion swirling around in my heart. I didn't realize until just now how much I wanted this. I never thought to have it—and so I convinced myself that it wasn't important. I can't believe I almost robbed us both of this moment. I cup his dear, beautiful face.

"You are my wildest dream come true, Stone. And for as long as I've known you, I've loved you. I accept your ring. I'll wear it so the world will know what our hearts told us a very long time ago…that we're each other's. And *only* each other's."

When he slips his ring onto my finger, I feel the tug of inevitability and the comforting weight of certainty's anchor. From that night in the bakery almost twenty years ago, until now, we've been moving toward this.

When I look back on our journey, I often wish we'd found our way to this sooner. But there's a part of me that knows what an impeccable timekeeper destiny is—and so, I wouldn't give back a second of it - not even the pain. Because…what to be loved forever by a man like Stone is a hell of an upside.

THE END

Author's Note

Dear Reader,

This story is special to me for many reasons. Jezebel, the biblical figure was my inspiration for the title. Her name has become synonymous with vice, treachery and sin.

But, when I started researching the woman behind all the myths and legends, I learned that nearly all of my perceptions about her, and what her name *should* stand for were misinformed.

Jezebel was a queen. One whose biggest crime was daring to behave just as the men of her time. She was ruthless, unapologetically ambitious, and believed in her right to rule.

Traditional historical texts often erase the contributions of women in their recounting of major events.

My study of history in college taught me that if I wanted to know the complete story, I'd have to read beyond the textbooks. And that I'd have to question the premise of every historical fact, I'd been taught.

That exercise made my life so much richer. I set out to tell the story of a woman who took that name, and turned it into a battle cry.

I hope you'll walk away from this story feeling empowered and of course, in *love*.

Dream Big, Dreamer. And happy reading!

Xoxo,
Dylan

Acknowledgments

As always, this part feels impossible to write.

There are so many people who are integral to this story making it into the world.

My beta readers are the first line of defense and they helped me shape and elevate the story. Thank you, Chele Walker, Sara Koelsch, Elizarey Reads, Lara Petersen, Marcia Golden Esders, and Amy Jackson—your early feedback and encouragement helped so much!

To the women who shared your stories with me so that I could make my characters as authentic as possible, THANK you for your time, your honesty and your trust.

To my editor, Lauren Clarke—you are a star. Having you as my partner in this process made all the difference and I am so grateful for the care and thoroughness you showed this manuscript.

To my colleagues who walk this very unique path alongside me, I'm glad to have you in my life and am grateful for your constant support.

To my Day Dreamers and my DREAM TEAM I LOVE you guys! You make my day, every single day! You inspire me to keep writing and I am so thankful for the parts of your day that you spend with me.

To all of the blogs who have tirelessly and graciously read and then promoted my work—you are my heroes. I couldn't do this without you.

To the readers who buy my books, who email, message and tweet me! Thank you SO much for everything. You're amazing and I write with your wind at my back every day!

Thank you to my family—my parents, my sisters, my brothers-in-law and my cousins—you are my village. Thank you for being wonderful and loving.

Finally, thank you to my husband and children. You are the heartbeats of my life. Thank you for inspiring me, loving me and supporting me. I love you all more than anything else in the universe!

Love,
Me

Also by Dylan Allen

RIVERS WILDE SERIES

The Legacy
Book one of the Rivers Wilde Series. An opposites attract, enemies to lovers stand-alone that kicks off this brand new series.

The Legend
This is a second chance at love story. Remington Wilde has loved one woman in his life and even though timing and family manipulations keep pulling them apart, it's a love worth fighting for.

The Jezebel
Regan Wilde and Stone Rivers were born enemies. But love has other ideas.

The Gathering
A delicious holiday novella with points of view from all six main characters including a scene from Tina and Tyson Wilde's point of view for the first time

The Daredevil: A Rivers Wilde/1001 Nights Novella
Tyson Wilde laughs in the face of danger and has yet to face a challenge he's not up to. Until Dina Lu walks into his life and threatens to turn it upside down.

The Mastermind: A Rivers Wilde/1001 Nights Novella
He lives under a golden spotlight. She's shackled to a past that must stay hidden. A fire-burning, second-chance romance novella.

THE SYMBOLS SERIES.

Then Came You
Set in London this is a workplace romance that features two people who are trying to outrun their pasts and protect their cynical hearts from more pain. But when their lives collide and their hearts and bodies yearn for each other, they'll have to decide if they are brave enough to fight for their love.

Still The One
This second chance romance features high school sweethearts who were torn apart by tragedy and treachery. Years later, when they realize that their feelings haven't changed, they embark on a mission to unravel the mystery surrounding her father's disappearance. But what they discover about their past might make a future together impossible.

Best for Last
This emotional, enemies to lovers, second chance romance features two people on a collision course with destiny. He's the heir to a British Dukedom, she's trying to find her place in this world. Opposites attract and sparks fly when they meet in a lush coastal city in Ghana. When serendipity reunites them, they'll have to reckon with their pasts to have the future they want.

STANDALONES

The Sun and Her Star
A friends to lovers, second chance at story. Angsty, emotional, sexy, and unforgettable. Graham and Apollo are two people who find each other just when they need to. What starts as a deep, abiding friendship grows into the kind of love that can move mountains. This story is a reader favorite.

Thicker Than Water
A friends to lovers and workplace romance that follows the love story between an undocumented writer and the movie executive who changes her life. This story is hopeful, honest, and achingly relevant. Go in with an open mind and prepare to fall in love.

The Sound of Temptation
A second chance forbidden romance that follows star-crossed lovers, a talented musician and the artist who becomes his muse. It spans nearly ten years and is a turbulent, exhilarating, heart pounding, and deeply intimate love story you will never forget.

If you've read my books and haven't already, please leave a review. Nothing fancy, but a line or two helps so much!

I love to hear from readers! Stay in touch with me at
    Dylan@dylanallenbooks.com

About the Author

Dylan Allen is a Texas girl with a serious case of wanderlust.

A self-proclaimed happily ever junkie, she loves creating stories where her characters chase their own happy endings.

When she isn't writing or reading, eating, or cooking, she and her family are planning their next adventure.

I love talking to you guys! Feel free to send me an email at Dylan@dylanallenbooks.com

Are you on Facebook? If you are, then PLEASE join my private reader group, Dylan's Day Dreamer.

It's where I spend most of my time online. My Day Dreamers get exclusive giveaways, sneak peeks, glimpses into my everyday, and lots of other fun bookish things! It's fantastic and my favorite place on the internet.

Discover More Blue Box Press Authors

Go to www.TheBlueBoxPress.com for more information.

Dylan Allen

Jennifer L. Armentrout

Kristen Ashley

Xio Axelrod

Steve Berry

Lexi Blake

Audrey Carlan

Marie Force

C. W. Gortner

Heather Graham

Donna Grant

Larissa Ione

Suzanne M. Johnson

J. Kenner

Randy Susan Meyers

Jennifer Probst

Kristen Proby

Christopher Rice

M.J. Rose

Kennedy Ryan

J.R. Ward

On Behalf of 1001 Dark Nights,
Liz Berry and Jillian Stein would like to thank ~

Steve Berry
Benjamin Stein
Kim Guidroz
Chelle Olson
Chris Graham
Tanaka Kangara
Jessica Saunders
Stacey Tardif
Suzy Baldwin
Grace Wenk
Dylan Stockton
Peggy Boulos Smith
Richard Blake
and Simon Lipskar

9 781968 707972